where
the
light
gets
in

www.penguin.co.uk

Also by Lucy Dillon

All I Ever Wanted
One Small Act of Kindness
A Hundred Pieces of Me
The Secret of Happy Ever After
Walking Back to Happiness
Lost Dogs and Lonely Hearts
The Ballroom Class

For more information on Lucy Dillon and her books, please visit her website at www.lucydillon.co.uk, her Facebook page at www.facebook.com/pages/LucyDillonBooks or follow her on Twitter @lucy_dillon or Instagram @lucydillonbooks

where the light gets in

Lucy Dillon

BANTAM PRESS

LONDON · NEW YORK · TORONTO · SYDNEY · AUCKLAND

TRANSWORLD PUBLISHERS
61–63 Uxbridge Road, London W5 5SA
www.penguin.co.uk

Transworld is part of the Penguin Random House group of companies
whose addresses can be found at global.penguinrandomhouse.com

First published in Great Britain in 2018 by Bantam Press
an imprint of Transworld Publishers

A CIP catalogue record for this book
is available from the British Library.

ISBN 9780593080368 (hb)
9780593077658 (tpb)

Typeset in 12.5/15pt Adobe Garamond by Jouve (UK), Milton Keynes
Printed and bound in Great Britain by Clays Ltd, Bungay, Suffolk

Penguin Random House is committed to a sustainable
future for our business, our readers and our planet. This book
is made from Forest Stewardship Council® certified paper.

1 3 5 7 9 10 8 6 4 2

To Jane Steele, with grateful thanks
for all the time you gave us

Prologue

Betty Dunlop wasn't scared of death, but then she hadn't been scared of the Luftwaffe, the Cold War, the threat of a nuclear winter, salmonella, cholesterol, or any of her three varyingly awful husbands.

Lorna Larkham, though, wasn't quite so relaxed about it. And the closer death glided towards Betty's bedside in St Agnes's Hospice, the faster Lorna's own heart beat inside her chest, so hard she had to force her legs from twitching, and getting up and running away.

The carriage clock beside her seemed to have stopped; how could it still be just seven o'clock? Lorna had arrived at six to start her volunteer shift, and the ward sister had intercepted her before she'd even got her jacket off, to warn her that Betty – ninety-three the week before and still roller-set and Ellnetted to the nines – had started to decline overnight.

'We knew something was up when she didn't ring for her cocoa.' The nurse put a hand on Lorna's arm, seeing panic freeze her face. 'She's still with us, though. Keep the music going, chat even if she doesn't reply. Let Betty know she's not on her own. I'm just down the hall if you need me.'

Discreetly, Lorna lowered her knitting to check Betty's hooded eyelids. Knitting had been one of Betty's hobbies too, something they'd chatted about when she'd first dropped in, to offer an hour or so of company. Lorna always

1

brought her wool bag along with her to the hospice; she found the rhythmic clicks and loops helped to fill the moments when the residents she was sitting with were half there, half not. Familiar noises for many of them, a childhood sound of mothers, aunties, darning and knitting, nattering away. As Lorna worked the rows, something of their characters seeped into the pattern: later, scraps of wool stuck between the needles reminded her unexpectedly of June's knowing eyes or Mabel's silk flowers. Betty, she already knew, would always be moss stitch: textured and Kelly green, the clean smell of Pears soap. She was about to turn her work round when an invisible nudge made her glance up.

Rudy, Betty's anxious dachshund, was stirring in his basket. Outside, the fat white moon had slipped out from behind a cloud, and the room felt chillier, as if someone had opened a window.

Lorna's pulse throbbed in her throat, alive and hot and determined. The music – some bland classical piece chosen by the last nurse – had finished, but Betty hadn't breathed out.

Panic tightened a notch in her chest with every hum of the self-levelling bed. Was this it? Was *this* it? She blinked, searching for clues she didn't want to see. Lorna had had 'end of life' training from the nurses, but she'd never been here before, not for real. The seconds in the room hung – then the sheets over Betty's shrunken frame rose, and the world carried on. For the time being.

Lorna let out a breath, a shuddery echo of Betty's, and gently touched the liver-spotted hand lying on top of the blanket, feeling the skin move under her fingertips. It was soft, and papery. Until quite recently, Lorna hadn't believed death would ever catch up with Betty. She was so bright-eyed, firmly engaged with life even in the hospice. But last week, they'd talked about Christmas, just gone. Lorna had told her about her surprisingly funny nights in the homeless shelter (more volunteering to avoid her sister Jessica's in-laws and their competitive board games) and Betty had confided what she'd been doing with her children, Peter, Susie and Rae. Her face had lit up as she described Rae's delightful Christmas cake and Peter's smart wool coat, but when Lorna had asked the nurse on duty when they'd called in, Debra had shaken her head. No visitors. Maybe that had been an early sign that Betty was beginning to slip away, like a sandcastle slowly falling back into the lapping tide.

'We're still here, Betty,' she said more bravely than she felt. It rattled Lorna, the sense of the outward Betty and her inner self invisibly detaching from each other. 'Me and Rudy. It's OK.'

Betty herself certainly wasn't afraid of what was coming. Her stories – and she had hundreds of stories – sparkled with careless courage: not just her nights shivering on West End rooftops, firewatching during the Blitz when she was barely older than Lorna's niece, but afterwards, when she'd married a soldier, upped sticks to Canada, only to ditch the soldier and his fists for an alcoholic Italian chef; then she'd run a bar and sold Avon make-up, had a 'surprise' baby at forty-four with a slick lawyer called Herb, moved back to Hendon with his cash when he died. Betty's life had been one exuberant leap of faith after another, landing on her small feet each time like a cat.

Lorna watched Betty floating back into the shadows of her memories, and heard that smoky voice in her head. 'Fear's good for you, darling,' she'd laughed, when Lorna blanched at her anecdotes. 'Shows you where the edges of yourself are.'

'I don't want to see my edges, thanks,' Lorna had said, chicken that she was.

'Why not?' Betty's eyebrows were magnificent, haughty like Joan Crawford's. 'Your edges might not be where you think they are.'

Lorna flipped through the CDs by the bed. Betty had her nailed. She *didn't* know where her edges were. In fact, she wondered a lot of things about herself, questions that she'd never ask because there was no one left to answer. Mum gone, Dad gone, and, with that, their little world had closed up behind them, leaving her and Jessica more alone than ever. Who was she meant to be? What traits or weaknesses, already brewing in her blood, might emerge as the years passed and she overtook her parents into middle age and beyond? Questions, and the blankness of never knowing, crept up on Lorna while she was sitting up late on nights like these, when the air swarmed with memories, hers and Betty's mingling in their shared silence.

Rudy circled in his basket and laid his head on his paws. Lorna slid Glenn Miller's big band orchestra into the player. If Betty's train was departing the station tonight, she'd want something with a bit of swing to take her on to the next destination. She pressed play and picked up her knitting, bracing herself for the last half-hour. Only thirty minutes. It wouldn't happen on her watch. Betty was too much of a dame for that.

She knitted and listened, two rows, three rows, four. 'I can never get moss stitch right,' Lorna murmured, just so Betty would know she was there. 'It always goes *too* lumpy.' But as the light moved across the room, she looked up and saw immediately something had changed. Betty's nose and cheekbones were sharpening as her breathing became phlegmy, and a metallic taste began to rise in Lorna's own throat. She glanced across to the button that would summon the nurse, but then steeled herself. Not yet. She could do this.

The old lady exhaled deeply, loudly, and Lorna wondered if she was seeing someone in her dreams that warranted a sigh. Someone stepping out of the wailing sirens and broken walls and dusty tea of her youth, where terror made everything vivid and fleeting, and ripe for the taking, right now. Holding out a hand, with a smile.

'Little Brown Jug' turned into 'Moonlight Serenade', Betty's favourite, and her hand twitched on the sheet. Lorna watched: which of her husbands would come for her? Which would she choose? Were her relatives approaching, her mother and father, a Victorian grandmother? That thought was comforting. That even if you were lying alone somewhere, or in a sterile hospital bed, there'd be familiar faces there, reaching for you with love, wanting to see you again. Yearning for you more than life.

Something hollowed inside her, dank and cold like a sea cave.

She rested the knitting on her knee for a moment, forcing herself to stay with the darkness. Lorna didn't know what her own mother's last moments had been like, and it haunted her. Whether they'd been peaceful like Betty's, whether there'd been pain, a struggle for air, regret and panic. It had been a heart attack: Lorna's father had found Cathy in her studio, surrounded by a pool of her own spilled ink, not blood. And then he'd died too, a year to the day later. Which was either a tragic coincidence, or – if Lorna and Jess were honest with each other – no coincidence at all.

Rudy lifted his head and whimpered. His ears pulled back, and he turned to her, quivering with fear.

Lorna realised her eyes were full and wet, and her attention snapped back to the responsibility she had here. The parched gaps in between breaths were getting longer.

At the start of the month, Betty had been alive enough to talk about her Agatha Christie-like plans for after her death with glee. 'I've put you in my will!' she'd confided as Lorna had been coiling her long hair under her winter hat, hurrying to catch the night bus. 'I'm leaving you something to remind you of me.'

Lorna had protested – there were rules about that and, besides, it wasn't why she came. But Betty would hear none of it.

'Nonsense. It's just a little something, and I want you to have it. I've no one else to leave it to. It's just to remind you to be scared once in a while, Lorna.' And she'd squeezed her gloved hand with determination. A squeeze that brooked no argument.

Lorna looked down at those fingers now, cold and stiff, all eight rings taken off by doctors, kept safe in a bag by the hospice staff. She'd heard all their tales apart from the ruby one, and she felt a stab of regret that she might never find out why Betty saved it till last. She didn't want Betty to go, but she'd done all the living she wanted to. It was so quiet, too simple for such a profound moment.

The moon moved behind the curtain, throwing a softer pool of light into the room, and the music changed again. Lorna's skin prickled; the air seemed to fill with big-band orchestras and invisible dancers, stepping soundlessly through an ethereal spotlight, swirling in a last dance before the blackout. 'I'm still here, Betty,' she whispered, 'with

Rudy,' then wondered if it was fair to try to keep Betty with her, if she wanted to go.

She willed herself to be calm, to be a comforting presence, but the fears edged through. What if Betty's eyes snapped open? What if she tried to speak? What if she needed help that Lorna couldn't give? Betty, what happened with the Italian chef? Why Montreal? Did loving life more than love make it easier to start again when the romance died, or was there one, one man you never forgot, one man who made every other seem that bit duller?

Rudy whimpered again, and then gave two short barks. And, her heart scuttling with panic, Lorna cracked.

She fumbled for the buzzer that would bring the night nurse into the room, gripped it in one hand to be sure, and pressed it as hard as she could. But as the nurse's footsteps clicked down the hall, followed by another swifter pair, Rudy lay down with his long nose on his paws and let out a low groan that brought tears to Lorna's eyes.

Her heart contracted and she longed to throw her arms open to catch the spirits in the room, which she couldn't see or feel, and beg them to tell her that everything was all right, that everything would be fine, that everyone was still there, just in a different form.

But she couldn't. And there would be no answer anyway.

As Lorna stumbled into the bright light of the corridor, she heard Betty's voice in her head, husky and alive.

'You know, Lorna, those cracks in your heart, where things didn't work out quite as you hoped, but you patched yourself up and carried on? That's where the light gets in.'

She turned back, and there was a slim shaft of moonlight slipping through the curtains.

Chapter One

'Here's to Mum and Dad,' said Jessica, raising her cup of tea in a toast towards the distant hills. 'Wherever they are.'

'Mum and Dad.' Lorna lifted her cup, took a sip and gagged. There had to be at least two sugars in there, and she hadn't taken sugar in her tea for years.

Lorna turned to her older sister to ask her if she was trying to make a point about her not being sweet enough, then saw the pensive way she was staring out into the distance, and decided to leave it. It was January, bitterly cold, and it had been quite a hike up from the car park; maybe the sugar wasn't a bad idea. They still had half a Bakewell tart to finish – Dad's birthday treat, brought in his honour – and the tea was to remember Mum, drunk out of her china cups with the tiny forget-me-nots, the last survivors from *her* mum's mum's massive china service. Mum had always had two sugars, maybe that was what Jess had been thinking of when she poured it. These small traditions were a bit like the cups, Lorna thought: fragments of a bigger picture. Like her and Jess. The last remnants of a family set that had dwindled, through breakages and carelessness, to just the two of them.

The wind coming off the hills really *was* cold. She hugged her parka more tightly around herself, and gazed out over

9

the rolling landscape below them, where orange-cagouled walkers and grey sheep roamed for their entertainment. The walkers were determined and sticking to the winding tracks, but the sheep seemed to be enjoying themselves more.

Mum would have picked out every tiny detail in this, she thought, and the scene in front of her morphed into one of Cathy Larkham's trademark pen-and-ink sketches: the stark trees, the hills serrated with paths, snow-dusted at the edges like a Bundt cake, the children wobbling along in bright wellies, the birds and the hopeful dogs, twisting back, watching for a thrown tennis ball. And the two women observing it all from a bench, one tall, one small, with their Thermos flask and their box of cake and their matching hats with bobbles. The bobble hats were another memorial touch: knitted by their dad's mum for a long-ago Christmas, found by Jess while she was empty-ing the house after he died. Blue for Jess, red for Lorna. Fat pom-poms on each one, bobbing when they moved.

The first time they'd sat here on this bench, overlook-ing the British Camp in Malvern, was the wintry day they'd scattered the ashes of Cathy and Peter Larkham, handfuls of ash mingling in the heavy casket in the same way their parents' lives had mingled, until it was impos-sible to see where one began and the other ended. In death, so in life. Or possibly the other way around.

Lorna made an effort to summon her parents in her mind. It was slightly harder every year and it bothered her that she always seemed to start now with their clothes – Mum's grey linen shirts, her pale arms under the rolled-up sleeves, speckled with freckles; Dad's green 'weekend' jumper that Jess had bought in one of her many efforts to drag him into the twenty-first century. He'd always dressed like a history teacher. Left to himself, Dad would have worn the same navy cords and two checked shirts in rotation for ever, his own school uniform. He dutifully brought out the weekend jumper every time either Jess or Lorna visited, but always with a shirt; the collar poked out of the crew neck as if it was fighting the enforced casualness.

A thought suddenly occurred to Lorna.

'Jess?' She turned to her big sister. 'Did Dad ever say why he wanted to be scattered *here* with Mum? I know they liked the area but . . . ?'

Jess was checking her phone – it was supposed to be on silent so they could focus on remembering their parents but Jess had three children with active social lives and a husband who referred every household decision to her, and she got twitchy if her phone didn't beep for five minutes. 'I think it was something to do with the view?'

'The view? Why? What's special about it?' Lorna scanned the horizon, trying to absorb any special details, any clue from the great beyond, but it was just . . . a nice view. She couldn't remember coming here as a family; they'd moved schools whenever Dad did – Brecon, Newcastle, Carlisle – but she couldn't remember a Significant Moment here in Malvern. The closest they'd been was Longhampton, about thirty miles further west.

'Dunno.' Jess looked up from her texts. 'Oh, no, wait – I do know. It was one of their places, before we were born. There's a photo of the two of them here, sitting on this bench, holding hands. Very seventies – Mum looks about nine, like she might take off if the wind got under her flares.' She paused and rolled her eyes. 'Dad's wearing his cords, obviously. The original ones.'

'I have *never* seen that photo.'

Jess put her phone down and sighed. There was a lot in the sigh. 'Well, I only saw it once. I was helping Dad with the paperwork after Mum died and he was looking through some of her albums. I'd never seen them before either. He couldn't remember half the people – they were mostly photos of Mum. She hadn't written anything on the back.'

'They knew and they really never considered we might want to know, one day, did they?,' said Lorna. After their mother's sudden heart attack, Dad spent most of his days leafing through old photographs, gazing at Mum's paintings and keeping everything exactly as she'd left it, in case it had all been a bad dream and she might walk through the door with his *Guardian*. Jess had been there with him more than Lorna had because soon after the funeral, in a fit of carpe diem, Lorna had enrolled on a Fine Art course in Italy. She'd always wanted to study art, secretly hoping the right course would unlock a hidden gift, but it hadn't taken long to realise this wasn't going to happen. The course was demanding, and Lorna had had to force herself to go back at the start of each term. Usually by reminding herself how much it was costing her to discover she hadn't inherited her mother's talent for life drawing.

'He said something about this being the bench where Mum had decided to give up teaching and paint full time. I think he might have proposed to her here too, I'm not sure.' A lot about their parents' life, pre-children, was a mystery to Jess and Lorna. It was a close marriage, bordering on telepathic; a web of smiles and in-jokes that didn't leave much room for other people. 'He got very emotional. His mouth went all flat, you know?'

'Oh no. He cried?' Lorna had never seen her dad cry until her mum died; after that the slightest thing set him off. A thumbed paperback, an old plate. On one sad occasion, a pair of shoes. It made Lorna feel even more useless that she couldn't even guess when to comfort him, let alone know what to say.

Jess nodded, then paused, cup at her lips. 'It's funny, I thought he'd talk *more* about Mum after she died. I mean, we were the only people who knew her as well as he did, but he didn't. I gave him lots of chances, but he wouldn't. It was like he'd gone into his own head. I don't think it even occurred to him that *I* might want to talk about her. My mother. Maybe I should have tried harder? Maybe if I had . . .' Her voice trailed away.

'Stop.' Lorna leaned her shoulder against Jess's. Losing both Mum and Dad within a year of each other had changed everything, too quickly. They'd dealt with it in different ways but the hardest part for both of them had been watching Dad crumble before their bewildered eyes; with one half of himself gone, he was so obviously a lover with a broken heart it was impossible to see him as their gentle, bumbling dad any more. He was a man, a man they couldn't heal. A stranger neither she nor Jess could burden with their own grief. 'You'd have been talking about two different people. His wife. Our mum.'

'When you think about it, Mum and Dad . . . we knew they met at university, they always had that wedding photo on the mantelpiece, but what stories do we know? We don't even know exactly why we're sitting here right now. There are so many questions I wish I'd asked . . .' Jess bit her lip. 'I tell Hattie and Milo and Tyra about how their dad and I met, how they came to be.

They love hearing it. We're all part of the same story. *Our* story.'

Lorna side-eyed her sister. 'Really? And how *do* you tell the story of how Hattie came to be? As a morality tale about young love overcoming all? Or as a warning about getting your contraception advice from someone's big sister at school?'

That broke Jess's stride. She frowned. 'I tell it as a story of how you can make things work out if you want it badly enough.' Then she conceded, 'And also about reading medication instructions, obviously. Anyway, Hattie's a different kind of sixteen. She's far more open with me about her life because I actually listen to what . . .' The words stuck in her throat, and Jess's blue eyes clouded over. Lorna knew what she was feeling: even now, years after, sadness could rush out of nowhere. Each passing year delivered new angles on grief as life moved you on, and you saw your old self differently: the pity was sharper because you hadn't realised it was pity-worthy before.

She leaned into her sister, feeling the softness of Jess's body under the parka, the warmth radiating outwards from her big, brave heart.

'You and Hattie are so different from us and Mum,' said Lorna. 'You don't have secrets, because you're *part of* her life. You two *enjoy* spending time together. Mainly in your role as her driver, but still. You and Ryan, you're just as close as Mum and Dad but you've always put Hattie in the middle. And now Milo and Tyra.'

'I'm not saying the way Mum and Dad brought us up was wrong, but if I got run over by a bus tomorrow, Hattie wouldn't be sitting here wondering *anything*. No secrets, no regrets, no *I love you*s we didn't say.' Jess turned her phone over; its cover was a black-and-white photo of her, Ryan, Hattie, Tyra and Milo, piled up in a mass of bare feet, white T-shirts and Ryan's family's toothy grin. 'That's what life's about, Lorna. Love, and honesty. And family.'

'Don't get run over by a bus.' Jess was veering danger-ously close to one of her favourite topics – how Lorna should get on with surrounding herself with a nuclear fam-ily like the Protheros. Lorna didn't want that, for various reasons, but Jess still tried to persuade Lorna otherwise whenever they met up. Jess had gone into teaching, like their dad; she had a mission to improve everything she saw. Maximise its potential.

'Like I've got *time* to find a bus to be run over by. But seriously, Lorna . . .' Her expression changed. 'You're part of our family, you know. This Christmas, we missed you. Ryan's family can be hard work, but you didn't have to spend it with waifs and strays.'

'I wanted to. It was fun. The dogs wore tinsel collars and there was no Cranium.' She changed the subject, quickly. 'So what are you doing later? Isn't tonight Ryan's five-a-side night?'

'It certainly is. First match after the Christmas break, always painful.' Jess tipped out the tea from her mug, and brushed the cake crumbs off her denim skirt. 'Do you want a lift to the station? Tyra's off to a party at four, then I need to drop Hattie at Wagamama for her evening shift. At least you can read all the way back to London.' She sounded briefly envious. 'I remember reading . . . for fun.'

'I'm not going back to London tonight,' said Lorna, gathering her bag and scarf and following her sister down the gravel path to the car park. 'I've got an appointment in Longhampton this afternoon.'

'Longhampton?' Jess looked over her shoulder, surprised. She'd trained herself never to look surprised if she could help it.

'Yup. I've got an appointment at a gallery there.'

'Oh? For work?'

Lorna was a Collection Administrator for a charity that loaned artworks to hospitals and other places with too many white walls and not enough joy. Her job was to match the art with the location, and then supervise the installation and collection of the paintings, sculptures, collages or whatever seemed to bring some positive energy to the space. Recently her boss had finally given her an acquisitions role, and Jess had been impressed with the budget Lorna had to manage, less impressed with the art she'd acquired. Jess preferred art to look like their mother's detailed illustrations: meticulously rendered nuggets of reality.

'No, not for work, for me. I'm thinking of buying it.'

Jess's expression said it all. 'Which gallery are we talking about? I can't even remember one.'

'That little one on the high street, next to that gift shop where we used to get birthday presents. It had navy walls and gold stars on the walls.' As a young teenager Lorna had drifted through its stained-glass door every time they went shopping in town, saving up her pocket money for treasures. Jess saved up for Clinique foundation and her driving test. 'It was where I bought that mixed-media portrait of a mermaid, the one I had in my room? The bakery that did the lemon tarts was on the other side?'

'Oh, yeah . . .' Jess seemed nostalgic for a moment. She liked lemon tarts. 'I do remember it. Did they sell anything of Mum's?'

'She let them have one or two, I think.' Cathy Larkham hadn't needed a gallery; once the series of modern fairy stories she'd illustrated for an old university friend turned into international bestsellers, she could have sold every one of her paintings before she started. And then, ironically, like Rapunzel, she rarely left the painting shed in their garden, drawing and colouring and creating worlds bigger than the one she lived in.

'And is this all definite?' Jess asked. 'Have you *signed* anything?'

'Not yet. But I've made up my mind. I need to move my life on, Jess. This is where I need to start.'

They were at Jess's car now, a 4×4 crammed with car seats and plastic cups, crisp packets and general child-related junk. The chaos, contradicted by the cocoon-like car seats, made Lorna twitchy: something about the relentless care required to keep these vulnerable creatures from harm, plus the mess. Ryan's company car was nothing like this: he drove a pristine silver Lexus, which he cleaned every Sunday morning, rain or shine, with a special 'semi-pro' cleaning kit. He'd done that ever since he and Jess bought their first house together, aged twenty-two. That also made Lorna twitchy, but for different reasons.

Jess put her bag on the bonnet while she searched for her keys in its tissue-flecked depths, then stopped. She sighed and said, 'I don't want to pour cold water on your plans, and it's great you're being more positive about life, but a gallery . . . do you think it's a good idea?'

'Why? You know I've always wanted to have my own gallery. And I've been waiting for the right one to come up, not rushing into anything. This is a decent little business, with room to expand, and there's accommodation upstairs. The whole thing costs half what I'm paying in rent now.' Lorna lifted her hands. 'I could live upstairs and fill the downstairs with my unmade bed, call it performance art, and still save money! There's literally nowhere smaller I can rent in Zone Three. I'm storing my laundry in the bath.'

'But your job – weren't they talking about promoting you?'

'No. They were talking about *re-organisation*. Our funding got cut at the end of the year, and we're all on freelance contracts now.' Lorna hadn't wanted to talk about that with Jess, not today, but Jess's expression had gone very school-teachery, whether she realised it or not. 'I mean,' she added, reluctantly, 'I've still got a role – just with fewer hours and less pay. And at the end of the day, I'd rather use my savings starting my own business than use them up subsidising my actual job. Anthony will give me work if I need it.'

'Oh, Lorna.' Jess was clearly struggling not to start making a bullet-point list of the reasons this was a terrible idea. 'I just . . . Longhampton? I know you're experienced in taking art into miserable places but . . . seriously?'

Lorna met her sister's gaze. Her eyes were concerned, but also haunted. Jess rarely looked haunted; she'd always reminded Lorna of a pre-Raphaelite model, untroubled and calm, with wide-set eyes and a serene resting expression. She made plans in the face of storms, and she saw them through. 'Why not?'

'Do you really want to go back there? After everything that happened?'

It hung in the air between them: the memories, the emotions, the younger versions of themselves that seemed like different people looking back, doing things they never talked about anymore.

'I'm thirty,' said Lorna, quietly. 'By the time Mum was my age, she'd found Dad, she'd had you and me, people were queuing up for her work. She was blossoming. Whereas I'm just . . . I'm just treading water. And fine, I'm not an artist, I don't have what Mum had, I've come to terms with that.' She stared over the car park, where a couple were trying to load an arthritic Labrador into the back of a Fiesta. Jess was one of the few people she could be honest with; one of the few people who knew how hard she'd wanted to discover some inherited talent, how hard she'd dug into herself, only to come up with nothing. 'So the next best thing is having a gallery where I can find people who *do* have talent, and encourage them and be responsible for bringing beauty into other people's lives.'

'But after what you went through with that shop in . . .'

'That was a learning curve,' she said stubbornly. 'And I learned from it. I'm not going to make those mistakes again. I can't afford to!'

She couldn't, either. Jess had put her inheritance into a bigger house, a trust fund for the kids, laying foundations for her family; Lorna had invested in a dream that hadn't worked out. First the Fine Art course, then a pop-up gallery. But there was a little left, enough for this final gamble.

'I need a challenge and this feels like Fate.' It seemed too glib, compressing nights of internet-scanning, brainstorming and budgeting into one small sentence. 'The price, and the location, and the connection with Mum . . . I'm giving myself one year, and I'm going into it with my eyes open this time. One year. So you'll have to buy at least fifteen birthday and anniversary presents from me, OK?'

19

Jess sighed and grabbed Lorna's hands. Gambles weren't her thing. She'd made one in her whole life, and it had come off, but she'd played everything very safe after that. 'I want this to work for you, Lorn, I really do.' She paused. 'But I *will* expect a family discount on the birthday cards.'

Two hours later, Lorna was sitting in a café that had been a tailor's the last time she'd been in Longhampton. She gazed across the main road at the gallery that had once inspired her to paint the bedroom she shared with her sister navy, with gold stars.

Like nearly everything from her childhood that Lorna remembered with love, it had changed. It was still an art gallery and the door was still stained glass, but the dark mystery had been stripped back to whiteness. White walls, white wood, white shelves, lots of white light. But there were bright colours just inside, vivid and intriguing against the blank background.

Lorna curled her hand around her coffee, served fashionably in a glass, not a cup (flat whites had reached Longhampton) and remembered the smell of the gallery then: oil paint and a Diptyque fig candle. Moments from her adolescence flashed through her mind like slippery fish: the familiar red and white pole of the barber's on the corner, the Saturday afternoon circuit of Dorothy Perkins to the big WHSmiths, to Topshop, to the café where Jess met Ryan and he bought Lorna hot chocolate deluxe with marshmallows if she pretended they'd been together all day, instead of letting the pair of them sneak off for an hour or two. There were four years between the Larkham sisters; at fifteen, when Jess started going out with Ryan, that was a huge difference. Jess would have been in as much trouble for abandoning eleven-year-old Lorna in town with hot chocolate and a dog-eared *Cosmopolitan* as she would for getting up to God knows what with Ryan behind the cricket pavilion.

There was a red To Let sign on the window above the main gallery frontage. Lorna had never noticed but there were at least two floors above it, as there were above all the shops along the high street. She knew now, from the business agents' details on the table in front of her, that the gallery's flat comprised a large kitchen-diner, a spacious reception room with feature fireplace and no fewer than four bedrooms and two bathrooms. And an attic.

A business, and a place to live. Not just to live either, to spread out. To enjoy her possessions instead of storing them. Lorna took deep breaths to stop the jitteriness spreading through her. She knew she should be studying the number of customers the gallery had, what the footfall was, what the hard facts were, but she couldn't. She couldn't stop looking at the original glass details in the door – curling ivy and mistletoe which hadn't been removed in the general Tippexing of the place – and feeling a weird certainty that this gallery had come available to her for a reason.

She saw her own reflection in the window of the café, and thought, I can do this. Betty had always insisted that good things happened to brave women. She'd put on red lipstick to summon up Betty's pizzazz, and angled her grey beanie the way her mum had, letting her straight blonde hair fall around her face like Faye Dunaway.

Her appointment to view with the current gallery owner was at five on the dot. Lorna finished the last centimetre of her coffee, blotted her lips on the white napkin so it left a perfect heart-shaped kiss, and walked over the road to her destiny to a big band playing in her head.

Chapter Two

There were only two other people in the Maiden Gallery when Lorna pushed open the door, and as she stepped in, both customers looked relieved and immediately began making for the exit.

The middle-aged woman sitting at the counter put down her crossword, and smiled. She had fine white hair in a candy-floss wisp around her head, and jaunty rainbow-striped glasses on a long chain. 'Hello there!' she said. 'Let me know if there's anything I can tell you about today's exhibition.'

Lorna assumed she was talking about the collection of massive close-ups of sheep's heads that lined one white wall. Whoever had painted those had clearly developed a keen interest in nostrils. Even though there was some-thing unsettling about them once you'd seen three giant sheep in a row, apparently ramming (ho ho) their heads against invisible windows, they were still a lot more inter-esting than anything else in the gallery: detailed close-ups of flowers, detailed close-ups of apple cores and, in a dar-ing break from the norm, half a wall of pastel canvases featuring silhouetted birds perched on telephone wires.

It was more like a dentist's waiting room than an art gallery, Lorna thought, and the excitement began to seep out of her. This definitely wasn't how she remembered the

Maiden Gallery. It no longer smelled of figs and paint and birthdays. It no longer had surprises wherever you looked, or paintings that stuck in your imagination. It didn't even have a black cat stalking around. All galleries needed a black cat.

But she didn't have to sell sheep's heads, she reminded herself. The sheep could be replaced with something better. Something fresh and new and as yet undiscovered.

Lorna pulled herself together and extended a hand. 'I'm not actually here for the exhibition, I'm here to view the gallery,' she said. 'I'm Lorna Larkham. Are you Mary? The agents suggested you could show me around.'

The lady put her pen down and a smile lit up her face as she pushed the glasses further up her nose. 'Ah ha! I'm Mary Knowles – lovely to meet you! Welcome to the Maiden! Everything is Maid-en Longhampton . . . Do you see?'

'Oh!' Lorna had genuinely never worked that out. 'Oh . . . right.'

They shook hands and as her gaze roamed further around, Lorna felt bad for dismissing the art on display. It wasn't all terrible. Just a bit *meh*. Beyond the initial room of sheep, she could see glass cabinets with handmade jewellery ranging from clunky to Supply Art Teacher, and items carved from wood.

'Do you want to look at the gallery or the flat first?' Mary enquired. 'The gallery is quite self-explanatory, I suppose, with the two front rooms, and then we go back a little way . . .' She stood up and showed Lorna through to the second room, which was much like the first but with a wall of tiny paintings of sheep in enormous felted frames, and more spinners with birthday cards. The floors were nice, though – thick oak planks that hadn't been painted white. Yet.

'This is our ceramics room,' Mary went on. 'We usually put Jim Timson's pottery in here but he's got a bad back and can't face the kiln until he's seen the specialist. So we're selling what's left from Penny Wright's last collection.'

Lorna peered round the corner into the back room. This at least was more like her memories: the pottery had always been in here, goblets with curling greenery like Viking celebration vessels, and enormous bowls that were only good for pot pourri. Now, there were two tables filled with wonky cheese plates. The ceiling sloped where some stairs ran above, and there was a boarded-up fireplace festooned with icicles made out of coloured resin.

Mary clapped a hand to her chest. 'Oh, sorry, they're left over from Christmas. I should have moved those by now. I've been rushed off my feet . . .'

Lorna privately doubted that, but she asked anyway. 'Were you very busy over Christmas?'

'Well, not so much, but I'm here on my own and I'm supposed to be running down the stock. My husband retired, and insisted that I gave up the gallery so we could both have some time off, and I said yes, so Keith went ahead and booked a whole series of golfing breaks, and then Jackie who used to pop in a few days a week got another job because I gave her notice, so I was on my own, which wouldn't have been a problem if we'd managed to move on, but I said I'd keep the place open until the agents found a new tenant, you see. And since then we haven't had any interest, which is disappointing, and . . .'

'Do you want to show me upstairs?' asked Lorna.

*

The stairs up to the flat were at the back of the gallery, past some shelves of mixed media collages that looked as if someone had emptied a Hoover bag on a glue-covered canvas, an office, and a pile of boxes marked 'Terry's Dream Unicorns – returns'. Although the carpet was threadbare, Lorna could make out thick wooden treads beneath them, and some of the tickling excitement began to return.

'Up we go!' Mary eyed the steep staircase with little enthusiasm, then began hauling herself upwards.

'You never fancied living here yourselves?' Lorna asked, giving Mary a discreet head start.

'Not really. We live out in Hartley, where we could have a bit of a garden. We could have taken in lodgers, I suppose, but Keith had a bad experience with a buy-to-let . . . Of course it's handy for storage.' Mary reached the top and got her breath back. 'Sorry it's so cold. I should have thought to put the heating on.'

She unlocked the front door and stepped back, so Lorna could see into the flat properly. 'This is it . . .'

'Wow,' said Lorna, because she couldn't help herself.

The dark narrowness of the stairs opened up into an unexpectedly large landing, light and airy, and echoing with lack of furniture. Ahead of them was the kitchen, with three long sash windows looking on to the main street, and a heavy pine table that had obviously been too much hassle to move out once it was there. Lorna's eye was drawn immediately across the kitchen to the perky red geraniums in the windowboxes of the house opposite; the kitchen was at double-decker-bus level, high enough to notice the furbelows and moulded garlands on the upper-storey façades.

'And that's a storage room, as you can see, but it's a

sitting room really.' A smaller room to the left was stacked with canvases and brown boxes, with a worn-out sofa opposite a fireplace. The stairs continued to wind round behind them, up to the second floor, and higher.

I wouldn't have enough furniture to fill this place, thought Lorna, and the idea thrilled her. So much space! An empty room, just for art and thinking and yoga. It would be *amazing*.

'I always forget how big it is. Two storeys and an attic. Excuse this mess.' Mary's boots were loud on the floorboards as she darted into the storeroom to tidy the stacks of paintings. They weren't messy, Lorna thought, quite the opposite. The rooms were full of inspiration, people's dreams and imagination. 'These shouldn't be here. We were supposed to have returned these to Donald. Trouble is, these artists, they look so *hurt* when things don't sell . . . Four bedrooms, two baths. Though I can't say what the bathrooms are like. We used one of them to store ice for the last proper private view . . .'

Lorna turned round slowly, taking everything in. She'd always had to share: first a childhood bedroom with snoring, fussy, constantly revising Jess, then with other friends in a student house, then flatshares, and then when she'd finally been able to afford a place of her own, it was so tiny that she could only have one friend round at a time. This was the lavish, airy space she'd craved for years – space to put up shelves for her ceramics, and set her clothes out on rails like a designer boutique, space to be alone, to hang everything she'd collected up on the walls. Space to let her own self spread out.

And it was cheaper than her current rent. So much cheaper it made her want to laugh.

'Have you run a gallery before?' Mary was speaking, and Lorna turned round. The friendly smile suggested she wasn't asking in an interviewing way, more out of conversation.

Even so, Lorna felt herself hedging around the question. 'No, not really. Well, I've, um, dabbled.'

That was a terrible answer. But she didn't want to go into all that now, and anyway, it was in the past. The pop-up in Shoreditch had never seemed further away than it did now.

But at the same time, Lorna could feel the strange tingle of belief again. And this time she didn't need anyone's second opinion.

Betty's funeral took place in a sombre crematorium miles from the hospice and even further from the colourful scenes of her long and dramatic life.

It was a quiet service. The only other attendees apart from Lorna were a couple of old ladies from the hospice, and three nurses. Debra had come in on her day off, to pay her respects to the smart woman who'd taught her daughter how to beehive her hair for prom – and, when Debra wasn't listening, told her how to stop a boy's hands from wandering. There were none of Betty's family there at all.

It came as a shock to Lorna, after her conversation with Betty about Christmas, to discover that Betty's children had predeceased her, many years earlier. Naughty little Susie, who loved trifle 'apart from the sherry', had been killed twenty years ago, in a car accident; clever Peter the accountant had had a stroke; Debra wasn't sure what had happened to Rae, other than that she'd never been on the hospice's radar.

'It's sad,' she whispered to Lorna as the coffin disappeared behind the curtain for the last time and the sound of Glenn Miller indicated discreetly that they could leave. 'Doesn't matter how popular you are, once you get over ninety, most funerals are like this – your mates are waiting for you on the other side, not here. Good on you for coming, though. Betty really appreciated your visits.'

Lorna had managed a weak smile. Getting a bus to Streatham and singing a hymn she didn't know seemed like the least she could do for a woman who'd given her the kick up the bahookie, as Betty would have put it, to phone the estate agent and put her money where her dreams were. The Maiden Gallery was now hers, to transform as best she could, sheep and all.

In the Garden of Remembrance, Lorna laid three red carnations on the memorial, blew a kiss up into the grey south London sky, and promised Betty that from that moment on, she would take a deep breath and do her damnedest to feel her edges, wherever they were. And also to wear lipstick as often as possible.

Before she left, Debra had given Lorna a note from the matron asking her to call in at the hospice next time she was passing, and she went the following morning, on her way to the bank to set up a new business account. Lorna had intended to let the volunteer organisers know about her move to Longhampton in any case – and to ask if there were any similar schemes that they knew of in the area.

At first, the volunteering had been a suggestion by a therapist she'd seen after her father died, as a way of working through her pain about their strained relationship at the end, her anger with herself that she hadn't been able to unlock his silent grief, the awkward silences filled with ticking clocks. But Lorna soon realised the problem wasn't *talking*: she enjoyed spending time with the patients she sat with. They weren't her dad, they weren't hosting glum elephants in the room that squashed all conversation flat. Some had great anecdotes; some had mastered companionable silence; whether they chatted or not, they all taught her something, and she would miss it, Lorna thought, as the nurse on duty walked her down to the matron's office. Probably more than they'd miss her.

Kathryn's office was a peaceful room with a view on to the special sensory garden, but though it was a drizzly day outside, inside it felt unseasonally floral. On the table by the door was a large vase full of scented tiger lilies but, after a moment or two, Lorna realised that even their pungent fragrance wasn't masking the even more pungent fragrance of dog, emanating from the wicker dog carrier by her desk. Inside which, she could just see, was Rudy.

The flowers weren't normally there. She was almost certain they'd been placed there by one of the nurses to minimise Rudy's presence.

'Now we've finally got Betty's paperwork sorted out, I can give you this,' said Kathryn, once Lorna was sitting in the easy chair opposite.

She slid a padded envelope across the desk. As Lorna began to demur, she said, 'I know there are rules, but Betty insisted she wanted you to have this . . . and that you'd understand what she meant.'

The envelope felt light, and when Lorna opened it, a thin tissue-wrapped sliver of something dropped into her hands. She unwrapped it carefully: it was a circular silver medal, on a blue-striped red ribbon. 'Is this Betty's? What is it?'

'A George Medal,' said Kathryn. 'Apparently, when she was just a slip of a thing, Betty ran into a Lyons Corner House that had been bombed, and dragged out two people seconds before it collapsed. Pretty impressive – they didn't just hand those medals out to anyone.'

Lorna could picture it: the wailing sirens and the dusty confusion, Betty shouldering her way past the officials to do the right thing. 'Did she tell you this?'

'No, we found a newspaper cutting, tucked in the back of an old photo album,' said Kathryn, shaking her head. 'I wish she *had* told us, don't you? That generation keep the oddest things to themselves. We knew all about Betty's divorces but she never mentioned her George Medal. Did she say anything to you about her war work?'

'Just that she'd been in the Blitz.' Lorna turned the medal over and over. It felt solid, a hard reminder of a fleeting moment, a breath of smoke. 'Shouldn't her family have it though?'

'You were at the funeral. There is no one. Anyway, she left specific instructions – she wanted you to have it. There's a card in there.'

There was. Lorna opened the envelope and read the note inside: *My dear Lorna, Put this in your pocket and remember – feel your edges!! Yours ever, Betty.* She'd signed it with a big Hollywood B, even though the writing was wobbly.

'That's wonderful.' She touched the worn ribbon, overcome; Betty hadn't kept this in a presentation box, she'd probably had it in her pocket too, reminding her to be brave every day, not just when bombs were raining down around her. 'I don't know what to say.'

Kathryn tapped the desk with her pen. 'There's another thing too.'

Lorna looked up. She hoped it wasn't the fox fur Betty had kept draped over her chair. 'I honestly can't take anything else. That's not what I volunteered for . . .'

'It's really a favour for us as well as Betty.' She nodded towards the basket by her feet. 'Now, I don't want to put you under any pressure, but we promised Betty we'd find Rudy a new home. I've been advised that the waiting time at the RSPCA is into weeks. They're always busy after Christmas, those poor puppies whose novelty's worn off. To be honest, Lorna, I'd rather not take him there if I can help it. He's already giving up.'

Lorna could only just make Rudy out in the darkness of the carrier. He was curled up at the back of it, his head tucked on his paws, turned away from a room that he no longer had any interest in.

'I'd take him myself,' Kathryn went on, 'but my cats barely let my husband in these days, ha ha!'

Lorna smiled but didn't laugh. She was trying very hard to drag the unreasonable side of her brain into line.

Lorna had never had a pet. She wasn't sure what you were meant to do with dogs, other than follow them around with a black bag and not, under *any* circumstances, let them eat Dundee cake. This she'd gleaned from the lady in the room next to Betty's who'd found out the hard way that dogs who eat fruit cake require expensive medical intervention. Dogs loved you, sure, but they also moulted, demanded attention and forced you to reorganise your life around their bladders. The responsibility wasn't something she particularly wanted to take on, not if she was about to move house *and* start up a new business.

More than that, the idea of taking responsibility for another creature's love bothered Lorna. It was an extension of how she felt about human relationships – they all had to end some time, leaving one party broken with loss. Her parents had had what most people would consider the perfect soulmate relationship, and yet look how it had turned out. Their love had been so all-encompassing that they literally couldn't live without each other. Dad had vanished without his Cathy. Mum hadn't had a best friend, other than Dad. Why would you want to start that, if misery was the inevitable end point? Surely it was better to live in a state of sociable independence with the world?

She looked into the basket. Rudy seemed to be pining in a very similar way for Betty. Sleeping in the hope of never waking up to his new, Betty-less life.

'If you'd like to read this letter she left . . .' Kathryn passed her a sheet of A4 covered in rambling handwriting. The agitation showed in the up-and-down lines; it was much less composed than the witty little card. 'I don't know if you can make it out, but she's left money – quite a lot of money, actually – in trust to cover his insurance. We're not making that public, wouldn't want someone unscrupulous taking advantage. We've all seen *Annie*, ha ha. But it's a factor, if you're thinking you might be able to take him on. He wouldn't cost you anything.'

Lorna was skimming the lines; she heard Betty's anxious care in every sentence.

> *. . . make sure Rudy's diet is low fat . . . vet says he's prone to back problems . . . careful walking him, as he's anxious about strangers, and other dogs, and thunder, and cars, and men . . . likes a small saucer of tea at bedtime, but no sugar because of his teeth!!!*

Her eye stopped at: . . . *please ask Lorna if she could help interview a new owner, as Rudy trusts her. He doesn't trust many people. She will know if they're kind or not.*

She glanced into the basket. Rudy's black eyes were observing her, alive and glittery with trepidation, and her heart wrenched. She hated to think of him being taken to a noisy rescue kennel, left there to be peered at in a concrete run – and passed over time and again? After the comforts he was used to with Betty?

This is why you don't want a dog, she reminded herself.

'How old is he?' Maybe it wouldn't be a long-term commitment. Lorna struggled between the voice in her head yelling *No,* and her desire to be the good person Betty and Kathryn and everyone at the hospice assumed she was.

'Six.' Kathryn pushed a folder across the desk. 'So he should be around for a good while yet. Betty kept him in very good nick – look at these dental records! I'd be happy if some of our patients in here had as many check-ups.'

Lorna eyed the dachshund, who'd turned round to face the room, and was now lying down with his nose on his paws, all the better to gaze up at her. He was sleek and dark chestnut, bigger than she remembered, now he was stretched out. It was amazing that he'd never made those smells while he'd been lying at Betty's bedside. Or maybe the lavender had been stronger in there.

'Have a think,' said Kathryn. 'One of the nurses says she'll have him for a few days. But if we can't get him into the rescue here, I'm not sure what we can do. Poor boy. It's like he's lost his spark. I'm not sure if it's not kinder to . . .'

She couldn't finish the sentence, and Rudy sighed, as if to underline the urgency.

Lorna didn't want a dog, but her conscience wouldn't

let her say 'yes, please' to Betty's George Medal, the talisman for the rest of her new life, and abandon poor Rudy.

Maybe it was better that he'd already given his heart to someone else. He'd never love her like he'd loved Betty, and she didn't have to be that One Person for him.

Oh Betty, you wily woman, she thought. You planned this good and proper.

Chapter Three

It was dark by the time the final box of Lorna's possessions was unloaded and stacked in the big room overlooking the town that she'd earmarked as hers. The street outside the gallery was grey and uninspiring, stripped of the remaining Christmas lights that had given the shop fronts a few traces of party colour last time she'd visited, and there weren't many shoppers left browsing the desperate 'Final Reductions!!!' sales. Those that were seemed keen to get home.

The gallery downstairs was still open. Mary had bustled upstairs while Lorna was directing the removal men – bearing a carton of milk, tea and biscuits 'to help you settle in!' – but even though she was itching to unwrap her own treasures from bubble wrap and start working out how best to display them, Lorna couldn't stop herself going straight down to see what a Saturday afternoon in her own art gallery would be like.

Very quiet, as it turned out. There was a single customer browsing the back room when Lorna came in, and she left soon after Lorna arrived, without buying anything. She did smile apologetically, though.

'How's it been today?' Lorna asked Mary as she turned the Open sign to Closed at six o'clock and locked the door.

'Not too bad . . . for January.' Mary always appeared

upbeat; it was partly down to her jazzy glasses. 'It gets better towards Valentine's Day – I try to encourage our artists to do something heart-based at least once a year. Some of them get a bit huffy about debasing their art, but a sale's a sale.'

She was going through her end-of-day routine, turning lights off in the displays and closing cabinets; Lorna watched, wondering if she should be making a list. As of Monday, this was her responsibility. It gave her a shiver.

Mary stopped, and turned to Lorna with a smile. 'I was thinking, shall we go through the admin and what have you now? Then you'll have tomorrow free to get unpacked, and hit the ground running on Monday.'

'Don't you want to get home?'

Mary flapped her hand. 'Keith's in Lytham St Anne's playing golf this weekend – it's just me and a Marks and Sparks ready meal. It won't take long; we're not a complicated business.'

'If you're sure ...' Lorna half wanted to get back upstairs, to start playing around with the big spare room she'd marked out as her 'creative space', but at the same time, her gaze was wandering around the walls. A few of the exhibits had biographies next to them, written by the artists, and Lorna wanted to study them properly now. Who were these artists? What did they create? And why?

'I'll make us a cup of tea,' said Mary. 'That's the first rule of owning a place like this, by the way. Get a reliable kettle and some decent biscuits.'

The back office was small, and nowhere near as messy as Lorna had expected. Shelves ran up one wall, lined with boxes labelled with the artists' names, and opposite them was a white desk with an ancient Mac, and a filing system that suggested IKEA had moved into the area since Lorna was last there. The only unusual thing she spotted was the stack of biscuit tins in one corner. It was at least fifteen tins high.

She retrieved Rudy from the flat upstairs while Mary made them tea, and watched from one of the orange office chairs as Mary talked her through a typical week in the Maiden Gallery. Filing, bank runs, opening times, rates, 'nice' teenagers who came in during holiday times to help out . . . The admin at least sounded straightforward.

'. . . and this is our database of local artists and artisan craftsmen and -women. You can say craftsperson if you like, but they never do . . . Wait, not that one. Oh, heavens!' Mary clicked several times on a mouse mat in the shape of a cookie before she managed to open a spreadsheet.

'Is everyone detailed on the computer?' Lorna had her own ideas about finding new talent but she didn't want to upset any established gallery regulars.

'Yes, but . . . Oh dear.' Mary kept clicking unsuccessfully until the right screen appeared. 'To be honest, I keep everything written down here.' She pulled a drawer open and removed a tatty A4 desk diary, full of Post-it notes and held together with elastic bands. 'I kept getting mixed up with the spreadsheets, and you know what artists are like – you don't want to be telling them someone else's sales details and who wants what. They're terribly competitive, some of them.'

'Absolutely,' said Lorna, making a mental note not to do that. Mum had never bothered too much about what other people sold, but then she'd been in her own world when she was in her studio. She didn't care how much her work fetched, or who bought it – but then she was lucky that Dad dealt with the mundane realities of life, leaving her free to wander round her imagination, untroubled by VAT or recycling. 'And do you have a mailing list? And regular customers?'

'Of course, here, look. We hold four exhibitions a year, and I suppose we could have more . . . Oh dear, you're going to think me very lazy . . . But, as you can see, some events are more successful than others. Just you try getting people out here during January. We even tried bribing them with wine. No joy.'

Lorna scanned the spreadsheet. She'd examined the accounts when the estate agent sent her the details of the gallery's turnover, but now she saw the numbers in human terms. What kind of paintings brought people out on cold nights, which artists had a following, who created art that touched people's souls. She'd always known no one *needed* a painting the way they needed loo roll; every individual item had to make someone fall in love with it. It was her challenge to find the art, then find its home.

'This exhibition looks popular,' she said, pointing to one event that had five times the attendees of the next – and a hugely profitable sales total. All the paintings sold, and a reserve list of customers who hadn't managed to secure what they wanted.

'Ah, yes. That was our last Joyce Rothery night.' Mary sighed and put on her glasses. She opened the desk diary at a page filled with business cards and handwritten Post-its. 'That was a *tremendously* fun evening. Gracious! Nearly five years ago now. How time flies . . . Yes, that makes our other events look a bit flat.'

'Who's Joyce Rothery?' It wasn't a name Lorna had heard before; she felt she should have.

Mary peered at her over the edge of her spectacles. 'She's probably the best artist we have round here. Haven't you come across her?'

Lorna almost said, But what about Cathy Larkham, but didn't. She wasn't sure why.

'Um, no, I haven't, actually. What's her style?' Was Joyce Rothery responsible for the herd of close-up farm animals in the main gallery?

'Oh, she's extraordinary – she paints the most beautiful oils. Huge following, locally and further afield. Let me find the pamphlet for her last event . . .' Mary flipped through the diary. 'Here, but this doesn't do her justice!'

Lorna scanned the brochure, wondering if it would feature something she remembered from her early teens, maybe one of the magical collages that had lodged in her imagination for so long, but it didn't. Joyce Rothery's work would probably have passed her by as a teenager; she painted landscapes, but so rich and heavy with energy they felt almost human in their emotions. According to the copy, Rothery worked on a variety of scales, and each composition lured the viewer straight into the frame; colours growled in one thunderous study of a cornfield, then hummed with tranquillity in another.

'Wow.' Lorna made a mental note to tell her boss at the art charity about these. What an impact these would have in a featureless atrium, or a tense waiting room. 'I bet these are incredible in real life.'

Mary nodded. 'Keith and I bought one of Joyce's seascapes years and years ago, before I even thought of taking on the gallery, and it was the best investment I ever made.

Not because of how much it's worth now, but because it's given me so much pleasure every day, just looking at it as I make my morning coffee. It's as if I'm right there, on the seafront in a gale. I've always felt she should be more well known than she is, but there you go.'

Lorna scanned the biography. *Born in Worcestershire in 1938 to a prominent local brewing family . . . trained at the Slade . . . exhibited at the Royal Academy Summer Exhibition . . . several important exhibitions . . . lives in the Yarley valley . . .*

She started to ask a question about prices, then looked up and saw Mary was staring down at the diary with a horror-struck expression. 'Mary?'

She slammed the book shut, then looked shamefaced, and opened it. 'Oh dear.'

'Oh dear, what?'

Mary pressed her lips together in a gesture that Lorna had already spotted as a nervous tic. 'I've got a confession to make. There are a few things I should have done which I haven't, because I didn't know what was happening with the Maiden.'

Lorna's heart began to sink; she knew too much about what might happen if you let 'a few things' slide with the Inland Revenue. 'Financial . . . things?'

Mary extracted a letter from the file, and when Lorna took it off her she could see there were several pages stapled together. 'It's from the Art Week organiser at the council. I had it in my head that this was happening in August, as usual, but I see now they've moved it forward into March.'

'Oh, I read about the town's Art Week – what a great idea.' Lorna's pulse returned to normal as she took the messy pages and flipped through the correspondence. Mary obviously liked buying filing equipment more than she liked using it. 'I take it the gallery's a regular venue?'

'Yes. The main Art Week is in the summer – well, it used to be – and then there's a pre-Christmas spin-off. It attracts a lot of people to the town, and the council's got this new Arts Director who's quite . . . um, keen to expand the whole shebang. I should have answered these when they arrived but Keith didn't want me to commit and, well . . .'

The tone of the letters was certainly very slick; Calum Hardy, Head of Communications, was no stranger to a mission statement. The headed paper had a logo and everything – LAW represented in various artistic styles – and one of the attachments featured photos from previous years' projects. Six-foot-high apples dotted around town, Make and Do tents in the town square. Lorna squinted. That looked like the famous installation of naked human beings, except in the Longhampton version the volunteers were clothed in army surplus gear.

'I expect you can miss it, if you explain it's too short notice?' Mary asked, anxiously. 'It's quite a lot of work . . .'

'No, honestly, Mary, it's a brilliant way to relaunch!' Lorna opened her notebook to a new page and wrote: *Organise Art Week exhibition*. 'What's the theme this year?'

'The same as every year, I suppose. Celebrating local art.'

Local art? For a split second, Lorna considered a Cathy Larkham retrospective. What could be closer to home than her mother? That would be a major splash: boxes of Mum's work were still in Jess's storage unit: same unseen. Dad had kept nearly everything, and Lorna could easily request loans from long-standing collectors. The dark shadows and sharp lines of her mum's illustrations would look incredible against the white walls of the Maiden Gallery. She could see it in her mind's eye: people admiring the work, moving slowly around the room, glasses chinking, conversation bubbling. A childhood memory of peeping from behind a door with Jess when Mum had a rare exhibition in London mingled with her own memories of openings she'd been to as an adult, except this time she'd be the one in charge, making the speech, hosting the event, listening to stories she hadn't heard before . . .

Then her natural stubbornness swept it away. No. She had to establish herself on her own terms, as her own person. Lorna wanted artists to trust her because she had taste, not because she had a famous artist for a mother.

'Well, that's easy,' she said, clicking her pen. 'We'll get Joyce Rothery on board – her first exhibition in five years!'

Perfect. Local, profitable, respected. Tick, tick, tick.

She wrote it down, then looked up to see Mary fiddling with her spectacle chain. 'What?'

'I don't know if you can, dear. We haven't been able to get in touch with Joyce for a while.'

Lorna's enthusiasm dipped as she glanced at the biography on the brochure. Oh no. Joyce was . . . what, eighty? 'How do you mean? Is she . . .' How best to ask this tactfully? '. . . still with us?'

Mary rolled her eyes. 'She's still got all her faculties, if that's what you're hinting at. And then some. No, she lives out in Much Yarley, but she never answers the phone and won't reply to letters. It was better when her husband was alive – he was a very nice chap, always answered the phone – but he died a few years ago now.'

'Oh. And you haven't seen her about?'

'I visited. Once.' The accompanying expression added, *And never again*. 'She's not a "do drop in" kind of person. But you could always try writing. Maybe if you told her you'd just taken over the gallery? She's . . .' Mary stopped herself and her cheeks went pink. 'Do you know, I was going to say she's a very nice lady, but I have to be honest, she's not. Joyce is . . . forthright in her opinions. It's not like we didn't *try* to stay in touch with her. She made it clear she didn't want to be in touch with *us*.'

'Well, there's nothing to say artists have to be sociable.' Lorna was sure she could persuade her. Already her mind was jumping with ideas – maybe getting the primary school involved, or holding classes in the gallery? Or some event in the town itself? Live-action pottery, or a huge Jackson Pollock-style splatter fest in the park? If she put together a strong programme, Joyce would want to be involved. Surely?

'Your best bet is to appreciate her work. But don't try soft-soaping her, whatever you do.' Mary helped herself to a biscuit and put the lid firmly on the tin. 'I must stop eating these. They're so moreish. Yes, she'll either help you or she won't, but I honestly can't tell you which. Mind you, if you manage it, then you're a better woman than me.'

The effort of being truthful *and* diplomatic was written plainly over Mary's round face. Lorna wondered if that was one of the reasons the long-suffering Keith was keen for her to give up the gallery.

Meanwhile, there was still a whole wall of other artists to get through.

'I'll put the kettle on again, shall I?' Lorna suggested. If all the Maiden's creatives required as much delicate handling as Joyce Rothery, it would be a two-pot job.

Lorna woke up on Sunday morning, and took a moment to remember where she was.

The room smelled different – of packing boxes and cleaner air and dust and . . . dog.

She rolled over and saw Rudy curled up in his basket by the window, his eyes squeezed shut even though Lorna wasn't convinced he was asleep. She'd considered putting his basket in the kitchen – start as you mean to go on, and all that – but he'd whimpered and looked so frightened that Lorna had relented. She felt the grip of responsibility for him, and she didn't like it. His anxiety made *her* anxious, and, to her shame, also irritated.

Because of Rudy's many and various phobias as listed in Betty's letter – and because Lorna wasn't confident about her own dog-wrangling skills should he encounter some or all of them – she decided to take him out before breakfast. Longhampton town centre was deserted first thing on Sunday morning. The signs on the shops were turned to Closed, the pavements were empty, and chairs were stacked on café tables; Lorna hadn't expected it to be bustling, but there were literally no other souls around other than her and Rudy, scuttling along the pavement as the first light appeared in the leaden sky.

I don't remember it being this grim, she thought, and shuddered.

Lorna tucked her spare hand into the warm depths of her parka pocket and glanced down at the little dachshund, waddling by her side on his short legs, his eyes darting left and right for any approaching hazards. Rudy's world was a dark and fearful place – black dogs, big dogs, aggressive dogs, police cars, bicycles, joggers, brooms and shopping trolleys. And men. Betty's RudyCare list didn't cover solutions to his phobias, just descriptions of them.

They followed the signs pointing towards the park, and Lorna peered into the windows of her business neighbours. A few were familiar – the WHSmith was still there, the family jewellers where starry-eyed local couples had always bought their engagement rings – but her eye sought out the freshly painted frontages, as well as traces of her past. There were signs that Longhampton's independent business scene was starting to blossom on the high street, with a deli, some new cafés and a bookstore breaking up the charity shops and chains.

She paused to admire a display of soft lambswool blankets in a homeware shop, and was mentally calculating whether she could afford one when she felt the abrupt tension on the lead.

Rudy was straining at the end of it, his whole body trembling with fear. Then he barked twice, and ran behind her legs, twisting the lead round her knee.

'Ow!' Lorna hopped in pain, and turned to see what he was reacting to: at the end of the street, a long way in the distance by the pub, was another dog owner with two black Labradors walking by his side. The man raised his hand in acknowledgement but the dogs didn't even look up. Even so, Rudy seemed terrified.

He barked again, a snippy, scared noise, then panted hard. His eyes were wide and his tail whipped furiously back and forth. Lorna was surprised to feel her own muscles clench with tension.

'Don't be silly. They're not coming near you.' She

crouched to comfort him but Rudy didn't respond with his usual friendly nose-nudge. Instead he lunged towards the Labradors, then barked, then hid behind her legs, as if he couldn't work out what to do.

Lorna didn't know what to do either; it panicked her. She scooped him up, tucking him into her coat. She could feel Rudy's heart beating through his ribs, and the hot scared gasps of his doggy breath as he wriggled. His coat was so fine that the trembling in his muscles made it ripple, and even though she couldn't understand why he was so scared when the dogs were miles away, a fierce urge to protect him overwhelmed her.

'It's fine, Rudy,' she said, spinning on her heel. 'We'll go somewhere different.'

She marched back down the street until the dogs were out of sight, then set him down again outside a smart artisan cheese shop that definitely hadn't been there seventeen years ago. He was heavier than he looked. The town was starting to wake up now, and a man inside the shop pointed to the sign, thinking she was waiting for him to open.

Lorna shook her head. A woman walked past on the other side of the street, thankfully without a dog, and the smell of grilling bacon drifted out of a café. Rudy was sniffing the air. Any moment now, she thought, a bicycle's going to appear and it'll be the same all over again. She didn't want that. She didn't want to see his fear again.

Lorna looked down at the dachshund, and he looked up at her.

'You can't go on like this, Rudy,' she said. 'We need to sort this out.'

He wagged his thin tail hopefully, then cowered as a car honked its horn, streets away.

The trouble was, she hadn't the first clue how to help him and it ripped at her heart.

She sighed. 'Come on, wee man,' she said. 'Let's go home.'

The one advantage of their early start was that Lorna was in the gallery's back office by ten, ready to tackle her monstrous to-do list. Rudy curled up on a pile of bubble wrap by her feet. His first walk, at least, was one thing ticked off it, Lorna thought, watching him snoring away happily, even if it had added another set of problems to the list.

Her main task of the day was to write a brilliantly persuasive letter to Joyce Rothery, convincing her to come out of retirement to relaunch the newly invigorated Maiden Gallery. There was very little information to be found on the internet about Joyce herself, but the passionate paintings made Lorna stare into her laptop, lost in their stories. How could paint on canvas make so many other pictures and emotions spring into her mind, she wondered, gazing at a moonlit row of terraced houses or a lone boat bobbing on a silvery sea. Paintings this good made her feel even more stupid for trying to paint herself. What a waste of time that Fine Art course had been – you could either do this, or you couldn't.

Dear Mrs Rothery, she typed, checking that was how Mary had addressed her in the past. It was still Mrs Rothery. Clearly being the main point of contact for her work hadn't loosened up the formality.

Forgive the intrusion, but I've recently taken over the management of the Maiden Gallery, and I would love to talk to you about the possibility of holding a retrospective of your work. I am a great admirer of your art, and understand that this year will be the thirtieth anniversary of your first solo exhibition . . .

Lorna wrote and rewrote the letter until she was happy she'd struck the right note of friendly professionalism, then printed it out on the headed paper, decided it would be better handwritten, copied it out again using an actual pen, and addressed the envelope according to Mary's page in the desk diary.

Then she slipped out and dropped it in the red postbox immediately outside the gallery, went back into the office and started making notes on all the other artists she had to introduce herself to. There were, according to Mary's files, nearly a hundred of them. Not all of them, Lorna hoped, were obsessed with barnyard animals and fruit.

She wasn't expecting an immediate response from the notoriously reclusive Joyce, but by Friday there'd been no phone call, and no reply in the post. What Lorna did get, however, was a chirpy email from Calum Hardy from the council, in response to her own about Art Week. It was constructed almost entirely from jargon.

Calum was very keen to talk to her about her plans regarding Joyce Rothery, as well as her other, madder, suggestions. It was only when she got to the part of the email when he suggested she set up a lunch for the three of them that Lorna began to wonder if she'd perhaps overplayed her hand.

'How long should I give Joyce to get in touch?' Lorna asked Mary when they were eating chocolate chip cookies in the back office. 'I'm worried this Calum is going to show up and want to see her.'

'Oh, I wouldn't take it personally,' said Mary. 'The mayor wanted to give Joyce the freedom of Longhampton last year and she refused to answer a single communication about it. Not even when he went round. Banging on the door for ages, he was.'

'You don't think I said something to offend her?' Had she somehow worked out that Lorna was another artist's daughter? Had there been a rivalry she was unaware of?

'No! You're so polite. I'm sure you didn't.' Mary peered at a portfolio from the Art College, open by the side of the desk, and recoiled at the contents. 'Ooh. Is that . . . what I think it is?'

'Yes,' said Lorna. She'd found a whole box of portfolios, sent in on spec and ignored, so far, by Mary. Lorna didn't intend to ignore them, even if some of the subject matter was a bit . . . risqué. The gallery needed fresh blood. Maybe not quite as literally as this artist was proposing. 'You know what? I'm going to go and see Mrs Rothery myself.'

'What harm can it do?' Mary replied, but she didn't look convinced.

Chapter Four

For a dog who'd barely been inside a car for the first six years of his life, Rudy took to Lorna's Fiat very enthusiastically. He was secured on the back seat in a new car harness, but it seemed to Lorna that he'd prefer to be behind the wheel, ideally honking the horn at passing dogs and giving them the Vs.

They'd driven about five miles out of town, and so far Rudy had barked at everything. The bigger the dog, the louder his bark. Lorna was starting to wonder if Betty had left her the medal in advance for the bravery she'd need to introduce him to polite society. If they could go everywhere by car, Lorna reasoned, Rudy would be fine. He was much bolder behind a windscreen than he was outside.

They'd left Much Yarley some way back, but the satnav was insisting that Lorna's destination was right ahead. There was nothing right ahead. Just trees. And sheep. They'd passed a few farm buildings, but on both sides of the road all Lorna could see were the usual greenish fields and, ahead, an orchard of dwarf apple trees, the bare branches starkly outlined against the pale sky. She didn't recognise it from her years in the town, but then their family had never been one for countryside picnics.

Lorna pulled into a lay-by, hoping that no one with a dog would walk past them and set Rudy off again.

'So where's the house?' she said aloud. She'd learned that the sound of her voice seemed to calm him. 'Is Joyce Rothery one of those back-to-the-land people who live in tents? Did she give the gallery a false address? Did her house get demolished to make way for cider apples?'

Lorna swivelled awkwardly to see if Rudy was hanging, rapt, on her words. He wasn't: he had his paws up on the back seat and was eyeballing an approaching man and his dogs, another two Labradors that had appeared out of nowhere. They were black and identical. Rudy's sturdy brown tube of a body was quivering with tension, then he let fly with a volley of hysterical yapping. She glanced in her rearview mirror, and spotted a lane that she hadn't seen before.

'This really isn't the answer,' she told Rudy as she flung the car into a three-point-turn, 'but it'll do for now.'

Half a mile down the pot-holed lane, just as Lorna was beginning to fear for her suspension, a house appeared behind a row of trees. She slowed, and then pulled over on to the grass. There was no other car parked outside, and no sign of life behind the dark windows. Only the beautifully carved wooden sign hanging from the iron gate suggested that she'd accidentally found Rooks Hall, the home of Joyce Rothery.

Rooks Hall was small, much smaller than the name suggested, but with a sense of grandeur, sitting in a magnificently wild garden that lapped around it like a queen's skirts. The thick black outer beams emphasised its higgledy-piggledy construction – there were no right angles anywhere, and if it hadn't been standing for about three hundred years already, Lorna would have assumed it was on the verge of collapse. A climbing rose circled the door, skeletal and flowerless now, and a faint air of neglect hung about the place, but not in a careless way – more a sense of nature running riot in good soil, flourishing too fast for a gardener to keep up with, even in the depths of winter. Leaves were scattered over the path, and white snowdrops and the very earliest purple-streaked crocuses were nosing through the borders.

Lorna turned to the back seat. Rudy was gnawing his paws.

'Stay there,' she said, nerves fluttering in her own stomach. 'I won't be long. Just hide in the footwell if anything comes.'

Rudy gazed back at her from under his eyebrows, as if he'd never so much as open his mouth without permission. Then he gave a half-sigh, half-groan and curled himself into a ball on the back seat, hiding his nose under his paws.

Lorna shouldered her bag, and crossed the road to the front gate. Up close, she could see flakes of paint scabbing off the iron curlicues, and when she lifted the sneck, she had to shove hard to get in.

The front door was half bobbly glass, half green wood. It seemed too dark inside for anyone to paint, surely? The glass was almost black with lack of light, and further obscured by a cross series of stickers warning off door-to-door sellers, junk-mail distributors, Jehovah's witnesses and carol singers.

Lorna blinked at the 'carol singers'. If carol singers came this far out of town, they deserved some Quality Street at least.

She knocked again, and this time yapping erupted from

inside the hall, but she couldn't make out any movement. Someone was in, but if they were, they weren't rushing to answer to the door.

Lorna bent down and lifted the letterbox. It was stiff and protected on the other side by a vicious spring, but she managed to push it open enough to see a grizzled Border terrier on the other side, bouncing up and down. There were a few letters scattered on the mat but the rest of the hall was in shadows, and she couldn't see further.

'Hello?' She tried to make her voice sound friendly. To the dog, and anyone else who might be listening. 'Hello, there? Anyone in?'

The Border terrier responded with a series of yaps so loud its whole body quivered. Then, without warning, it launched itself at the letterbox, white teeth bared. Lorna yanked back her hand as fast as she could and nearly toppled over.

The flap snapped shut and the dog carried on yelping indignantly.

She stood up and rubbed her hands together. This wasn't going as planned. Maybe Joyce Rothery wasn't in. Or maybe she didn't answer the door, just like she didn't answer her post. Lorna had, in the past, had days when she couldn't face people either, and had refused to let anyone into her room. Until Jess had more or less barged the door down, because technically it was her room too.

I'll leave a note, Lorna thought, and reached into her bag for her notebook.

She was trying to think how to start when suddenly, without warning, the letterbox snapped open again, from the other side, revealing four spiky fingers.

'Who the hell are you?' came a voice. It snapped like the letterbox.

Lorna jumped backwards, startled, dropping her book.

'Hello,' she said and then her mind went blank. The sense of expectation emanating from a few inches away was very disconcerting.

'If that Kia's sent you, you can bugger off,' the voice went on. It was an elderly voice but it bristled with pluck, much like the Border terrier. 'I'm *fine*. I've been feeding myself for nearly eighty years, and I don't need any more patronising about drinking enough bloody tea, then about how often to go to the loo. So, off you toddle, young lady. Go and find some old dodderer who needs your help, because this old dodderer doesn't.'

'I'm not . . .' Lorna started, but the letterbox had slammed shut again.

She stood up, awkwardly. Indistinct movement on the other side of the glass suggested that Mrs Rothery had concluded the conversation was ov-*ah* and was shuffling back down the hall.

Lorna was reluctant to admit Mary had been right but it was clear Joyce didn't welcome visitors. However, she wasn't Kia. She presumed Kia was the unlucky social worker assigned to keep an eye on Joyce. Lorna had met a few patronising social workers in the course of her volunteering, and a few had talked to the volunteers as if they were senile, never mind the old people. But Lorna wasn't there to patronise Joyce – she was there to talk about her art.

She wobbled, then thought of the George Medal, sitting on her bedside table where she could see it every morning. Betty Dunlop wouldn't put up with this. Betty would remind her that she'd more or less promised Calum Hardy that she'd deliver a Joyce Rothery retrospective and she'd better get on and jolly well deliver it.

She opened up the letterbox, steadying herself with her free hand. 'I don't know who Kia is,' she called through into the hall. The air smelled of dust, and green plants. 'My name's Lorna Larkham. From the gallery? I wrote to you a few days ago – Mary Knowles suggested I come and talk to you about your work?'

There was a pause. The shuffling stopped.

'They're beautiful paintings,' Lorna went on. 'Very powerful.'

She held her breath, and crossed her fingers.

Nothing happened. Then, after a long moment, Joyce shouted, 'I don't know what you mean.'

'Mary's retired and I've taken over the gallery.'

Lorna paused, wondering if this was really the most professional way to go about it, yelling a business proposal through a letterbox. Still . . .

'Could I come in, maybe? And have a chat?' she shouted hopefully.

Joyce didn't reply, and Lorna wondered if maybe she'd gone too far, but then there was a sudden cry, and a mad thunderclap of barking.

'Bernard! Don't get under my *feet*!' And a thud like someone falling against the wall, the slither of books, something hard tumbling on to the floor.

'Are you all right?' Lorna called. 'Mrs Rothery?'

There was no response.

She pushed the letterbox further open and tried to see inside, but the angle was wrong. She could just make out the old lady in the hall, and the side table, and the dog bouncing around her, barking. Had she slipped? Was she hurt?

'Mrs Rothery? Hello? Can you let me in?'

There was a cough behind her. 'Can I help you?'

Lorna spun round. A man was standing by the gate, and for a moment she wondered if it was the dog walker she'd passed earlier – but it wasn't. This man was about her age, in a black jacket with some kind of slogan T-shirt underneath, and a messenger bag slung over his shoulder. There was a red Prius next to her car; she hadn't heard it pull up.

'Actually, yes, I'm rather worried about this lady here,' she said. 'I think she's fallen. We should probably call someone?'

'Yes, me!' he said. 'I'm her social worker. Keir Brownlow.'

He was holding out a hand to shake, but Lorna wasn't sure this was the time for formal introductions, not with a potential broken hip situation unfolding a few feet away. She shook it uneasily. 'I'm Lorna Larkham. Shouldn't we get in there and check she's all right?' She indicated the door.

'Oh! Yes, of course. Hello, Joyce! Be with you in a minute!' he called in a clear, rather patronising voice, and started searching in his messenger bag. 'I'm sorry I'm a bit late,' he added, 'but I wasn't sure you were coming today. I didn't have any of your details, just that you might be calling round before lunch. I've been out all morning with one of Jackie's clients who's just been admitted to hospital with pneumonia. Sorry if you've been waiting. Please don't put in a complaint, we're understaffed!'

What? She frowned. 'I'm not sure I'm who you think . . .' Lorna began but her words were lost in the sound of crashing from inside.

She spun and dropped to her knees to look through the letterbox again. 'Don't try to move! Are you all right? Joyce?'

'It's *Mrs Rothery*!'

The old lady had fallen against the side table and – from the jarring, jangling noise – pulled her old-fashioned telephone over with her. The dog was going mad, barking and leaping about. Her skinny ankles were exposed under her slacks, and she looked vulnerable and suddenly much less ferocious.

Lorna stood up quickly. 'We need to get in there. Have you got a key?'

'No, I haven't. She's able to open the door herself, and she refuses to give us a spare set.'

'Then how are we going to get in? She's not moving!'

Keir stepped back and started sizing up the small bay window at the front, masked with a set of dark curtains.

'Good luck with *that*,' said Lorna. She thought she could hear the old lady groaning, and the dog was hysterical, bouncing around like a rubber ball. Apart from anything else, she couldn't listen to that whining for a lot longer. He sounded like a boiling kettle. 'We'll have to barge the door.'

Keir gazed at her, horrified, through his thick glasses. 'I don't think that's the *first* option, surely?'

'It is if she's broken her hip!'

'No, I'm sorry, I *cannot* get authorisation to break someone's door, just like that. It's criminal damage. We've been taken to court for less . . .'

Lorna squinted through the letterbox. Joyce was slumped on the floor, one arm out, the other clutching her leg. The Border terrier had stopped yapping to lick his mistress's nose with worried tenderness. 'Don't worry, Mrs Rothery,' she called. 'We're on the case. We won't be a second.'

'I'm fine,' she croaked unconvincingly. 'Go away.'

At least she's conscious, thought Lorna. 'We'll go away, just as soon as we've made sure you're all right,' she offered. 'Then we'll both bugger off. How about that?'

The old lady's response was lost in more barking as the dog returned to the door to see off the intruders.

She stood up and dumped her bag on the step. 'Right,' she said. 'You mind that, I'm going round the back.'

'What?' Keir had got his phone out, dithering over whom to call.

'There's often a way in through the back door. I used to walk a Jack Russell for an old lady who kept a set of keys in the peg bag on her washing line. Don't ask,' she added in one breath. 'You stay there and keep an eye on her, keep her talking.'

She set off to the sound of Keir calling through the letterbox in the sort of 'old dodderer' tones Joyce would find most annoying. It would, Lorna suspected, irritate her enough to distract her from any pain.

As she'd hoped, the back door of Rooks Hall was easily accessible. The back garden was as wild as the front, but it led out towards open fields and a copse that was probably swarming with rabbits. There was a large shed at the bottom of the garden – that must be her studio, she thought. What a view.

Now wasn't the time for that, though. She looked around. Where would you hide a key? No peg bag, no plant pot, no 'discreet' metal acorn . . .

Lorna's eye fell on an old Lyon's Golden Syrup tin, placed not quite unobtrusively enough by the back step. Sure enough, inside was a set of keys, and she wasted no time in unlocking the door and letting herself in.

'Hello?' she called as soon as she was inside. 'Mrs Rothery,

59

it's Lorna, from outside.' The kitchen smelled musty, of old teabags and dried dog food, but it was light, with a stripy roller blind over a big window that framed a perfect landscape view of the hills and with an original starburst clock over the cooker. It was neat and tidy, not quite what she'd have expected from an artist who painted wildernesses in emotional colours.

Don't be nosy, thought Lorna, but she couldn't help taking in the details of a solitary life: the mini tin of beans, the pillboxes, the empty calendar, the decades old fabric fading on the kitchen chair seats, geometric silver and spearmint. The single mug in the sink.

She made her way to the door that led, she guessed, into the hall. The dog was pelting back and forth, barking at Keir at the front, then back to the kitchen door, and she opened it carefully. Still, Lorna managed to clunk the terrier's head by accident with the door as she let herself in. It let out a yelp and carried on barking.

The hall was dark, with framed paintings on the red walls and monochrome tiling on the floor. And lying in the middle of it, under a fallen table, was Joyce Rothery.

'For God's sake,' she croaked as Lorna crouched beside her. 'Make it stop.'

Lorna lifted up the table and set it back against the wall. 'Make what stop? The pain? Are you in pain?'

'No, Keir.' She flapped her hand towards the letterbox. 'Make him stop. Telling me to "breathe through the pain", and what have you. I'm not soft in the head or giving birth. I know how to *breathe*.'

The letterbox clattered. 'I'm only trying to help.' Keir sounded hurt.

'He's only trying to help,' said Lorna, diplomatically.

'But men often say useless things at times of crisis. Can you sit up? Do you think you've broken anything?'

'I heard that,' Keir huffed. 'But carry on.'

'Good of you.' Joyce huffed with effort as Lorna tentatively guided her into a sitting position. She was small but strong under the loose blue tunic, not quite the bird-like frail thing Lorna had expected from the view she'd had through the letterbox. 'Ouch! I've bruised something, I'd say. But nothing worse,' she added. 'I'll be fine.'

'Can you move your fingers? And your toes?' The hands were arthritic, but didn't seem as if anything was broken. Lorna checked Joyce's eyes for signs of concussion. 'Sorry for staring,' she went on, 'I've done a First Aid course.'

The beady eyes were taking in every detail of Lorna's face in return, not caring if the inspection made her uncomfortable. Joyce was a handsome woman, rather than a pretty one: she had a strong nose, clear blue eyes and high, solid cheekbones. She wore her years like the long turquoise pendant round her neck – proudly. 'I don't care for being stared at like that. It makes me wonder if you're one of those loony religious types. Or if I've got lipstick on my teeth.'

Lorna tried not to react. At least this proved there was nothing much wrong with Joyce, other than a bit of shock.

'Shall I call an ambulance?' Keir called through the letterbox. His eyes were just visible, his eyebrows beetling with concern.

'Why?' Joyce called, scornfully. 'Are you worried you're going to get into trouble with your boss?'

'No! I'm concerned about you, Mrs R. You're very hard to take care of.'

'Did you just call me Mrs R? You impertinent child.'

Lorna stifled a smile.

'I suggest you go and spend your time and effort on people who need care,' Joyce went on. She looked at Lorna. 'Quite outrageous.'

'Should I let him in?' she asked. 'He does need to see you.'

Joyce huffed, and then she dropped her voice. 'I'm perfectly all right, young lady,' she said. 'I have no desire to be "on the radar" for these people. How would you like some do-gooder trying to tell you how to live in your home?'

She looked Lorna straight in the eye, with a frankness that Lorna recognised from other supposedly old dodderers who had held very firm views on how they intended to depart this life. Betty, for one. She knew better than to argue with it.

'Then let him in and he can report you're fine,' she replied, under her breath. 'Why don't I take Bernard for a quick walk? Then when I come back, I'll insist Keir leaves with me.'

Joyce Rothery was a hard woman to help, but she was smart enough to know a deal when she saw one.

'Don't be longer than ten minutes,' she said. 'And don't let him loose. There's a lead by the front door.'

'Well, I take my hat off to you,' said Mary when Lorna returned triumphantly a few hours later. 'You've succeeded where the great Mayor Barry Williams failed. You've entered the house of Joyce Rothery.'

Lorna unclipped Rudy's lead from his harness and let

him trot over to the desk, where he flopped in the basket Mary had brought in from home. Keith hadn't let her replace Fudge their cocker spaniel as 'it was a tie' and she said she wanted to make Rudy feel as welcome as Lorna. 'I wouldn't go that far. We didn't even talk about her art. I just walked her dog up the lane, she instructed me to call her Mrs Rothery, *not* Joyce, and I said I'd pop back over the weekend to take Bernard out again.'

'Bernard?'

'Her Border terrier.'

Mary raised her eyebrows. 'So now you're her dog walker. I suppose that's one angle we didn't try – and it would be a nice outing for Rudy. How did he cope?'

'Rudy stayed in the car. I'm not sure he's ready for Bernard just yet.' Lorna couldn't help feeling torn about that. The social worker, Keir, definitely seemed to think she was someone else, someone who was *supposed* to be walking Mrs Rothery's dog, and she hadn't exactly put him straight about it. Well, no. She hadn't put him straight at *all*. Her conscience pricked her. Should she? His card was in her jacket pocket.

But what then? He'd get in touch with the right person, and she'd lose her chance to gain Joyce Rothery's trust. Lorna already had a mental image of them bonding over their favourite artists, the dogs snoring at their feet by the fire. Hmm, the dogs. Putting aside Joyce's own prickliness, it would take a bit of work to get Rudy and Bernard to make friends – from the growling Rudy had set up in the car, she'd decided it would be safer to walk Bernard up the lane on his own – for now. But maybe a feisty pal was exactly what timid Rudy needed, she argued.

Plus, if Lorna was honest, she didn't want to come clean. Keir looked the type to be powerfully disappointed, and Joyce would think she was a complete chancer.

'So what happened while I was out?' she asked instead.

'Belinda Shapiro dropped off some more of her painted wine glasses.' Mary pulled her lower lip wide, exposing her lower dentures in a show of awkwardness. 'Sorry. I said you'd have them. I find it very hard to say no to Belinda.'

'How many painted wine glasses have you sold?' Lorna racked her brains for Belinda Shapiro in the sale lists she'd seen. The name didn't ring a bell. She couldn't remember seeing any wine glasses either, painted or otherwise.

'What, ever?'

'Yes, ever.'

Mary looked evasive. 'Well . . . You know that big box in the stockroom upstairs?'

The pair of them looked round the empty gallery, and the yellow sheep's eyes stared back. If the wine glasses weren't on display to leaven the barnyard domination, Lorna concluded, they must be very, very bad.

'Oh, Calum Hardy called too,' said Mary, hastily changing the subject. 'He wants to come round to interview you for the local paper about your plans for the gallery. And Art Week. And of course, yourself.'

'When?' asked Lorna.

Mary looked apologetic. 'Um . . . early next week?'

'Great!' Deadlines were good. There was a lot you could achieve in a few days, she told herself.

Later that evening, Lorna lay flat on her back on the brand-new yoga mat and stared at the blank canvas leaning by the fireplace in the biggest spare bedroom. She'd decided this room was going to be kept empty for yoga and 'mindfulness' – and maybe some artistic inspiration floating up from the gallery below.

But instead, she felt overwhelmed. How did artists know where to start? How did they summon up the courage to make the first mark on that perfect whiteness? What did it feel like to have that finished version in your mind, and believe you could bring it out for everyone to see? Her course had focused on traditional life drawing, and it had taken Lorna hours to start a single piece – she'd fiddled around getting her pencils exactly right, the light, the angles, while everyone else was sketching away, their vision taking shape on the paper like stop-motion animation. There'd been no excuses: the best teachers, the perfect light, no pressure, as much inspiration in the beautiful Italian countryside as anyone could ask for.

And yet there'd been nothing harder in that whole pointless year than the starting. Once the first stroke was down, Lorna had known she'd never be able to transmit what she saw in her mind's eye. Creativity, she'd come to realise, was an instinct that threw out ideas like sparklers, a unique filter only you saw the world through, whatever you wanted to call it. Her mum had it – her mum was *made* of creativity – but Lorna didn't have it, or the confidence to fake it.

She sighed and turned her head, so she could look out into the night sky and the stars caught in the neat grid of the sash windowpanes. They were beautiful old windows. The darkness outside made her feel weightless and free, as if she could float away out into the night, over the hills and up beyond the glittering heavens. In the half-light of the silent room, without anyone there to tell her who Lorna Larkham had been or should be, Lorna closed her eyes and willed the secret hopes and wishes and dreams that *had* to be hidden inside her flow out with each breath.

This room might show her a way to be creative. If not drawing classically like her mum, then maybe collage? Or sculpture? Or abstracts?

Nothing came. No flash, no spark. Nothing.

For God's sake. What was *wrong* with her? Here she was, her heart empty and open, in a place full of memories, in her own space for the first time, alone but with everything in front of her. Surely that sort of infinite possibility, that sort of *fear*, had to spark something?

But it didn't. Lorna only felt numb, and a bit thirsty.

'Bollocks,' she muttered, and got up to make another cup of tea.

Chapter Five

Driving towards Much Yarley again on Sunday morning, braced with some ideas from the internet about helping anxious dogs make new friends, Lorna started to feel a strange sense of déjà vu. Some of the landmarks seemed familiar but she wasn't sure whether it was because she recognised them from the previous visit, now she wasn't focused on the satnav, or from her childhood.

She and Jess hadn't had a particularly active social life – or rather, she hadn't. From more or less the moment they'd moved to the town, Jess had been glued to Ryan Prothero's side, and Lorna had tagged along, but not every time because there were limits to even her boredom threshold. It was worse when Ryan turned seventeen, and acquired his first car. Sitting in the back of his Renault Clio listening to Ryan and Jess run through their extensive list of soppy pet names while driving laps of Longhampton's one-way system was *awkward*. No wonder she'd preferred to spend her weekends in the library, or Longhampton's perfunctory town museum, or doing the loop of the shops, avoiding the Goths by the war memorial.

Every so often, Dad would bung Jess a tenner to take Lorna along to one of Ryan's Young Farmers' Club events. Strictly speaking, Ryan wasn't a young farmer – his dad had a farm-machinery business which kept both Protheros in matching Range Rovers – but his best mate Sam 'Ozzy' Osborne was a fifth-generation son of the soil, and that gave them all access to an active social calendar of ploughing matches and discos in barns, sometimes with a chicken or two wandering through during the slow dances.

Lorna wondered if Much Yarley was where Ozzy's dad's farm had been as she passed a field of cows. It rang a faint bell. They definitely had cows, she remembered that, because of the secret Ozzy had confided in her, in the dark corner of one post-ploughing-match disco. He'd told her that he was glad his brother Gabe ("Big Ozzy") was going to inherit the farm, because the thought of raising cows, just to slaughter them, made him sick. Ozzy's sweet cider breath had been hot against her ear as he leaned in close so no one would hear him, and Lorna's stomach had flipped first because the Lynx-and-teenage-boy smell of his shirt was so exotic, and then because she realised he'd just shared something very secret indeed. Lorna knew next to nothing about farming but even she knew Ozzy's dad would go ballistic at the idea of his son getting all vegetarian about the cows.

Lorna had a secret too, but one she didn't want to share: a raging crush on Ozzy that was inappropriate for a just-thirteen-year-old, given that he was seventeen, a sixth former. She hadn't told anyone – who was there to tell? Their parents didn't initiate conversations about that sort of thing, and Jess was prone to random acts of Big Sisterliness and might stop her seeing Ozzy – with whom she had a genuine friendship – 'for her own good'. Her school-friends, the academic violin-playing types with nice hair, were sniffy about the YFC crowd, but when Lorna gazed up into Ozzy's brown eyes, soft and trusting like the cows on the farm, her whole body glowed. Nothing, and no one, in Lorna's life had come close to that moment. She'd felt important and warm, as if she was sitting in the sun. Trusted, and understood. And it scared her as much as it warmed her inside.

Funny how four years mattered so much then, she thought as she turned off the main road towards Rooks Hall. The next time she'd seen Ozzy had been in London, when she was just back from the humiliating experience of her art course and temping until she worked out what to do next. She'd been having a drink with her flatmate Tiffany, a student nanny whose pragmatic mum had instructed her to have one cocktail a week in an expensive bar 'because you never know who you might meet', and she wouldn't have recognised Ozzy if he hadn't given up trying to catch her eye and marched over to where she was standing. In place of the checked shirts and jeans she'd been used to, he was wearing a suit and glasses, and had had his brown curls cropped short, and when Lorna said, 'Oh my God, Ozzy!' he'd looked pained and said, 'Can you call me Sam, please?'

Sam. She'd always thought of him as Sam, even though she'd never heard Jess and Ryan use his real name. His name wasn't even Sam: it was Samson. Big Ozzy's real name was Gabriel. Their mother, Mrs Ozzy, was a church-warden, like many Mrs Osbornes before her. Another little detail he'd shared, and she'd stored in her heart like pressed flowers or train tickets.

It turned out, as they shouted over the clamour in the bar, that Ozzy – *Sam* – had got himself a job with a prop-erty developer in Islington; he'd told her what he did, but it was noisy, and she'd been distracted by how easily he wore his new city clothes, and then distracted again by how on earth she could spin her awful year abroad. They'd had several drinks, during which time his accent came back a bit, then when he had to leave to go on somewhere else, she'd missed the moment to get his number, or even ask where he was going. A date, she'd assumed, embarrassed by her disappointment. Lorna hadn't seen him again until her father died, and all the Osbornes were at the funeral. Kindly and solid in their church suits, Ozzy – Sam – tanned in a slightly different way to his brother Gabe, who was now working full time on the farm.

'Ozzy was always going to leave,' Jess had muttered as they stood in the line outside the church and shook everyone's hands. 'He was never going to be a farmer.'

'I know,' Lorna had muttered. She knew that because they'd made a promise to one another, she and Sam, one late night just before things went properly wrong.

'If you ever come back and find me here,' he'd said, lying back on the hay bale as they gazed up into the star-dotted night sky, 'shoot me. I'll do the same for you.' He'd pretended to spit on his hand before holding it out, and she took it, and shook it, and wished she was just two years older, so maybe he would kiss her instead.

Lorna knew he remembered because when the Osbornes reached them in the line, Sam had leaned forward to kiss her cheek, London-style, and he'd whispered, 'Don't shoot me this time, obviously.' It had made her laugh on a day when she'd felt completely blank with grief. Only Sam could do that.

If only that *had* been the last time she'd met him. Lorna winced. It still made her cringe, thinking about it, so she pushed the memory away before it could start rolling out in her head.

A herd of cows crossing the road ahead made her slow down, and finally stop. They were fine-looking beasts, small and black with a thick white stripe down their bellies, like a football top. The man driving them across into the field opposite was assisted by a collie but they didn't seem to need much intervention as they ambled over into the next field, tails swishing and flicking. Their peaceful expressions made Lorna feel irrationally envious.

She swivelled in her seat, already anticipating Rudy's aggressive fear-response to the herd but he was sitting up, watching them with curiosity, not fear.

'Oh, right,' she said. 'So you're fine with cows but not Labradors? Where is the logic in that?'

Rudy wagged his tail and farted happily.

'Are you absolutely sure that the countryside is appropriate for that dog?' Joyce Rothery gave Lorna a suspicious look from just around the doorframe. 'I can see three pot holes from here in which you could quite easily lose the poor little bugger.'

At least they weren't conducting the conversation through the letterbox this time. Joyce had opened the door far enough to pin Lorna to the doorstep with a look, while keeping Bernard, who was also peering round inquisitively, penned back with one leg.

From the way Bernard's ears were vibrating, he seemed to be wagging his tail hard behind the door at the prospect of another trip out. Lorna hoped he was transmitting positive dog vibes to Rudy who didn't look quite so keen. But so far, Border terriers seemed to be on Rudy's short list

71

of acceptable dogs. She had a small bag of cheese pieces to encourage positive associations, if necessary.

'I can't walk him in town,' she said truthfully. 'Rudy's scared of pretty much everything. His first owner was an old lady with a terminal heart condition so she didn't get out with him much. Rudy misses her, and the country-side's very new to him – it's set him back a bit.'

Joyce's pursed lips relaxed slightly. 'Poor chap. What a big change.'

'We're doing our best, aren't we?' Rudy looked up from under his smooth eyebrows. His coat had started to shine again, and Lorna hoped it wouldn't rain. 'Shall I take Bernard out then?'

Joyce seemed less sure about entrusting Bernard to Lorna than she had been a few days ago. 'Whatever that inter-fering fusspot Keir might have told you,' she said, 'I am perfectly capable of walking my own dog.'

'Of course you are.' Lorna tried to sound positive and non-patronising. 'But it's best to give bruises a chance to heal. It would be a shame if Bernard was bouncing off the walls and got under your feet again. How are you feeling, by the way?'

'Don't start, please. I'm *fine*.'

Bored with the human chat, Bernard had spotted a blackbird in the hedge opposite, and lunged forward with a joyous bark, wriggling past Joyce's leg. If Lorna hadn't managed to get one fingertip under his collar, he'd have been across the road and away. She looked up, and Joyce was gripping the doorframe, shaken, and suddenly vul-nerable, despite her proud attitude.

'Let me run some of this energy off?' Lorna suggested. 'Do you have a lead? Or maybe a lasso?'

Joyce regarded her for a second, then said, 'I'll get it.'

She was gone a moment, during which time Bernard and Rudy sniffed each other in wide circles, and when Joyce returned, holding an extending lead designed for a much bigger dog, she said, with a cynical arch of her eyebrow, 'It's quite a coincidence, isn't it? You running the gallery where I used to exhibit my paintings, and being Keir's Cinnamon Trust volunteer.'

Ah ha! So Keir thought she was a Cinnamon Trust volunteer. Lorna knew what they did – walk dogs for older people – from her hospice work. Plus, Joyce had hopefully read the letter she'd sent. Two interesting facts.

'Isn't it?' Lorna smiled; then she mentally warned herself not to tell any outright lies, just to make things easier. She pulled the draft programme she'd prepared out of her bag. 'I thought you might like to read this – it's about the programme of events I'm planning this spring to bring the Maiden Gallery right back into the heart of town life. Including the Art Week exhibitions? I thought we could—'

Joyce took the paper from her, and handed her the lead. 'Don't let Bernard get into any foxes' you-know-what,' she said, and closed the door.

With Rudy and Bernard racing ahead of her on leads like a small husky team, Lorna set off up the lane from Rooks Hall towards the public footpath.

Bernard seemed to know where he was going, and Lorna soon realised why Joyce had given her a lead suitable for a small horse: he had the pulling power of a dog ten times his size. After a tentative sniff or two of his new friend, Rudy kept up with more gusto than she'd expected, and she found herself lengthening her own stride to stay with the two dogs. When Bernard stormed down a gravelled siding, she and Rudy followed, and after a few hundred metres of high hedgerows, the path turned again and they were walking alongside a field, edged along the horizon with a perfect line of trees rising like harp strings against the pale blue sky.

This is beautiful, thought Lorna, struck with the cleanness of the light, and got her phone out to take a photograph. It was a chilly day, and she had to peel off one glove to touch the phone screen, then juggle both extending leads in one hand, while holding the glove. It was only a matter of time before a hard tug on one lead made her lose her balance.

Rudy's sniffy circling and Bernard's exuberant wandering had tangled up their leads and now Bernard was yanking Rudy around on his harness in a way that he clearly didn't like. Bernard carried on bouncing, but Rudy's ears flattened as a growl came from him. She'd never heard *that*.

'Hey, hey, lads.' Lorna shoved her phone back in her pocket. The leads had retracted now, leaving the tangle even harder to sort out. There was no alternative; she'd have to unclip them. 'Don't you two move while I do this, please . . .'

Even before the words had left her mouth, Bernard spotted movement in the field and he lunged at it, pulling Lorna's fingers straight out of the loop on his collar. Without a backward glance, he was pelting across the pasture in hot pursuit of something . . . Lorna squinted: a brown rabbit. Even though he looked like a teddy bear with his funny stiff-legged gait, there was a murderous purpose about the way Bernard was fixed on the bunny, and Lorna's heart sank. 'Bernard!' she howled.

The rabbit was quick, zigzagging from one side to another, but the Border terrier was determined and stir-crazy and had pest control in his blood. When the rabbit made a dash for the hedge, so did Bernard, and then both were out of sight.

'Bernard! Come back here right now!' she yelled, pointlessly, clipping Rudy on to his lead. She set off at a trot but she was no match for them, and after a few minutes of running and yelling Lorna came to a breathless stop at the place in the hedge where they'd vanished, put her hands on her hips and tried to work out what to do next.

The field looked empty, but it dipped and hollowed out near a small wood, so there could be sheep somewhere around. They clumped together, Lorna knew that, so it didn't mean she mightn't run into a whole flock of them any moment. She started walking briskly towards the wood. The rabbit had probably headed home, with Bernard in hot pursuit.

'Bernard? Bernard!' she called, and then stumbled in shock as a gunshot ripped across the still morning air. Then another. Then a third. She'd never heard a real gun before. It sounded harsher than on television, brutal and metallic.

Lorna froze where she was, and a hot acid rose up her throat. She could smell the cordite. Something had died.

Two pheasants rattled up from the trees ahead, and a man strode out of the woodland, a shotgun on his shoulder. Lorna assumed he was a gamekeeper or a farmer from the dark green jacket and boots, and the furious expression.

'Was that your dog?' he yelled, jerking his thumb behind him. 'Loose in the field?'

Was that?

'No! I mean, yes – have you shot him?' She felt sick. Oh my God. What was she going to tell Joyce? 'You shot him? He was only chasing a rabbit!'

'In a field of pregnant ewes? Yes, I bloody did shoot at him, you stupid bitch.'

Rudy was trembling by her feet and now he started barking fearfully as the man advanced on Lorna. She picked the little dog up and shoved him into her jacket for safety, feeling his panic blending with her own.

'Where is he?' Lorna's legs trembled with adrenalin, but she made herself walk towards the man. 'There aren't any sheep in this field. You're lying.'

'So? He shouldn't be loose.' The man's eyes were narrow, and a cold anger tightened his face. 'It's townie morons like you who cause thousands of pounds' worth of damage to—'

'It was an accident! He wasn't off the lead on purpose, I'm not *stupid*.' Lorna scanned the field, trying not to cry with shock. Poor Bernard – hyper and daft and sweet, he couldn't be *dead*. 'Where is he? You just shot him and left him to die?'

The man's lip curled contemptuously.

'Simon! Oi, Simon!' The blart of an engine made them both turn round. 'I've got him.'

Someone was coming up from the other side of the field, bouncing over the tuffets on a quad bike. The driver was steering with one hand, because the other hand was gripping the scruff of a very much alive Bernard. Relief flooded Lorna's body, and she ran towards the bike.

'I'm so sorry,' she cried. 'I'm walking him for someone and he got away from me, and I *know* it's dangerous to let dogs off their lead . . .'

'Yeah, yeah. You're lucky – the sheep are in the upper field. This one nearly got himself stuck down a rabbit hole, though. Didn't you?' He gave him a shake, but Bernard wriggled round to try to lick him.

The quad-bike driver was younger than the other man – he had a beard but a thick, trendy one, and he was dressed in the padded gilet, checked shirt and jeans uniform of every Young Farmer Lorna had ever met, male or female. The only concession to the bitter wind was a navy trapper hat, rammed down over his dark hair, and when he pushed the brim back with a strong hand, revealing wind-reddened cheekbones above the beard, Lorna squinted in surprise.

A rush of recognition, orange and red-gold like lava, coursed through her, sending her centre a little off-balance, just as it always had done. That a face could feel so familiar, and so full of possibilities at the same time, as if she and he had known each other over and over in previous lives but not quite this one yet.

'Ozzy?' she said.

He pulled off his hat, and there he was. That specific arrangement of thick straight eyebrows over long-lashed brown eyes that had always struck Lorna as being the perfect balance between strong and pretty for a handsome man's face. But now there was that distracting beard, and a roughness there hadn't been before, and, in the second he recognised her, just a fleeting recoil that made her think that maybe he was feeling as awkward about this unexpected meeting as she was.

'Sam,' he said impatiently. 'If you don't mind, Lorna.'

The beard was a half-decent disguise but Lorna would have known it was Ozzy just from the way he walked over to her once he'd jumped off the quad bike. He was smaller and finer-featured than his older brother Gabriel, but he had a physical presence – not defiant, exactly, but definite. Sam was a man who occupied his own space like a boy standing on a wall, challenging anyone to knock him off it. Little Brother Syndrome, he'd once called it, and asked her if Little Sister Syndrome was the same.

Lorna had told him it wasn't. She'd positively benefited from Jess's make-up and wardrobe, although obviously Jess hadn't always been aware of it at the time.

'Hello, *Sam*,' she said, and for a moment, she nearly hugged him. Just in time she held out her hand. Then she pulled off her glove and reoffered her bare hand. There was formal, and there was formal between old friends. 'Hello, there.'

He smiled, just, and when their skin touched Lorna felt the old warmth spread through her; she knew she wasn't thinking straight from the shock Bernard had just given her, but she couldn't recall any – *any* – of the witty things she'd planned to spit out, were she and Sam Osborne ever to meet again. Instead, her stupid mouth was smiling. *Why?* Why was she smiling when his mate had pretended to shoot Bernard? Why was she smiling when the last time they'd met, she'd promised herself that was the last time *ever*?

Ozzy – Sam – scratched his beard and forced out a better smile. It was crooked, as if he was trying too hard to make it look natural. His hand was warm, and he held hers for a second too long before shaking it and letting go.

'Remind me. What did we say about finding each other back here?' he said.

Damn. She should have been quicker off the mark; she could have got in with that. 'I could say the same.' Lorna shaded her eyes against the sunshine. That was a good point . . . what was *he* doing here? With a beard? On *a quad bike*? 'I really am sorry about the dog. It was an accident; he slipped off.'

Bernard was looking annoyingly docile under Sam's arm, as if butter wouldn't melt in his shaggy face.

The man in the green jacket butted in, before the conversation could get going. He pointed his finger at Lorna. 'Next time we see a dog in this field . . . bang.' He made a gun-cocking gesture and stormed off towards the woods.

'Yeah, OK, Simon, she's got the message,' called Sam, and turned back to Lorna with a shrug. 'We've had a few dogs loose and it's coming up to lambing. Simon's had a run-in with a couple of owners already.'

'You're . . . working for him?' Lorna hazarded.

'No! He's one of the farm managers.'

'And you're . . . managing property round here? Your boss bought a country estate?'

'No. Are we playing Twenty Questions? You can just ask me.'

Rudy wriggled inside Lorna's jacket, and she extracted him, setting him on the ground and making a big show of attaching him to his lead. 'Why aren't you in London, telling flaky people like me how to run their businesses?'

Nuts. She hadn't meant to say that, and she certainly hadn't meant it to sound so snippy. But out it had come, on a little gust of bitterness. The exact words.

'Whoa.' Sam stepped back, raising his hands. 'I take it you're not still in the urban art game?'

'Nope,' said Lorna. 'That ship has sailed. Like the *Titanic*.'

He smiled, then looked uncomfortable.

'You were right.' Lorna forced herself to sound blasé. 'If it makes you feel better. The overheads *were* ridiculous, and maybe I did make a few . . .' Quite a lot. '. . . bad choices. But you live and learn. It was an . . . experience.'

He shrugged. 'I'm a numbers man. That's all. I wasn't judging anything else . . .'

Bad idea to mix business and pleasure. The memory flared in Lorna's mind like a bee sting. His tone, the flush, the awkwardness, the pure *ugh* of the whole thing.

They looked at each other, surrounded by fields and birds and open sky. It was so surreally different to the last time they'd met that Lorna made herself revisit that last conversation: then, they'd been surrounded by artisan gins, tattooed hipsters and loud music. She'd initiated the meeting, ostensibly to ask Sam's advice about her business plan – a pop-up gallery for graffiti-inspired urban art in an East London arch – but also because she wanted to see him, as an adult, with her new adult confidence. His business advice had been blunt, but then . . . Lorna squirmed away from the emotions that oozed through the memories. She'd held it together until he'd left the restaurant, discreetly paying the bill on his way out, and she'd gone home determined to prove him wrong, even though in her heart of hearts, she suspected Sam knew what he was talking about. On every level.

'If it makes *you* feel better,' he said, 'I'm not pleased to be right. Anyway, no need to keep guessing, I'm back here. It's our farm,' he added, jerking his head towards the hill when she looked confused. 'Hello? How much of your early life have you blanked out? You don't even remember where we live?'

'No!' Lorna looked in the direction and could just make out the tips of brick buildings on the horizon, a spire in an animal shape, probably a cow. 'I never went to your farm.'

'You did! You went to at least one ploughing match in our upper field.'

'Was it your upper field? They all look the same to me. Are you confusing me with my big sister? She often pretended to be interested in ploughing matches.'

'Nope,' said Sam, deadpan. 'I can honestly say I've never confused you with Jess.'

'But *why* are you back? I'm assuming it's just a holiday – if you're really back then obviously hell has . . .' Lorna stopped, the laugh stuck in her throat. *Frozen over.*

Maybe something hellish *had* happened. It would take a disaster to prise Sam's Oyster card from his hands.

'Hell has frozen over, were you going to say?' He met her eye unflinchingly.

'Yes.' She faltered. 'Yes, I guess so. I'm sorry, Sam, is everything all right?'

Sam held her gaze for a moment longer, then glanced down at his boots. 'Dad's not been well for a while. Gabe had taken over the farm, then the daft beggar got in the way of a baler last summer. He was in hospital for two months, told he wouldn't be able to work full time again, so Dad phoned me. Basically, come back or he puts the farm up for sale. It's been in the family for four generations so . . .' His accent had slid back into the local patterns, Lorna noticed. Curvier and softer, but with a trace of apology, as if he knew *she* knew it wasn't really how he spoke. Sam had never had as much of a local accent as Ryan or his brother, even before he moved to Fulham.

'Oh. Wow. Poor Gabe. I guess . . . well done, you.' Lorna didn't know what to say. It didn't make sense – well, Sam wanting to help his family out made sense, but as a farmer? The cows! He used to do anything to avoid being on the farm when the wagon came for market – was he now handling the abattoir calls?

'Is it still a . . . beef farm?' She couldn't remember if it was dairy or beef cattle. All she remembered was the way Ozzy had described the soft gummy snuffles of the calves, the playful joy with which even the older cows kicked up their heels in fresh straw.

'We had both, but we've packed the dairy side in. Not enough money in mass-produced milk.' He turned his attention back to Bernard, who was nibbling the zip of Sam's gilet. 'We're diversifying.'

'Great!' Lorna didn't know what to say. It was just too . . . odd, seeing Sam here like this. She felt unprepared, discombobulated, and he didn't look much calmer. It wasn't one of the many scenarios she'd rehearsed in her head.

Her instincts muttered *get out, get out,* and she busied her hands with Bernard's lead. Rudy was patiently waiting by her feet, sniffing at the ground with interest. It was probably his first time in a sheep field. He was unfazed by sheep poo. And, Lorna noted, unfazed by Sam. 'Anyway, don't want to keep you from what you were doing, you're obviously busy.'

Sam lifted the terrier down, holding his collar until

Lorna had him clipped on. 'And why are *you* back?' he asked casually.

'I've bought an art gallery.'

'What? You're kidding? Again?'

'Different time, different place. I know this is going to work.' She straightened, defences rising. Sam didn't need to know about the one-year plan.

'Well, you know where to come for some advice you can ignore.'

Lorna forced the corners of her mouth upwards; she didn't want to hear all that again. 'Brilliant. And you know where to come for some art you think is crap. Anyway . . .' She flapped her arms, ending the conversation. 'I need to get back. It's good to see you. Sorry about the dog, won't happen again.'

'Lorna, don't be . . .' he started, grabbing at the changing mood. Then he seemed felled by awkwardness too. 'Good to see you. Let's have a drink in town. Catch up.' Sam lifted a hand to shield his eyes from the sun and she couldn't quite make out his expression, whether he meant it or not. 'I haven't heard from Ryan in ages, be nice to find out what the Protheros are up to.'

'Child transport, mainly,' she said. 'It's all about the logistics.'

'Great.' Sam smiled, more naturally this time, and his brown eyes crinkled at the edges. He looked older; the strong eyebrows made sense on his face now, the beard gave him a solidity his personality had had long before his body caught up.

Lorna wondered if she looked different to Sam, or if he still just saw the awkward little sister pretending to like homebrew scrumpy. Had she said something that had stuck in Sam's memory for nearly twenty years, the way his confession about the cows had stuck in hers? No, the thing he remembered first about her was her promise to leave. And here she was.

It wasn't just the cow secret, though. Millions of fragments of Sam had stuck in her mind like splinters: thousands of tiny comments, glances, jokes, songs, evenings she'd hoarded up, hooking into her own memory until it was impossible to separate them out from her own. He'd always been there, in her tapestry. But his recollection of those years was probably very different. Everyone's was. It was probably just as well you couldn't see how out of focus you were, in their version of your own past.

Lorna lifted her hand. 'Bye, Sam,' she said and walked off with the two dogs before she could spoil it by saying anything else.

Chapter Six

It had been the politest 'no' Lorna had ever heard, to the point where she'd thought Joyce was leading up to saying yes. It would have made such a perfect story in the catalogue notes too: *After saving her dog Bernard from being shot, Lorna Larkham was able to persuade Joyce Rothery to curate a retrospective in her newly reimagined Maiden Gallery* . . .

But Joyce had said no. A non-negotiable no. When Lorna had dropped Bernard back, and asked Joyce if she'd read her ideas about Art Week, and whether she'd had time to consider the letter she'd written her about a retrospective, the answer was brisk and definite.

'I normally ignore letters,' she'd said matter-of-factly, 'but since you've been kind to Bernard, I'll tell you straight, Miss Larkham – I'm not interested in any exhibitions, or retrospectives or whatever you care to call them. I've drawn a line under that part of my life. I'm no longer an artist. So thanks for your interest, but if that was the ulterior motive for these walks, you're free to stop coming now.'

Lorna hadn't known what to say. She'd stammered something about that being fine, that she understood, but it had felt as if she'd made a faux pas by even asking. Surely artists were artists? For ever? Her mother had never stopped, she'd been consumed by creativity from the moment she woke up until the very last moment of her life – you couldn't retire from it.

And the implication that she'd only been walking Bernard to connive her way into Joyce's favour – it made her cringe.

'The old biddy!' said Mary, when Lorna passed on the news. Then she looked ashamed. 'Sorry, mean of me. I suppose it's her choice. So, *are* you?' she added. 'Going to stop walking Bernard?'

'I can't, can I?' Lorna reached for the biscuit tin, Mary's friend in times of stress. 'I'll look like a total opportunist! No, of course I'll keep going,' she went on. 'It's a nice walk, and Rudy seems to be OK with Bernard. It's good to go somewhere where we don't meet many people.'

Sam on his quad bike roared across her mind. They'd seen each other, and got it out of the way, but she'd come here for space, to be herself, not try to pick up threads of the past. She didn't need Sam Osborne continuing to lecture her about how to run her life.

'Well, you tried. And there are still plenty of other absolutely *top-quality* artists on our books.' Mary brushed crumbs off her scarf; it looked very like the box of unsold silk-printed scarves Lorna had come across in the stockroom, under the box of unsold painted wine glasses.

'I need to come up with something different for Calum Hardy now,' she said glumly.

'I'm sure you will!' Mary gestured to the front of the gallery. 'Incidentally, I've had so many lovely comments this morning about your window display!'

Lorna had spent Sunday afternoon reorganising the broad gallery window to showcase the few pieces of non-agricultural artwork she had to offer: a set of collage seascapes by a retired vicar from Much Langton who described them as 'a serendipitous orchestration of the found and the construct', four blue porcelain bowls which she'd filled with polished pebbles and frothy gypsophilia, and some studies of seashells in pastel frames. To bring the display together, Lorna pinned one of her own craft projects down the middle: a child's mermaid tail she'd made at a machine-knitting night class a few years ago.

'But I must ask,' Mary went on, 'where did you find this lovely mermaid's tail? I don't recognise it, and I'm sure I'd remember selling it.'

'It's mine.' Lorna had to admit it had turned out well, after the tutor had helped her . . . quite a lot. The scales were worked in different colour wools, and she'd sewn sequins on at random so it glittered. It had been her attempt to find a creative spark, albeit with a pattern. Lorna could not go off pattern. 'It's not as hard as it looks,' she added.

'I think it's exquisite.' Mary touched the scales admiringly. 'In fact, do you know, I'd like to buy it for my granddaughter. Would you give me a staff discount?'

'I've been meaning to talk to you about this – shouldn't *I* be paying *you* to be here?' Mary's continued, unpaid presence in the gallery had been niggling at Lorna; she didn't want to take advantage. 'I know we haven't been busy, but I do appreciate your help, and . . .'

Mary flapped her hand. 'Oh, no, it's rather fun when you don't have to worry about the bills. You can pay me in mermaid tails. That is, if that gentleman in the window isn't going to snap it up first. Look! He's been staring at it for ages now. Coo-ee! Why don't you come in?'

Coo-ee, thought Lorna with an inward smile, watching

Mary beckon through the glass. Who still said *coo-ee*? But the smile faded when she saw who was peering into the gallery.

It was Keir Brownlow, staring right at her and looking seriously pissed off.

'Mary,' she started, 'I don't think he's . . .'

She was already opening the door, practically dragging Keir in off the street. 'Come on in,' she was saying. 'Would you like a closer look at our lovely mermaid tail? It's bespoke!'

Lorna froze. Keir's pleasant face was red and as near to cross as she imagined he got. He looked pained, as if getting this mad wasn't something he enjoyed. He disentangled himself from Mary's grasp. 'It's actually your colleague I'd like a word with.'

'Ah! This is Lorna, she's the owner of the gallery.' Mary gave her a theatrical wink. '*And* the knit-smith in question. I will leave you two to it!'

She shimmered off to the back room, trailing a cloud of White Linen.

Keir and Lorna regarded each other without speaking for a moment, then he whined, in a voice sharp with disappointment, 'You know what I'm going to say, don't you?'

'No? Is there a problem?' Lorna hated being caught doing something she shouldn't be.

'A problem? Don't you think it's a *problem* if someone lies about who they are, in order to gain access to a vulnerable member of the community?'

'I'm not sure what you . . .'

'You're not from the Cinnamon Trust.' He was clenching his fists. 'Are you?'

Keir's injured expression seemed to be hoping she'd say

she was, and Lorna almost wondered how quickly she could apply once he'd left the shop, so it wouldn't be a lie if she did say she was, but . . .

Jess's disapproving face floated into her mind.

'No,' she admitted. 'I'm not.'

'So when you let me assume you *were* someone who was security checked and recommended to us, so that I gave you access to our client's home, you were knowingly and deliberately misleading me and, in effect, the social services? It's a criminal offence!'

'Now, *wait* a second.' Lorna raised her hands. 'Did *you* ask me for any ID? Did you even mention the words Cinnamon Trust? I was there for perfectly legitimate reasons. *You're* the one who didn't do the checks. If anyone's screwed up here, it's you.'

Keir squirmed but he wasn't finished. 'You didn't say you weren't. That's just lying by omission; it's how scam artists get started. They win the trust of vulnerable people and then when they're comfortable with the abuser, they steal their life savings. And more than that, their faith in other people! Which, when you're a vulnerable adult like Mrs Rothery, is way more precious.'

'Oh, come on . . . Do I look like a confidence trickster?' She didn't even query the vulnerability of Joyce 'I'm fine' Rothery.

'You certainly had me fooled,' Keir retorted, as if he was the epitome of streetwise social workerdom.

Lorna suppressed her snort, for the sake of his pride. 'I wasn't trying to fool anyone . . . Look! Joyce sold most of her paintings through this gallery.' She swept a hand around the shop floor. 'That's why I was there – I was visiting her to talk about staging an exhibition of her work.'

'Her work?'

'Yes,' said Lorna patiently. 'Joyce Rothery is an important local artist. Didn't you ever notice the paintings in her house?'

'Not really. I've never managed to get inside. She keeps me on the step.' Keir's bluster dropped a couple of notches, at which point Mary appeared with a tea tray.

'Have a cup of tea and calm down, Keir,' said Lorna. 'Let's start this conversation again.'

Keir pushed his thick glasses up his nose, dropping his messenger bag by a jewellery cabinet. He took the mug Mary was offering him, cupped it in both hands as if it was a precious gift, then sank down on a decorative pouffe that wasn't actually for customers to sit on. He didn't notice it wobble.

Mary started to herd him off it, but Lorna shook her head. If it broke . . . it broke. It wasn't that nice to begin with and Mary was resisting all overt attempts to return it to its maker.

'I'm in a whole world of trouble because of you,' he moaned. 'You realise that while we were dealing with Mrs Rothery, the *real* volunteer phoned my office to apologise for missing the meeting? So when I came back and told my boss that I'd met the dog walker, and you were very nice, and you'd obviously been trained in gaining access to properties in emergencies, guess who got bollocked?' He pointed to himself, just in case she hadn't got the message.

'How could she bollock you?' asked Lorna. 'We saved Joyce from lying on that cold hall floor for who knows how long. Does it matter who I was?'

'Yes! Totally! I got an *hour's* lecture about confidentiality, client security, responsibility for safeguarding.' Now his anger had burned out, Keir looked close to tears. 'I nearly got put on a disciplinary because of this. I'm already on an unofficial warning, and this is my first placement. I was a mature student,' he added, before she could ask, 'I'm not totally wet behind the ears.'

'But why did you tell your boss I got us in? Why didn't you just say *you* found the key round the back?'

'Because I didn't!' His big eyes widened, horrified. 'I had to document Mrs Rothery's fall, and my visit, and the outcome. What if she'd reported me?'

'Oh, he simply had to, Lorna,' Mary chipped in. 'You can't fib. What if something had gone missing or Joyce decided to press charges? My friend Benita had to go to court to get her mother's savings back from the cleaner social services were sending. Wasn't the first time she'd done it, either. The social worker in charge lost her job for not checking the references.'

Keir's face drained of colour.

Lorna looked up just in time to see a couple approach the gallery door, take in the drama unfolding inside, and then hurry away. 'I'm sorry you got into trouble because of me,' she said. 'If it gets your boss off your back, you can tell her I've got a DBS check – I've volunteered in a hospice for the past few years.'

'What kind of volunteering?' He narrowed his eyes.

'I was a befriender, visiting patients who didn't have family or friends.' She reached for the notepad on the desk and copied Kathryn's contact details from her phone, then handed it to him. 'Kathryn's the matron, she'll tell you I'm not in the habit of burgling old ladies. She'll also vouch for my dog-walking reliability.'

He scrutinised it. 'Thanks. I'll ring her, if you don't mind. At least I'll be able to tell Sally I checked you out.'

'Tell her Rudy sends his love.' Lorna tried a small smile. 'Tell her we've nearly cured his nervous flatulence.'

Keir took off his glasses and cleaned them. With his spiky blond hair and round eyes, he looked like a guinea pig, nervous and squinty. 'Sorry for yelling. I'm *drained*. It's bad enough dealing with Mrs Rothery on a good day, without this too. Not going to lie, I reckon I've been landed with her because everyone else has given up.'

'God loves a trier!' said Mary. 'And you'll be pleased to hear Lorna is going to carry on walking Mrs Rothery's dog regardless.' She offered him the biscuit tin. Keir took two chocolate cookies. 'So that frees up your real volunteer to help someone else!'

'Can I put you on the official walking list, then?' he asked. 'We liaise with the Cinnamon Trust but I've got my project. It's part of my final assessment.'

'Why not?' said Lorna. She hadn't got round to making contact with the local hospice; this would save her time.

'Great! We're calling it Operation Walkies – a lot of our elderly clients have dogs or cats and, to be honest, they tend to take a lot better care of their pets than they do of themselves. And some reckon if we find some unwashed dishes in the sink or something, that's it, they'll be carted off to a care home, so they don't let us in.' Keir seemed more animated now. 'Sally, my boss, had this great idea that if we buddy up our housebound clients with a dog walker, or a cat . . . a cat stroker – whatever it is you're meant to do with cats – it's a way of keeping an eye on them. Discreetly, like.'

'So you make the dog walkers spy on the old people!' exclaimed Mary.

'No! Not really . . . well, yes.' Keir dunked his biscuit and looked guilty. 'But for the right reasons. And the dogs get walked. Everyone's a winner.'

'I think it's a good idea,' said Lorna. 'The hospice tried to let their patients keep their pets with them as long as they could. It's how I got to know Rudy. He had quite a few friends at St Agnes's, didn't you?' Rudy was lying in his basket, his chin on the edge so his nose drooped down over it. He was still recovering from hanging out with Bernard. 'We had Pets as Therapy dogs coming in too, to be stroked and just be . . . doggy and calm.'

Lorna thought of Joyce in her isolated cottage, in the middle of nowhere, with only Bernard. How would anyone know if she fell again? How many other older people lived like that? 'I don't mind walking a few more dogs in town, if they're close enough. I'll be taking Rudy out anyway.'

'But no big dogs,' said Mary, nodding protectively towards Rudy. 'My little pal here is very nervous. Sorry,' she added to Lorna. 'Keith won't let us get another dog. Says he's still finding Minky's hair in the en suite.'

Lorna felt she was getting to know Keith quite well, in the brief time she'd known Mary.

Joyce's refusal to consider involvement in Art Week had thrown a rather inconvenient spoke in Lorna's planned meeting with Calum Hardy later that week.

With some help from Mary, the internet and what material she could find about previous events, Lorna had brainstormed as many ideas as she could for a community art project to replace her retrospective idea – which now seemed insanely presumptuous. What had she been thinking? Of course it was Joyce's right to decide. The best she could come up with was inspired by a game her mother had once played with her and Jess – with, Lorna tried not to remember, mixed results.

'You give everyone pens and paper,' she explained to Mary as they sat sorting through a box of jewellery made from spoons, 'and ask them to draw each other.'

Mary stopped. 'Right,' she said doubtfully. 'What if you're not very good at drawing? I can't do noses. I just can't.'

'It's not about being accurate,' Lorna insisted. 'It's about capturing people's character. We'll have a proper artist in the gallery, drawing customers, and the customers can draw the artist. It's . . . conceptual, and local.'

'And he will be kind, will he? Or she?' Mary touched her own nose, self-consciously. 'They won't do horrid caricatures?'

'It's art,' said Lorna confidently. 'Whatever it is, it is.' And she started typing it up very quickly on the laptop in the office, to make it look as if she'd spent hours preparing, instead of just fifteen minutes.

Calum dropped by just after four. In person, he was the exact opposite of Keir, and reminded Lorna uncannily of an art dealer called Jackson with whom she'd had a fling in London, to the point where she had to ask a few loaded questions about New Cross to establish Calum wasn't his brother.

But then maybe most London art types were like Calum: good-looking in a groomed, almost Edwardian manner, he wore a tweed waistcoat over a green shirt rolled up at the sleeves. It revealed a tattoo on his inner arm, of a cherub with a quiff that matched his own.

Things got off to a positive start when Calum walked in, already admiring the facelifted gallery. 'So, I really like what you're doing here.' He gazed round the main room, nodding with approval. 'It feels . . . different?'

'Thanks.' Lorna smiled politely. It *should* feel different. She had spent most of her evenings that week rollering the walls, and now two sides of the room were a warm, matte grey that made the paintings – half as many as before – stand out better. The entirety of the Maiden Gallery had been taken down, swapped around, rearranged and, in some cases, boxed up to go back from whence it came.

That hadn't been without some weeping and wailing from Mary. What was on display was only the tip of the craftberg. Lorna had painstakingly combed through the unsold stock that had built up over the years, trying to find items that she loved (there was an undiscovered hoard in the cellar, a Tutankhamen's tomb of painted goblets and insipid pastels). She wasn't looking for masterpieces, just items that made her feel something, whether it was joy or admiration, even confusion. If it didn't make her feel anything other than 'why?' then it had to go, regardless of whether or not the creator was a personal friend of Mary's – and many of them were.

'We've had a reappraisal of the gallery's direction,' she added, fielding a dark look from the office where Mary was lurking, waiting to bring a tea tray out.

'Yup, I love how you've curated this.' Calum picked up a painting on glass and admired it. 'There's a real cohesion here.' He used the word 'curated' a lot. He also wore yellow trainers and took photos of everything on his phone. Lorna felt a lot less anxious about Art Week now she'd met Calum in person. This, she could deal with. She'd met it before, in London, and it had, in the main, been a lot of Emperor's New Moustaches.

When they'd done a slow tour of both rooms, Mary sidled out with refreshments, vanishing before Calum could recognise her as the elusive previous owner.

'So, let's talk about Art Week?' He perched on the desk, raised his eyebrows and tried to sip from a misshapen tea-cup. The handle was too small, and stuck on a slant, and Calum frowned as he tried not to spill herbal tea on his waistcoat. 'Got a theme?'

Too late, Lorna realised the cup was from a box of grotesquely awful pottery they'd been arguing over when he arrived. Mary had made the tea in it on nervous autopilot.

Calum tried to hold the cup more comfortably and failed. 'Quick suggestion? Don't make it ceramics. What the hell is this, if you don't mind me asking?'

The potter responsible for the tea set was 'a sweet man in Florham, his wife left him for the tree surgeon'; Mary had argued hard for Bob's unhappy ceramics to be spared the chop as they were 'all he had left'. 'It's a think piece,' she said swiftly. 'It's responding to the concept of *hygge*. Challenging the usual comforting sensation you get. Deliberately. On purpose. It's called a . . . hic-cup.'

Calum looked surprised, but examined the wonky handle with renewed interest. 'Clever! So, Art Week – you were talking about a Joyce Rothery retrospective?'

'Change of plan,' said Lorna. 'I read around about previous Art Weeks and what the vision is for the future, and I realised it's not in the spirit of community to focus on one artist, however amazing she is.'

He raised a 'tell me more' eyebrow.

'I loved the mission statement about involving local people in the creative process themselves,' she went on. 'So I was thinking about a You Are the Artist event!'

'You Are the Art. You Are the Artist.' Calum nodded, as if digesting her internal thought process. 'I like that. Go on?'

Lorna outlined her idea, trying not to outline the problems with it too. She skimmed over the minor detail that she'd never managed to draw more than someone's head before giving up, or that she'd made her mum cry when Jess drew Lorna's massive feet so she looked like a duck, and Lorna had jabbed her with a pencil so hard the lead snapped off.

Fortunately, Lorna was better at pitching than she was at sketching.

'Soooo, there's potential there,' said Calum when she'd finished. 'I'll roll it around in the office, see where we get to.' He didn't look as thrilled as Lorna would have liked, but she'd learned that people like Calum never let on when you'd had a good idea.

The main thing was, she'd met him. She'd demonstrated her own command of art jargon and, despite feeling a bit underdressed in his company, she liked Calum.

'I'll reach out to Sarra at the local paper,' he was saying, as they made their way to the door, 'and she'll drop by and interview you. You've got linked up with the council website? And what about your own website? You've got a social media manager? No? We can hook you up there. What else? You're on the fliers, and the mailing list for events . . .' Calum scanned through his phone and then looked up with a smile. 'I think that's it. Great to meet you, Lorna.'

He held out his hand and shook hers again. 'You've got some good energy here, you know? That's what this town needs. Fresh energy. Get everyone creating!'

'Thanks.' Lorna felt rather emotional. Calum was the

first person who'd given her gallery – and her ability to run it – whole-hearted support.

When the bell finished jangling, Mary reappeared at the office door with a tray of knobbly crockery.

'When I've washed these up, do I put them back on a shelf or pack them away?' she asked plaintively.

'Shelf.' Lorna strode towards the ceramics room, and the remains of Bob's deformed tea service of heartbreak. 'We just need to rewrite this description . . .'

Later that night, Lorna retreated upstairs to her thinking room for some positive manifestation. After her conversation with Calum, she felt genuinely excited: anything was possible. And with Mary helping her – Mary seemed to know everyone in town, and now *she* didn't have to organise Art Week, she was almost enthusiastic about it – they could come up with an exhibition that would bring customers back to the Maiden Gallery, maybe even from further afield. It would be the centre of fresh and inspirational creativity. She'd have made that happen.

Lorna reached for her pen and opened a new page in her notepad, pointing and flexing her toes in the bed socks she was wearing to keep warm. She hadn't yet put curtains up in her empty room, and the night sky was framed by the sash windows, a deep blue with a perfect half-moon sitting over the roofs. Longhampton town centre was quiet at night, and she could hear the creaks and clicks of the old house as the cold air outside nipped between the floorboards, through the worn sashes. She loved the silence and the space, and never felt scared on her own. Her soul was keeping her company, stretching out and yawning, like a beast that had been hibernating for years, now coming back to life and ready for adventures.

It was moments like these that Lorna felt closest to her mum. When thoughts zipped and spun around in her head, it reminded her of sitting in the studio when she was small, colouring in a pattern Cathy had quickly scribbled on a blank page, the two of them engrossed in doing the same thing. As she got older, Lorna was allowed in less and less often, and she missed that sharing feeling.

She was leaning back, imagining how she could cover the gallery awning in lights, when Rudy's head nudged her back and she jumped. He liked to be where Lorna was, even if it meant creeping in to a room soundlessly and curling up just within of reach.

'Hey, Rudy.' She reached around and stroked his silky ears. No, she wasn't on her own. Rudy was just enough company, undemanding as he was.

'You want to come and sit on my knee?' she asked in a babying voice, but when she lifted him on to her legs, he slid off in a dignified manner. *I'm not a toy,* his reproachful eyes seemed to say, but he sat down again not far away, and when Lorna turned back to her pad she felt him slink back and curl up near her. When he breathed out, the heat of his body pressed against hers, and she felt honoured. If the limits Rudy's needs put on her day were sometimes annoying – the abruptly terminated walks when he took fright, the coaxing with treats just to look at distant dogs – these moments of trust made her ashamed of her impatience.

Next to her on the floor, Lorna's mobile rang and she reached a hand out without looking.

Please let it be someone positive, she thought, but then realised that it could only be Jess. She loved her sister, but she didn't want to speak to Jess right now; she'd only ask her questions about the business or tell her about Tyra's ballet class, or Milo's latest run-in with the tooth fairy, or Hattie's mocks – Lorna needed to keep her inspiration going.

Or it could be Sam? 'Let's meet up for a drink,' he'd said. Had he meant it?

Lorna turned the phone over to see who it was and, in doing so, managed to press the answer button by mistake; and then it was too late to hang up.

With a mental groan, she put the phone to her ear, but before she even had time to say, 'Hello, Tiffany,' a frantic voice was already gabbling.

'Oh my God, Lorna, I'm so glad you answered!'

Lorna crossed her legs and braced herself. 'Are you having a crisis, Tiff?'

'HOW DID YOU KNOW?'

Because I've never picked up a call from you that didn't involve a crisis of some kind, Lorna thought, but wisely chose not to say.

Chapter Seven

Lorna kept a very specific photograph of her friend Tiffany on her phone, one taken when they were on a last-minute bargain holiday in New York two years previously – the last holiday, in fact, they'd been on together.

Both of them were wearing plastic devil horns, glittery red lipstick and even glitterier silver eye shadow. Ninety minutes after that selfie was taken, most of the glittery eye shadow was smeared down Tiffany's face, the horns were being paraded across the Brooklyn Bridge by two complete strangers from Limerick on a stag night, and Lorna was doing some very fast talking to the owner of the bar they'd just been asked to leave.

She kept that photo as Tiffany's identity on her phone to remind her of many things, specifically never to go on holiday with Tiff again. No matter how good the hotel deal was.

'Lorna, where are you?' Tiffany demanded now.

'In Longhampton, in my new flat.' Lorna got up off the floor and made her way out of the thinking room. Tiff's agitated tone made her want to stand up, and be ready for whatever was coming. Also she wanted to keep the thinking room uncontaminated with drama. 'What's the matter? You sound stressed.'

'Things are a bit weird. Listen, Lola, I need a favour.'

Ah, the nickname. Nicknames meant complicated favours. Lorna wandered through to the kitchen, hesitated at the mint tea caddy, then opened the fridge. There was a half-finished bottle of white wine in there, a cheap one she'd found in the cellar in a box marked 'Stephanie – Private View'. She unscrewed the top and sniffed it. Lemons, and a note of dishwasher tablet. Perfect.

'What kind of favour? If it's money, then I wish I could help, but I'm totally skint. I'm drinking leftover booze I found from the last party here.' She looked at the bottle, and wrinkled her nose. 'It's actually *called* "Girls' Night Out Chardonnay".'

'It's not always money.' Tiffany sounded affronted. 'Lorna, can I come and stay with you for a few nights? I'm about to be kicked out.'

'What?' Lorna elbowed the fridge shut. Tiffany was a live-in nanny, in the sort of smart area of London that she'd thought existed only in Richard Curtis films. Tiff's accommodation was part of the deal, and in Lorna's opinion, she earned every penny. 'Has something happened with the Hollandes?'

'Sort of.'

There was a pause. Lorna thought she could hear some kind of disturbance going on in the background. 'Tiff? Is that someone shouting?'

'Yes, it's Sophie, she's . . .' Tiffany started coolly, and then the sound of a plate smashing made her squeak in panic. 'Oh, God, I thought she said she'd do this calmly!'

'Do *what* calmly?'

'Sophie found a text on Jean-Claude's phone at the weekend, and since then it's been like World War Three.' The words tumbled out in an undertone, almost as if

Tiffany was crouching by the stairs trying to spy on what was going on while not drawing attention to herself. 'For someone who does nothing apart from shop and get her hair done, she's suddenly the most efficient woman in town – she's got a lawyer, she's moving back to Paris, she's taking him to *les cleaneurs*, all in the space of two days . . .'

'And you know all this *how*?'

'Because I'm trapped here! You can only spend so much time walking a pair of under-fives around the park. And,' Tiffany added, 'because I've got one of those instant translators that I use with the kids. I tell you what, I've learned some interesting words in the last week.'

'But how does this affect you? Surely you've got a contract – they can't just make you homeless! What about the children?'

'Well, that's the thing. Granny arrived this morning, direct from Paris, to whisk *les enfants* away on a special holiday. And without *les enfants* . . .' There was a pause which sounded as if it was being filled with some Gallic gesture.

Lorna stared at Rudy, who had got out of his basket to stare at her. 'Are you doing that annoying Gallic shrug thing?'

'What? How did you know?' The last live-in job Tiffany had had, with two high-powered American fund managers, made her say 'ossome' and high-five everyone in sight. She was quite absorbent when it came to her families.

'I just . . . knew. Look, Tiff, they can't chuck you out. That's your home.'

'No, I *can't* stay. Sophie has made it, um, preeetty clear to me that she'd prefer it if I left as soon as. She said it would be easier to deal with the house. It's rented.' Tiff dropped her voice and whispered, in a gossipy tone, 'Her papa pays for it. *And* the school fees. *And* her Pilates lessons.'

'How do you know that?'

'Oh, the things I know. Anyway, please? Please can I stay with you for a night or two? Seriously, I need to get out of here before I'm dragged in as a character witness. Maybe to a murder trial.'

Lorna squeezed her eyes shut. She hated saying no to her friends, but she also hated the thought of sharing a bathroom with Tiff ever again. Sharing her kitchen. Sharing her precious, lovely silence that it had taken her years to find. 'Wouldn't it be easier to stay with your mum?'

'Mum?' Tiffany sounded incredulous. 'Are you kidding? I can't tell my *mum* I've walked out. You know what she's like – she paid for that training course. She'll go insane. Don't make me beg you for somewhere to go. I'm your best friend,' she finished, martyred. 'Come *on*.'

'It's not that I don't want to help you out. I just . . . I just need some space to get my head together. I'm trying to get the gallery off the ground, working all hours, and . . .'

There was a crashing noise so loud that even Lorna could hear it, followed by a woman's shriek of barely controlled French rage.

And then another crash. And a man's howl of pain.

'Please?' said Tiff, in a smaller voice. 'I can leave straight away and be with you by tonight.'

'You can't wait till . . . ?'

Crash.

'Do you *want* to see me on *Crimewatch*? Do you?'

Crash.

Lorna sighed. She didn't want to see Tiffany on *Crimewatch*, no. 'Fine, come.'

'You're a star! Give me your address and I'll get a taxi at the other end.'

Lorna reached for her wine, then put it down. 'I'll meet you at the station. The taxis go home at six.'

When Lorna's alarm went off the next morning, the flat felt different again. Not the doggy presence this time. Now it felt occupied.

She turned her head on the pillow to slap the ringer on her Mickey Mouse clock down. She couldn't hear the first arrivals on the high street, which usually stood out in the flat's silence, because now there was a background sound of someone singing and probably dancing in the kitchen downstairs to Radio One, opening and slamming shut drawers to locate cutlery and crockery, running the hot tap until the boiler rattled in surprise at the extra work.

On the plus side, there was the smell of toast and coffee.

Lorna had to concede that that was one thing in Tiffany's favour as a flatmate: she didn't slob around in bed until all hours. She'd trained herself out of lie-ins when she'd opted for childcare as a career. She also made excellent coffee. Usually with the expensive beans Lorna used to hide in her lunchbox, but even so.

She leaned over to see if Rudy was still asleep in his basket. He was – his nose tucked under his paws, exactly as he'd been since Tiffany had crashed into the flat the night before, along with her six bags, one suitcase and, troublingly, a guitar case. He looked as far in denial about the new addition to their household as Lorna felt.

'It's only for a few days,' Lorna whispered. She told

105

herself not to be so mean, curling her resentment up into the duvet. Despite her dramatic personality, Tiff was popular with her agency and worshipped by the children she looked after; they'd find her another live-in job by the end of the day. There would be wealthy families begging to have her and her six bags of junk shipped into their *Elle Decor* houses.

Lorna heard feet coming up the stairs, followed by a cursory knock on the door. 'Are you awake yet?'

'No.'

'Yeah, you are.' The bedroom door was kneed open and Tiffany appeared, bearing a plate piled high with toast and two mugs of coffee, which were spilling on the carpet. 'Budge up, your flat's bloody freezing.'

'It's not freezing. You're just used to millionaires paying the heating bills.' Lorna wriggled into a sitting position as Tiffany made herself comfortable on the bed.

'Whatever. This place is massive.' Tiffany gazed round at the paintings Lorna had hung in her room. She'd chosen her favourites, the ones she wanted to keep closest: a detailed Victorian engraving of a bustling Paddington Station, an abstract in dreamy lilacs and gold, and the one painting of Cathy's Lorna had chosen to wake up to every morning – a magnificent Queen of Cups standing proud over a roiling sea of marine detail. 'Your spare room's about the size of our old flat.'

'Don't exaggerate.' Lorna paused for effect. 'The spare room *and the kitchen together* are about the same size as the old flat.'

'Are you planning on taking in lodgers?' Tiffany went on. 'Because you could get, what? Four people in here. Coining it in.'

Lorna folded a piece of toast in half. She had to admit, it was actually quite nice to have someone else make you breakfast. 'Nope. It's for me.'

'What? You're crazy. Do you know how much you could be making doing Airbnb?'

'Don't care. I'm enjoying the peace and quiet. I can do what I like, when I like, and there's no one to give me a hard time about anything.'

'No one?' Tiffany nudged her. Now she was safely out of the French family war zone, last night's jumpiness had vanished, to be replaced by her normal cheeky confidence. 'Still?'

'Meaning?'

'I mean, you let things fizzle out with that chef who was after you?'

'It didn't fizzle *up*.' She reddened. Last time she'd spoken properly to Tiff she'd been vaguely seeing one of the chefs from the restaurant opposite her flat; Max was cute, half-Kiwi, and he could chop an onion in under ten seconds, but he was also keen to settle down, and Lorna wasn't. She couldn't imagine being with Max for ever, so why set him up for the inevitable heartbreak?

Tiff looked disbelieving. 'But he wanted to take you to Paris! To show you his galettes!'

'I'm sure some other girl's enjoying them by now. I've got a dog instead. As you can see.' Rudy had waddled into the room, emboldened by the smell of toast. 'I prefer him, to be honest. He never ever tells me how to reverse park.'

'You know, after what I've seen of relationships these past few months, I think you've got the right idea,' said Tiff. 'You're independent – just you and your big old sausage dog. Hello, doggo!' Tiff waved at Rudy and he stared back, startled. She chucked him her toast corner, and nudged Lorna to pass her another bit.

Lorna offered her the plate, and they ate toast in silence, while Rudy was hoisted onto the bed to nibble Tiffany's leftover crusts. Tea and toast felt like the better of the old times. Sometimes they'd spent entire Sundays watching boxsets on her laptop and working their way through a loaf of bread with a jar of Nutella. Tiff claimed she'd had a lecture confirming Nutella's nutritional value, and Lorna's course, a sensible degree in Sociology, didn't have a counter argument.

A weekend sensation spread over her morning mood, making her feel sunny inside. Except – she suddenly remembered – it wasn't a weekend. It was Thursday, and Mary was away playing doubles golf with Keith.

'I've got to get up.' Lorna sat bolt upright. 'I've got so much to do. Are you any good at mopping floors?'

'The best.' Tiffany nudged her. 'Thanks for letting me stay, mate. I'll get on to the agency this morning – I'll be out of your hair before you know it.'

Lorna nudged her back. 'No rush,' she said, and meant it. 'It's good to see you.'

Her memory gave her a brief flash of the bathroom from their shared house – the smeary mirror, the cascading windowsills, the piles of towels – but she decided to ignore it. For the time being.

True to her word, Lorna went back to Much Yarley a few days later to walk Bernard again. The weather had turned grey and gloomy, and a few degrees colder, but she realised Bernard had got used to a little extra exercise. It felt cruel to stop – and she didn't like the thought of Joyce coping with his excess energy in the house.

There, she thought to herself, that's what owning a dog's done to you. It's made you walk in the bloody drizzle for the sake of other people.

If Longhampton town centre was grey, there was no sign of spring arriving in Much Yarley either. The sky over the fields that she drove past was colourless and everything else was a washed-out green, with nothing budding in the hedgerows apart from the odd scrap of litter. Even the sheep on the hillside looked grubby.

Lorna collected Bernard from the door and took him and Rudy up the lane towards the Osbornes' land. She didn't see Sam, or Angry Simon, but still kept both dogs on the lead, despite Bernard the psycho teddy bear's insatiable desire to dive into the undergrowth in search of rabbits. Rudy didn't have a lot of clearance for his short legs, and Lorna was trying to keep him as clean as she could, since she'd wrestled him into a woollen jumper she'd started to knit while the gallery was quiet.

Lorna had struggled to follow the pattern, but it felt like something nice to do for the little dog, who didn't ask for much. He shivered a lot, and she worried that he was cold or scared. She had strategies now for dismantling his anxiety, but none would work overnight, and she'd read on the internet that swaddling nervous dogs helped to calm them down.

Plus, as Tiffany pointed out, Rudy looked very cute in a jumper.

'Are you going to knit him a hat next?' Tiffany had asked, in all seriousness, as Lorna tugged the front legs into place. 'That would look so cool with a beanie. Sophie bought one of these for her friend's Shih Tzu – it cost nearly a week's wages. It's another world, Lorn, seriously.'

They'd spent the next hour looking on the internet for patterns to knit dog hats. There were lots. The best ones, they agreed, were the hats for dogs with cats' ears on them. The gallery had indeed been very quiet.

Joyce Rothery, unsurprisingly, didn't share Tiffany and Lorna's feelings about dogs in clothes.

'What on earth is that poor dachshund wearing?' she asked when Lorna returned Bernard to his owner, tail wagging and half covered in mud from where he'd barged through several puddles. Rudy was clean, and his tail was whipping happily.

'It's a jumper. I couldn't find a coat in the pet shop that fitted his back, so I tried to make one myself. He's a funny shape.'

'You made it, did you?' Joyce pursed her lips in what could have been a smile. It was sort of amused. Then she gestured towards Rudy, with an impatient flick of an arthritic hand. 'Let's have a look.'

Lorna dutifully picked Rudy up and lifted him so Joyce could inspect her handiwork. The old lady ran her hand over the ribbed section at the back, where Lorna had tried to knit a skull and crossbones. It hadn't worked. It looked more like a smiley face.

'I know there are a few places I went a bit wrong,' she admitted, as the knobbly fingers went straight to every single one of her mistakes. 'I normally knit squares.'

'I can see . . . You've dropped a stitch or two here.' Joyce poked a finger through the hole that Lorna had tried to tack together as a 'feature' and wiggled the loose ends. 'Still, on the plus side, you won't lose your sausage dog. He'll leave a trail of yarn behind him wherever he goes and you can reel him back in. Or maybe that's the plan?'

'I don't think it's a bad first attempt,' said Lorna stiffly. 'It's not easy teaching yourself to knit from YouTube.'

'From you *what*?' Joyce inserted maximum disdain into each syllable and an audible 'h' into 'what'.

'From the internet. Anyway, I've got another on the go, in stripes this time. Red, white and blue. Rudy's first owner was very patriotic. I think this one'll be better,' she added, but it didn't sound convincing. 'I like it, anyway.'

Knitting always reminded her of where she was at the time, and Rudy's jumper, Lorna knew, would remind her of the first weeks in the gallery – the excitement, the bursts of ideas, the panic, the smell of the fresh paint. The liberating sense of being herself, and being responsible for the small, hairy life sitting under the desk.

Joyce stopped stroking Rudy's ears – she'd moved on from the jumper – and glanced up. 'Have you got it with you, this other jumper?'

'Yes. It's in my bag.'

'Well, I'd better have a look at it,' she said, 'so your poor German sausage isn't forced to put his little legs through the wrong holes.' She stepped back, opening the door two inches wider.

'Are you sure?' Lorna knew Joyce's eyesight was failing; Keir had confided in her that it was one of the reasons she was on the social services' radar, living on her own so far from a neighbour. Surely her knitting would be even more erratic than Lorna's? But it was the first time Joyce had invited her inside. How could she say no?

Bernard had already barged his way back in, and Lorna could hear him running around the kitchen, slurping from his water bowl and skittering across the tiles to check nothing had invaded his kingdom while he'd been out. He'd be getting everything covered in mud.

'Come in, if you're coming in,' said Joyce impatiently. 'You're letting the heat escape.'

The sitting room at Rooks Hall was small but stylishly furnished, with a low grey sofa along one wall, and two high-backed armchairs on either side of a tiled fireplace where a fire was burning. It smelled Christmassy, maybe from the logs in the basket by the grate, and the two hammered silver dishes of dusty pot pourri that sat on the pale oak sideboard.

Lorna was surprised by how modern the room felt; the cottage's olde worlde exterior had led her to expect heavy antique chests and musty carpets, but the furniture was mid-century and elegant. The walls were a perfect mushroom colour, a subtle shade that changed as the light moved. Piles of books sat next to each chair, thick reference volumes of art and places. It was a room to live in, a room that had been loved.

'Sit yourself down,' said Joyce, indicating the chairs by the fire. 'Don't worry about dog hairs, Bernard's not allowed up. Now, hand over your knitting.'

With a slight groan, the old lady settled herself on the chair nearest the window and accepted the scrap of knitting from Lorna's hands. Lorna perched on the edge of the opposite chair and watched her take the needles easily into her hands, running her fingertips up and down the rows, her thin lips moving as she counted the stitches. While Joyce communed with the wool, Bernard sauntered in from the kitchen, his ears still flecked with burrs that had stuck to his ears while he terrorised the hedgerows. He gave his owner's feet a quick sniff; then he curled up into a ball next to the tapestry footstool and went to sleep, a teddy bear once again.

Rudy stayed very close to Lorna's ankle as she sat further back in her chair. She could feel the anxious rise and fall of his ribs slowly lessen until he too let out a huffy grunt and curled up against her foot.

Lorna glanced around the room, trying to absorb as many details as she could without looking nosey. There were pictures everywhere, but arranged in a clever way that didn't overwhelm the space – something Lorna was never sure she'd got quite right in her own flat. She'd expected heavy oils, like Joyce's own work, but there were more abstracts than oils, studies in colour and shape, and a trio of understated but intense block prints that changed the more Lorna looked at them.

But the painting that drew the eye most was the one hung above the fireplace, and she could tell immediately it was one of Joyce's own: a striking coastal landscape of a simple white cottage set near the edge of a cliff, the surging tide flicking foam on to the streaked rocks, while a thunderous purple sky loomed overhead. The house itself was small and still, a quiet spot in the centre of the storm, and it gave Lorna a familiar, snug feeling.

'Our old house,' said Joyce, concentrating on the knitting. 'Mine and Bernard's. The first Bernard, obviously. The human one.'

How did she know Lorna was looking at it? 'Is it in Wales?'

'Pembrokeshire.' Joyce glanced up, suddenly interested. 'Do you know the area?'

'We used to go there on holiday.' The memory was

113

unfolding inside Lorna the longer she gazed at the painting, like a fern spreading out tendrils of forgotten smells and sense. 'Me and my mum and dad, and my sister. We used to stay in a cottage a bit like that.'

'Oh, yes, there are lots. Old fishermen's cottages, mostly. Simple but solid. Do you like it?'

'Yes, it's making me think of . . .' Her voice trailed away as the images appeared, somewhere between her head and her heart.

Lorna remembered the thick stone walls and the hollow roar of the wind in the chimney at night, listening from under a pile of scratchy wool blankets, next to a snoring Jess. The wilder the storm, the cosier the bed felt. They'd been scraped-together holidays – damp holiday homes borrowed from their parents' wide circle of friends – but between the squabbles and sunburn there had been moments like nuggets of sea glass in Lorna's memory: when Mum had charmed some mackerel from a fisherman (swapped for sketches dashed off in an exercise book) and Dad had cleaned and cooked them on the beach, right in front of them. Frowning and concentrating, as neat as possible 'out of respect for the fish'. They'd eaten them together, the four of them, sharing the surprise of Dad's skill.

'It looks . . . safe,' she said, remembering her mum singing and washing up while she and Jess dried their sand-gritty feet by the cottage fire. She had a good voice, and Lorna couldn't remember hearing her sing much at home after that. Why? Dad had sung too. Them singing, the coal fire, the spread of warmth over her clammy skin – safe, that was the feeling. Safe inside the arms of her mum and her dad and her sister, under a blanket, dozing to the sound of singing. A shared memory, created by the four of them.

'Do you think so? Most people look at that and say something ludicrous about what it must have cost to heat the place. Or how *cold* it must have been in winter.'

'I think it looks snug. Like when you're watching a storm coming, but you're tucked up inside.' And that was the sense memory replaying in her imagination now, Lorna realised. A safe fear. The sea-salt smell of the white cottage filled her mind, and she blinked away tears as she felt her hand in her mum's again, Jess on the other side, holding her dad's as they ran four abreast, barefoot, along the deserted beach – a family, having fun together. Together.

She turned her head; Joyce was looking at her. She wiped her eyes hastily with the back of her hand. Maybe Joyce's eyesight wasn't sharp enough to spot her tears.

'It *was* snug, you're exactly right,' said Joyce matter-of-factly. 'We were very happy there.'

'I can tell,' said Lorna. 'I would be too.'

They sat in silence for a few more moments while Joyce continued to poke and pick at Rudy's jumper. Lorna racked her brains for something intelligent to say. None of the easy conversations she'd relied on in the hospice – 'Tell me about these lovely grandchildren!' or 'Have you been watching the tennis/Olympics/*Coronation Street*?' – seemed appropriate here. She wanted to talk about Joyce's paintings, but now they'd had the 'no' conversation she didn't want to make it look as if she were being pushy.

But then Calum Hardy popped into Lorna's mind and the ambitious side of her knew that getting Joyce Rothery in would be a real coup, and this was her chance.

Do it, urged the brisk Betty voice in her head. What's the worst thing she can say? No? She's already said that.

What are you scared of? It's only words. Count to three and ask.

Nggh.

Lorna struggled, trying to find a way of phrasing it, but she couldn't. The fear of Joyce's disapproval, combined with her awe of the lady's talent, tied her tongue.

Fortunately, Joyce spoke first. 'You've gone wrong with this row.' She began hooking the wool out in loose loops, carrying some on the tips of her fingers while she dived in and out with the needles, resetting the pattern.

'How can you tell what to knit without the instructions?'

'It's only counting.' Joyce's movements were nimble, even though her fingers seemed arthritic. 'Counting and feel. There.' She flipped the jumper over, felt it, then flipped it back and added a couple of stitches.

'Oh! Could you show me what you just did?' Lorna leaned forward without thinking, so close she could smell the old lady's scent. She wore L' Air du Temps on the silk scarf round her neck.

'What did I just do?'

'You started the leg. Can you knit a leg hole for me, so I can copy it? It's so much easier when someone can show you where you're going wrong.'

There were now firm lines of knitting around the edges of Lorna's attempts, anchoring the whole thing together.

Joyce looked at her quizzically, saw she wasn't faking her enthusiasm, shrugged and demonstrated the stitches. 'You go here, and here, and count *carefully* this time, don't just guess and hope for the best.'

Lorna watched; experience made Joyce's economic movements elegant. Flick, loop, flick, loop, and there, something solid was created from nothing. It was perfectly logical but magical at the same time.

'What are you staring at?' Joyce didn't take her eyes off the knitting, even though Lorna wondered how much she could actually see. 'Never seen an old biddy knitting before?'

'Not as well as that,' she answered truthfully.

Joyce snorted at the compliment and handed back the dog jumper, now with two leg holes established. 'You do the other two and bring them with you next time,' she said with a beady look over the top of her darkened glasses. 'I warn you now, though, I've high standards. I don't accept sloppy workmanship.'

'I'll do my best,' said Lorna, and when she waved good-bye at the door, there was a glimmer in Joyce's eyes that hadn't been there before. Curiosity, maybe.

And as Lorna drove away, there was something sprouting in her own heart that hadn't been there before. A small leaf, or a ray of morning sun. This time, she thought, checking both ways as she turned on to the main road, it felt as if Joyce actually wanted her to go back.

More than that, she did too.

Chapter Eight

The second weekend in February started before dawn for Lorna and Tiffany, while the world outside the gallery window was still dark, and only the most devoted owners were stumbling down the high street towards the park, their dogs nosing gleefully ahead in matching reflective jackets.

It was a big weekend for the Maiden Gallery. This was Lorna's first chance to make some money and drag the month's takings back into line with projections, via strong card sales, men looking to spend money for the sake of it, and hopefully some extravagant impulse buying of gifts. In other words, it was the weekend before Valentine's Day.

'So, that's everything,' said Tiffany, casting a critical eye over their early morning efforts. She'd made her 'special' strong coffee, and with Lorna's motivational playlist on loud, their resulting surge of effort had transformed the gallery into a romantic wonderland. It helped that Mary was away playing golf with Keith again because they'd moved everything. Paintings had been rehung in eye-catching clusters, the glass cabinets sparkled with jewellery, the card spinners were restocked, and one wall had been temporarily smackeroo-ed with potato-print lipstick kisses. 'Anything red, anything pink, anything with hearts, flowers, dogs or pigs. Is that it?'

Lorna tied the last Lover's Knot on to the papier mâché stag's head that she'd given up on selling or persuading Mary to return. His antlers were decorated with every ring in the gallery, tied to red ribbons of various lengths. He looked rather festive. 'Anyone coming in for a card, convince them that a piece of art is a much more long-lasting Valentine's gift than roses.'

'Especially if it's a piece of art with roses on.'

'Exactly.' Lorna glanced sideways at the bland flower close-ups that she'd brought out of stockroom exile for the occasion. Today was their best, and last, chance. 'And if they choose jewellery, we've got a *lot* of hand-decorated containers to put it in, for a reasonable giftbox charge.'

'Got you,' said Tiffany with a jaunty fingerpoint. She bent down to stroke Rudy, who was watching them from the safety of his basket under the desk. 'And a bow for sir? Maybe we could pop Rudy on the desk and have him selling Valentine's cards for pets?'

It was a good idea, and Lorna toyed with it for a millisecond, but Rudy's naturally anxious expression stopped it dead. He only relaxed in his basket in the gallery when it was just her, Mary or Tiffany about – luckily for him, that was most of the time. Today, she hoped anyway, it would be far too busy.

She picked him up protectively and he pushed his sharp nose into her armpit – his little sign of trust. 'No, I think there'll be too many people here for Rudy. But make a pet card display anyway. We need to give people lots of reasons to spend money.'

'Take it from a nanny who always had to buy cards for Mummy *and* Daddy *and* the doggies,' said Tiffany, efficiently dealing out cat and dog cards from the main pile as if she were at a Las Vegas casino. 'There is no limit to people's madness when it comes to Valentine's Day, and *no one* who can't have a card sent to them.'

The first customer was already peering through the door, wallet in hand, when Lorna turned the Open sign around at nine o'clock – a harassed man who 'didn't want to make the same mistake as last year'. He left with a pair of silver cockleshell earrings, plus a rose canvas as back-up, and the rush continued at a steady pace through lunch, thanks to the hand-painted window display, which promised 'personal service to find the perfect gift'.

Lorna was relieved to see the amount of old stock flying through the till, but what really gave her a buzz every time was finding something special for each customer, a treasure she knew wouldn't end up at the back of a drawer. Talking to customers about what they were drawn to also made her look at some of Mary's favourites in a new way: one lady absolutely adored Bob's wonky pottery which Tiffany had filled with Love Hearts.

'Aw, it's like me and my bloke,' she said, hugging two lumpy hic-cup mugs to her chest. 'Bit off centre but we love each other just the same.' Lorna made a mental note not to be so snobby in future. Not until she was in profit, anyway.

They worked through without a lunch break, and Lorna was just coming in from taking Rudy out for a quick spin down the street behind the gallery when Tiffany grabbed her and bundled her towards the back office.

'Someone to see you.' She nodded towards the front of the gallery, where a man in a heavy jacket was standing by the counter, squinting critically at a canvas of a sheep's head. He angled his head, frowning at the sheep, and Lorna realised it was Sam. She hadn't recognised him immediately, not with the beard. Her chest suddenly felt light and tight – not exactly with excitement, more from panic that she was about to say something stupid.

And then, a funny sort of pride that he'd seen her new venture, and seen it so busy too. Just goes to show, she thought defiantly, I'm not totally clueless about art.

'Who's that?' Tiffany leaned over. 'Don't tell me he's one of the artists you were talking to on the phone the other day. Because if it is, you can sign me up for a full-time job. I would have *no* problem talking to him about his creative impulses.'

'He's not an artist, he's an old friend.' Lorna wondered what kind of artist Tiff thought Sam was – a blacksmith? A rugged woodworker? She could sort of see that.

'Aye aye.' Tiffany raised her eyebrows. 'What type of friend?'

'You've met him! Sam Osborne. We met him in the bar at Colbert? He's my brother-in-law's best mate,' she added, when Tiff's face went blank. 'The property developer? I've known him since I was eleven. It's not like you're think-ing, so stop it.' She knew she was protesting too much, and Tiffany's disbelieving expression made it clear that it wasn't convincing.

'How many of these old friends have you got?' Tiffany angled her head to see past the jewellery cabinet. 'I love a country boy. Is he a farmer? I bet he'd look great stripped to the waist, a scythe over his shoulder . . .'

'That's *Poldark*, Tiff. Not actual farming.'

'Are you sure?'

Lorna shook her head and walked through the gallery.

Her heart felt as though it was beating high up in her throat, but she tried to look relaxed. Two quick, unseen clenches of the hands, a friendly smile. There. Relaxed.

'Hi!' she said. As she got closer, she could smell the fresh air clinging to Sam's coat. It swamped his shoulders, making him seem broader. 'I can do you a discount on that! And we have about ten more if you want a different kind of sheep.'

'Its eyes are wrong,' he said, pointing at the beady yellow marbles. 'Jacobs don't have yellow eyes.'

'Maybe it's not Jacob's sheep! Maybe it's Walter's!' said Lorna, and winced at herself.

Sam looked askance. 'Is that the best you can do?'

'That's my only sheep joke.'

'Well, I won't hold it against you, I've got no art jokes.' He gestured round the gallery. 'Looks good! I was in town and thought I'd pop in to see what you've been up to.'

'And do you approve?' She couldn't help sounding a bit snippy.

Sam raised his eyebrows. 'Well, at least I know what these paintings are meant to be of. I've already had reports – you sold a birthday card to one of Mum's WI cronies and she got the rest on the grapevine. I know, I know.' He lifted a hand in a 'what can you do' weary gesture. 'That's Longhampton. Not much going on. Any gossip . . . Not that you're gossip, obviously.'

'Oh, come on.' Lorna hadn't missed the jibe about the art; just because Sam 'knew what it was meant to be' didn't mean it was good. That just confirmed her worst suspicions. 'We both know you can get in the local newsletter by wearing a hat.'

'At least it takes the heat off me for ten minutes,' said Sam.

'Why? What's the gossip about you?' Was there gossip? About why he'd come back?

He looked cross with himself. 'No,' he said, in a way that didn't encourage further questions.

'So,' said a voice behind her, 'can we interest you in a Valentine's card? We have some beautiful examples.'

What? Lorna spun round.

'Doesn't have to be for a lady friend.' Tiffany had shimmered up behind her, farmer-charming smile in place. 'We have cards suitable for anyone. A good friend, your mum, your dog, a favourite cow?'

'My *mum*?' Sam looked horrified at the same time as Lorna said, 'A *cow*?'

'I don't judge.' Tiffany tilted her head. 'You country folk. Takes all sorts. So, what's it to be? Something for the wife? Or girlfriend? Or both?'

'Tiff, a lady over there's looking at the eggshells,' said Lorna, pointing in the direction of the ceramics. 'Tell her everything looks better in groups of three. Unless she wants to put a piece of jewellery in it, in which case steer her to the silver cabinet.'

'Will do!' She lingered for a moment, giving Sam a shameless up-and-down look, until Lorna nudged her and she sashayed off.

'So . . .' she said and her mind went blank. There were quite a lot of big questions that seemed too big for casual chit-chat. Are you married? Why the beard? How come Jess and Ryan haven't mentioned you for ages when you were once round there every other weekend?

'Who's that?' he asked conversationally. 'I don't recognise her as a local, so I'll have to report back to Mum that there's someone new about the place.'

'That's Tiffany. She's a nanny. You met her, in that bar?'

Sam looked blank. 'Did I? Should I have remembered?'

'I don't know. Should you?' Tiffany had the kind of wicked eyes that people (men) seemed unable to walk past. Whenever she and Lorna had gone out when they were living together, she'd been asked so many times if she was a model that Lorna had started to wonder if she had some kind of secret life. Tiffany always retorted that she looked like the DD + M&S lingerie lady. 'She's in between jobs at the moment, and I've got plenty of room so she's staying here. What? What are you smiling at?'

'Just a lot of information. I wasn't asking if you had three kids stashed away upstairs.' He paused and tilted his head. 'Oh no. Do you?'

'Three kids of my own? No,' said Lorna, and waited a beat. 'There are four.'

Sam's face registered quick shock, but then he rolled his eyes.

'Good to see your sense of humour's still as crap as ever. So, anyway, how about that drink? I've got a few things to do in town, but if you're free later we could have a pint in the Jolly Fox?'

Really? Lorna wanted to tally up the day's takings, and she definitely needed to go through the stockroom and replenish the displays for the Sunday opening. And there was no food in the fridge and the laundry basket was overflowing, and she needed to talk seriously to Tiffany about what was actually going on with her agency, and how long she was planning to stay. And she didn't want any more advice about art from Sam Osborne.

'Yes,' she heard herself say. 'Why not?'

*

124

Lorna couldn't remember what the Jolly Fox public house at the end of the high street had looked like when she lived in Longhampton, but Sam assured her while they were waiting at the bar that it had changed beyond all recognition – and not for the best.

Looking round it now, she was pretty glad she'd never been to the old version if this was an improvement.

'You must remember the horse brasses they had over the optics?' he said, pointing to the mirrored cocktail shelves that now reflected the customers back at themselves through a fence of exotic-coloured spirits. 'And the so-called draught ales that we reckoned were just Jim's home brew? And the booths? Come on,' he added disbelievingly when she looked blank, 'you *must* remember the booths.'

'Sam, I was thirteen when we left Longhampton,' Lorna pointed out. 'I never set foot in this place.'

'Oh, come on, you did. The average age of the drinkers was probably just over seventeen, and that included the old codgers playing dominos in the snug.'

She shook her head impatiently. 'Don't you remember? I looked about ten, so I always got carded. Jess used to tell bouncers I worked for a plastic surgeon and got discount Botox, but I couldn't even get in with her fake ID.'

'Ha! Of course. The fake ID . . .' The barmaid appeared, and Sam ordered her cider and his Guinness, then leaned on his elbow, appraising her in the same cool manner that had turned her insides to water the time they'd met up in London. He'd looked so much older, a finished man; she'd thought up until then that she looked adult, confident and independent, but obviously he hadn't seen that, not the way he'd spoken to her.

'It's funny,' he said, 'I always think of you as being the same age as us.'

'Not at the time you didn't.' She'd forgotten – until now – how sore it had felt being left behind, part of the 'us' only when it suited them. 'You just think it now because you want to think you're four years younger than you are.'

'Ha! No, that came out wrong, I'm sorry. I meant you always seemed old for your years, or maybe we were immature . . .' He realised he was digging himself in deeper. 'Jeez, shut up, man.' He held out his wrist for a slap – something Jess used to make Ryan do, as a running joke – and for a second he was the old Sam again, familiar as a faded T-shirt.

It was confusing, thought Lorna, suddenly unable to meet his gaze – it was easier to look at his reflection in the mirror. Forget the beard, there was something new about him that hadn't been there before. An edginess, a fidget in his movements, as if he wasn't entirely comfortable back in the brand new checked shirt and jeans. Something else was different. Maybe Sam was struggling too, finding some things unchanged while some things were transformed beyond recognition. Like the farm, like his plans. Maybe like her.

It had to be that, thought Lorna, and in trying to avoid meeting his eye in the mirror, caught her own reflection. Her hair was messier than she'd thought and her raspberry lipstick, hastily applied in the reflection of a framed print on the way out of the gallery, had already worn off. She glanced away; she never looked the way she thought she did in her head.

Sam spotted the sudden movement. 'What?'

'Those mirrors.' She nodded at them, embarrassed. 'Who wants to see themselves getting pissed?'

'I think it's so you spot anyone trying to steal your handbag or pinch your bum. I mean, you can change some things but the clientele . . .' Their eyes met in the reflection and Sam smiled, a sweet smile that reached his brown eyes. Lorna realised she'd missed him. Not him, maybe, so much as the possibilities of her crush, the memories that trailed behind him like clouds. For a long time she hadn't been able to think about Sam at all but here he was, and *here*, when they weren't trying to be city escapees, it was easier than she'd expected.

She enjoyed the sensation of her own smile spreading across her lips, seeing it reflected in his.

The moment stretched between them, and then Sam coughed. 'There's a table over there – do you want to sit down? There's something I need to get off my chest.'

'Yes,' said Lorna, and her happiness deflated. She wasn't sure she wanted to hear whatever it was.

There weren't many people in the pub, and plenty of seats to choose from. They sat down under a reproduction poster of a Longhampton railway station that had never been that pretty in real life, at a table small enough that their knees almost, but not quite, touched underneath. Sam put his pint down dead centre on the beer mat advertising the local craft ale, and looked straight at Lorna. He had a disconcertingly clear stare; she'd always felt as if he could see inside her mind. It made her want to think of frantic scribbles to protect her less noble thoughts.

'So, let's get rid of the elephant in the room,' he said.

Lorna poured her cider carefully, though her hand was wobbling. 'Which elephant?' she said, and nearly added,

I didn't know you'd gone into elephant farming, but stopped herself.

'The last time we saw each other . . . I was a bit of a dick. I'm sorry.'

Something twanged in Lorna's chest. What exactly was he apologising for? The rather smug business advice, or . . . the other snub?

'I shouldn't have said what I did about your pop-up gallery.' Sam scratched his beard. 'I'm sorry. What do I know about art, compared with you? When I got home, I nearly came back to apologise but I didn't want to make it worse. You had the art background, not me. I just knew about the money.'

'Well, if I'm honest, both aspects were a bit . . .' Lorna stared at her glass. It had seemed amazing at the time. When Zak the artist she'd 'discovered' was explaining it to her. Zak the next big thing, for definite. Ha. 'I'm sorry I said what *I* said. You were right.'

'How much did you lose?'

'Let's not discuss that.'

He winced for her. 'Look, we can all do things perfectly in hindsight. It's not so easy in the heat of the moment.'

The heat of the moment. Lorna's mental defences finally cracked under the pressure of the memories. It had been a corner table in a nice restaurant Sam was expensing. She'd felt like his equal, finally, with her own money, her own plan, her own file of paperwork. She'd been asking for his advice, and he'd given it with all the confidence of a thirty-year-old in a thousand-pound suit.

So Sam's 'advice' hadn't been what she'd wanted to hear, but she'd tried to accept it, telling herself he was only giving her the benefit of his financial experience, he didn't understand how the art world worked. And he'd smiled and said that was the end of the boring work chat, and he'd ordered another bottle of wine while she was still smoothing her ruffled feathers, putting her brave face back on. More wine arrived, and was poured, and they'd talked about Ryan and Jess – the present-day Ryan and Jess with their three kids, not the old stories – and it had felt as if something fresh was starting. Sam was looking at her in a different way, so different that Lorna had let herself reach out her hand as he was speaking, and she'd touched his beautiful smooth cheek.

That was all she'd done. She'd rested her fingertips on the line of his jaw, the way she'd dreamed of doing for years and years, and he'd – it made her shrivel inside even now – he'd taken her wrist and said, gently, 'That's not a good idea, Lorna.'

As though she were a teen who'd drunk too much cider and overstepped the mark.

So yes, she could have done things better. She looked away.

Sam didn't wait for her to speak. 'It's in the past,' he said, and made a whisking gesture with his left hand. Lorna noticed he still wore the signet ring he'd taken to wearing in London. So he hadn't jettisoned *every* pretentious detail of his previous life.

'In the past.' But here they were, and the past was all around them.

'Have you seen Milo and Tyra recently?' he asked. 'I have to confess I've been a pretty crap godfather. Must be well over a year since I last saw Ryan for a beer.'

'Oh, they're fine. Same as always.' Lorna focused on her drink. 'Tyra's six going on twenty-six, and Milo's into monster trucks. He'd probably love a go on a tractor. There you go! Instant brownie points! He'll be really excited to have a farmer for a godfather.'

Sam's smile was polite but this time it didn't reach his eyes.

'Sorry, did I say something stupid?'

'No. Nope, I guess I am a farmer.' He stroked his chin again; clearly a new nervous tic. 'Just feels odd, hearing you say that. I think of Gabriel as being a farmer, or Dad. Not me.'

'You mean you still think of yourself as a property developer? Please God, no. It's sooo pre-recession.'

He managed a weak laugh. 'It's more than that though, it's more . . . who I am. Farming's not a job, is it? It's not about nine to five, it's living the farm, living the land.' He drank more of his pint. 'I'm not expressing this well. Sorry.'

'You and Gabe, though.' Lorna shrugged. 'You're made of the same DNA. OK, so he went to Hartpury but you had the same basic upbringing. No reason you can't do it just as well as he can, in your own way.'

'You'd say that about you and Jess, would you?' He raised an eyebrow. 'She could do what you do? Just because your dad was a teacher, she's had to be one? Just like your mum was an artist, you *have* to be good at it too?'

It pricked, right at the deepest point of Lorna's inner soul. Sam didn't mean it the way she was hearing it, but couldn't he see that not being like her mum, not having that understanding, was the thing that tormented her most?

Why would he know that, though? She'd never told him. She'd just hoped he understood, somehow. Because he *knew* her.

They looked at each other for a moment, while a gang from the rugby club made their way over to the bar, young men with tattoos and training tops, barging and bantering like bullocks. Lorna scrambled for words, because she could tell from the way Sam was looking at her that he was expecting her to say the right thing. The trouble was, she didn't know what he needed to hear, and what she wanted to say – What are *you* doing back on a farm you couldn't get away from fast enough? – wasn't helpful.

And then her phone rang. The selfie of Lorna and Tiffany flashed on to the screen and she picked it up.

'Sorry for interrupting your hot date at the Yokel Arms,' said Tiff, 'but your niece has arrived at the flat.'

'My *niece*?' Tyra popped into Lorna's head, in her sparkly gold wellies and pink mac.

'About sixteen? My height? Blonde hair.' Tiffany dropped her voice. 'Not really blonde. More mouse.'

Not Tyra, Hattie. Lorna glanced up at Sam.

'That's Harriet,' she said to Tiffany, and instantly Sam put his pint down and looked enquiring.

'She looks just like you! Same eyes, same manner-isms. It's uncanny.'

'Thanks.' Hattie was very pretty, with long legs and peachy teenage skin that she preferred to cover with too much make-up. 'I didn't know she was coming. Do you want to put her on?'

'Not sure that'd help,' said Tiffany. 'She's been here in the kitchen rearranging your junk for the past half-hour. She even washed up, can you believe? I let her, obviously. Doesn't want to chat, and believe me, I'm *very* good at getting kids to chat. I don't want to panic you, but I'd say she's definitely upset about something.'

'Did you say she arrived half an hour ago? Why didn't you call me?'

'I have been *trying* to call you,' said Tiffany. 'But you don't seem to be answering your phone.'

It had been on silent. Now Lorna looked, there were several missed calls – Jess Home and Jess Mobile, as well as Tiffany Mobile. Lorna racked her brains. Had she agreed to have her for a weekend? Surely not – Jess had one of those family calendars with separate columns for her, Ryan, Hattie, Tyra and Milo. There would have been a reminder phone call, at the very least.

'Why do you think she's upset about something?' Lorna asked. 'Has she said something?'

There was a pause, as if Tiff was moving further into the hall. 'Just a hunch,' she said drily, 'but she hasn't stopped crying since she got here.'

Chapter Nine

When Lorna walked into the kitchen and saw the girl sitting staring morosely into a Snoopy mug, she did a double take: Hattie was so like photos of herself during her arty adolescence she was almost a ghost, albeit in a hoodie and Camden Market harem trousers instead of jeans and a Stone Roses T-shirt.

Hattie had dyed her light brown hair paler, and it hung around her face in a fine curtain, as vanilla-blonde as Lorna's had been naturally at that age. But the way her gaze was boring into the mug, as if she could levitate it with the sheer force of her unhappiness – that intensity was pure Jess. Jess had got that from their mother, who could stare at a canvas so hard Lorna half expected to see hot singed dots appear. Hattie was leaning on her elbows, her chin hidden in her hands; one sleeve was pulled up over her palm like a little girl, and the other had fallen down, exposing a slender white arm, with the faded whorls of a henna tattoo snaking downwards and a few fraying friendship bracelets round her bony wrist.

The long fingers covered with silver rings, the mascara-spiked eyelashes, the hunched shoulders . . . half-Jessica, half-Lorna. It was hard to see anything of robust country lad Ryan there at all.

Tiffany was sitting next to her, and there were two

mugs and the remains of a chocolate cake between them on the table. As Lorna walked in, Tiffany leaned back on her chair and said casually, 'Hey, you're back! Cup of tea? I've just made one.'

Lorna wanted to respond in the same relaxed manner but there was something about Hattie's defensive posture that set her nerves jangling. This clearly wasn't a spur-of-the-moment social visit. Rudy must have felt it too because he was sitting by Hattie's feet, close enough to almost-but-not-quite rest his chin on her trainer, something he never did with strangers. When Lorna approached, his body deflated, as if he was relieved she was back.

'Hey, Hattie! What a nice surprise. I didn't know you were coming.' She sat down next to the teenager, and when she hugged her, Lorna felt Hattie's bones under the sweatshirt. Strong and fragile at the same time. 'Every-thing OK?'

'Yeah.' It was barely more than a breath.

'Does your mum know you're here?' she asked, looking over at Tiffany, who shook her head.

'No.' Hattie glanced up, her blue eyes huge in her heart-shaped face. 'Don't ring her yet. Please.'

'OK. Well, I'll have to give her a ring at some point,' said Lorna. 'She'll be wondering where you are.'

'She won't care.'

'Oh, she will,' said Tiffany. 'I don't even know your mum, and I know she will.'

'Just a quick call.' Lorna stood up and reached for her phone. Jess would be going out of her mind; if she could have attached bungee ropes to her kids to keep them in sight, she would.

She tried to ignore Hattie's plaintive protests as she

made her way into the hall. There was a message on her locked screen from Sam: *Hope everything's OK with Hattie. Say hi from me – tell her that her mum was much worse at her age! Great to see you – you owe me a beer. Keep in touch. S.*

Lorna stared at it. Was she disappointed there was no 'x'? Relieved that seeing Sam again had been easier than she'd expected? It hadn't been anything like she'd expected. He'd been nothing like as tricky as the last time they'd met, but nothing like the old Sam either.

She didn't have time to think much further because Jess picked up on the second ring.

'Lorna? Be quick!' Her sister's voice was high with tension. 'I need to keep the phone free. We're having a nightmare.'

Lorna sat down halfway up the stairs, so she could still see into the kitchen, but Hattie and Tiff couldn't hear her. Tiff, veteran of much parent-child conflict, had turned on the radio.

'I might be able to help you with that,' said Lorna. 'Hattie's here.'

'Oh, thank God. Thank God.' Jessica covered the phone, and said to someone, 'She's at Lorna's. I know, I know! I know, I'll tell her. Ryan, that's not helpful.' There was a break in her voice when she carried on, and it jolted Lorna. 'We've been out of our *minds*. I wanted to call the police but Ryan kept saying I was over-reacting, and it would only make things worse . . .'

'How long have you been—'

Jess didn't even let her finish. 'Since this morning! I've been ringing her all day but the little madam hasn't been answering her phone. She stayed at a friend's house last

135

night, but I asked her to be back here first thing, because I was taking the kids into town to get Ryan's birthday present. Then we were going out for dinner together tonight to celebrate. She knew that, we do it every year. It's Hattie who usually chooses his cake!'

Argh, Ryan's birthday, thought Lorna. She never remembered Ryan's birthday till it was too late, not even when she had a shop full of cards. Jess remembered everyone's. She had a special birthdays and anniversaries book.

'So what's going on? It's not like Hattie to make everyone panic like this.'

Hattie was a model teen – Saturday job at Wagamama, grade A student, half-hearted flute player, bit on the skinny side but then Jess was always on one diet or another so biscuits were hard to come by in the Prothero household. The young woman at Lorna's kitchen table looked positively mutinous when she wasn't crying. Not like Hattie at all.

There was a telling pause on the other end, and the acoustics on the phone changed, as if Jess was moving into a different room for privacy. 'Well, to be honest, she's been really moody recently. Not wanting to do things with the kids, answering back to her dad . . .'

'Whoa. Hattie answering back to *Ryan*?'

'I know. I get that it's not much fun, trying to find ways to spend time together that works for the little ones as well as her, but we're a *family*, we do things together. I thought she enjoyed it. And I can't believe she'd miss Ryan's birthday. I just . . . I just have no idea what this is all about. Why wouldn't she let me know if she was going off somewhere? Why wouldn't she think we'd be worried *sick* not to hear from her?'

Lorna could think of at least four reasons off the top of her head, starting with friendship fallout, a non-approved piercing, adolescent hormones or a broken heart. And maybe a reluctance to spend Saturday night in a pizza chain with two under-eights and her mum and dad – a dad who often broke out some spontaneous dad-dancing when he was particularly happy. It wouldn't be too hard to find out which.

'Oh, teenagers,' said Lorna, vaguely. 'You know how bad we were.'

'Were we, though? We wouldn't have got away with flouncing off for a whole day. We definitely wouldn't have got away with answering back . . .'

'Jess, you *had* Hattie when you were only a couple of years older than she is now.'

Silence.

'Look,' said Lorna at the same time as Jessica said, 'With Ryan, who I'd been with since I was fifteen and have been ever since,' in an outraged tone.

The smell of toast drifted through from the kitchen and in the distance the town hall clock chimed – eight o'clock. The start of the evening, thought Lorna, but it felt like the end of it.

Her brain slid disobediently sideways. Where had Sam gone after she'd left him at the pub? Home, or to a friend's house? Did he still have friends here? Did he have a local girlfriend? Or one in London? Somehow they hadn't talked about him at all.

Jess sighed. 'Sorry. We've been so lucky with Hattie. She's never given us a day's worry. God. I sound like someone's mum.' She paused, then groaned. 'But I am, aren't I?'

'She's safe and sound and eating cake here, so just have

a glass of wine and enjoy what's left of Ryan's birthday.' Lorna straightened one of the framed prints running up the stairs – a collection of vintage fashion prints she'd never had space to hang before. 'I'll talk to her. Maybe she'll tell me if something's up. I bet it's nothing, Jess. She can help me in the gallery tomorrow, and I'll put her on the train home for supper.'

'Have you got room? Where will she sleep?' That sounded more like Jess: identifying problems, so she could solve them.

'There's loads of room here. Tiffany's in the spare bed, but Hattie's fine on the sofa, so long as she doesn't mind random linen.'

'Tiffany's there? What happened to wanting some time and space to yourself?'

'You can't plan for other people, can you?' Lorna could hear animated voices from the kitchen – a snatch of laughter over the music. That was a good sign. 'Tiff's not staying long. Just till she gets another placement.'

'I hope Hattie didn't interrupt your girls' night in.'

'No, actually, I was out – I was having a drink with Sam Osborne.'

'Ozzy?' Jess sounded surprised. 'Is he in Longhampton?'

'Indeed he is. Taken over the farm from Gabriel.'

'No!' Jessica sounded surprised. 'The farm, seriously? Didn't Ozzy used to talk about emigrating at one point? Just to make sure his dad couldn't rope him into calving?'

'Like I say, you can't plan for other people – Gabriel fell under a baler and couldn't manage the farm by himself, so they persuaded Sam to come back and take it on.'

'Oh, that's sad. Well, maybe ten years in London changed his mind about the joys of country life. Must be quite nice for you both then, having a familiar face around. Where did you go? The Jolly Fox?'

'How did you know?'

'Where else is there? Do they still have those velvet booths where lads would try to get their arms around you?' Jess went on nostalgically. 'And the toilets with the condom machine with the graffiti about Tracey Jenkins?'

'I don't know, Jess. I'd only just got my drink when I had an emergency call to come home and deal with the surprise arrival in my kitchen. Do you want to speak to your daughter, by the way?'

She walked back into the kitchen with the phone. Tiffany was showing Hattie how to do some complicated plait on her hair, and they seemed to be getting on like a house on fire. But when Lorna offered Hattie her mobile and mouthed, 'It's your mum!' she looked panicked and shook her head so hard she pulled out most of the plait.

Lorna joggled the phone. 'Just let her know you're OK. She's worried about you.'

Reluctantly, Hattie took it, and closed her eyes. 'Hi, Mum. Yeah. I'm fine. Yeah.' There was a long pause. 'I'm *fine*. My mobile was out of charge. Sorry.'

Tiffany and Lorna exchanged 'yeah, right' looks over her head. She'd been on her phone the entire time – texts, WhatsApp, flicking away with an expert thumb.

Jessica was clearly talking a lot, not that Hattie was responding. Her eyes stayed tightly shut, but the movement under the lids suggested she was trying not to cry. She twisted a strand of hair round her finger and chewed the ragged end. Eventually, she said, 'Yeah, Mum, gotta go, sorry I missed Dad's dinner, love you, bye, bye. Bye,' and handed the phone back to Lorna.

'. . . your daddy and I love you very much,' Jessica was still saying. Lorna waited a beat, then coughed.

'Hi, Jess, me again. So I'll let you know what time the train gets in tomorrow, shall I?'

'Thanks, sis. If you could try to find out what this is about . . .' Jess sounded vulnerable; she wasn't used to asking her little sister for help. It was always the other way round.

'I will.'

While they were speaking, Hattie got up from the table and left the room. She was so light that her feet made no sound on the stairs, not even the second one from the top that always squeaked, and it was only the click of the bathroom door upstairs that let Lorna know where she'd gone.

And then the lock clicked across and they both heard that.

Later, when Lorna was making up a bed on the sofa from the spare pillows and a crocheted blanket that was more decorative than functional, she tried to winkle out what had happened.

'You don't have to tell me the whole thing,' she said as Hattie stood chewing her hair. 'But I promise I'll do my best to help, whatever it is.'

'It's nothing,' Hattie muttered, and looked heartbreakingly like the little girl in pigtails that Lorna had pushed on swings and carried to feed ducks. So heartbreakingly like that little girl, in fact, that Lorna couldn't bear to probe, and instead made her a hot drink and warned her to grab the bathroom before Tiffany got up, or else she'd be waiting hours.

Hattie wouldn't reveal anything the following day either, even though Lorna tried to create plenty of quiet moments together, and Tiffany focused her not-inconsiderable nannying skills on Hattie in between persuading men to buy handmade jewellery.

'I thought she was going to say something earlier when she was showing me the photographs on her phone,' Tiffany whispered as they watched Hattie gift-wrapping at the desk. 'She's taken some amazing photos of the town.'

'Which town?' Hattie was a skilful gift-wrapper; it was satisfying watching her smooth the paper to a neat crease, twirling the ribbons ruthlessly on a scissor edge.

'Dur. *This* town. Dogs in the park, and the fancy railings – she must have been wandering around for hours before she came here last night. It's so cold, poor kid!'

Lorna opened her mouth to speak, then closed it. It didn't make sense. Why hadn't Hattie just come over? No, wait. Thinking about it, it was obvious why not – because Lorna would have phoned Jess immediately, and Jess would have tanked straight over to get her. Hattie clearly wanted to be on her own, and Lorna could understand that, even if she didn't know why.

'So what did she nearly say?'

'She started to say something about not wanting to be at home, then she clammed up. Kids always tell you eventually but you have to let them come round to it.' Tiffany shrugged. 'My guess is that it's a boyfriend her dad doesn't approve of, or maybe a falling-out at school. She trusts you; she'll tell you in her own time. Hey, you know what?

If all else fails, offer to do an exhibition of her photos here. I told her to post them to Instagram but she went shy and said no, they were rubbish and everyone would laugh at her.'

At least *that* was more Hattie-like. 'Well, thanks for trying, Tiff.'

'No problem.' Tiffany turned her head. 'You're a very arty family. Your mum, you, now Hattie!'

'I'm no artist,' said Lorna, automatically. 'I just find it.'

'Yeah, yeah,' said Tiff.

The rest of the day passed in a steady chain of sales, and Hattie relaxed over tea, joining in with Tiffany's tales of nightmare babysitting with some hair-raising stories of her own about Milo and Tyra that Lorna hadn't heard. It was only when Lorna was putting her on the train home, armed with a coffee and a magazine and some cards from the gallery for Valentine's Day, that the teenager suddenly threw her arms around Lorna's neck and squeezed her tightly.

'Thanks, Auntie Lorna,' she said, her voice muffled. 'Sorry if I got in the way.'

'You didn't get in the way, you were a big help!' Lorna held her at arm's length so she could see in her face that she meant it. 'Come back any time. Just call me first, so I can get a proper bed made up. And tell your mum and dad you're coming.'

A cloud passed across Hattie's open face. 'They're going to go mad, aren't they?'

'Only because they worry about you.'

Hattie dropped her gaze to the tips of her white DMs, and her hair swung in front of her, a shield over her expression.

'Let me give you some advice,' said Lorna. 'Get your apology in first, and just tell the truth. I know your mum. She *needs* to *know* stuff. Whatever it is that's happened, let her help you with it. That's all she wants to do – to help you.'

'She won't understand.' It was a painful mumble.

Lorna sighed. 'The thing is, Hattie, me and your mum – we loved *our* mum, but we didn't talk to her that much about our problems. She found it hard – she was an artist, as you know, and I guess her head was often . . . somewhere else. So if Jess is asking questions it's only because she worries about what you're not saying. She'll be imagining some awful things! She's got a much better imagination than me . . .'

It was an attempt at humour, but Hattie didn't smile.

'But you know she'd go to the ends of the earth to help you.' Lorna bit her lip, gripped with sudden love for the awkward girl who looked so like she had once. 'I would too, if you asked. So . . . please ask. Ask us anything.'

The train appeared at the end of the platform, and the few evening passengers around them began to step forward. Still Hattie said nothing. Oh God, thought Lorna, panic rising inside her, I've run out of time, I've failed, Hattie's going home with nothing solved and everything a mess.

And then Hattie lifted her head and said, with tears in her eyes, 'I wish I could but even Mum can't fix this,' and pushed her way onto the train before Lorna could ask her what she meant.

Valentine's Day arrived, and there were no cards for Lorna on the mat when she and Rudy returned from his special dog-avoiding morning walk. Not that she was expecting any, she reminded herself.

'The post hasn't been,' said Tiffany. 'Don't panic.'

She was barely visible at the kitchen table behind a huge vase of red roses that had arrived before Lorna and Rudy had even left. The deliveryman had informed her that they were the biggest bunch of the day. 'I needed them out of the van to make room,' he explained, shoving them in her arms.

'Who said I was panicking? I'm not expecting anything.' Lorna filled Rudy's breakfast bowl, conscious of his adoring gaze directed at her. Her, or the bowl. That was all she needed. 'Still no clue about your floral overture?'

'Absolutely none.'

Lorna didn't believe that. Tiff was glued to her mobile, obviously waiting for a follow-up call from someone. Someone very generous, very smitten, and very mysterious. She nearly always had a boyfriend of some description, and sometimes more than one, but generally she was happy to go into details. Too much detail for Lorna, usually, but she seemed strangely reticent about this.

The landline rang and they both jumped, but Tiffany's hand was quickest.

'Hello?' she said, and the way her face froze, then relaxed with relief, gave Lorna's suspicions another twist. Why was no one telling her anything these days?

'OK, I will. No problem.' Tiffany rolled her eyes, and handed the receiver over. 'It's your social worker.'

'My . . . ?'

'Keir Brownlow.'

'Oh. Calling to see if you got his floral tribute?' Lorna shot back, pressing the phone to her chest.

'Ha ha. Come on, Rudy, let's go downstairs and open up Mummy's gallery.' Tiffany swept out, Rudy under her arm, his short legs dangling like a child on a ride at Alton Towers. For some reason, Rudy didn't seem to mind Tiff carrying him round. He seemed calmed by her aura. Maybe it was her executive nanny training, Lorna thought, a special module on Neurotic Dogs of the Rich and Famous.

'Hello, Keir.' Lorna topped up her coffee from the cafetière. She'd been expecting a call from Keir about signing up to the dog-walking rota, something she hadn't had time for yet. 'How are you?'

'I need a favour. Urgently.' He sounded stressed, and his voice echoed, as if he were in a corridor. 'Can you go round to Joyce's and collect Bernard this morning?'

'Yes, why? What's up? Does he need to go to the vets?'

'No, Joyce is in hospital. He's been on his own since seven last night.'

'What?' Lorna put her coffee down. 'What's happened? Is she all right?'

'She fell again yesterday, at home. Probably over Bernard, though she's denying it. Luckily a neighbour was dropping off the village magazine and heard Bernard going nuts, but the ambulance had to come out and bring her into the hospital for some checks on her hip. The geron-tologist couldn't get round to her until this morning and apparently she's been creating merry hell all night about the bloody dog. I offered to go over, but she wouldn't have it – told me to call you. She said you'd know what to do.'

Lorna had to smile. Joyce, dismissing Keir with a flick of the hand, even on a hospital trolley. Poor Keir, always wanting to be the knight in shining armour, and no one ever letting him.

'Can you believe she said under no account was I even to try to walk it? I mean, him?' he went on grumpily. 'She asked if you could go over. It's all she's bothered about – doesn't care about her own condition.'

Lorna could picture Bernard searching through the house, trying to find his mistress, worrying and barking and stressing out. He'd done his best to protect Joyce but Keir was right, he probably was the cause of her fall, weaving around her feet in play. Lorna had nearly tripped over Rudy herself, more than once. 'No problem, I'll head over there now.'

'Thanks, Lorna.' The relief in Keir's voice was palpable. 'That's made my day way easier already. You wouldn't believe the forms I'm going to have to go through with her. Wish me luck . . .'

'Keir!' He'd almost gone, but she caught him in time. 'How's Joyce? When will she be able to come home?'

It was a question she almost didn't want to ask, and Keir's long pause said more than client confidentiality allowed him to.

'I think she's going to be fine,' he said carefully. 'But as for coming home to her own house . . . let's play that one by ear.'

A fresh crop of snowdrops had popped up by the front door since Lorna had last been out to Much Yarley, their drooping heads like fat jade-tipped pearls against the wintry soil. Bernard's furious barks were ricocheting off the tiled hall floor as she approached the path. It sounded as if he was doing circuits from front door to back, roaring away any intruders.

The barking ceased the second Lorna walked through

the door, and was replaced by a joyful panting. Bernard bounced around her legs, tail wagging, thrilled to see his walking companion, eagerly looking past her to see if his friend Rudy was there too. They were quite a pair, the apprehensive dachshund and the gung-ho terrier. Lorna thought that between them they had a whole balanced doggy personality.

'Calm down!' she said, trying to get a lead clipped on Bernard's collar. 'We'll have a walk then we're going into town. You'll like that. Town's full of stuff to bark at. I just need to get some things for your . . . for Joyce.'

Inside the house felt wrong. Lorna sensed Joyce's affront still lingering in the house, a crossness like firework smoke in the air. The orderly world of Rooks Hall had been invaded: in the sitting room, the armchairs had been pushed to one side, and the stacks of books knocked over, the titles spilling in tipsy piles, hastily nudged under the chair by an impatient foot. A china cup of cold coffee was left by the fireplace, next to a heap of knitting – the knitting Joyce had been doing last time Lorna had visited. She felt a sudden sharp fear that maybe it wouldn't be finished.

From this, thought Lorna, gazing round at the paintings, to a fluorescent-lit hospital ward. That would be worse for Joyce than the physical discomfort. Rooks Hall was more than a home, it was an extension of her creative mind: the sophisticated palette of colours on the walls, silvery taupes in the curtains and woven rugs, sharp reds and ochres picked out in the gallery of paintings. Joyce's personality was everywhere: in the threadbare patches on the chairs' arms where hands had rested and the painted nails had tapped along to the radio, the postcards on the mantelpiece, the knitting.

Lorna paused in front of the painting of the Welsh fisherman's house above the fireplace, the low white haven above the crashing waves, and an echo of her childhood came back to her – Mum, pinning up sketches in every holiday cottage they rented, so their rooms felt like home. Joyce needed that too, she thought, and made a note to take her a card from the gallery. Something colourful to look at on her bedside table.

Her hand hesitated over the knitting – would Joyce want that too, in hospital, to take her mind off the tedium? Did she need other things, a toilet bag or pyjamas, a book to read, things from upstairs, in her bedroom? Keir hadn't said but maybe she should save Joyce the embarrassment of asking, and just do it.

Or maybe she shouldn't, maybe it would make Joyce think she'd been prowling around. Lorna was torn. Joyce Rothery was a private person, that was the one thing she knew for sure about her. Fiercely private.

She wavered. Bernard was restless in the hall, scratching to get out. Lorna's eyes wandered around, drinking in the detail of the paintings she hadn't felt able to study properly with Joyce sitting there, watching her. Everywhere she looked there was something intriguing, drops of colour and texture and light. This was the perfect chance – maybe the only chance she'd get – to explore the fascinating corners of Joyce's artistic mind. To see whether she even had any of Lorna's mother's illustrations in her collection. That thought made her tingle. Had they met, two artists living in the same area? Did Joyce know her? Did she rate her?

But even as Lorna thought it, she saw the Welsh cottage again, and shame swept the temptation away. *Stop thinking about yourself.*

Joyce had trusted her with her two most precious things: her dog, and her privacy. She wasn't going to betray either of those.

Lorna picked up the knitting, and the ball of sea-green wool it was attached to, and led Bernard out into the garden, locking the door to Rooks Hall behind her.

Chapter Ten

The nurse who took Lorna down to see Joyce on the geriatric ward informed her that since Joyce had no serious injuries, she'd been put in a room with three other elderly ladies until she could be discharged.

'Social services need to make sure home's nice and safe,' she explained as Lorna scurried to keep up with her rapid pace down the corridor. 'No real damage done this time, definitely not to her vocal cords, anyway. But there's a duty of care, see . . .'

The three other patients were asleep, their heads tilted and toothless mouths open like dozing turtles, but Joyce was sitting bolt upright, fighting the green hospital gown and the plastic tray with an untouched lunch on it with all her might. She was glaring at the juicebox in particular. It had a *straw*.

'Visitor for you, Joyce!' said the nurse, then immediately corrected herself. 'Mrs Rothery.'

Joyce looked up, and managed a wintry smile when she saw Lorna. 'Thank you, Kelly.' Her eyes were bright in her face, but she looked smaller, more vulnerable in the hospital gown instead of her usual tunic and earrings. Her silver hair was flattened to one side where she'd been sleeping, and Lorna felt a protective urge to fluff it up for her. A protective urge that she hastily suppressed.

'Hello, there!' she said in a low voice, so as not to wake the others. 'How are . . . ?'

Joyce raised a warning hand. 'Absolutely fine, thank you very much, no need to go through that rigmarole.' She indicated the chair by the bedside and Lorna obediently sat down. 'First things first – Bernard. Is he all right?'

'I walked him down the lane, and now he's back at the flat having a nap with Rudy.'

That was sort of true. Lorna had been towed up and down the lane for half an hour on the other end of Bernard's lead while he lunged and barked at everything in sight, from trees to squirrels to gusts of wind. Although Lorna strayed as close to Sam's farmland as she could, she hadn't seen any sign of human life – not Sam, Gabe or their dad. And then she'd kicked herself for straying up there in the first place.

'Good. Good.' Joyce folded her hands, and unfolded them. Then, just as Lorna was beginning to wonder if she was really all right, she squared her thin shoulders and looked straight into Lorna's face, her deep blue eyes urgently conspiratorial.

'Thank you for taking care of Bernard. I thought it better to leave him where he was until you could intervene, rather than let Keir attempt to walk him.' She elongated Keir's name with a withering sigh. 'By the time he'd consulted his committee about the ethical way to walk a terrier, or indeed if a pedigree terrier was even ethical *in and of* itself, I expect Bernard would have been on the other side of Longhampton with a trail of carnage in his wake.'

Lorna wasn't sure she could come up with a quick answer to that, so she reached into her bag for the knitting. 'He's fine. I'm happy to have him. Just concentrate on yourself.

The nurse said you could be sent home any moment, but I've brought you some distractions, just in case.' She put the needles and wool on the side table, along with a copy of *The Times*. None of the magazines in the hospital shop seemed appropriate. 'I hope it's all right – this is the knitting you left on the chair by the fire? I've got my own dog jumper here too – I'm stuck again on a leg hole. I don't know if you could have a look . . .'

Joyce turned her head with interest when she saw the half-finished work. If she were being honest, Lorna hadn't planned to bring Rudy's new jumper for Joyce to check – she carried it in her bag all the time, anyway – but she'd noticed how a new energy came into the old lady's eyes when she was straightening up Lorna's puckered stitches into something approaching neatness.

'Only if you feel up to it,' she added.

'Of course. That little chap needs a warm jumper in this weather. Hand it over.' Joyce gestured to the needles, and as soon as Lorna passed them, she started running her fingertips along the stitches, counting silently and twisting the wool around her fingers to get the tension right.

It left Lorna with nothing to work on herself, since Joyce's knitting was way too complex for her to tackle, so she racked her brains for some conversation to fill the silence.

'So, we had a busy weekend in the gallery!' she said. 'Thank goodness for Valentine's Day. We sold a lot of cards and almost all the silver jewellery. We even sold a few paintings.'

'Ones you liked?'

'Um, yes.' They'd all been from the bland end of the spectrum, but they were money in the till.

'And you're closed today, I suppose, to recuperate from

your sales drive?' Joyce frowned at the stitches, then poked the needle into the first loop and began unpicking Lorna's uneven work.

'No, the gallery's open as normal. My friend Tiffany's helping out for a few hours.'

'And who is Tiffany?'

'My old flatmate. She's a live-in nanny – well, she was until the family she was working for broke up and she was out of a job.' Something about the rhythmic clicking of Joyce's needles encouraged Lorna to carry on talking. 'It's an awkward time to look for a full-time position, apparently, but she's got some savings, and she's good at talking to people – so the gallery suits her.'

'And are you enjoying having her stay? You told me the other day that you wanted some time to yourself.'

'Um . . . yes.' That sounded less than enthusiastic. Lorna hurried to justify the 'um'. 'To be honest, it was nice being on my own, but Tiff and I have lived together before, so I'm used to sharing space with her. We don't get under each other's feet.' Apart from the pyramid of toiletries crammed on to the bathroom windowsill, and the heap of laundry piled on top of the washing machine. 'Well,' she conceded, 'she's more of a piler, whereas I'm a putter-awayer. But there's lots of space so it's not so bad.'

Joyce flicked and pulled the loops on the needle. 'Describe her to me, would you?' she said, without looking up. 'I like to picture people in my head.'

'Well, Tiff's shorter than me, dark red hair. The colour of black cherries. She's had it all colours of the rainbow since I've known her, though.'

'And what was your favourite?'

Lorna was surprised by the question; Joyce didn't often

ask questions during their conversations. 'Candyfloss pink. She looked like a merry-go-round horse. But when she started her nanny training they made her dye it brown.' She racked her brains for piquant details, since Joyce probably wouldn't accept Tiff's star sign. 'She tries to juggle things you shouldn't really juggle, like raw eggs, and when she's drunk, she thinks she can speak Spanish. She can't speak Spanish. When I think of Tiffany, I smell Chanel No. 5. She wears it because it was her nan's favourite,' she added, 'not because she thinks she's Marilyn Monroe.'

'So . . .' Joyce turned the jumper over, and inserted a needle meticulously into the next row. 'In this flat above the gallery, there's you, and there's this runaway Mary Poppins, and your German sausage dog. What else?'

'Nothing, just another two bedrooms upstairs. I've got the master bedroom with an original coal fireplace,' she continued. 'Tiff's in the spare room, which has roseprint wallpaper and a view of the church spire. It's cosy. Then there's another room with old stock in that I should probably get a bed for, in case my niece comes to stay again. My niece Hattie stayed this weekend,' she added, hoping she was creating an interesting mental collage for Joyce. 'She's sixteen, blonde, legs like Bambi, eyes like Snow White. Then one more bedroom that I'm saving as a creative space.' Lorna counted on her fingers to make sure she hadn't left anything out. 'And there's a box room between the two bedrooms on the top floor. An estate agent would count that as the fifth.'

'So you've had quite a houseful this weekend!'

'I did. But it was . . . quite nice,' said Lorna. 'Except there was a bit of drama with Hattie. She lives near Evesham – she hadn't told my sister she was coming. And between them, they used all the hot water but I didn't have time for a bath so . . .'

Out of the corner of her eye, Lorna saw the blue uniform of the nurse appear at the other end of the ward, with doctors ready to do the rounds. She checked her watch. It was nearly three.

'Sorry, I'm going to have to go in a minute. I promised Mary and Tiff I'd be back before the end of the day. We're hoping to do some last-minute Valentine's business before the shop shuts! Is there anything else you need?'

'Yes.' Joyce glanced over to the door, and saw the nurse. 'There is something actually.' She sat further upright in the bed, wincing with the effort.

'If it's Bernard, then it's really no problem,' Lorna started, but Joyce stopped her.

'I know what's happening, I'm not gaga quite yet, so please hear me out.' Joyce's eyes darted to the door, then fixed on Lorna. 'I overheard Keir and the nurses talking about me while they were here earlier. I pretended to be asleep, of course. The plan is for them to send a team of do-gooders into my house to check it's safe for me to return. Without even asking me!'

Lorna tried not to react too much; had Joyce really heard this? Or had she been asleep? 'That's good, though, isn't it? They want to make your house safe so you can go home.'

'No, that's not it, don't interrupt.' The hand was raised again. 'It's going to take a while, by all accounts, Keir having to tick every one of his ridiculous boxes, so in the meantime they want to send me to Butterfields for what they called "respite care" – you've heard of Butterfields?'

'Is it the care home on the outskirts of town? With the long drive that you can see from the road?'

'Yes, it was a very elegant house once upon a time.' Joyce's eyes turned distant. 'Some beautiful carved oak panels. My husband used to know the owners. Anyway,' she recovered crossly, 'it's not very elegant any more. It's run down and awful and doctors send you there to *die*. I have no intention of setting foot over the threshold. I've known friends have "respite care" in those places, perfectly fit and healthy when they go in – and they haven't come back.'

'But if Keir doesn't think Rooks Hall is safe . . .' Lorna's brain was skipping ahead, trying to work out what Joyce wanted. 'It would be awful if you tripped again and hurt yourself this time. Surely it's better to let them fix what needs fixing so you can stay there as long as you can?'

'Lorna, I intend to stay in Rooks Hall until they carry me out, feet first.' Her stiff fingers tapped the bed sheet emphatically. 'I am *not* going into that care home. Or, even worse, Monnow Court, where they won't let me take Bernard with me, and in any case, I just . . . I won't.' A shadow of fear broke through her determination, and Lorna could tell the old lady was scared. Scared of dying, of frailty, of her dignified independence being stolen from her. A cold finger traced down Lorna's spine.

The nurse was approaching now, and she caught Lorna's eye and pointed to her watch.

Lorna made a 'two seconds?' face. The nurse nodded, and turned to the first bed, picking up the clipboard at the foot of it, and pulling the curtains around to murmur at the sleeping patient in a tone Joyce would have called patronising if she'd had more energy.

'So what would you like me to do?' She leaned forward. 'Talk to Keir about staying in here until the house is ready?'

Joyce wrinkled her nose in horror. 'I can't stay here; they need the beds for old people. No, I will give you any painting of your choice from my house . . . if you let me and Bernard stay with you, in the flat above the gallery, until we can go home.'

It took Lorna a moment to process what she'd just heard. She stared at Joyce, unsure whether she meant what she was saying.

'Any painting,' Joyce repeated in a low, clear voice. 'Or if you wanted to hold that retrospective you were talking about, I will lend you as many paintings, on a temporary basis, as you require.'

'But . . .' Lorna's brain spun. Joyce? In her flat? Lorna wasn't sure that was going to work. It was hard enough sharing space with Tiff, someone she'd known for years – someone who'd known *her* for years too. Joyce was a stranger, and elderly, and vulnerable. And would Bernard get on with Rudy full time? Would Joyce need medical care? What if she fell? Would she be responsible?

But the paintings, roared a voice in her head. Come on, Lorna, *the paintings*. This is a gift from the gods!

The nurse was approaching the second lady in the ward; Joyce would be next. 'Do we have a deal? I'm mobile, I'm coherent, I don't need looking after.' Joyce smiled, a thin, bittersweet smile. 'One meal a day and you can have what-ever sleeping pills they give me. We'll split any codeine.'

It was a flash of naughtiness that Lorna hadn't been expecting, and it cracked something inside her.

'You don't have to give me a painting.' It felt wrong, taking something valuable in return for a favour she should have offered freely. An old lady, scared of her own fragility – hadn't she seen that time and again in the

157

hospice? Hadn't she always wished she could help? 'If it's only for a few days . . .'

'No.' Joyce's finger jabbed the bedclothes. 'It has to be a proper arrangement, Lorna. I will not have anyone feeling sorry for me, thank you very much. You can do something for me, and I will do something for you.'

'Can I think about it?'

Joyce leaned to one side, and grimaced towards the door. 'Time's up.'

'What?' Lorna twisted round, and yes, there was Keir in his parka, talking to another nurse while juggling a huge file. Papers were spilling everywhere, and the nurse was helping him catch them. 'Oh . . . typical.'

'It has to be your idea.' Joyce arched an eyebrow. 'If he thinks I've bullied you into it, he'll say no. So make it convincing.' And she sank back into her pillows, and smiled.

Lorna could hear Keir's approach before he reached the bed; he was apologising in his familiar rambling manner.

'. . . so short-staffed right now, with Jackie on maternity leave again, it's taken me for ever to deal with the paperwork. Oh, hello, Lorna!' Keir seemed pleased to see her when she turned around. 'Joyce, you're looking so much better.'

Lorna noticed he didn't call her Mrs Rothery and, for once, she didn't enforce it.

'So how are we feeling?' he enquired.

'I am feeling bruised but positive, and Lorna here is feeling delighted with her gallery sales,' said Joyce. 'I can't say how *you're* feeling, of course.'

Keir made an 'oh, you' face, and went on, 'I've got some details with me, you'll be pleased to hear – firstly about the aids we can supply to your house, and secondly, a

brochure about your minibreak. I'm afraid Butterfields was
full but I've pulled some strings and managed to get you a
special room with a garden view at Monnow Court – that's
nice, isn't it? You can watch the birds having their lunch.
The staff put out fresh seed every day . . .'

Joyce made a strangled noise. 'There's been a develop-
ment on that front, Keir.' She turned to Lorna. 'Lorna's
made the most generous offer.'

'Um, yes.' Two pairs of eyes were fixed on her. 'I thought,
rather than go to the expense of Mrs Rothery taking up a
care-home room, she could stay in my flat. While her
accommodation is being assessed.'

'What?' Keir corrected himself almost immediately. 'I
mean, are you sure?'

'Absolutely.' *What am I doing?* 'I've got lots of space
and the bedroom and bathroom are on one level so much
easier for Mrs Rothery to manage. You can check it out
if you want.'

'But . . .' He seemed flustered. 'Normally we're happy
to discharge patients to family members but you're not . . .'

'My family are all dead,' said Joyce briskly. 'And I don't
have any medical requirements, you said so yourself. The
district nurse can visit if she cares to.'

Keir looked at Lorna and then back at Joyce again.

'It would be an honour to have the gallery's most famous artist to stay with me,' Lorna explained. 'I'm hoping
Mrs Rothery can advise me about our Art Week exhibition
and perhaps go through some of the portfolios I've been sent.'
She glanced at Joyce. 'I would appreciate her expertise, as
well as her company.'

Lorna knew she was pushing it, but she sensed Joyce
was amused. Well, hadn't she wanted a deal?

'If I feel up to it,' Joyce sighed. 'I might be able to glance through a portfolio or two.'

'Good,' said Lorna.

'Good,' said Keir but he sounded very confused.

'Good,' said Joyce, and touched the postcard Lorna had propped against her water glass. It was one of Cathy Larkham's inky sketches from a Welsh beach.

When Lorna got back to the flat there was a red envelope lying on top of the junk mail behind the door, and her heart leaped into her throat.

Even though she told herself she didn't want a card from Sam because that would just complicate things, Lorna's hands trembled as she turned it over to check the address.

Was it from Max the chef? Had he found out where she'd moved to? Despite her rational thoughts about commitment, she felt a twinge of pleasure that someone had cared enough to find a card, put it in the post.

And Sam had been in the shop. He had seen what amazing cards they had . . .

The writing on the front was unfamiliar but the writing inside wasn't.

It was from Jess. As per their arrangement for the past twenty-one years.

Lorna tried to ignore her own disappointment as she trudged upstairs to the sound of two hysterical dogs running circuits round her flat.

Chapter Eleven

Keir Brownlow came round the following morning with his safety checklist, and admitted that he had some concerns about Rooks Hall, and whether it could be made safe for Joyce to go home.

'I've said for *ages* that the house won't meet safeguarding criteria,' he said, drinking tea while Lorna moved her things out of her bedroom to make space for Joyce and the mobility aids Keir had dragged upstairs. 'The place is freezing at the best of times, the ambulance team thought they could smell gas, and Joyce refuses to let anyone in to check – we spoke to the landlords and apparently she makes it impossible for them to do much.'

Lorna put a vase of chalky white tulips on the bedside table. 'But if she's a private tenant, aren't her landlords legally obliged to make it safe?'

'They are, yes, but I don't know if she's even got a formal tenancy agreement – she's been there years. A colleague who lives nearby says the landlords who own most of the houses down Joyce's lane are turning their housing stock into holiday homes. So they'd probably rather Joyce moved into sheltered accommodation anyway.'

Lorna frowned. 'So where are the locals supposed to live, when all the pretty cottages are holiday homes?'

'Don't start me,' said Keir forlornly. 'I'm stuck with my

parents. Believe me, no one's praying for a housing crash harder than my mum.'

After he left, Lorna carried on making the room, with its small en suite, ready for Joyce. She put a radio by the bedside, moved an easy chair near the window so Joyce could read and see over the rooftops, but she hesitated over the art in there. What would she like? Was there any point trying to guess? Was she revealing too much about herself in the Queen of Cups, in the soft abstract?

Lorna decided to leave it exactly as it was. Let Joyce read into it what she wanted.

Tiffany came upstairs shortly afterwards to find her making up the spare sofa bed with new linen for herself. She seemed touchy.

'Can you help me with this duvet?' Lorna asked. 'Or are you watching to see how it's done?'

Reluctantly, Tiff took a corner and started pulling the cover over. 'Keir says Joyce Rothery's moving in with us – is that right?'

Lorna let the *with us* go for the time being. 'Yes, just for a day or so, till she can go back to her own house.'

'Why?' She widened her eyes until she looked almost cartoonish. 'What happened to *I want to be alone*? What happened to all that aggro you gave me about bathroom rotas? And not leaving junk in your Thinking Room? And not using your good coffee?'

Tiff had been in a funny mood ever since the roses arrived – and she still hadn't told Lorna who they were from, which had put Lorna in her own funny mood.

'Because Joyce is scared of going into the care home, even for a few days. And I don't blame her.' She shook out the pillowcase. 'It's only until her landlords fix some handrails and checks the gas. She won't be here long.'

'Are you sure it's a good idea?' Tiffany seemed less than enthusiastic. 'Sophie's grandmama came to stay while her kitchen in Paris was refitted. She was there *four months*. The entire house smelled of mothballs by the end.'

'Yes, I'm sure. Joyce is an amazing artist, and an interesting woman, and she doesn't have anyone else,' said Lorna sharply. 'It's all right for you, with your huge bunches of Valentine's roses – not everyone has a rich boyfriend to take care of them.'

Tiffany went red.

'Still no idea about who they were from?' Lorna pressed on. It came out more pointed than she'd meant, partly because Tiff had been so coy about them, partly because she didn't see why she should have to justify her favour to Joyce, but Tiffany suddenly squinched her eyes shut and clenched her fists.

'What? What did I say?' Lorna felt bad immediately. She reached out and touched her friend's arm. 'Tell me – what's up? Who sent you those flowers?'

'I can't tell you. You'd . . . Forget it.' Tiffany pulled away, and gave Lorna a sorrowful glare that she couldn't read. 'I'm taking the dogs for a walk,' she said over her shoulder. 'Rudy! Bernard!'

Rudy was curled up on a pile of blankets. He looked up at Lorna, and then towards Tiffany, and bravely followed her out on to the landing.

Lorna had wasted no time in getting in touch with as many local artists as she could, in an effort to give the gallery an infusion of new work, and there was no shortage of aspiring artists eager to be represented on its walls. The more modern ones emailed links to their websites, but some still sent in work in portfolios or on CDs. Lorna was only halfway through the pile of discs that had been opened, filed by Mary in one of her many storage boxes and promptly forgotten. Some she thought were interesting, some terrible; some she honestly couldn't tell whether they were good or bad. A few were plain worrying.

It was the hour before closing, and she was trying to tick off a few more before Keir arrived with Joyce. Outside, the first drops of rain were flicking against the windowpanes and the back office felt cosy. Tiffany was long since back from her walk with the dogs, and now Rudy was asleep under the desk, while Bernard was chasing tennis balls up and down the stairs. Lorna eased off her boots and began clicking through an endless parade of abstracts called *Refractions XII – XXX*, which seemed to be the inside of someone's skull during a series of debilitating migraines.

Blue, green, yellow fractals.

The works represent the intersection of tangible shape and temporal confusion, in order to challenge the viewer's perception of artistic practice . . .

They reminded Lorna uncomfortably of the art she'd tried to sell in London. It had been challenging too.

'That's a bold use of colour.'

She spun round on the chair. Joyce was standing right behind her, wrapped in a heavy black coat with a deep fur collar, the colour of old snow. She'd appeared so silently that for one surreal second, Lorna wondered if she'd died in hospital and this was her last earthly visit before moving on to a higher plane.

But then Joyce coughed, and pointed at the screen. 'Although how big is it? How on earth can you tell anything from that little snap?'

Lorna scrambled to her feet. 'Hello! Joyce, I'm sorry, I didn't hear you come in. Where's Mary?'

Joyce leaned nearer the computer screen. The smell of fading perfume and locked wardrobes intensified. 'Mary scuttled out as soon as she saw me. She's gone to help Keir.'

'Where's he?' Lorna looked round – the gallery was empty, the Closed sign still swinging on the door from Mary's exit.

'He's trying to find a place to park. *What* a performance. Do you mind if I . . . ?' She indicated the chair Lorna had vacated. Underneath it, Rudy wagged his tail and Joyce nodded at him as she sank into it. 'What do you call this?' She flicked a finger at the screen.

'It's a submission. An artist based in . . .' Lorna studied the CD case. 'In Bromsgrove.'

'Hmmph. Are they all like this?'

'Mostly. Would you like me to . . . ?' Lorna pressed the space bar, moving the images on.

They peered in silence at the screen, the headachey yellows and greens merging into one another. Lorna began to feel embarrassed, somehow responsible for the art. I should know what to say, she thought. Joyce will know whether it's good or not – I don't. Her confidence wavered.

'And this is how artists send their work nowadays?' Joyce asked. 'On a computer?'

'Some do. Some send links to their websites.' She

paused. 'I prefer the old-fashioned portfolios, to be honest with you. But there's often more context on the website. Who they are, why they paint. Subtitles, in other words, to give you a foothold.'

'But how can you tell what it feels like?' Joyce rubbed the air between her arthritic fingers. 'The texture, the canvas . . . ?'

'You can't,' said Lorna, 'I think this is how it comes. It's computer generated.'

They stared at the final image. It was so busy and angry, Lorna felt her eyeballs hurting. 'What do you think this is about?' she asked, emboldened by the fact that Joyce wasn't actually looking at her. She tried to phrase it in such a way that it wasn't obvious she didn't know.

'Well, it's playing with the idea of colour and rhythm,' said Joyce. 'And I suppose there's a sort of tonality about it. Is this the type of work you represent here now?'

'No,' said Lorna.

'Do you like it?'

Something important was hanging in the balance between them. Was it good? Was she missing a genius in the making? Lorna thought of the art she did know she liked, instinctively – Joyce's safe white house, the contemplative portraits she'd seen a few days ago – and found her answer.

'No,' she said honestly. 'It's giving me a headache.'

There was a long pause, in which she wasn't sure if she'd said the right thing. Then Joyce sighed. 'Me too. Well, that's a relief,' she said. She gazed round the office, her pale eyes taking in the shelves lined with artists' files, including her own. 'I've never been in here, you know. Quite the nerve centre.'

'Let me take you upstairs,' said Lorna. 'Before Keir comes in here and tells me off for making you sit in a room he hasn't health and safety checked.'

Joyce's first evening as Lorna's guest was spent closeted in her bedroom with Bernard. She was 'worn out by the day', she said, and just wanted to listen to the radio, then sleep.

'Of course! Absolutely fine!' Lorna's cheeks ached with smiling. She'd smiled and smiled while Keir was there to reassure him that he could report back to his dragon boss, and felt she had to keep smiling to compensate for Tiffany's mood, which was still hanging over the place like fog. 'I've put a radio by the bed, can you see? That's the on button. And there's a carafe of water, and I'm sure you know how the electric blanket works. Would you like me to bring you some tea later? A snack?'

'No, thank you. I'm fine.' Joyce was settled in the chair by the window, her knitting on her lap. The lamplight shone through her fine white hair, exposing the palely freckled scalp beneath. Lorna looked away; it felt like a too-personal thing to notice.

She scanned the room for anything she'd forgotten. 'You're sure there's nothing else you need?'

'Very sure. Just some rest.'

Lorna's eye fell on a photo she hadn't moved from the chest of drawers – a framed snap of her and Jess on the beach in Wales with Mum and Dad, the camera balanced on a rock and the four of them only just in focus. Jess had been in charge of running back while they counted down from five, and her mouth was still open in loud instruction, while Dad and Lorna were clearly saying 'two'. Mum was smiling, mysteriously, at Dad.

Don't move it, she told herself. Draws more attention to it.

'And it's fine for Bernard to sleep in here,' she added, 'I've put one of Rudy's cushions in.'

'Thank you.' Joyce smiled thinly. She did look tired. 'And where will you be?'

'Oh, on the sofa bed. I'll be fine.' She'd never slept on the sofa bed but it was only for a few nights. 'Right then. I'll . . . leave you to it. Shout if you need anything!'

Lorna smiled once more and then turned to go. At the door, she heard Joyce say, 'Lorna?'

She turned, expecting a 'thank you'.

'Is this you?' Joyce pointed not at the photograph, but at a pencil sketch on the bookshelf. It was of Lorna and Jessica, aged about three and seven, doing a jigsaw on holiday, their heads bent together, Jess's dark curls mingling with Lorna's straight blonde hair. Jess had found it with their mother's things and given it to Lorna after the funeral. The tenderness meant Lorna could only look at it for a certain amount of time. She rationed it.

'Yes,' she said, 'my mum drew that.' She paused. 'She was an artist. Cathy Larkham?'

'I thought so,' said Joyce, ambiguously, and nodded, half to herself. 'It sings with love.'

Their eyes met for a long moment, and Joyce *knew*, Lorna thought. Joyce understood something that she wasn't quite sure she understood herself.

Lorna was still thinking about the sketch – and her mum – when she walked into the kitchen and saw the pile of washing up by the sink. Tiffany was texting on her phone at the table but she flipped it over when Lorna walked in. There were coffee mugs on the table, and the breakfast bowls were still on the side where they'd been left, crumbs and buttery knives everywhere. How could Tiff sit there texting someone, and not take ten seconds to load the dishwasher with her own dirty plates?

'I don't want to start making house rules,' said Lorna, flicking on the kettle. 'But can you not leave cups by the dishwasher? They're going to start mounting up, with three of us here.'

'OK,' said Tiffany, surprised.

'Maybe I should do a rota,' Lorna went on, despite herself.

'If that's what you want.'

I wish I could just go into that white room and lie down and look at the stars out of the window and think about Mum, she thought, then realised she couldn't, because it was full of stuff she'd had to move out of the sitting room to unfold the sofa bed. Most of it Tiffany's.

The kettle boiled and the phone rang on the wall. Tiffany jumped on her chair, nearly spilling her tea. 'Can you get that, please?' she said, even though she was nearer.

Lorna frowned. And that was another thing – why wasn't Tiff confiding in her about whatever it was that was going on? Didn't she trust her?

'Please?' Tiffany repeated.

It was an old phone, obviously left there by previous tenants, and talking on it tethered the speaker to the wall by the window. Lorna looked down at the street below as she answered. Outside the gallery, someone in a Barbour jacket was looking into the window – was it Sam? She'd been thinking about him on and off all day – it was his birthday at the end of the month, and she'd been wondering it if would look too keen to take him out for a drink.

'Hello? Lorna? It's Jess.' From the sound in the background, there was an impromptu recorder recital going on at the Protheros'.

'Hi, Jess.' She said Jess's name for Tiff's benefit and saw her shoulders slump back to normal. 'Thanks for the Valentine's card. I see you didn't even get Ryan to write it this year. Slipping. Did you like mine?'

'I did! Cute!' She moved on too swiftly and Lorna knew she'd barely noticed the card she'd spent ages choosing. 'Listen, I'm ringing to ask a favour.'

Lorna returned her gaze to the man outside the shop, willing him to look up so she could see his face. The dark hair was familiar, and was that a beard? She angled her head against the windowpane. Was Sam staring into the shop in the hope of seeing her? Why didn't he look up?

'. . . would that be all right?' Jess had finished speaking.

'What? Say that again?'

'I don't know what you did with Hattie while she was there last weekend but she's incredibly keen to come back. She even suggested getting the Friday-night train.' Jess made a clicking noise.

The man made a visor of his hand on the glass to see into the darkened gallery, then gave up and walked away. Lorna flattened herself against the window to see but she couldn't tell whether it was Sam. When she turned, Tiffany was frozen at the table, staring at her with big eyes.

'What?' she mouthed.

'Is someone downstairs?' Tiff gestured.

Lorna shook her head. Jess was rattling on in the bossy

tone that made her habitually zone out, and the strange, hunted expression on Tiffany's face was too weird to ignore.

'. . . from Wagamama, so maybe you could give her some money for helping you out in the gallery? Lorna? Are you listening to me? Lorna!'

Lorna dragged her focus back to the phone as Tiff pushed back her chair and went over to the window. 'Wait, sorry – are we still talking about Hattie?'

'Yes!' Jess sounded aggrieved. 'Are you checking your emails while you're talking to me?'

'No!' That was something Jess did, sometimes when Lorna was actually there in person. 'Of course I'm not. I'm listening.'

'So? What was the last thing I said.'

'Hattie . . . wants to come here this weekend?'

Tiff wandered back to the table and stared at her phone. Just behind her, on the landing table, the extravagant bunch of red roses glowed in the dim hall light. Funny that Tiff had put them out there, rather than kept them in her own room. And she'd barely mentioned them since, almost as if she didn't want them. Why was that?

'Yes! And?'

'You want me to give Hattie some cash because she's packed her job in at Wagamama?'

'No, she's been made *redundant*. They've laid all the students off.'

Oh, was *that* the reason for Hattie turning up out of the blue last weekend? Had she been sacked, and had to make up an excuse? Jess was the sort of mum who would probably march round there and demand explanations.

Lorna felt bad – she'd meant to find a moment to

ring Hattie. Should she say something now? It felt wrong, keeping things from her sister, but if that was all it was . . .

'Between you and me, though, it's a relief,' Jess went on. 'That business last weekend, Hattie running off, missing Ryan's birthday . . . I think she knew this was coming and didn't know how to tell us. As if we'd be worried!'

Really, though? Jess sounded so relieved Lorna didn't want to raise any doubts. 'Well, I'd love to have her, if she wants to come. She's the best wrapper I've ever seen.'

'Thanks, sis.' Jess sounded relieved. 'I know it's short notice but—'

'You're welcome,' said Lorna, and it was only when she put the phone down, after some quickfire information about Tyra's swimming badge and Milo's nits, that she realised she was going to have to buy another bed.

Rudy had spent his life working to a regular and relatively uneventful timetable, and he made it clear with every inch of his elongated body that he didn't like change. All the extra noises and unfamiliar smells in the flat needed investigation, and when Tiffany had gone to bed, he wandered from room to room until he found Lorna lying on the sofa, her feet sticking out from under the spare duvet, waiting as usual for sleep to finish its rounds of everyone else in the world and find her.

She heard rather than saw the little dog enter, and dropped her hand to dachshund level, which he sniffed, and then licked with a delicate tongue, his gentle greeting. His wet nose tickled her fingertips. And since she was feeling rather unsettled herself, Lorna lifted Rudy up and let him curl into the narrow ledge of unoccupied sofa in front of her body. On top of the duvet, not under it. She had limits.

'This is just a dream,' she told him. 'You never get to sleep on the sofa.'

He curled up against her, warm and compliant, and Lorna felt comforted.

Her mind drifted through the events of the evening. Tiff's mysterious behaviour, Joyce arriving, settling into her bedroom, reading her art like the secrets in her palm. And then Hattie. Was that really the whole story, that she'd snuck away to Longhampton to avoid telling her mum she'd been sacked? Something didn't feel right.

Sam's face floated up, as it had done so often for so long, but now, with that beard, the face of a different man again. The flat line of thick brows framing his dark eyes was just the same; Lorna traced the the curl of disappointment that it hadn't been him, peering into her gallery, then traced another curl of shame at the way he'd politely repelled her approach.

She stared blankly at the windows, where the thin curtains were letting moonlight drift across the walls. You're not thirteen any more. You're an adult, and so's he. You barely know him as a man. You have no idea what his personal life was like then – or is now.

I need a reason to call him, she thought, then rolled her eyes at herself. Rudy wriggled further backwards, pressing his bony spine into her leg. Then it popped into Lorna's head: Hattie was staying the weekend; it would make perfect sense to ask Sam if he wanted to spend time with them? He was her niece's godfather, after all.

Rudy moved, growling very low under his breath, and Lorna heard the sitting room door move. A thick wedge of dim light fell into the room, closely followed by the sound of feet on floorboards.

Oh God, was it Joyce? Was she sleepwalking? Was she in need of medical attention? What if she fell? The responsibility of what she'd taken on suddenly weighed on Lorna.

She sat up quickly, so fast Rudy nearly tumbled off the sofa, and reached for her mobile as the door opened.

'Hello?' she whispered. 'Joyce?'

But it wasn't Joyce, it was Tiffany.

Without her make-up on, and barefoot in her polka-dot pyjamas, she looked much younger, and Lorna could see, even in the half-light, that she'd been crying.

'Tiff?' she whispered. 'Are you all right?'

She shook her head. 'No. Lorna, I need to talk to you about something. Something bad.'

Chapter Twelve

Lorna shifted over on the sofa to make room for Tiffany, and she slipped under the duvet, tucking it tight around her legs. She frowned at the pattern, as if she wasn't sure where to start her story.

'Let me guess,' said Lorna. She had a few ideas of why Tiff was finding this so hard. 'Something to do with those roses?'

Tiffany looked up, surprised. 'How did you know?'

'Because you've *never* had flowers and not made a huge song and dance about them.' She tried to sound teasing, hoping it would make Tiff smile. 'I remember every single tacky petrol station bouquet you ever got from Jim the Crim.'

'He wasn't a crim,' Tiff said automatically. 'He just used his mum's disabled parking badge once or twice.'

'Yeah, yeah. So you say. Who are these from?' Lorna nudged her. 'They're gorgeous; you'd normally be shouting it from the rooftops.'

Tiffany hugged her knees. 'You have to promise not to judge. It's . . . a real mess.'

'Is it someone I know?' she said, to get the ball rolling.

'Sort of.'

Wait. It couldn't be Sam, could it? whispered a weaselly voice in her ear. He'd noticed Tiffany that day in the gallery; he could have popped back in to chat while Lorna was out walking Rudy and Bernard. Why wouldn't he fancy Tiff? She was smart, petite, confident – the sort of woman Sam had probably dated while he was working in London . . .

Tiffany suddenly grabbed her hand and looked right into her eyes, her own wide with distress. 'You've got to believe me when I tell you that I absolutely, *definitively* did not mean this to happen,' she blurted out. 'None of it. I'm so embarrassed.'

'Tiff, don't be dramatic, it's just flowers. Who sent them?'

Her gaze dropped to the duvet. 'JC. He must have found out where I was from the agency. I asked them not to give out my new address . . .'

'Hold up.' Lorna raised her hand in a stop sign. 'Who's JC?'

'Jean-Claude.' She reached out for Rudy but he buried himself deeper into the duvet. 'The dad of the family I was working for.'

'You're kidding me?' Lorna's relief that it wasn't Sam was swiftly replaced with shock. 'You've been having an affair with your boss? In his *house*?'

Tiffany looked horrified. 'An affair? No! Sod off!'

'Then what? Why else would he be sending you flowers?'

'Because . . . because he's trying to get me to go back. And I can't.'

'Why? What's happened?'

'Ngggh.' Tiff grabbed her face with her hands, then looked up and said, in a rush, 'He's been having an affair, with his PA. I know, cliché. He talked me into providing an alibi for a weekend away when Sophie was in Paris and he was meant to be here. That's one thing.' She held up a finger. 'Then Sophie worked it out, and made me give *her* an alibi. I know, it's mad. That's two. Then there was the nannycam I found in the bathroom – my bathroom, not even the kids'! – *three*; then the fact that I'm supposed to talk to them in English and they all bitch about me in French, four; and five, the final straw, Sophie put me on a diet because I'm fatter than her friends' nannies and it's making her look bad.'

Lorna's jaw dropped.

'Anyway. They each found out about the other when I got my dates wrong on the calendar, so all hell broke loose. But they've clearly made up and realised they can't control the kids without me, because they've been ringing and ringing, trying to get me to go back like nothing happened but I can't.' Tiffany lifted her hands, then let them fall again. 'I can't do it any more. I'm *done*.'

'OK, so find a different family. This lot sound pretty hard work, to be honest, the rows and affairs . . . Not everyone's like that, surely?'

'They're not the worst. The things I've heard from my mates . . .' Tiffany let out a shuddering sigh. 'Lorn, I don't want to be a nanny any more. I can put up with the kids, but it's the parents. The constant goalpost shifting, and the *can I just tell you something*s, and the spying, and the pissy way they demand receipts for coffee while they're buying a second ski chalet . . . Ugh! It's killing me.' Her eyes were wild.

'They must miss you, though, if they're sending you two hundred quids' worth of premium English roses.'

Tiffany gave her a contemptuous look. 'Yeah. No.

Sophie sent me a voicemail with the children crying in the background. *Oh Tiffanneee, les enfants miss yooooou, zey are crying for yooooou.* No, they're not, Sophie. They're crying because you won't let them eat fruit sugars.'

Lorna tried not to smile. 'Why didn't you tell me?' She nudged Tiffany. 'I thought you loved your work. I mean, I've left jobs before. I jacked in a *very* good job to do this. One I actually liked. I wouldn't have judged.'

'I didn't tell you because it would make it real.' Tiffany chewed her lip. 'And you'd just moved here, and you kept going on about how you wanted your space, and I didn't know how long I'd have to stay . . . Plus I wasn't . . . I'm not looking forward to telling my mum.' She glanced up from under her thick eyelashes; Lorna had never seen her look so scared.

Lorna wanted to say, She'll understand, but she knew Tiff's mum well enough to know this would *not* be the case.

'At Christmas, she told the whole family over lunch that my next job will be with William and Kate,' Tiffany went on. 'She's got a framed photo of me in my uniform on the sideboard, she's so proud. And she's still paying off the loan she took out for my fees. It was massive. I'll have to pay her the money back, and I don't know how I can.'

'Oh.' That was more serious. Lorna liked Mrs Harris – she was loud and friendly and had regularly dropped in on their flat share with Tupperwares of food to find out how Tiff's hunt for a rich bachelor was going in West London. But she'd made it clear that just as they'd found the money for Tiff's brother's dentistry degree because 'dentists never go poor now there's Instagram', Tiff's nanny qualification was a similar long-term investment.

'Plus the agency are on my case, twice a day. I'll probably end up owing them money too, specially if I've broken my contract. And . . .' She splayed her hands on the duvet and Rudy wriggled further away. 'I've let the kids down! They weren't so bad. But at least they'll get another nanny soon. Sophie isn't going to handle them solo much longer.'

'That it?' Lorna asked. 'Did you steal their spare change too? Any towels and/or dressing gowns in your suitcase that you want to tell me about?'

Tiff looked up miserably. 'Do you hate me?'

'Of course not, you doughnut. Would you like me to?'

'Well, I hate myself. Lying, and whatnot.'

'And what does hating yourself achieve?'

'It makes me feel less of a cow. I've let everyone down. And I'm actually crap at the thing I thought I was good at.' She pushed the hair out of her mournful eyes. 'This isn't exactly where I saw myself at this stage in my life. I mean, I wasn't on Mum's career trajectory but I hadn't planned on bailing so soon.'

'You've jacked in your job, not set fire to an orphanage,' Lorna pointed out calmly. 'There must be temp work you can do here in the meantime. Or some bar shifts – you've done loads of that. And just talk to the agency. Tell them how unreasonable the Hollandes were. What harm can it do?'

'But I can't afford to pay you any rent.'

'We'll work something out. I've budgeted to cover this place until the end of the year. Makes no difference whether you're here or not. You can help me with Rudy's anxiety training, if you want. And Keir's still pushing me to join his Surveillance Dogs for the Old thing. Volunteer for that – he'd be made up.'

179

Tiffany managed a smile. 'You're sure?'

'Yeah. Course.' Lorna reached over and hugged her. Old friends. She felt a hungry nostalgia for those times, the boxset Sundays, the nights getting ready together, the night buses home. Those days slipped past so quickly, while you were planning a future that never turned out the way you expected.

'It'll be better in the morning,' she said. 'Go back to bed.'

Around the second coffee break of the day, Keir dropped by on his way to a care meeting. He wanted to pass on the news that he'd spoken to Joyce's landlords, and to the occupational therapist at the hospital, and the soonest the builders could come in and do the necessary work was now 'early next week'. He was *not* impressed with the reception he'd had from the landlord.

'I told him it was urgent,' he huffed, 'but he was so rude! He actually said he was doing Joyce a favour putting these safety aids in, then implied she was trying to fake a compensation claim for her fall.'

'That's outrageous.' Lorna felt furious on Joyce's behalf. 'I bet he hasn't done repairs in there for years.'

'Probably just looking for excuses to get Joyce out.' Keir sniffed; he had a constant cold. 'The cottage further up the lane had a Range Rover outside, couple of holiday-makers unloading Waitrose bags from the boot.' He lowered his voice. 'How's she getting on?'

'Fine,' said Lorna. 'She's . . .'

'Right behind you.' Joyce emerged from the back room, her knitting bag in hand. She was dressed in a chic grey skirt and jumper, a yellow silk scarf like a splash of sunshine around her neck. She didn't look like someone who'd recently been in hospital.

'Joyce?' Lorna jumped. How much had she heard? 'How long have you been there?'

An imperious flash of knobbly fingers and rings. 'Fifteen minutes or so. I've been making myself comfortable in your back room.' Joyce leaned forward, her eyes sharp with interest. 'Now, I do like that pottery. Inspired by Troika? Almost illegally so. Who makes it?'

Keir rushed over to her. 'Joyce! Did you go down those stairs on your own? You need to be careful . . .'

'I'm *fine*, for heaven's sake.' Joyce brushed off his hand and made her way over to the gallery desk. 'It's good for the hips to attempt stairs once a day. I don't want to get home and find I can no longer get to my own bed.'

'But they're so *steep*.'

'Nonsense. I've had friends who moved into bungalows and promptly died.'

Lorna suspected Joyce had just made that up. From the way her gaze was sweeping around the new watercolours, it seemed the gallery's display was interesting her. Lorna wondered which pieces, exactly.

'That's rather intriguing.' Joyce gestured towards a large canvas by the window: green trees against a metallic foil sunset, with a distinctive path winding up a hill. 'The forest going out of town, is it?'

'Yes, the artist came in yesterday and left it on spec. It's inspired by the woods just beyond the park.' It had been the first artist interview Lorna felt had gone well; the young painter, Corey, had just graduated from the local art school and wasn't too cool to be thrilled by Lorna's enthusiasm for his work. He hadn't even had time to write a wildly pretentious description of his creative process.

Joyce nodded. 'I rather like it. Just on the cusp of abstract and representational.'

'And there are dogs hidden in there! You can make them out, in between the leaves and branches. Fourteen, the artist said.' Mary had reassured Lorna that 'dogs sell anything in here'.

'Really? I can't see ... my eyes.' Joyce didn't even attempt to squint, and Lorna wished she hadn't said anything. It was easy to forget about Joyce's failing sight; she seemed to glide through the world like a tweedy swan.

'Another reason not to be running up and down stairs!' Keir interrupted. 'We need to take care of ourselves!'

Lorna winced at the 'we'. She already knew Joyce wasn't a 'we' person.

'We?' Joyce enquired. 'Don't *we* have some old people to go and look after?' And Keir remembered his morning meeting and left.

Joyce settled herself in the back room of the gallery with her knitting and a cup of tea that Tiffany and Lorna refreshed every hour or so. She insisted there was nothing she needed, and passed no comments to the browsers, until Lorna put her head round, just after lunch.

Joyce was staring into space, but when Lorna coughed, she snapped back to reality. 'Oh, hello. Lorna, before you ask again, if it's not too much trouble, there *is* something I need.'

'Of course, what can I do?'

Joyce held up a half-finished dog coat on her knee – very Bernard, in crisp black and white stripes. It was perfect and, as far as Lorna knew, she'd only started it that morning. 'I forgot to bring my wool with me, in the rush.'

'Oh.' It wouldn't have been something Keir would have thought to pack, knitting wool. 'Would you like me to go and buy you some more?' She gestured towards the street. 'There's a lovely new craft shop down by the town hall . . .'

'No, I need the match. I thought, if you were taking the dogs out later, you might go by Rooks Hall and collect it? And perhaps you could check they locked the door?'

Lorna hadn't planned to, but there was something about the way Joyce asked that made her think she was worried about her house, whether it was still standing without her in it. 'Your wool stash is in the trunk by the fireplace, isn't it?'

'It is. Thank you, Lorna. You're very kind.' Joyce smiled, a real smile that lifted the tiredness in her face. Lorna was touched by it. Joyce had perked up overnight, like a wilting tulip in fresh water, from simply being in the gallery, amongst the art and the colours, and the murmur of conversation.

'My pleasure,' she said, and meant it.

A car was already parked in front of Joyce's house when Lorna pulled up outside – a Land Rover she hadn't seen before.

Keir's words sprang into her mind. Was this the bolshie landlord? Or someone else, who'd noticed the house was empty? The car was too muddy and agricultural to be a holidaymaker.

Lorna got out and was halfway up the drive when she had a better idea. She went back to her car and lifted both Bernard and Rudy down from the back, then led them up to the front door, quietly opened it with her key and unhooked their leads, letting them both loose like rockets down the hall.

Bernard barged into the house, barking with delight to be home, with Rudy close behind, tail wagging as he trotted on his short legs after his friend. But it took Bernard nanoseconds to work out that someone was in the house, and then the yapping turned up several notches, followed by the sound of male yelling.

'Get off! Get off, you little sod!'

Good, thought Lorna, gritting her teeth as she followed, phone in hand. If that was the landlord, he deserved it, going through Joyce's things without permission, and if it was a burglar . . .

She dialled the first two nines on her mobile before heading towards the sound of the barking upstairs.

'Don't move!' she yelled. 'The police are on the way!'

'Why?' replied an exasperated man's voice. 'For God's sake, call them back and tell them not to come.'

Lorna ran up the narrow carpeted stairs and on to the landing, where the dogs were bouncing around as if it was the best game ever.

Standing in the bathroom, wearing a pair of paint-stained overalls and wielding a power drill, was a pissed-off-looking Sam Osborne. A radio play was burbling in the background and there was a thermos of tea on the windowsill. Meanwhile Bernard was humping the air around his leg, tongue lolling out with careless joy, while Rudy tried to copy him without having the first idea what Bernard was doing.

'Get these two out of my bloody way!' He waved his

free hand. 'There's wet adhesive and everything in here. They'll get hairs on it.'

'What are you doing here?' Lorna stared at Sam. Normally a man doing DIY was quite a sexy look but Sam didn't seem 100 per cent in control of the power drill. He held it as if it might suddenly start whirring round at the handle as well as at the bit. And they definitely weren't his overalls. They were the overalls of a much bigger man.

'What does it look like I'm doing?' He seemed evasive, as if he'd been caught doing something he didn't want her to see. 'I'm fitting handrails. What are *you* doing?'

'I'm walking Joyce's dog.' Lorna's brain slowly made connections. 'She's staying with me at the moment while her . . . Wait. Are *you* Joyce's landlord?'

'Hang on, let me pause this.' Sam jabbed at his phone, the source of the radio play. The voices stopped, mid-argument. 'The farm owns all the houses down this lane. Well, we did – Dad sold a couple. We've still got four. At the moment.'

The shabby, intimate details of the bathroom leaped out at Lorna – an old plastic shower cap drying over the taps, the pink hand soap on the basin, brown etched deep in its long cracks. For once, Keir was right to be concerned: this wasn't a safe place for an old lady. The ancient iron bath was high-sided with creepy claw feet, the dilapidated extractor fan on the frosted window looked loose – everything needed securing.

Lorna stared at him, remembering what Keir had said about the rudeness he'd experienced. Had *Sam* been rude to Keir? She wouldn't have thought so, but then he hadn't held back with his advice to her, had he? The professional,

London-hardened Sam was very different to the soft teenager she'd preserved in her memory for so long.

'And you're doing the safety work?' There was a plastic grab rail in a B&Q box, some screws, a rubber mat. 'I thought the builders were supposed to be coming next week?'

'They are, but I thought I'd come over, see if I could make a start. Builders round here charge a fortune. Spend most of the morning standing round talking about what they need to do tomorrow.' He scratched his beard, as if he didn't want to go into details. 'It's Gabe's department, managing this sort of thing, but he never negotiates. He was at school with half of them.'

'So were you.'

Sam gave her a look. 'Yeah, but I was the smartarse who went to London, wasn't I? I think they get together and see who can rip me off the most.'

Lorna looked round, distracted by the crimson candlewick dressing gown, the watercolour of fishing boats in a harbour, the splayed toothbrush in a glass. 'Are all the houses this . . .' She wanted to say 'dated' but thought it might be rude, so settled for '. . . old-fashioned?'

He raised an eyebrow. 'Before you judge, bear in mind not all the tenants refuse to let us in, like Mrs Rothery. We're renovating two at the moment. The tenancies finished and rather than renew the lease, we decided we'd take a break and do them up. Holiday lets, that's where we're aiming to make some money. We're even looking into doing something with the farm, for townies wanting that country experience – rent your own chicken for the weekend, feed a lamb, milk a cow, kind of thing.'

'So you're pimping the cows out now?'

'Ha ha.' But Sam was too busy measuring the bath to see her expression was more shocked than sarcastic. 'Obviously Mrs Rothery's lease is long-standing, so we're doing what we can for her,' he went on. 'Mind you . . .' He sucked his teeth. 'I've got the list the social worker emailed over but there's only so much you can do. Grab rails are fine, but you get to the point where it's just safer for everyone to be in a more modern place.'

'Maybe Joyce wants to stay in the home she's been happy in for so many years.'

Sam gave her a funny look. 'Yeah, I get that. But when you've called an ambulance for your brother falling down the stairs because he's too proud to use a stair lift, you start thinking differently about safety.'

His bluntness gave Lorna a cold feeling. 'Isn't that up to her, though?'

'Maybe. Maybe she can train this dog here to call the ambulance . . . Anyway, now you're here, give us a hand, will you?' He nodded at the bath. 'Sit in here and tell me where you'd want a grab rail to go, if you were a bloody-minded old lady.'

Lorna climbed into the bath feeling as if she hadn't ended that conversation very satisfactorily. Sam held the plastic rail in place, and when he leaned over her, she could smell his aftershave and the warmth of his skin.

'That social worker said Mrs Rothery was staying with a friend for a few days. Didn't realise the friend was you,' he said, marking a spot on the wall with a pencil.

'I've been walking Bernard. I suppose we've got to know each other through that.' She couldn't quite place Sam's tone: was he interested? Annoyed she hadn't said? 'And the art, of course.'

'Oh, right. She knew your mum?'

'No, I don't think so.'

Lorna was going to tell him more but she stopped. She didn't feel like explaining about the deal they'd struck, or Joyce's fear of the care home. For the first time ever she wasn't sure she trusted Sam with her secrets – and that was something she'd never thought. Ever.

And she couldn't explore that unsettling thought properly, because it had suddenly occurred to her how sad it was that her mum hadn't known Joyce. Two artists in the same small community. They could have been friends, they could have challenged each other, supported one another in that mysterious, dark forest of imagination. If Mum hadn't kept herself in her bubble with Dad . . .

Sam leaned over to pencil in another mark. His face was within touching distance above her, the hairs of his forearm darkening the skin where his checked shirt sleeve rolled back, but instead of the excitement Lorna always imagined she'd feel, being so close to Sam and free to let something happen, she sensed her soul rolling up protectively around her.

Sam stopped scribbling on the wall and glanced down at her, lying in the bath. 'You OK?'

'Fine,' she said, because words weren't fitting the hollowness in her heart. Was it the house making her feel so lonely?

In another room upstairs, the dogs were playing: barking and running and skittering. Rudy had never played before, being an old lady's dog, but now he was puppyish in Bernard's company. Lorna wished she could wind the clock back ten minutes, so she and Sam could have started this conversation with a laugh, watching the two dogs scamper ineptly. It might have ended better.

'How's Hattie?' He went back to the task in hand. 'Did you ever find out what all that was about, her turning up like that?'

'Ask her yourself. She's coming to stay this weekend,' Lorna heard herself say. 'Do you want to come out for a meal? Or are you busy? I guess you *are* busy, with the farm and stuff, and probably finishing this . . .'

Sam stuck the pencil behind his ear and regarded her thoughtfully. 'That'd be nice,' he said. 'When?'

And despite everything, Lorna's heart swooped in her chest, like one of the dark birds in the trees outside, then settled somewhere different in the pit of her stomach.

Chapter Thirteen

Saturday was always a good day for business, and even with a faint mizzle greying the high street outside, this was no exception.

Hattie had arrived in a better mood than last time, and was eager to help out. She was kept busy on the till, selling cards and a number of grown-up colouring books, while Lorna booked in several items to be framed by Archibald the framer in Hartley.

Another of her money-spinning initiatives was 'creative framing'; Betty's medal had been set in a beautiful red mount, and now hung in the kitchen to inspire Lorna to be brave and pile on the lipstick. She'd also had five of her old cocktail rings mounted and framed, the fruitgum-sized stones encircled with an old beaded necklace of her mum's that Lorna loved but never wore; it came back looking amazing, so she'd got Archibald to make some more for a display suggesting how a boring pile of keepsakes could be turned into a Mother's Day gift to last for ever. Five people had already brought in a shoebox full of cards and photos, and Archibald was making bigger frames.

Mary left before lunch to play golf with Keith; she seemed unusually edgy with Joyce sitting in the back room, knitting like a machine on the small chair by the window.

'Don't you two get on?' Lorna noticed Mary had avoided the back room all day, even though the biscuits were in the office beyond.

'Oh no! No, nothing like that! Goodness, no!' Mary seemed flustered, although it could have been the dangerously low level of Hobnobs in her system. 'It's just that . . . Well, Joyce makes me nervous. Doesn't she make you nervous?'

'Not nervous. Conscious of talking nonsense, maybe.' Lorna wouldn't say she'd got to know Joyce – her polite reserve was just how she was – but since her arrival in Lorna's flat, the mood had shifted from cordiality to something cautiously approaching personal. In her hospital bed, in her worn leather slippers by the bedroom door, in her spartan bathroom, Lorna had glimpsed what lay beneath Joyce's shell, but she knew Joyce had also intuited private details about her – how could she have failed to? The family snaps in her bedroom, the art on the walls. It wasn't their conversations so much as the quiet moments that seemed to be building their connection, the vapour trail left between each exchange about portfolios or the arrangement of canvases.

At three, there was a lull and Lorna made tea for Joyce and Hattie. Joyce took her cup, and showed Lorna her finished dog coat. It was a new one, a flawless Aran, knitted entirely without a pattern.

'I can see it in my head,' Joyce said, offhandedly when Lorna expressed her astonishment. 'Don't ask me to write it down.'

'Aren't you bored of knitting coats?' Lorna offered Joyce a biscuit from the tin. 'Are there other things you could knit?'

Joyce shrugged. 'I have a few ideas . . . We'll see.'

Lorna watched the old lady's expression; her eyes were somewhere else, like Hattie's. Mulling over ideas, stretching and testing them.

What colours and shapes is she seeing? she wondered enviously. How is her artist's mind working? But Lorna's thoughts were broken by Hattie, slouching past, eyes glued to her phone.

'Don't forget, we're having dinner with Sam tonight,' she said. Hattie nodded vaguely, but didn't look up from the screen.

Lorna let out a low breath, and when she looked back she saw Joyce was watching them both with a hawkish expression, and she wished she knew what she was thinking.

Sam had chosen the venue for dinner: La Dragon, Longhampton's new fusion restaurant. It was the third most popular eatery in town, according to TripAdvisor, behind the new burger joint and the evergreen Italian time warp that was Ferrari's Trattoria and Pizzeria. La Dragon was located opposite the Memorial Hall where Lorna and Jessica had had exactly four tap-dancing classes before Lorna twisted her ankle and Jess refused to go on her own.

'This is nice,' said Lorna, looking around the red-checked tablecloths and trendy silver lampshades. Sam was paying. He made a point of telling them when the menus arrived, as if it might affect their choices – which seemed a bit London Sam to Lorna.

'Isn't it? I have to tell you, Hattie, it wasn't always this nice.' Sam winked at Hattie, who was warily nibbling a piece of lava bread. 'It used to be a greasy spoon snack bar called Snax. With an "x". Wall-to-wall plastic tables, and the waitresses were two sisters called Mavis and Doris. They only sold food that could be deep-fried or microwaved.'

'This was when microwaving was an exciting new concept in Longhampton,' Lorna explained. 'Before then, everything was just deep fried.'

'Wow.' Hattie looked over her shoulder. A couple were having an awkward date in the corner table, where a jukebox had once been stuck on Wham's *Make It Big* for a whole year.

To Lorna's relief, Hattie's mouth curved into a smile. That was when she looked like Ryan – when she smiled, all wholesomeness and square teeth. 'When was this?'

Sam glanced over at Lorna and pretended to think. 'When did microwaves arrive in Longhampton, Lorna? Ooooh, what . . . five, six years ago?'

She laughed. 'No! More like . . . ten.'

'Auntie Lorna and I moved to the big city around the time of microwaves,' he told Hattie solemnly. 'When we came back, everything had changed. There was an internet café.'

'It's true,' said Lorna, as Hattie looked between them both, enjoying the back and forth. 'We used to go to discos in barns and sit on hay bales.' She shook her head. 'Because no one could afford chairs. So sad.'

'Really?'

'Oh yes,' said Sam. 'And we didn't have Spotify either, so everyone just had to hum tunes from the hit parade. You know beatboxing? We had to do that just so people could dance.'

To give him his due, Sam was making this much easier. He had an easy way with Hattie, even though by his own admission he hadn't seen her since Milo's christening, and apart from making a big deal about it being his treat, he'd been much more like his old self-deprecating self.

'Doris and Mavis,' she said nostalgically. 'They were twins, weren't they?'

'Yes, identical twins.' Sam poured the wine. 'You could only tell them apart by their warts. And Doris called everyone duck, while Mavis had a thing about Roger Moore. We used to call her . . . um, Miss Moneypenny.'

'No, you didn't.' Lorna frowned, amused. 'That's not what you called her.'

Sam winked. 'I'm editing.'

'Ew!' Hattie giggled, and when the teenage waitress slouched over in her daffodil apron, Lorna was pleased to see Hattie smile up at her and order a sizeable meal.

The food was better than Lorna had expected, and so was the conversation. They chatted about modern art, and Hattie's plans for sixth-form college, but any attempts to get Sam to talk about the farm or what was happening in London were headed off, and instead the conversation returned again and again to Sam and Lorna's teenage years, particularly as the wine bottle emptied, and was replaced, and was half-emptied again.

It was nice to reminisce with Sam, Lorna thought, and to catch him looking nostalgically, almost shyly, at her as they wandered down familiar anecdotal paths, avoiding the hard parts. The easiest memories were their shared ones of Jess and Ryan, two people they both loved very much. Lorna told Hattie how Ryan had felt like a big brother to her, how he'd taken real care of her and Jess, and although she vaguely registered Hattie's hunching shoulders, she put it down to teenage mortification that her parents had once been spotty, lustful adolescents too, snogging in Renault Clios and failing their driving tests.

'Funny to think your mum and dad fell in love next to eighty cows, isn't it?' She tried to catch Hattie's downcast eye. Hattie had been stirring the remains of her ice cream round the bowl for five minutes now while they talked about DJ Holstein, the Hip-hop Young Farmer from Builth Wells. 'I don't know who had the biggest cow eyes – the cows, or your dad looking at your mum!'

'Yeah, we always knew they'd end up together,' said Sam. 'Even if you weren't exactly planned, the way they dealt with it . . . Just goes to show, when two people really love one another, it doesn't matter what life throws at them.' He stared into his glass, then looked up, right at Lorna. 'Gives the rest of us hope, eh, Lorna?'

Lorna didn't know how to read Sam's ambiguous expression. Did he mean . . . he hadn't found anyone? Or that she was that person?

'And they're still mad about each other.' She focused on Hattie instead. 'Jess always says, as soon as she found Ryan, she knew he was the man for her. For all her life.'

Whatever Sam was starting to say was lost in the sound of metal scraping on tiles, as Hattie shoved back her chair and dashed out of the restaurant with a sob. Other diners watched her go, knives and forks suspended in mid-air. The door opened and slammed, and she was gone.

Lorna and Sam stared at each other, shocked.

He lifted his hands helplessly. 'Was it too much?' he said. 'Telling her she was a bit of a surprise? Didn't she know?'

'God, yes. Jess *told* her she wasn't planned,' said Lorna. 'She's the only unplanned thing Jess has ever done.' Then

195

it dawned on her. Oh no. Did Hattie have an unplanned accident of her own? She threw her napkin on the table and got up. 'There's something going on. She's been acting funny for a while. It's not you, I promise.'

'OK. Well, I'll be here.' He looked awkward.

'I don't know how long it'll take.' Lorna was conscious of the entire restaurant pretending not to listen in on their table. 'If you want to go home . . .' She mangled a smile. 'We don't seem to be able to get through a whole evening, do we?'

'I'll wait,' he said. 'If there's anything I can do? I remember what it was like to be that age. Confused.'

Their eyes locked, and Lorna wished she could read minds. That, or ever know what to say to Sam Osborne.

'I'll see if she'll talk to me about whatever it is.' She pushed back her chair. 'Wish me luck.'

Hattie was across the road, sitting on the brick wall outside the Memorial Hall, rocking gently and crying.

Lorna sat down and wrapped an arm round her narrow shoulders, and Hattie turned into her. Her body shook with each gulped breath, and Lorna's heart ached with a need to soothe away her distress. 'What's the matter, Harrietta?' She stroked her soft hair. She hadn't called her Harrietta since she was a toddler. 'Come on, you can tell me.'

'I can't.' Her voice was muffled up against Lorna's jacket.

'Now, you *can*, come on.' She put her hands on either side of Hattie's head, lifting her tear-smudged face. She was so soft, so pretty. 'You nearly told me last time you were here. Whatever it is, it's not going to get better if you ignore it. It's not going to go away.'

196

She tried to keep her voice calm but her mind was racing over the possibilities, and circling back to one. Was Hattie pregnant? It would explain the paleness, the fear of telling Jess and Ryan. They were so ambitious for her, Lorna knew, Jess especially. They had such dreams.

'I understand if you're scared to tell your mum and dad,' she went on. 'But they love you so much, and I'll help you. Whatever it is that's happened, we'll find a way to talk to them about it. I promise.'

She held her niece's face for a long minute, then Hattie chewed her lip, and said, 'You have to swear not to ring Mum straight away.'

'We'll talk it through first.'

There was an unbearable pause, then Hattie said, 'It's Dad.' Her eyes were huge in her face, almost superhuman with pain. The words spilled out in a messy rush. 'I saw him in Costa Coffee in Hereford with another woman. They were holding hands. I know something's going on and I don't know how to tell Mum.'

'What?' Lorna was stunned. *What?* Of all the things she'd been expecting, predictable, loyal, reassuringly dull Ryan cheating wasn't even on her radar. 'Tell me slowly – start from the beginning. Why were you in Hereford?'

Hattie hugged her knees. 'With work. I wasn't meant to be there. My manager sent me and Tia over to the Hereford branch because they needed extra staff for taste-testing. And after our shift we went to get a latte and Dad was in Costa – with this woman. He didn't see me. I pretended I didn't want a coffee and ran out.'

Her anxious red-rimmed eyes said: Should I have stayed? Did I do the right thing?

'It was definitely him?' Lorna was struggling with her

own shock. Ryan was the most trustworthy of trustworthy husbands – it was almost a running joke how devoted to Jess he was. 'He wasn't just with . . . a work colleague?'

'It was a Saturday. He'd told Mum he had an away bowls match.' Hattie looked scornful, then upset. 'This girl was really pretty. Dad was staring at her like . . .' She mimed slack-jawed lust. 'And he didn't look like himself. He was wearing a new jacket and his hair was spiky.'

Lorna pushed aside the grim image of a dolled-up Ryan. 'And what was this woman like?'

'Young. In her twenties, I think.' Hattie's lip curled. 'She had long blonde hair and a Michael Kors handbag.'

Lorna hesitated, then asked a question she already knew the answer to. 'So you haven't told your mum?'

'No!' Hattie seemed to be swinging between disgust and absolute misery. 'What am I supposed to tell her? "Dad's cheating on you?" What if he denies it? What if she hates me? What if I've got it wrong?' Her voice rose into a squeak.

'OK, OK, that's fair enough.' Lorna rubbed Hattie's back, calming her like a baby. 'Have you got any other reason to think he's seeing someone? Has he been acting odd? Has he . . .' She racked her brains. What did people who had affairs do? Apart from get alibis from the nanny?

Hattie shook her head. 'I told him I needed to borrow his phone one night and there was someone on his messages called P. He'd deleted most of them but there was one left, and it said, *So good to see you at the weekend xxx.* Kiss, kiss, kiss. You don't say that to a work colleague, do you?'

'No.' Lorna groaned inwardly. 'You don't. And have you spoken to him?'

'Why? I don't want to be in his company. I couldn't even go to his stupid birthday party! What a hypocrite, making us play happy families while he's sending kisses to some homewrecker. It's gross.' Hattie looked up at Lorna from under her fringe. 'I thought you might . . . You might . . .'

'I could tell your mum? Right.' What was she supposed to do? Lorna took a deep breath. Sam was coming out of La Dragon's door.

'Everything all right, ladies?' He had their jackets over his arm, Lorna's bag over his shoulder. 'I've settled up, so if you want to go somewhere a bit quieter, maybe the Red Lion? Or . . .' He looked between the two of them. 'Maybe you just want to go home?'

'I need the loo,' Hattie announced, wiping tarry mascara smears from under her eyes with the side of her finger. 'Where is it?'

Lorna touched her arm. 'Walk to the back; it's by the coats. We'll wait here for you, OK?'

She and Sam watched as Hattie marched back inside, her skinny legs bird-like under her padded jacket. She probably hadn't been eating, Lorna thought. The worry must have been awful, weighing on her shoulders, day after day.

Ryan. It just didn't make sense. Her heart rate was still racing. What a total fucking idiot. How could he do that to Jess? She was the ideal wife. His soul mate, but not in that suffocating way their parents had been. She was kind, professional, long-suffering, *gorgeous* . . .

'So what's happened?' Sam sank down on the wall next to Lorna and dropped his voice. He seemed concerned, brotherly. 'Boyfriend trouble?'

Lorna considered for a moment; should she tell Sam? Hattie hadn't exactly sworn her to secrecy, and who else knew Ryan and Jessica? No one knew them like she and Sam did. And Sam might know what the hell was going on.

That thought didn't cheer her.

'Hattie caught Ryan with another woman.'

The twinkle left Sam's eyes instantly. 'What? You're joking! Ryan? Is she sure?'

Lorna shook her head, watching his expression for clues. None of it made sense. 'Of course she is. He's her dad.'

'What did she see?'

'Secret date in a coffee shop. Blonde girl, younger, the usual clichés. Ryan didn't see her. He doesn't know she knows.'

He let out a long breath. 'Wow. And what's she going to do?'

'She doesn't know. Well, *I* don't know what to do. I can't imagine how much strain she's been under!'

'Poor kid.' Sam made a tsk noise, gazing back at the red neon dragon over the door. 'Poor kid.'

Lorna looked at him closely. 'Do you know anything about this?'

'Me? What? No, no idea.' Was Sam's expression suddenly shifty? 'I've barely seen Ryan since the christening. What with leaving . . . leaving London, dealing with the farm.'

She wanted to ask him more, but Hattie was coming back, her long pale hair making her look like a miserable angel as she edged her way between two parked cars.

Sam spoke quickly under his breath. 'So what are you going to do? Are you going to tell Jess?'

'I'll have to, won't I?' Lorna felt sick.

'Why not ask Jess to drive out and collect Hattie tomorrow, then tell her together? It's always better to do that stuff in person.' He touched her arm, as if speaking from experience. 'I just can't believe this. Maybe there's an explanation?'

'Like what?' Lorna felt hopelessly inadequate. This wasn't anything she'd experienced at home. In their family, men didn't cheat on you, they worshipped the ground you walked on until you died, and then they pined away, missing you with every breath.

Tiffany was way more knowledgeable about this kind of thing, she thought. Sophie Hollande doubtless had a few choice strategies for dealing with cheating husbands. Maybe Tiff could advise.

Lorna sighed. 'It'd be nice if there was an explanation. But from what I hear, there usually isn't.'

Chapter Fourteen

Lorna promised Hattie she'd sleep on it before she rang Jess. Not that she slept – she lay wide awake, with Hattie's shattering words going round her head on a loop. Just a few words, and everything flipped upside down. She struggled to compose a bearable way of telling Jess, but her mind kept going back to the day Ryan told the Larkhams that he'd got their brilliant elder daughter pregnant.

Everything had changed after that. And it had only taken a handful of words on that occasion too.

Ryan had worn a jacket, as if it might make a difference; his shoulders at least looked grown-up. Trapped on the sofa, because no one had warned her this was about to go down, Lorna had watched the four of them as if it was a film, not real life happening right there in front of the six o'clock news on mute, with the ice-cream van chimes pealing outside. A bad film, at that, since neither her parents, nor Ryan and Jess, seemed familiar with the lines they had to say. Ryan stammered through their plans to keep the baby while Jess gripped his hand and gazed at her stunned parents from under her thick dark fringe.

'I love Jessica, Mr Larkham,' he'd said, over and over. It hadn't crossed anyone's mind that he might not. 'I'm going to make everything right. For ever.'

Dawn light smudged the wall opposite the window,

and in her memory Lorna saw the scene laid out in a tableau like a highly coloured Victorian morality painting.
The defiant young couple who already looked like a family unit, the bewildered father, the deeply embarrassed
younger sister finally realising what had been going on
when the phone was constantly engaged, next door's cat
sloping back home with the gossip. And their beautiful
mother, sitting there in her painting shirt, curiously glassy.
That was where Lorna's attention had been transfixed: the
strange absence of her mother, and the way her dad kept
glancing anxiously at her, not at Jess.

Rudy pawed at the sofa as the town hall clock chimed
six, and Lorna let him sneak up on to her duvet again,
because replaying that weird day, seventeen years ago, was
taking her down some other alleyways, into feelings she
hadn't let herself remember in a long while. The emotions were sharp again now, though, over-tangy like the
synthetic strawberry tarts in the café, tarts she'd never
eaten elsewhere in case they weren't as good. She'd felt
sick when she'd heard Dad talk about the job he'd been
offered the following term in Hay-on-Wye. She didn't
want to move away from Sam. It had been proper, I-can't-
breathe panic, because how could she tell anyone what
she felt about him? And guilt – guilt that she was thinking
about herself, even in the middle of her sister's drama.
Worst of all the unpleasant palette of fresh emotions
had been a new shame – that even as Jess might be ruining her life, Lorna was experiencing a spicy kind of
excitement at the drama of it, a curiosity about what might
happen next.

And that was the first time she'd pulled herself up short
in shock, because even then, at thirteen, she'd had the

sense that this wasn't something good inside her. It felt bad and wrong, but at the same time . . .

Lorna stroked Rudy as he buried himself into her side, and she dragged her mind back to the present.

Hattie had to have got it wrong. It didn't make sense. Ryan had stuck by Jess exactly as he'd promised. Every anniversary, every birthday, he'd bought her a new charm for her bracelet, and he'd loved her in the same reliable, tea-in-bed, clear-to-see, simple way. Why would he cheat? When did he have time in his car-cleaning rota?

They make time, said a voice in her head. Especially the boring ones.

Lorna texted her sister after breakfast, and at ten to eleven, Jess's black Golf pulled up outside the gallery, as Lorna was loading yet another pile of towels into the washing machine in the kitchen. Jess reverse parked in one confident movement into a tiny space Lorna would have driven straight past, and got out, gazing around her at a high street that was coming back to life in her memories. When Jess saw the goldfish sign hanging next door where the gift shop had been, she looked at it for a few beats, then smiled affectionately as if remembering something nice.

High above, Lorna watched Jess smile, and her stomach knotted up. She looked so happy – a strong woman, capable, loving, in control of her world.

'Is that her?' asked Hattie, and Lorna said, 'Looks like it,' in as normal a voice as she could manage.

Tiffany had taken the dogs out, and Joyce and Hattie were sitting on the sofa knitting. Joyce had offered to get Hattie started on a square, to give her something to do, and now Hattie was six rows down. The stitches were tight and tense, but neat.

She stopped and looked at Lorna. The mood in the kitchen had been calm, but now Hattie's nerves were almost visible, radiating off her the same way Rudy's coat rippled with anxiety.

Joyce's needles clicked on unperturbed, thickening the navy line of her striped dog coat, loop by calm loop.

'Have you dropped a stitch?' she asked, leaning over to inspect Hattie's knitting without stopping her own movement. 'Oh, that's easily fixed. Maybe we could loosen this out a bit too . . .' She took the needles from Hattie, showing her where the gap was and then flipping it back with a delicate probe of the needle tip. When Joyce gave Hattie the needles she carried on again, as if she could knit away the trembling in her hands. She wrapped the trailing wool several times around her thin fingers, doubling, tripling the tension.

Lorna didn't want to wait for the doorbell. 'I'll go down,' she said, and Hattie looked relieved.

Joyce's deft fingers kept knitting.

Lorna opened the front door to see Jess checking her phone, and she smiled as she looked up from it, which made Lorna feel even worse because she knew it would be Ryan she'd be texting, to confirm she'd arrived safely.

'Hi!' she said. 'I feel as if I've stepped back in time – can you believe that terrible butcher's is still going over the road?'

'I know,' said Lorna. 'I think it must be a front for something.'

'Do you want to tell me what this is about now?' she said brightly. 'Before I come in?'

'Um . . .'

'I take it it's something to do with Hattie?' Jess nodded upwards. 'Whatever it is she's done, I'm not going to go mad, but tell me now, before I see her, so I can get my face prepared.'

When Lorna didn't reply at once, Jess's breezy manner disappeared, and Lorna could tell she'd been practising it on the way over. Hattie, and her happiness, was one of the few chinks in her armour.

Suddenly Lorna really didn't want to take her sister upstairs, to explode her whole world in front of an audience. 'Listen, why don't we go for a coffee?'

Jess tried a brave smile. It didn't come off. 'Really? It's that bad?'

Lorna pulled her jacket from the peg by the door. 'Let's go for a walk. Coffee's the one thing that's improved round here.'

They wandered down the high street, past the butcher's and the cafés they remembered and the delis and glitzy nail bars that definitely hadn't been part of Longhampton's shopping experience when they'd been teenagers, and turned towards the town gardens, where the flower beds glowed with early spring colour, bulbous tulips waving above the purple pansies like cheerful deely-boppers.

Lorna bought Jess a cappuccino from the coffee cart parked next to the iron gates and they followed the slow-moving parade of dog walkers and pushchairs around the paths, until they reached the Victorian bandstand, scene of much teenage drinking and now a Heritage Beacon.

'Blimey, they've cleaned this up,' Jess observed as they

settled themselves on the recently repainted steps. 'What happened to the graffiti about Donna Phillips?'

'Who knows?' Lorna poured sugar into her latte. 'She's probably a councillor now. Her first act of power being to remove her personal details from the bandstand.'

'Ha!' Jess leaned back, looking around the park. 'This is a lot nicer than I remember.'

'This bit is. Others . . . not so much.'

'Right, let's have it.' Jess sighed and hugged her knees. 'Hit me with the bad news. Is it about the gallery? Are you in debt already? Have you got the Revenue after you?'

'No.'

'Good. Are you ill?'

'No!' Lorna twisted round to stare at her sister. 'That's your first assumption? One, I've messed up my taxes; two, I'm ill?'

'I just want to get that out of the way. Is Hattie . . . ? Oh, no, she's not pregnant, is she?' Jess's expression suddenly tightened. 'I mean, as far as I know there's no boyfriend on the scene but . . . I know I can't exactly be mad with her, but you never want your kids to make the same mistake as . . . Not that she was a mistake . . .'

She knuckled her own head, and Lorna was glad they weren't having this conversation in the kitchen, with Hattie there.

'I'm not saying Hattie was a mistake,' said Jess firmly. 'She was the best thing that's ever happened to me and Ryan. The best. Apart from Milo and Tyra, obviously. Equal best.'

'Hattie isn't pregnant.'

Jess's shoulders slumped with relief. 'Thank God.

Don't take that the wrong way. But she's got so much ahead of her – her last report from school was outstanding. Did I tell you she's going for county netball trials next term?'

'You said. I know, she's a bright girl. She's great.'

'So what's the matter? Hattie's fine, you're fine . . .'

It was clear that Ryan didn't even figure on her list of potential crises. Lorna took a deep breath and steeled herself but before she could speak, Jess groaned. 'Oh, no. Don't tell me Hattie wants a dog? She was going on and on about that dachshund of—'

'No!' She had to get it out. 'It's Ryan. Hattie told me that she saw Ryan in Hereford a few weeks ago with a woman. They were having coffee, they looked very . . .' How had it looked? Was it fair to put words into Hattie's mouth? She hadn't described exactly what she'd seen, and Lorna hadn't pushed her too hard – how could she? 'It wasn't a business meeting,' she finished awkwardly.

'What?' Jess had resumed drinking her cappuccino, and she paused with it halfway to her lips. 'Ryan?'

Lorna nodded.

'I think you've got some wires crossed. Ryan hasn't been anywhere near Hereford.' Jess shook her head, dismissing it. 'Neither has Hattie, come to think of it.'

'She was sent over there for work a few weeks ago. She saw Ryan in a Costa. In the window. Holding hands with a young blonde woman.'

'No. That's not . . . Is she absolutely sure it was him?'

'I think she'd recognise her own dad.'

'And did he see her?' She corrected herself. 'This man.'

Lorna shook her head. 'I don't think so.'

Jess leaned back. 'She must have made a mistake. Ryan's

been mad busy with work this past month. No, it must be someone who looks like him.'

'Hattie's adamant it was. That's why she's been so stressed. She hasn't known how to tell you, or whether she should.'

'But she told *you*?'

'Easier than telling you.'

Jess slumped. 'True. So how long have you known about this?'

'Only since last night. Sam and I took her out for dinner – at a new place, used to be that café with the twins? We were talking about how you and Ryan were such a well-matched couple, how we knew you'd get married, even then, and . . .' Lorna heard it in her head, from Hattie's anguished point of view. It must have been like punching a bruise. 'It was too much for her.'

Jess turned away and stared out at the park. 'Well, yes, obviously, if that's what she thinks she saw but . . . honestly, Lorna, she's made a mistake. Poor Hattie, worrying about how to tell me. So that's what that weird behaviour's been about. Poor baby.'

Lorna side-eyed her big sister. Jess wasn't even considering there might be something it in. But then her whole marriage was built on Ryan's honourable nature. Their amazing bond, the one she'd waved in the doubters' faces for nearly seventeen triumphant years. In a way she was relieved Jess hadn't broken down at the news, but this calmness was unsettling in a different way. *Could* Hattie have been wrong? Would she really get that upset if she wasn't sure?

'Jess,' she started tentatively. 'You know, if there has been, um . . . If Ryan has done something stupid, then you can always talk to me. I won't judge or anything. I'm always here for you.'

But Jess carried on staring out at the park, her eyes fixed on two old people walking two even older basset hounds towards the footpath that led up into the woodland area. All four were moving in happy slow motion, ears and chins swinging.

'I know, Lorn,' she said. 'Thanks.' Without turning her head, she put her arm round her shoulder. 'Poor Hattie's been a bit neglected lately, with me and Ryan running around after the littlies. Bet that's what this is all about. I'll take her out this week, spend some quality time with her.'

The sun emerged from behind a cloud, sparkling on Jess's impressive selection of diamond rings just under Lorna's nose. One for each child, a stack of adoring gemstones.

Later that night, when Hattie and Jess had gone home, and Tiff and Joyce had retired to bed, Lorna tossed and turned on the sofa, her body as uncomfortable as her conscience. Even Rudy gave up, slinking off the sofa to lie on his cushion. When the town hall clock outside chimed half past one – the 'go to bed' call, before the chimes ceased for the night – Lorna threw off the duvet and went into the kitchen to indulge in the one thing she knew would calm down her racing thoughts.

Not wine, or chocolate, but a colouring book.

Adult colouring books were Lorna's guilty pleasure, a slightly tacky habit not even Tiffany knew about. Like squirty cream and plastic cheese, it was something she knew she shouldn't like but did. A lot. The calming simplicity of following the lines was comforting, like the

colour-by-numbers books her mum hated, where everything would turn out right, so long as she matched the
paint with the numbers. Anyone could be creative then,
even her.

Lorna opened the tea-towel drawer where she'd hidden
the pick of the colouring books from the rack downstairs,
and sat down with the jar of felt tips. Even arranging the
shades in a rainbow cheered her up. She pulled out a cerise
pen – cerise, the colour of discos and fizzy pop – and
started to colour the Mona Lisa in more upbeat shades.
She looked cheerier with a stripy shirt. And Debbie Harry
blonde hair. She paused, then gave her some dark roots.
Edgy.

She was taking such care to get the texture of the pen
strokes even that she didn't notice the kitchen door opening and a figure appearing in the shadow of the hall. It
was only when the chair opposite squeaked on the floor
tiles that she realised she wasn't alone, and nearly jumped
out of her skin.

Joyce coughed apologetically on the other side of the
table. 'Sorry, I didn't mean to startle you,' she said. 'You
seemed lost in the moment. Do you mind if I join you?
I've given up on sleep for tonight.'

She was wearing a long paisley dressing gown, a beautiful burst of deep purple and rich red swirls. Lorna hadn't
seen her wear it before, and the extravagant colour was a
surprise after Joyce's muted daytime clothes.

'Of course! I'm just . . .' She moved her arm to hide the
colouring book. She was embarrassed to be caught with
it – she'd noticed Joyce peering at the display rack downstairs, and she hadn't smiled as most people did when they
realised what they were. She'd looked rather despairing.

'Drawing?' Joyce supplied, tilting her head to see. 'Oh, I didn't know you sketched.'

'I don't.'

The moment hung between them. I want her to take me seriously as a gallerist, Lorna thought, cringing. How can she, when she knows I treat Old Masters as outlines for colouring-in?

But there was nowhere to hide the book. And in the middle of the night, in the kitchen, Joyce didn't seem like the intimidating force she sometimes was. Lorna could see her pale, sun-spotted neck in the wrap of the unexpected dressing gown, the blue vein in her wrist. The softness of her silver hair, undressed for bed. A stranger in a stranger's house, dependent on a complicated bargain.

Lorna moved her hand. 'To be honest, Joyce . . . I'm colouring in.' What the hell. After the day's revelations, this one seemed very minor league. 'The Mona Lisa, as dressed by Boden.'

There. Busted.

'Oh!' Joyce peered over. 'How funny. She suits a stripe. Is this one of Harriet's little sister's books?'

'No, they're for adults – colouring to encourage mindfulness. You can colour in everything from Old Masters to Hollywood film posters to random patterns. I find them soothing when I can't sleep.' Lorna shrugged. 'Something about choosing the right colours, and filling in the boxes, and seeing something emerge . . .'

'Like colour by numbers? For *adults*?'

'Yes, I suppose.'

'My son used to love those,' said Joyce. 'I must confess, I liked watching the colour slowly eat up the numbers as he painted. Lovely blocks of colour flooding out the digits.'

'Yes!' said Lorna. That was exactly how it had felt. She'd forgotten that feeling, of seeing colour and shape overwhelm the black lines and numbers.

A son, though? Joyce was talking again.

'It's interesting, isn't it?' she went on. 'Giving people the choice to fall in line . . . or not. To create something of their own within a trusted framework, or share in the joy of the original by exploring the artist's original experience.' She made a satisfied 'hmmph' noise.

Lorna stared at her punk rock Mona Lisa. She suddenly looked like a modern art statement.

'I should have written that down,' she said wryly. 'I could have put a label next to the books and presented it to Calum Hardy as an Art Week experience.'

'Indeed,' said Joyce, and reached for the pot of pens, examining them with interest. 'I'm sure you've come up with something interesting, though.'

'I don't know. I'm not particularly creative. I just want the gallery to be represented.' She bit her lip. 'I don't want to let it down.'

Lorna realised Joyce was looking at her, reading every detail of her face with her sharp artist's eyes. What was she seeing?

'Would you like something to colour?' She couldn't remember what else she'd hidden in her drawer. Maybe a book of Vogue covers?

'Do you have any plain paper? I'm not good with lines these days.'

Lorna kicked herself. Of course – Joyce's eyesight. It was easy to forget; she'd arranged the room cleverly to avoid any accidents. Easy access in and out, everything within reach.

'Let me find you some,' she said.

There was a pack of printer paper on the dresser, and Lorna handed a thick wedge to Joyce, who examined all the pens one by one, eventually selecting a pale blue.

'Periwinkle,' she said. 'I always think that's the exact colour of comfort.'

'Cup of tea?' The strange middle-of-the-night mood felt companionable now.

'Yes, please.' Joyce started doodling on a blank sheet of paper. The nib moved confidently across the page, sketching out a long wave of hair, a pointed tip of a nose. A watchful eye.

Hattie.

The pen stopped, and the spell was broken. Lorna looked up to see Joyce staring at the page.

'How funny,' she said. 'I didn't expect that.'

'What? To draw Hattie?'

'No.' She squinted at the page. 'To draw at all. I haven't felt like doing that in such a long time.'

'Oh.' Lorna wasn't sure what to say, but a flame of excitement flickered under her ribs. *In such a long time.* Was this the beginning of something? In her very own kitchen?

Joyce picked up a grey pen and added a few tentative lines around Hattie's hair, blending it out, adding two more lines – Hattie's hand, always pushing the long strands behind her ear.

'Did you stop drawing because of your eyesight?' Lorna asked. If Joyce was frustrated because she couldn't express herself the way she used to, there were other art forms that didn't need such precise attention to detail as sketching. She wondered if she should suggest a trip to an art-supplies store before Joyce went back to Rooks Hall – something might grab her attention.

'Not really. It's more that I haven't had any . . .' Joyce stopped, and patted her chest, as if the right words were eluding her. 'Art comes from here, you see. From inside.' She tapped her head, then looked wry. 'Not so much up here. Although obviously you can make it come, if you have to.'

'And something inspired you today?' It came out before she could stop it.

'Harriet.' Joyce's eyebrows beetled, acknowledging the uncomfortable air in the house. 'She's a sweet girl, I can tell that. So transparent, poor thing, you can see straight inside her. I gave her some knitting to take home.' She paused. 'It's good for taking your mind off things, knitting. Don't you find?'

Lorna felt as if Joyce was looking straight into her now too. She dropped her gaze to her jazzy Mona Lisa, then turned the page, embarrassed at her safe choices. The next black and white offering was Millais's moon-faced Ophelia, floating ecstatically down the stream like a human bouquet garni.

'Did you run out of art you wanted to make?' she asked instead.

'Yes, I suppose so.' Joyce sighed, and reached for a yellow pen. This time she didn't uncap it straight away. 'Since Bernie died – my husband – I haven't felt . . . moved. You need to be moved to create. You need something to say. Otherwise it's just bathroom art like those terrible close-ups of cows and flowers that people—' She stopped, obviously remembering that half the gallery downstairs was covered in exactly that. 'I didn't mean to be rude. Sorry.'

215

Joyce didn't look sorry though, Lorna thought. But she didn't feel embarrassed.

'Those pictures don't do much for me either, if I'm truthful,' she said. 'But some people do like them. That was my job, you see. Finding art that made people feel happy, or calm, or just . . . better. You can't always decide *for* people what should make them happy, can you? That's up to them.' A few weeks in the gallery had rammed home that message: there was no money in snobbery, either.

Joyce gave her an inscrutable look. 'And what do you like?'

'Art that makes me feel what the artist was feeling,' said Lorna. 'Sometimes art that shows me what *I'm* feeling, even if I don't know it.'

'I like that answer.'

'Just the truth. So, was your husband an artist?' There, in their dressing gowns and slippers, Lorna felt she was talking to Joyce the same way she'd talk to any other friend of a friend. Or a grandmother of a friend of a friend.

'No, he was a manager.' Joyce uncapped the yellow pen and began drawing something else, something graphic, the pen jerking and flattening in a very different way to Lorna's careful shading. 'Bernie's art was outside – his garden. When we moved to Rooks Hall, he mapped out every bed and square inch of lawn in marker pen on one of my canvases. I painted it in. Our aim was to have something in bloom every single day of the year. Every. Single. Day.'

She punctuated the words with strong lines on the page.

'Like living sculpture.' Lorna pictured the overgrown beds at the cottage, weeds and flowers tumbling together over boundaries like splattered paint. Once it had been tended and neat, just as Joyce had marshalled storm clouds of oily colour on canvas. They'd both lost their gardener, Joyce and Rooks Hall. Suddenly Lorna understood exactly why Joyce was so reluctant to leave her house. Why she hated leaving it on its own.

'Exactly that. I preferred his work to mine. Bernie's compositions changed all the time, from sunrise to noon to dusk. And textures for every sense, not just sight – we chose colours and scents; he found the right plants from everywhere. Ronan had an area too.' She paused, and then, in a quieter voice, added, 'Our boy.'

It was a delicate moment, a tipping point in the conversation.

Lorna trod carefully. 'Does Ronan . . . live locally?'

'He died when he was eighteen. A silly accident. He went away on a gap year, volunteering in remote places, and one day he was in a car crash. Not a serious one, but miles from a proper hospital. It was the infection that killed him. He died before we even knew he was hurt.'

'Oh! Oh, I'm sorry, Joyce.'

The grief was visible in Joyce's body, the sudden tension in her shoulders as if a weight had been loaded on her back, the pen in her hand too heavy to move.

Lorna recognised the pain, but also the shapeless guilt hanging over it, of not being there, of not sharing the final breath, not hearing the last word. Knowing someone was alone. 'I can't imagine how hard that was,' she said softly. 'I wasn't there for my mother, or my father. At the end. I wish so much I had been. Even if it was awful.'

It hung between them; then Joyce shook her head. 'Funnily enough, that gave me plenty to express for a while, but after that . . .' She started drawing lines. When the pen shook, she made the next line follow the wobble, until the page was covered with bulges spreading the sadness out across the blank paper like a map contour. A map of grief.

Lorna watched the pen, feeling as if she was seeing something more than drawing, and hearing more than Joyce was actually saying. Quietly, she began to colour Ophelia's hair, floating in the stream, the same pale ashy blonde as Hattie's. And her own.

Chapter Fifteen

Lorna spent Monday morning hovering over every telephone she walked past, expecting it to ring. She was braced for anything – Jess in tears, Hattie in tears, even Ryan in tears at being caught out – but the only call she had was from an artist who wanted to come in to show her his watercolours of haunted pebbles.

Calls, plural. He phoned a second time, thinking he was speaking to a gallery in Hartley this time, and Lorna let him outline the Maiden Gallery's new owner's stupidity and rudeness for five minutes before putting him straight, and driving a mental stake through his head. She really wasn't in the mood for being told she had no artistic vision, not this morning.

'Was that Jess?' asked Tiffany, bearing a tray of tea.

'Nope. Another artist who thinks I should be honoured to share his mad fantasies with the town.' Lorna wrote MARTIN ALLENSMORE in capitals on her Never Deal With page. There were two ceramists and someone who made ironic models of dogs out of cat hair there already. She rammed the pen back in the pot, and the top fell off. 'Should I call her? I thought I'd have heard something by now.'

'Won't she be at work?' Tiffany handed Lorna her peppermint tea and went over to where Joyce was sitting in the chair from the back room. She was knitting another dog coat in two kinds of wool. 'There you go, Joyce, milk, no sugar. I'll put it here, don't want to interrupt you.'

'Too kind.' Joyce was at a critical stage with the final leg hole and didn't look up.

'Probably.' Lorna stirred the teabag. 'Do you think I should call Hattie instead then?'

Tiffany stopped, her hand in the biscuit tin. 'No! *Definitely* don't call Hattie.'

'Why not?'

'Because she'll realise you don't know what's going on. And that'll just confirm in her head that something *is*. Trust me,' she added when Lorna looked bewildered, 'I've done a whole module on teenage paranoia.'

'I'm sure your sister is dealing with it in her own way,' said Joyce, finishing off the final stitches. 'She seems a very capable woman. Now, scissors?'

Lorna sighed and opened the stationery drawer. Jess was capable. At *work*. She'd had no experience of crises like this, unlike Lorna who'd entered and exited relationships on a pretty much yearly cycle since she'd left school. Jess had only ever had one falling-out with Ryan – when he went to Birmingham to work for his big brother, Craig, who had a building company, instead of applying to university as planned. They were only apart for a few months, but it felt like years.

After Jess and Ryan's baby bombshell, Dad's initial threat to drag them all off to Hay-on-Wye came to nothing, thanks to Lorna's pleas not to separate her from her schoolfriends (by which she meant Sam). Dad was worried about Jess's prospects, but Mum loved the studio they'd built on the side of the house; none of them really wanted to leave. The Protheros, on the other hand, decided Ryan needed a dose of reality – if he wanted a family, Mr Prothero insisted, he'd have to learn how to provide for one. It seemed ridiculous now, and if anything, it had only solidified their determination to get married, but Ryan's dad had been adamant. Ryan went off to learn how to project manage shop fittings while Lorna suffered Jess's sulks, their father's bewilderment at the sudden explosion of his hitherto low-maintenance family, and Mum shutting herself in her studio for days on end. The summer dragged on to the sound of 'Yellow' by Coldplay, over and over from the room upstairs, and the smell of Pot Noodles, which Jess ate by the pallet-full.

Lorna stared out of the gallery window, over the shelves of glass fishes and the smooth porcelain bowls, into the street, and something about the familiar shape of the shop doorway opposite brought back the shapeless gloom of that summer. She'd spent most of that holiday hanging around the gallery to escape Jess's furious moodiness and the smell of rehydrated pork flakes. And, of course, hoping she'd bump into Sam.

'. . . would be fine. Lorna? Lorna!'

She looked up. Tiffany was holding up a dog jacket; the way Joyce had blended the colours made it look like tiger stripes. 'We can sell these for Mrs Rothery, can't we? They're works of art.'

'Um, Tiff, you do know Joyce is an *actual* artist,' said Lorna. She tipped her head imperceptibly to remind Tiff that Joyce was there.

'I think *these* are *actual* works of art,' said Tiffany.

'Perhaps. If you displayed them on cats and called them a post-modern commentary on transexuality.' Joyce's expression was straight but Lorna – *now* – was starting to tell when she was joking. It had taken time to spot the slight downward cast of the eye, the dry lift at the end of the sentence. 'A cat in dog's clothing. Rather political.'

It went over Tiff's head. 'I don't think we could get that on a cat? But we'll display them on Rudy. What would you like us to charge? I think you could easily ask twenty quid. They're bespoke!'

'Oh, heavens, no. Charge whatever you like, but give the money to charity,' said Joyce, reaching for her tea. 'Bernard came from that rescue place on the hill. Give it to them.'

'Of course,' said Lorna, and although Joyce was pretending to be dismissive about her efforts, there was a glimmer of . . . pride? Even knitting, even half-blind, Joyce was head and shoulders above the rest of the artists here.

They'd only had two customers since the gallery had opened, but Lorna didn't mind. Her brain was still worrying away about Hattie and Jess, yet sitting there with Joyce knitting and Tiffany rearranging the cards, and some tea on the go, with lemony sunshine spreading though a gallery that was really starting to look like hers . . . it felt nice not to be on her own.

Then the gallery phone rang on the desk.

Joyce and Tiffany both looked up, and Lorna reached for it. Could it be Jess calling from work? She tried to sound as normal as possible. 'Hello?'

'Is that Lorna Larkham?' It was a man's voice.

'Yes?'

'Lorna, this is Calum, Calum Hardy, from Longhampton Art Week?'

'Oh, hello, *Calum*,' she said, for the benefit of Joyce and Tiffany. 'How nice to hear from you!'

Tiffany perched on the desk and made an 'ooh' face. Joyce put down her knitting needles.

'Is this about my Art Week proposal?' Lorna went on. She was pleased Joyce was here to witness this – anything that made her look like a thoughtful and discerning gallerist had to help her plans to host Joyce's eventual retrospective.

'It is.' Calum coughed. He didn't sound as friendly as the last time they'd spoken. 'Listen, we're busy people, I'll get to the point – we need to discuss your submission. This . . . artists drawing customers, and customers drawing artists concept.'

'Great! Hang on a second, Calum . . .' She winked at Tiffany and put the phone on to speaker, so they could hear the conversation. 'That's better. So! Did you like it? I really wanted to open up a dialogue about how art and artists are perceived, and how art is—'

'Lorna, let me stop you there,' said Calum. His voice sounded distorted on loudspeaker. 'When I say, discuss, I really mean . . . we don't think it's going to work.'

Her face fell. 'What?'

'Yeaaaah, I suppose we expected, with your art-in-the-community background, that you'd have a more . . . I've got to be honest, I thought you'd come up with something stronger than this.'

Tiffany's 'ooh' face morphed into an outraged 'sod off!' one. Lorna didn't even want to look at Joyce. She could feel her cheeks flaming as humiliation turned her hot and cold inside.

'What do you mean?' she managed.

'Well, for a start, how many people do you have in your shop now? Be honest.'

'Two,' said Lorna evasively.

'That aren't staff.'

'Um, one.'

'Right. And how do you think that one person would feel if there was an artist in there too? Drawing her as she walked around?'

Joyce raised her eyebrows sardonically.

'I think she'd be fine with that,' said Lorna.

'Well, I ran it past a few folks here and they were very *not* fine with it. It lays us open to all sorts of problems, as a council. Minorities and so on . . .'

'Dogs?' she blurted out, frantically trying to think of something else. Her eye fell on Rudy, asleep by a canvas. 'Dogs painting with their . . . paws.'

Oh God. Where had that come from? Joyce and Tiffany stared at her in horror.

'Was that a joke? Look, I appreciate you're trying to be flexible, Lorna, but you were already late for the deadline, so I'm afraid you're going to have to sit this Art Week out. If you wanted to help, you could always volunteer with the—'

'Wait!' said Lorna, pushing through her embarrassment. 'I've got other ideas.'

'Was that your best one?' He sounded very doubtful.

'I've got notebooks full.' She hadn't, he knew she hadn't, but Lorna couldn't let Calum Hardy write her off like that in front of Joyce. 'Please, Calum. I'll email something over first thing.'

There was a long pause.

'Please? This is *so* important to me.'

He sighed. 'I've got a meeting to finalise the budget tomorrow afternoon. I'd need it in front of me by lunch. And this is just because it's you. And I like you.'

'Fine. I won't let you down, Calum.' She swallowed, and wished she could take him off speakerphone and have this conversation without an audience, but it was too late now. And anyway, she felt as if she was speaking to Joyce as much as to Calum Hardy. 'I'm passionate about this – I want to show people art's not something to be scared of, it's something that's all around us, something that brings us together as human beings. And I want to bring local people right into the creative process, defining our town. That's what Art Week is about, for me.'

She knew it sounded cheesy but it was true.

Joyce was watching her, though she'd started knitting again. Click, click, click, her eyes never dropping to the needles, the fingers moving on their own as the pattern formed in her head. She's doing it now, Lorna thought, she's making art right here in the gallery. She thinks she's given up art but she hasn't really. She can't. She's a true artist; that's what they do.

The bell jangled as a couple came into the shop, and Lorna grabbed it as an excuse to wind up the call.

'I'll email you something by tomorrow lunchtime,' she said, quickly. 'Thanks for giving me another chance, Calum, I really appreciate it! Speak tomorrow!'

And she hung up before he could change his mind. Adrenalin was surging around her, as if she'd just presented in front of a hall full of people, not two.

The couple meandered round to the ceramics cabinet, and Tiffany let out a long whistle. 'What a knob. What does he think he's doing? Running the National Gallery?'

'I'm sorry you had to hear that, Joyce,' said Lorna.

'At least your idea was fresh.' Joyce looped the wool round a finger. 'From what I read in the paper, Art Week's normally an excuse for the fat cats in the council to drink warm white wine in front of the Mayor's wife's amateurish watercolours of their holiday cottage. As for Calum Hardy . . .' She sniffed, and started a new line. 'As Tiffany says: what a knob.'

The word dropped precisely from her lips, without a flicker of reaction.

Tiffany looked horrified, but Lorna smiled. Joyce's timing was perfect.

Having promised Calum a brilliant new idea, Lorna's brain promptly went into white noise mode. She spent the rest of the day alternating between scribbling down terrible ideas, and staring at the phone, which still didn't ring. Whatever Jess or Hattie were talking about, they weren't including her.

At four o'clock, there was a commotion at the door as Keir Brownlow arrived in his usual whirlwind of papers, direct from the council offices two streets down.

'We'll have to rush,' he announced, juggling his file, his phone and a large takeaway coffee as he elbowed his way in. 'I've got Shirley parked outside on a double yellow – she's dropping us then going back to the hospital to do the day-care run.'

'What are you talking about?'

'Joyce.' He stared at Lorna. 'You didn't get my email?'

'No!'

'What?' Keir dumped his bag on the desk and checked his phone. 'I rang you at . . . No, wait. I rang *Shirley*. Nuts. Sorry. I've managed to get the occupational therapist out to Rooks Hall this afternoon – she needs to check the safety fittings with the landlords, and myself, and Joyce, ideally, so we can sign off on Joyce going back and getting out of your hair by tonight.'

'Hello?' Joyce waved a hand from her chair. 'I'm here. I'm not just in the third person.'

'Of course you're not! Hello, Joyce!' He bustled over to her, sorting out forms as he went. 'I was just saying to Lorna, we can take you home this afternoon. Your land-lords have everything sorted out. You'll be glad to get back, won't you?'

He was speaking in the exact tone Joyce found most annoying; Lorna could tell that from the formality that had returned to the old lady's posture. The shoulders were back; the sharp chin was up.

She'd relaxed. It was only now the guard had gone back up that Lorna realised it had inched, carefully, down.

'Well, what kind of answer can I give to that?' Joyce asked, drily. 'Without offending Lorna here?'

Keir looked momentarily horrified. 'I'm sure you've had a lovely time surrounded by all these lovely cows,' he said, then winced. 'The paintings, I mean! Not . . . not, um . . . Can I trouble you to check over these documents before we go? Or would you prefer me to read them to you?' He offered her some forms from his folder.

Joyce gave him a withering look, and then glanced over his head, a 'for heaven's sake!' glint of despair in her eyes, and Lorna felt included in Joyce's tiny gang of one. She smiled. It felt nice.

'Joyce, we don't mind. Of course you want to get home to Rooks Hall. Tiffany can help us pack . . . Tiff? Tiff, are you busy?'

Tiffany breezed in from the back room, and Keir dropped the pile of papers he was trying to sort while holding a pen in the other hand.

'Hello, hello!' she said. 'What was that about packing? Aw, Joyce! Are you leaving so soon?'

'I'm afraid so,' said Joyce. 'Shirley is on a double yellow.'

Keir coughed. 'Ah, Tiffany, before you go – I've something for you!'

'Really?' Tiffany turned back.

'Yes, two more dogs need walking in the town area,' he said, handing her one sheet of paper, 'and here's the details about the charity job.' He passed her another, and blushed. 'They need someone with parent–child experience, as well as office skills. I spoke to Sally, said you'd be perfect.'

'Thanks, Keir.' She beamed at him. 'Can't believe you remembered.'

He seemed flustered. 'No problem. I might have made out you've had a bit more office experience but . . .'

Tiffany patted his arm. 'Don't worry, I can type. I owe you one!' Outside, a car honked its horn. 'Oops, better get a move on.'

As they'd been speaking, Joyce had got to her feet – painfully, Lorna realised – and was preparing herself to go. She seemed more fragile than she'd looked upstairs in the kitchen, calmly teaching Hattie to knit while Lorna and Tiff bustled around.

'Would you like me to come with you?' Lorna didn't even know why she said it; it was instinct more than anything else.

Keir looked at them both. 'You can have an advocate

for the meeting with the OT and the landlords, if you want, Joyce. It's a lot to take in on your own.'

Joyce waved her hand. 'No, no. Ridiculous. I've taken up quite enough of Lorna's time – I expect she's got things to do tonight. Family matters to attend to, and such like.' She raised an eyebrow as she said it, and it wasn't unsympathetic. Joyce saw everything, emotions in colours, the shadows of secrets passing across faces.

But she said, 'I'm happy to come if you'd like?' Sam would be there, in his odd new role as reluctant landlord. Maybe Ryan had called him about the weekend's events. Maybe he knew something. A shiver ran through her and she held herself carefully to stop Joyce catching it.

A skittering of claws on the stairs announced Bernard's arrival in the gallery.

Keir slapped his forehead as the terrier bounced with joy around his mistress's legs. 'Oh God!' he said. 'I didn't tell Shirley about Bernard. I don't know if she's legally allowed to take him. Let me go and talk to her.'

He rushed out, and Lorna moved towards the stairs, wondering how quickly they could pack Joyce's belongings. Shirley would have to do a lap of the block, at least. There was a cough behind her, and she turned.

'Thank you for having me,' said Joyce, but before Lorna could reply, went on, 'We need to discuss payment.'

Lorna flushed. 'What? No, no. Honestly, it's fine . . .'

Joyce fixed her with a clear gaze. 'No, we made a deal. I promised you something in return for your keeping me out of that godforsaken old folks' home this last week. And you did. What would you like?'

She's asking me to put a price on a kindness, thought Lorna. I can't do that. Her paintings are worth thousands.

What I gave her – tea and a bed and more family drama than she bargained for – should have been given freely.

'An idea,' she heard herself say. 'An idea, for Art Week. Something Calum Hardy will love.'

Shirley honked her horn again, and Joyce's thin lips curved into a smile. 'All right,' she said. 'We'll speak in the morning.'

There was no phone call from Jess that night. Nothing from Hattie, no Instagram snaps to interpret, nothing on Facebook. No texts, no emails.

Rudy curled himself up in his basket, missing his boisterous terrier friend. He didn't even bark when two pigeons landed right in front of his nose on the window ledge.

'It's quiet on our own, isn't it?' said Lorna to herself.

At the kitchen table, Tiffany looked up from her job application. 'Yeah, I know. Weird, when you think about it – Joyce didn't say much, and Hattie wasn't here long, but it still feels strange without them. Bernard, mind you – he was noisy. Do you think Joyce liked being here?'

'I don't know.' Lorna's mind was picturing Joyce back at silent Rooks Hall, sitting on her own by her fireplace, alone with the memories of her son, and her husband. And the flowers in the beds outside, reminding her of buds blooming, dying, blooming again – life going on long after the gardener had been scattered to the winds.

Should she have gone back with her? Did she have a duty of care as a friend now? Or was that pushing Joyce's limits? She'd been keen to make it a deal, not a favour. Lorna got up from the sofa, where she'd been pretending to go through an artist's website, and picked up the sketch of Hattie from the table.

It was rough, but the lines were bold and confident; Joyce had caught Hattie's whole soul in a few instinctive strokes. Her smooth forehead seemed bowed under the burden of her thoughts, and Lorna's heart twisted with its perceptive beauty.

She could see her sister in Hattie's face. They'd promised never to have secrets, she and Jess. Not after their childhood spent feeling lost in their parents' world of tender secrets, safe in their family love but feeling oddly apart. So why wasn't Jess calling her? What wasn't she telling her?

Does she think I'll gloat? Lorna wondered. That I was right, about not letting someone in, in case they broke your heart?

Tiffany coughed at the table. 'Can I make you a cup of tea? Or run you a bath, or something? You look shattered.'

Lorna realised she was glad to see Tiff there at the kitchen table.

She'd wanted an empty flat, yes, but the thought of dealing with her thoughts now, in a silent room – it would be awful. She'd found her space and claimed it as her own but she was happy to share it with these women: the friend, the artist, the sister, the child turning into a woman . . . They made her life feel richer, little figures populating the background of her story like the fairies and elves in her mum's illustrations, the signature butterfly that always rose up into Cathy's sky.

'Thanks,' said Lorna. 'I really mean that.'

Tiff tilted her head. 'Why don't you phone Joyce, check everything's all right? She'll pretend she's not bothered but I think she'd like it.'

'I think I will,' said Lorna. 'But in the morning.'

Chapter Sixteen

In the event, Joyce phoned Lorna before she could make the call to see how the move home had gone. Before she'd even had her breakfast, in fact.

The phone rang at half past seven, when Lorna was just finishing her allotted fifteen minutes in the bathroom before Tiff colonised it for the next hour. She dashed out in her towel to answer it; she was jumpy, in case Jess called with the Reasonable Explanation that Lorna still couldn't devise, despite bending her imagination in many improbable directions.

'Good morning!' Joyce sounded as if she'd been up for hours. 'Did I wake you?'

'No, no,' Lorna chirruped. Joyce had strong views about early rising. 'Been up for *ages*.'

She made a hmph noise. 'Anyway, as promised I have a solution for your Art Week issue,' Joyce went on. 'But you'd better come now if you're going to get it to that rude man for the morning. Oh, and the dog's being a tinker. A walk may be in order.'

Lorna recognised an instruction when she heard one. 'I'm on my way.'

Someone had been busy in the garden of Rooks Hall while Joyce had been in Longhampton with Lorna. The long grass had been mown, the borders trimmed back to moderate wildness, and the moss swept off the doorstep. Lorna noticed the remains of hollyhocks and clematis climbing the walls as she picked her way up the uneven path – now she knew about Joyce and Bernard's joint plan to create their year of flowers, the garden felt different. More like an old photograph, with ghosts lingering just out of shot.

Joyce was waiting for her at the door, a small figure in red against the darkness of the hall. She was leaning casually against the frame, but Lorna could tell she was steadying herself; behind her, lurking, was the metal shape of a walker, and a white grab bar drilled into the wall by the stairs. The impertinent changes to Rooks Hall had begun, and there was no sign of Bernard.

Lorna tried not to let her reaction show in her face but Joyce was sharp when it came to body language and saw her flinch.

'You've noticed my so-called improvements?' Joyce rolled her eyes dismissively and then shuffled down the hall into the sitting room. 'I don't *need* a walking frame, by the way. Or a commode,' she threw over her shoulder. 'I'm *fine*.'

'Well, if it helps you stay here . . .' Lorna followed, keeping Rudy on a short lead, taking everything in with quick glances: slippy rugs, gone; speckled mirrors, cleaned; dead pot plants, removed. There was a chemical smell in the house: new glue, freshly drilled screwholes, Dettol – lots of it. 'Who came to do the work? The landlords?'

'No idea. There's a number by the phone.' Joyce didn't alter her slow course, but waved a hand behind her.

Lorna checked, there was a card: *Osborne Property Services*, and a number. *Gabriel*, it said. Not Sam. If Gabe was in charge, why had Sam been round that day, doing the DIY? Gabe's injury, presumably. Or maybe he was just impatient to get it done; or didn't trust anyone else to do it properly.

Joyce had disappeared into the sitting room. Lorna let Rudy off to go and find Bernard, and went in after her.

The change was even more obvious here. The higgledy-piggledy piles of art books had been removed, and an NHS walking frame was bossily positioned next to the armchair, although the plastic hadn't been removed. The paintings were still there – the dramatic landscapes, the textured abstracts, the story of Joyce's life in oils and watercolours – but something undefinable was now present: a sadness? A sense of supervision? There was a kettle and cups on a small table, to save unnecessary trips to the kitchen; boxes of tissues, and photos that had been brought down from upstairs. It felt like the rooms Lorna had visited in the hospice. Full of a long life, but compressed into a much smaller space, as if everything precious had to be kept very close. Closer and closer.

The familiarity caught in her chest.

But Joyce was talking, and she didn't seem sad. Her eyes sparkled as she nodded towards something propped up against the bookshelf, thickly covered in bubble wrap. A painting, obviously, but of what, Lorna couldn't see.

'There you go, for you.' Joyce waved her hand in her lordly gesture. 'Probably not what you're expecting, but you may find it helpful.'

Lorna touched the thick wrapping – it was a painting. A big one.

'Joyce, this is far too much,' she said. A quick search of auction prices one night, while doing the very dispiriting monthly accounts, had revealed what Lorna had guessed: Joyce's originals were fetching thousands, if they ever came up for sale. Suddenly the deal felt wrong. As if she was taking advantage.

'Don't tell me you've started valuing paintings by *weight*, Lorna. Goodness me.'

Joyce seemed more like her old self, defiant in her red cashmere jumper, as if she could dress her way back to full health. Her head tilted, testing Lorna's reaction, and Lorna suddenly, desperately, didn't want to be caught thinking the wrong thing.

'It would be rude *not* to accept it,' Joyce informed her, loftily. 'I needed somewhere to recuperate in peace with my dog; you provided that. We had a deal. Don't treat me like an old dodderer, Lorna. Do me the courtesy of letting me honour my end of it.'

'But we didn't exactly give you a peaceful place to stay, did we? And you left me that lovely sketch of Hattie. That's enough, really.'

'This is for your Art Week project, then. I've been associated with the Maiden Gallery for most of my career. I wish it to be the centre of positive attention for once. Aren't you going to open it? Aren't you *interested*? Oh, do come on!'

Lorna couldn't help catching Joyce's excitement. 'OK,' she said, and began unpicking the bubble wrap.

'It's been in storage for several years,' Joyce said as Lorna struggled with the tape. 'I had to sweet-talk Keir into carrying it in from the shed for me. He started talking about risk assessments . . . Honestly. What a wet lettuce that lad is.'

Lorna laughed at the thought of Joyce's 'sweet-talking',

then stopped, suddenly, as the final layer came away to reveal the artwork underneath.

It was the bandstand in the park. But instead of the brooding canvases she'd come to associate with Joyce, this was simple, almost childlike in its joyfulness. The bandstand sat at the centre of the painting, its distinctive gold columns outlined against a cloudless blue sky, and from its domed shape swirled a rainbow of colours and textures – the music, in other words, blended into the flowers and lawn and benches of the park like an invisible sound wave. Lorna could feel the bold flourish of brass in the golden curls, and the percussive rhythms in the bouncy splashes of rat-a-tat red dots. The bandstand was empty but the park felt full of life.

It was happy, thought Lorna. There was happiness in this work, in every tiny brushstroke, in every shining butterfly wing, every uplifted flower head. The colours were singing.

'I painted it for Ronan,' said Joyce quietly. 'We used to go to listen to the bands on a Sunday, when he was a tot. He'd ask us what colour the trumpets were, and we'd say, "They're golden, darling, they're brass." And he used to shake his head and say, "No, no, no, they're red! Red like tomatoes!"'

'Red? You mean they . . . sounded red?' Weirdly, Lorna could see it.

'Not to me – they were always golden, like the sun. But yes, to him they were bright red. And flutes were pale blue,' Joyce went on, 'and cymbals were glittery purple like a magpie wing . . . You get the idea. Ronan loved colours. He would sit in my studio with my crayons, listening to music, and sorting out the rainbow into instruments.

236

Kandinsky, of course, had the idea first but we let Ronan think he'd discovered it. We played a game all the time – what colour is happiness? What colour is sleep? What colour is love . . . ?'

Her words fell away, too flimsy for the emotions they had to carry, and Lorna felt a lump in her own throat.

They stood gazing at the painting, and Lorna suddenly spotted the little boy in the corner, the only figure in the whole composition, peeking out from behind a tree. Dark tufty hair, mischievous smile, waving a small hand. Ronan. Joyce had drawn him in, the way her mum had always put her and Jess somewhere in the background too.

She was about to tell Joyce that, then stopped and observed Joyce instead, the sad and loving way she knew that painting like the inside of her heart. Why? Why would you put your child in the background?

Because they were always hiding in your mind, even when you were locked in your studio, painting. Even when they thought you were shutting them out, you were making them immortal.

Oh.

'Anyway, that's by the by . . .' Joyce fidgeted with her gold rings. 'I thought perhaps this could be a starting point for a community art happening, or whatever it's called these days. A public painting, sharing the colour of music, perhaps?'

A volley of ideas struck Lorna in a glorious burst, one after the other. 'What if we could set up easels by the bandstand and have paints, and sponges or brushes or something, and maybe get a band to play? And have people interpret what they hear?'

Joyce shrugged. 'It's up to you, you're the curator.' But there was a ghost of a smile on her thin lips.

'Oh, not easels . . . maybe a big mural?' Lorna's mind was spinning. 'Maybe . . . different contributions running into one another? Like sections of an orchestra playing together?'

'I think there's something there,' said Joyce. 'Now, would you take Bernard out? He's getting under my damn feet.'

There was no sign of the Border terrier, but there was a mist across Joyce's face, and Lorna touched her arm. The old lady didn't flinch.

'Thank you, Joyce,' she said. 'I won't let you down.'

Calum Hardy was hugely enthusiastic about the proposal Lorna emailed to him with five minutes to spare, for reasons she hadn't expected.

'How did you *know*?' he asked, all charm now she'd delivered something he liked.

'Know what?'

'About the school band project? Cock-up with planning meant it clashed, and we were wondering how on earth we could combine it with Art Week without – how can I put it? – being upstaged by tots with trumpets. But this is genius. Kids playing, lots of parents there watching, plenty of interaction, *fantastic* visual for the local paper. Well done, Lorna. I knew you'd come up with a winner.'

'Thanks . . .'

Calum was still talking. 'And somehow – somehow! – you've managed to get a contribution out of Joyce Rothery! To be honest, we were starting to wonder if she'd died – this is major news. Can you get her along too?' He sounded buoyant. 'Get her to splat the first splodge?'

'I don't know about that.' Joyce had insisted that *wouldn't* be happening.

'We should definitely have lunch to discuss. What's your diary looking like for the rest of the week?'

'Not too bad.' Was he being flirty? There was definitely a flirtier note in his voice. Lorna twirled the pen around her fingers. Lunch with Calum might be quite fun. Compared with Sam's hot-and-cold personality, at least she knew where she was with someone like Calum. If the conversation dried up you could always talk about obscure artists or how Instagram was destroying/reinventing photography.

'How about next Monday? We want to make this the central weekend project, so I'd love to get started on some planning with you asap.'

'Great!'

'Can't wait,' said Calum, and when he hung up, Lorna felt as if she'd just stepped off a holiday flight.

'Who was that, dear?' Mary leaned into the back office from the gallery, where she was dusting the ceramics.

'Calum from the council. He loves my revised idea.' Lorna was trying to keep an eye on Mary – she was only working a few days a week, but Lorna kept finding stuff, hidden away in boxes in the cellar, most of which Mary was very evasive about. She sometimes wondered whether she was bringing in her secret unsold stash from home, box by box, before Keith discovered it. It would certainly explain the accounts, which were increasingly hard to reconcile.

'Oh, hurray!' Mary frowned. 'What is it, exactly?'

'I'll explain when I get back.' Lorna pulled on her jacket.

'Do you mind holding the fort for an hour or two? I need to take some things over to Archibald's to be framed. I think these ladies in the gallery need some help?'

Two women were cooing over Joyce's knitted dog jackets, displayed on toy Westies Tiff had found in a charity shop. The tiger-striped ones in particular were drawing a lot of attention, and Mary had noted a couple of requests from customers for specific models – as yet, Lorna hadn't decided whether to pass those requests on to Joyce. 'These two again! They said they were thinking of buying more. You should tell Joyce that,' she added. 'Tell her that she's got a new lease of life in the gallery!'

Lorna opened her mouth to say, 'I don't know how she'd take that!' and then thought: Why not? Whether Joyce considered her knitting art or not, her coats were creative and beautiful and brought people pleasure. That was art.

The idea surprised her with its certainty. It hadn't come from the part of her brain she expected it to.

'See you later, Mary,' she said, and picked up the bag of treasures, rings, curls of hair and cards, someone's private cloud of memories to be framed in time for Mother's Day.

Spring sunshine had brought out the café's pavement tables for the first time that year as well as yellow primroses in the hanging baskets, and Lorna felt optimistic about the day as she loaded Rudy into the back of the car. Archibald liked dogs and Lorna was trying to introduce Rudy slowly to new experiences – in this case, men with white beards like Santa. Rudy was looking jaunty in his Breton jumper, specially customised to fit his long back.

'Betty would have loved you in a stripe,' she told him, and he whipped his tail.

'Lorna!'

She looked over to see Sam waving at her on the other side of the street. He was wearing a suit, very similar to the one she'd seen him wear that night in London. The same one, in fact. 'Stay there!' He dodged around the slow line of cars crawling towards the traffic lights at the end of the high street.

Lorna closed the boot and waited for him to cross. Joyce hadn't mentioned her meeting with the landlords and the occupational therapist – did Sam want brownie points for fixing Joyce's handrails? No, wait. *Ryan*. Had he called Sam and given him *his* side of Hattie's story – if there was one?

Then suddenly he was there, in front of her. He smiled, and she smiled back, automatically, then wondered if she should. 'You off somewhere?' he asked.

'Just to the framers. Are *you* going somewhere, dressed up?'

'What?' Sam looked down and did a double take. 'Oh, no, meeting at the bank. Nothing exciting. Funny to think I used to wear this every day and now it's dressing up.'

'Nice suit,' said Lorna. It was. It made him look less farmer, more landowner. Apart from the beard. That still took some getting used to.

'You're too kind – it's getting a bit tight round the waist, thanks to Mum and her baking.' Sam tugged at his belt ruefully. 'No time for the gym either . . . Anyway, I was hoping to catch you,' he went on. 'Two things – any news from Jess?'

She shook her head. So Ryan hadn't called him in a guilty panic. Good. 'No, nothing.'

'Nothing?' He raised an eyebrow.

'No, she was very calm about the whole thing. She's convinced Hattie made a mistake. And she would know – I mean, Ryan, cheating? Come on.' Lorna shrugged. 'Jess is sure it's nothing, so if she thinks that . . . What? Why are you looking like that?'

Sam hiked his eyebrows even higher, and Lorna felt a sudden doubt – her instinct was to believe her sister, even though she too had a feeling there was a lot more to it than Jess wanted there to be. Jess had an understandable phobia of being talked about; 'rise above it' was one of her favourite sayings.

'Because Hattie was so upset,' he said simply.

'Teenagers can be dramatic. Even Jess said Hattie probably wanted a bit of attention. The little ones do take up most of their time and . . .'

She stopped. That was unfair. Hattie wasn't a drama queen, not like that.

Sam didn't look convinced either. He was holding her gaze, reading her face with that kindly concern she knew so well, and she tried hard not to encourage the tingling running down her neck, along her arms. It felt like fine rain, invisible but still there. Did he know something she didn't?

'Should I call Ryan?' he offered. 'I didn't suggest it before, in case . . . well, in case you thought I was interfering, but if you think there's something he might tell me . . .'

'No, don't. Don't. Jess will know we've been discussing it. Best leave it.'

'You won't let me try to talk to him?' He gave her a keen look. 'I love those guys. I want to help, if I can.'

'I know.' And Lorna knew he did; Sam's loyalty to Ryan, when the whole town was talking about him and Jess, and the way he'd taken care of them both at their mum's funeral, stepping in to help Ryan when their dad was dazed with grief – he was a gentle man at heart. But Lorna knew her sister; when Jess said she didn't want to discuss something, that was it.

She smiled, brokenly. 'What was the second thing? You said there were two things?'

Sam gave up. 'The second thing was, what are you doing on Friday night?'

Two offers in the space of an hour. What was the world coming to? 'Are you asking me out?'

'No, don't get your hopes up, I'm asking you *in*.' He looked apologetic in advance. 'Mum wants to know if you'd like to come round for dinner. Just us – me, Dad, Gabriel, Gabe's wife Emma. Maybe their kids too, if they're not out at some party or other.'

Lorna had never been invited round to the Osbornes' before. 'That would be nice. Would you like me to bring anything?'

'Ear plugs?' He seemed relieved to move on to safer ground. 'An open mind? Dad's got very entrenched since he retired. Promise me you'll ignore at least half of what's said.'

They stepped to one side to allow a lady with a Yorkie to pass, and inside the car Rudy started barking like a crazed thing, his wet nose bumping against the glass. He still wasn't relaxed around most other dogs, despite their best bribes, and his fear set Lorna on edge too.

'I'd better go,' she said. 'Before he bursts.'

'Great! See you Friday night, about six? Farmers are early to bed, unlike you arty types.' Sam hovered for a second, as if unsure about what came next. Was he leaning forward to kiss her cheek?

'Friday night,' said Lorna, and got into the car, flustered at the thought of being early to bed with a farmer.

Chapter Seventeen

Pat Osborne's farmhouse kitchen had been a favourite hang-out for the local Young Farmers when Ryan and Sam were leading players on the local scene: there was always cake in the tin, dogs by the Aga and the occasional bottle of cider from Mr Osborne's unlocked beer fridge. None of these items were available at the Protheros' house, Jess reported; when their family business took off, Ryan's parents had upgraded to an executive home on the outskirts, where you had to remove your shoes at the door and remember to put coasters under everything.

Lorna couldn't decide whether she should make an effort for a kitchen dinner at the home of someone she'd known for twenty years, or whether not making an effort would offend Sam's parents. Her teenage thinking tangled up with her adult thinking, and in the end she put on some clean jeans and her studded boots that made her feel like Stevie Nicks. You couldn't go wrong with boots, she thought, then spent half an hour searching in the wine merchant's four doors down from the gallery until she found a bottle that cost enough to look polite but not so much that it looked flash.

The early evening drive through the country lanes felt like moving through a postcard – the road took Lorna past orchards and pasture fields where cattle grazed in the fading light, and the clean air smelled of wood and smoke. As she got nearer the farm, her attention was caught by some smaller cows in the field nearest the house: the sturdy little black cows with a thick band of white around their middles like humbugs. They were so pretty, she thought, and wondered if she should have revised some cow breeds to make conversation with Sam's dad.

The satnav had brought her a funny way, not past Rooks Hall, and the turning into the farm came as a surprise: there was an arch, leading into a wide yard, surrounded by Dutch barns stacked high with bags of feed. She parked next to a tractor, carefully avoiding the chickens strutting across the cleanly swept cobbles, and got out. The barns were showing signs of age, but the farmhouse itself was attractive, with arched curves of paler bricks surrounding the windows and a weathervane perched jauntily on the roof like a fascinator.

'Hello!' Sam appeared from an outbuilding, in jeans and a jumper. A farm cat ran out after him, looked both ways for Labradors, then crossed the cobbles in a streak of darkness. 'Right on time. How are you?'

He leaned forward to kiss her cheek; it was an automatic gesture that they both realised they had to commit to, once started. The air that brushed against Lorna's face smelled of aftershave and Persil and something else, something that hadn't changed in twenty years. It was half a polite kiss, half a hug, and Sam's shoulder pressed against hers. He got a little closer every time, a little more relaxed.

'Fine, thanks. I brought this.' Lorna offered him the bottle of wine. 'Good to see there's a decent wine merchant here now.'

'*Apparently*, it's been there over a hundred years.' Sam pretended to look embarrassed. 'Who knew?'

'Well, I guess if it didn't sell Diamond White then how would we have known it was there, eh?'

They stood for a second, smiling, feeling the past wash around their ankles like the edge of a wave. Sometimes, Lorna thought, it was as if there were two Lorna and Sams – the smart, capable adults who'd connected as near-strangers, briefly, and disconnected just as quickly; and the teens who had grown up together but never connected at all. Two versions of themselves, running simultaneously. Her heart shifted, softening again. She'd seen the old Sam in his concern for Hattie and her sister. Maybe they could go back, after all.

'We should . . .' He gestured towards the house, and Lorna nodded, and followed him. At the door, he touched the small of her back, briefly, like a secret.

The Osbornes' kitchen was exactly as Lorna had imagined it would be. There was an ancient cream Aga on a tiled hearth, fiddleback chairs around a heavy pine table that looked as though it had been there since the Armada, and a couple of plastic dog beds by the door, one containing an elderly black Labrador with a snow-white muzzle and eyebrows. When Lorna and Sam walked in, it lifted its head, saw Sam and thumped its tail twice, then settled its nose back on its paws.

'Ah, finally! Skiving off in the office again, eh?' The stocky man at the table put his beer down as they came in; his tone was bantering, his eyes weren't. Lorna recognised Gabriel, Sam's older brother.

'Says the man who hasn't shifted from here since lunch,' Sam retorted evenly. His tone was bantering too but Lorna caught a flash of irritation as he leaned into the fridge – she saw his hand touch a beer bottle, but then he took a Coke. 'Can I get you a drink, Lorna?'

'Yes, please. Coke's fine,' she said as Gabriel replied, 'I'm working from my phone, en' I? That's technology.'

Gabriel had always been broad-shouldered and strong for his age, playing rugby for the town when he was still in his teens, but now his checked shirt strained over the top of his jeans and his nose had a beery flush. Lorna sensed a narrowness to his eyes that hadn't been there before, as if he was sizing everything up and not finding what he wanted. He and Sam had seemed very different back then; fifteen years on, only the dark eyes gave any clue they were related.

Sam handed her a can of Coke and a pint glass with a faint air of apology. 'Bills still need paying, Gabe.'

Gabriel raised his hands in mock-surrender. The fingers were chubby and something about them gave Lorna the creeps. 'You're the brains, little bro. Who's this then?'

Sam addressed her, not him. 'Lorna, you remember Gabe, I'm sure,' he said. 'I did tell him you were coming for dinner. He's got a lot on, must have slipped his mind.'

Lorna leaned forward to shake his creepy hand – what else could she do? – just as he said, 'Well, hello, Lorna! I wouldn't have known you.'

'Is that a compliment?' It didn't come out as lightly as she'd have liked.

'It's been a while.' Gabriel smiled at her, his eyes almost vanishing into his red face. 'How old were you when that clever sister of yours got herself up the . . . ?' Sam coughed, Gabriel corrected himself with a smirk. 'When we last saw you? About twelve?'

'I left when I was thirteen,' she said before Sam could interrupt again. 'Jess was seventeen. And engaged to Ryan. They've been married for nearly seventeen years now.'

'All's well that ends well, eh?' said Gabriel with a wink, and Lorna noticed a flicker in Sam's jaw. There was real tension between the two of them, beyond the standard issue brotherly squabbling she remembered from years back.

How had it felt for Gabe? she wondered. First, you've got a straight A little brother who makes it clear he's too good for the farm. But that doesn't matter because you've got the job for life. Then you fall under a baler and that same little brother comes back in his fancy suit and starts telling you how to do the job you've been training for since you could drive a quad bike.

The worst of both worlds. For everyone involved.

'Sam! Out of that fridge!' Mrs Osborne appeared from the pantry, wiping her hands on her apron. She was neat and never stopped moving, with the last Princess Diana haircut in existence, unchanged since Lorna had last seen her. 'Oh, Lorna! You've caught me on the hop! I'm sorry. How are you, love?'

'Very well, thank you, Mrs Osborne.' Lorna offered her the bottle of wine. 'I wasn't sure what we were eating.'

'Wine! Posh!' said Gabriel. 'We're simple folk here, beer would've done.'

'Don't be silly, Gabriel. Sam often gets us wine. Very kind of you.' Mrs Osborne put it on the sideboard carefully. 'Sit down. I'll call Dad now you're here.'

Sam and Gabriel exchanged loaded glances as Mr Osborne was summoned from wherever he was (the cow shed) and they settled around the table. Sam's mother lifted a steaming pie out of the Aga, and while they were still marvelling at its size, she surrounded it with dishes of roast potatoes, peas, broccoli, mashed potatoes and gravy.

'No boiled spuds, Mum?' asked Gabriel, lifting a lid.

'And you wonder what I meant about my suit.' Sam raised an eyebrow at Lorna, offering her the first plate.

'This smells delicious,' she said. Her voice sounded different in the kitchen – shyer, more like her old teenage self.

Mrs Osborne beamed as the men piled into the food. 'How's your sister, Lorna? We still get a card from her and Ryan every Christmas. And the kids? Three now, isn't it?'

Lorna tried not to look at Gabriel. 'All fine, thank you. Hattie's been helping me out in the gallery. Sam mentioned you'd called in for cards?'

'I have indeed. Isn't it lovely that you and Hattie are keeping it in the family with your art, just like us and the farm!' Mrs Osborne's cheery expression faltered. 'It was so sad about your dad, Lorna. Very sad, especially so soon after your mum. You've been through the wars.'

'We have. Lots of happy memories though.' It was her stock response. No one knew what to say; to lose one parent was bad enough, but to lose two . . . It was touching when an elderly couple couldn't live without each other, but Cathy and Peter hadn't even been sixty. There was an uncomfortable drama about it, an extravagant emotion.

'You'll notice lots of changes with the farm,' Mr Osborne announced.

'Yes!' It wasn't a real question, of course, just a chance to open up a favourite topic, but Lorna didn't mind going with it.

'Got to move with the times, Dad,' said Sam, as if he knew where this was heading.

'Know how long we've been here this year?' Mr Osborne pointed at her with his knife; Mrs Osborne nudged him and he dropped it. 'One hundred and fifty years. All in the same family.'

'Wow.'

'Not many farms round here can say that.'

'And that's why we're adapting,' said Sam. 'Diversification, everyone's doing it.'

'Diversification.' Mr Osborne poked at his pie. 'Don't feel like farming to me. Feels more like playing about.'

Sam helped himself to peas without making eye contact. 'Times change, Dad. We need to diversify if we want to go on for another hundred and fifty.'

It had never struck Lorna before how weird it was, being part of a farming family – taking on that obligation to keep the farm going, no matter whether you wanted to or not, because that's what your family did. And Sam's dad being forced to stay here and watch his sons change everything he'd worked for, being reminded of his own time slipping away with each harvest brought in.

She suddenly felt claustrophobic. The copper pans on the side, the rows of blue and white plates lining the Welsh dresser, the ancient cookbooks. Everything in this kitchen had been here for *years*. Even the dogs were replaced with identical black Labradors.

'For instance,' Sam explained, turning to Lorna, 'we're renting out some pasture to a farmer over the way for his beef herd, and we've turned over a few fields to bird seed.'

'Bird seed? What, for bird feeders?' She sensed this was a conversation only she would be contributing to. Gabriel remained silent, brooding, not part of either side; Pat kept smiling and eating her supper in small regular forkfuls. Mr Osborne looked positively wounded.

'Yes! It's an expanding market. And some for racing pigeons, special high-energy mixes. I looked into growing sunflowers for the seeds but we're a bit far north for that.'

'Shame,' said Mrs Osborne. 'I'd have loved a field full of sunflowers, wouldn't you, Len? Makes a change from cows, left, right and centre!'

'Not for me. Had to get rid of my dairy herd, no money in 'em, apparently.' He sounded morose. 'Broke my heart, that did. Day they come and took the girls away.'

'All about volume production now,' said Sam. 'None of us want that, Dad. Even if we could have afforded the machinery, you'd have hated seeing it.'

He would have hated it, Lorna thought. Sam was dutiful but he drew the line somewhere.

'What about the cows outside?' she asked, wanting to get the old man talking about something he liked. 'The lovely stripy ones? Are they yours?'

'Yes.' Mr Osborne's eyes lit up. 'They're Belted Galloways. Beautiful, ent they? Lovely creatures, Belties.'

'Very succulent,' said Gabriel, a loaded fork halfway to his open pink mouth.

Lorna blanched. 'You eat them?'

'Course. What else they for, cows? You a vegetarian?' Gabriel went on, back in the conversation. 'Dad! We've got another veggie! Call the steak police!'

'Gabriel! Enough! Now, what *I'm* enjoying is the holiday accommodation.' Mrs Osborne cast dark looks around the table, and continued brightly, 'We did a bit of B & B when the boys were young, but Sam's come up with a plan for making money from the cottages we used to rent out. No one round here wanted them, being so far out of town, so we've done up a few and it's really taking off, isn't it?' She looked proudly between her boys. 'Gabriel manages them, and Sam does the fancy marketing. You quite enjoy it, don't you, Sam? Not quite what you were doing up in London, but a bit like it, eh?'

Gabriel muttered something under his breath and Sam glared at him.

'How many cottages are you renting out?' Lorna asked Mrs Osborne, just to be polite.

'We've got three on the website, and there are three more to do. Well, four. Mrs Rothery's still in Rooks Hall, bless her. Although I shouldn't think she'll be there for much longer.' The corners of Mrs Osborne's mouth tilted downwards sympathetically. 'She had a fall recently, poor dear. I popped in to talk to her about Butterfields – my mother-in-law's there. Lovely place.'

'Gave you an earful, didn't she?' said Gabriel. 'Reckon you should go back and have another little chat. Old cottage like that's no place for someone her age.'

Lorna bristled. Joyce wasn't old; she was barely eighty and acted a decade younger. 'I don't think she feels ready to give up her independence just yet. She's very active for her age.'

'Sam says you know Mrs Rothery, Lorna?' Mrs Osborne turned to her with interest. 'Is that right? How did you meet her?'

'She's an artist – she sold her work through my gallery.' How did they not know that?

'And Lorna walks her Border terrier sometimes,' said Sam. 'Mum, did Gran ever get someone in to walk Wispa?

Because Lorna's friend Tiffany volunteers for a charity that helps old people exercise their dogs. Any chance we could get someone to walk a very old collie, Lorna?'

It was a brave attempt to divert the conversation, but Mrs Osborne had heard what she wanted to hear. She fixed Lorna with a direct, farmer's-wife smile. 'Well, now. Maybe you could have a chat with Mrs Rothery, then? Tell her it's so much better to move into one of these retirement homes while you're still up to making friends and settling in. No point hanging on in that cottage – it'd be the best thing for everyone if she made a move while she's got some oomph left.'

'Mrs Rothery has more oomph than I do,' said Lorna, struggling not to glare at Sam.

Inside, she was seething. Was this the point of her invitation tonight? Had Sam set this up, so his mother could ask her what he couldn't? So the Osbornes could eject Joyce from her home, to get on with making more money from it?

Sam wasn't looking at her, on purpose probably. She felt angry with him, but also with herself. What a cheap shot. He'd always been about the bottom line, Sam. He hadn't even *tried* to understand about the art when she'd explained her pop-up gallery; he'd just torn holes in her sums, made it all about the money. And that was the difference between them. She had art and creativity in her veins, and he had money.

'It's the best cottage, Rooks Hall,' said Gabriel. 'Put more parking in at the front, and you could easily let it to sleep eight.'

'More parking?' Lorna knew what was coming; she just had to hear him say it so she could hate him completely.

'Tarmac over the garden.' Gabe smiled; there was a fat shred of broccoli stuck in his gappy teeth.

By keeping her patient and courteous dad at the forefront of her mind as a kind of talisman, Lorna managed to make small talk for the rest of the main course, and an apple pie with double cream, but when Mrs Osborne offered her some tea 'to wash it down', she pushed her chair from the table.

'So sorry, I've got to get back,' she said. 'I've left my dog on his own.'

Sam met her gaze and she knew he knew Tiff was in the flat with Rudy but she didn't care. She was too disappointed with him, and she hoped it showed in her eyes.

'Thanks so much for a delicious supper,' she went on as the Osbornes slowly got to their feet. 'Don't get up! Sam'll see me out, won't you, Sam?'

'Hey, hey, hey,' crowed Gabriel, 'Sammy boy!'

'Give it a rest, Gabe.' He followed Lorna out, and when they were out of earshot in the shadowy yard, she turned to him, struggling to compress her bitterness into one sharp, unemotional sentence.

She couldn't. It was all she could do not to throw her head back and let the contempt spill out. She hated Gabriel, and she loathed herself.

Sam sighed. 'I know what you're going to say,' he said. 'And no, is the answer.'

'How would you know what I'm thinking? That's the only reason you invited me, isn't it?' Lorna jerked a thumb back at the cosy kitchen window. 'To help you get Joyce out of her home so you can start turning it into an over-priced holiday cottage.'

'Of course not!' He ran a hand through his hair. 'Why would I have spent all last weekend drilling holes in my own fingers to make the place safe for her if I thought that?'

'Because you're legally obliged to!' Lorna couldn't believe Sam would do something like this, but then . . . maybe he would. He couldn't have done so well in business if he hadn't got that ruthless streak. 'I can't believe I have to say this, but please don't kick her out. That cottage is Joyce's *life*. Her husband designed the garden for her, it's where she created her art, it's . . . everything to her. Are you surprised she doesn't want to move to some care home where she can't even take her dog?'

'Butterfields *does* let—'

'There's no room at Butterfields at the moment. There's only Monnow Court, where she can't take Bernard!' Lorna held up her hands to stop him. This evening had started with so much happy nostalgia; now she was feeling as small and hopeless as the old Lorna, not as creative as her mother, not as clever as her sister. Nothing had changed. Nothing. 'And thanks for sticking up for the mother of your godchild when your brother was making out she was a sleazy under-age mum, by the way,' she added. 'Oh no, wait. You didn't.'

'Lorna, please don't . . .' Sam sighed, and turned away so she couldn't see his face. 'I'm sorry about that.'

'Not as much as I am.' She stared at him. Who *was* he?

The light from the kitchen window dimmed as someone – his mother? – drew the curtains shut, and another cat streaked across the yard, disappearing into the barns that once held shuffling, cud-breathed cattle. Lorna wanted to go dramatically, but she knew that once she stormed off, that would be it. There would be no recovering this moment and she desperately wanted Sam to show her how wrong she was.

His voice, when he spoke, was carefully controlled. What he said made her heart sink. 'You have no idea how hard this has been for me. You think I was happy to come back here . . . to this?' He lifted his palms. 'It's the last place in the *world* I want to be. But you do what you have to do. We all do. You know that.'

Lorna wanted to back down and sympathise, but she couldn't. She was too angry still. 'What? Evict old ladies from their houses?'

'Don't be so melodramatic. The alternative was evicting *that* old lady from *her* house.' He jerked a thumb towards the farm. 'We'd have had to sell. Seriously. Where would Mum and Dad have gone, at their age?'

'It's not the same thing.' Even as she said it the rational side of Lorna's brain was arguing his point, reminding her of the spectres chaining him to this place, to his family, to a life he hadn't chosen and didn't want. But the heartbroken side was in control now, riding roughshod over reason.

'You know, the one thing I always believed about you was that you were kind,' she said passionately. 'I can't see how you could be so kind to animals, and so cruel to an old lady with nothing left but her memories.'

And before she could see the hurt on Sam's face, she got into her car and drove away, without looking back. All the way home, Lorna replayed the conversation in her head, but she couldn't make herself feel bad about saying what she'd said.

She'd meant it.

Chapter Eighteen

Lorna's Art Week briefing with Calum Hardy was as sparky and borderline flirtatious as she'd expected, mainly because she'd provided him with a centrepiece to the whole Art Week, one that the design team were 'excited to run with'.

'We are *all over* Paint the Music,' he assured her over Ferrari's special lunch offer (pasta plus one glass of questionable wine or beer). 'It's on all the posters, journalists are loving it, and we're in talks to get the local television news team down to join in! I know! It's like real-life *Anchorman*. Make sure you get your hair done.'

And he actually winked.

Calum was so enthusiastic that Lorna felt guilty about taking credit for what had been, really, Joyce's idea.

'Would you like to come along and join in?' she suggested when she called round later in the week to walk Bernard, update Joyce with the latest developments and get more advice on her knitting. 'Maybe, if you felt like it, you could start us off? Put in the inaugural brushstroke?'

She held her breath as Joyce carried on knitting. She had discarded the book of patterns and had begun a dog coat of her own design, with silver butterfly wings and a sort of scaly pattern, and now she focused on her needles as if the answer could only come once she'd finished that row.

The clock ticked on the mantelpiece, a metronome to Joyce's stitches. The old lady said nothing, but Lorna had come to realise that meant she was thinking. Joyce didn't waste words; they were as carefully chosen as the colours in her paintings. She wondered if she'd made a faux pas – was a community splodgy project a bit beneath Joyce, as a proper artist? Maybe it was too personal, to celebrate Ronan's idea in public.

Oh dear. Lorna winced and fumbled her own stitch. It had been ages since Joyce had pulled a protracted silence on her; since her stay in the flat, they talked easily, from the moment she walked in to the moment she closed the gate behind her.

Bernard sat up and scratched his ear; hairs flew off in every direction. He badly needed a haircut. Joyce knitted on.

Had she heard? Was she going deaf?

'The thing is, I'm not creative,' Lorna gabbled. 'I can *guess* what you would do, but I don't think I could . . . get it *right*, somehow. I don't really want to ask another artist to begin this piece when it's your idea.'

'Lorna, of course you're creative. Everyone is. And you of all people should know there's no right or wrong with art,' said Joyce, still not looking up. 'You paint what you feel.'

'But people need to know roughly what they're *doing* before they join in. They need some practical instruction.' She didn't want to beg, but now the idea of running this event without Joyce's guidance was making her feel panicky. What if it didn't start right? It could so easily turn into an unholy mess. 'I never know where to start. It's why I like colouring books!'

Rudy snored at her feet. He didn't mind waiting for his walk, unlike Bernard who had sauntered over to the window, and was staring impatiently into the fields, growling at birds.

'That's the experiment. Provide the materials, let them explore the process.'

'Calum Hardy doesn't want an experiment.' Lorna put her knitting down. The tension had gone lumpy and she'd dropped a stitch somewhere, throwing the whole pattern out. 'He wants something colourful he can put up in the town hall. He wants a photo opportunity of inter-generational art participation, not an empty canvas and seven people standing round refusing to make eye contact with volunteers holding sponges. That's what I've promised him.'

And I have no idea how to do it! How *do* you paint a trumpet's noise?

'I mean, even if you just showed me first . . .' she blurted out. 'So I've got an idea. Your painting, it's so immediate and perfect – I want to convey something like that but I can't, and it puts me off starting.'

Joyce looked up and saw Lorna's panic. 'But you *can* do that.'

'I can't, Joyce.' She swallowed. 'I've wanted to be an artist all my life, and I've trained at some good places. And I've realised . . . I'm not. I need your help. I don't want to let that beautiful painting down.' Joyce had shared something heartbreakingly personal with her, and Lorna was offering this raw glimpse of her own heart in return. 'I don't want to let *you* down.'

Joyce met her gaze. She seemed different this morning, in a way Lorna couldn't quite put her finger on. There were two unopened letters on the hall table, one in a brown envelope, one handwritten. She hoped Gabriel bloody Osborne wasn't ending her tenancy, after everything she'd said to Sam.

'Oh, for heaven's sake, what a fuss,' said Joyce. 'We'll start it off together.'

Lorna felt her shoulders relax with relief.

'But, please,' Joyce went on, 'no big fanfare about me being there. This is your idea. It's not about me. And if it rains, I'm not coming.'

'Oh, Joyce. This means so much to me,' said Lorna. 'Thank you.'

'No gushing, please. Now tell me,' Joyce changed the subject as easily as she flipped her needles and began a new row. 'What's happening in that flat of yours? When is Hattie coming back for more knitting lessons? Has Tiffany told her mum she's left her job yet?'

Lorna gave up trying to knit and talk at the same time. She shoved her needles into the wool. 'Tiff's temping for the council's childcare programme, and she's helping Keir set up this scheme where old people carry cards to let people know if they've got dogs at home, in emergencies. Her mum's gone on a cruise, so she's put off telling her about the nannying. I haven't heard from Hattie, so I think everything's OK . . .' She paused, guilty at how long it had been since they'd spoken. 'Or my sister. I don't know whether to call or not.'

'I think you should call her,' said Joyce. 'What have you got to lose? If you don't mind my saying so. You never know what's round the corner.'

Lorna looked at her, surprised. What was in those letters? she wondered. Should she tell Joyce about her dinner with the Osbornes?

Joyce resumed her knitting in a 'and that's your lot' manner. 'Now then, I think Bernard would like to go out.'

The gallery was what passed for busy when Lorna got back.

A retired couple was browsing in the back room, picking up the ceramics very carefully, and another couple was admiring the metal tree sculptures that an artist had delivered the previous week. A young woman was chatting at the desk with Mary, while a boy and a little girl – belonging to her, Lorna guessed – were rotating the card spinner, pointing at the different cards.

'Ah, Lorna!' Mary seemed relieved to see her. 'This lady was asking me if we do these dog coats for a pug?'

'It would be the most incredible wedding present for my sister-in-law,' said the woman. She seemed friendly and wore a couple of lumpy felt brooches on her cardigan that Lorna recognised from Mary's previous stock. So someone *had* bought them. 'It was the striped ones that caught my eye. Her dogs are called Bumble and Bee, so you know – bumble bee, perfect!' She grinned. 'I would knit them myself but I just don't have time, what with these two.' She nodded towards to the children, heads together at the spinner.

'This lady is a keen knitter,' said Mary. 'She thought we ran workshops!'

'Yes, I saw someone knitting in here last week? An older lady?'

'You did, she's actually an artist.' Lorna took off her bag and put it by the desk. 'Joyce Rothery?'

'Oh, right. Great!' Clearly the woman hadn't heard of

her. 'But have you thought about knitting workshops – as art?' she went on. 'It's a domestic art form, like needlework.'

'Isn't it just darning?' murmured Mary.

'No, it's a whole thing,' said Lorna. Some of the artworks she'd delivered to hospices had been delicate needlework or tapestry; they had a calming, therapeutic impact, as if the artist's patience had been stitched into the pattern along with the thread. 'William Morris and Arts and Crafts and all that.'

'Craftivism!' The customer pointed and nodded. 'What I really want to get into is yarnbombing – where people group together and create whole knitted scenes, then put them up overnight so it's like a magical surprise? I wish I could find somewhere to do that locally. I can't knit enough on my own. It'd take years.'

Something about the woman's enthusiasm touched Lorna. Plus she'd been mad enough to buy one of the furball brooches from the shop. A sensation was unfolding in the back of her mind, like a half-forgotten dream coming back to her.

'Maybe we should look into that,' said Lorna. 'Let me take your details and I'll let you know if we can get people together.'

The lady scribbled down her name – Caitlin Reardon – and some contact details, and called her two children over. 'Have you two decided on a birthday card? It can't be *that* hard.'

'This is for my friend Alex,' said the little girl carefully, and reached up to put a card on the counter. It was a pug in a party hat. The boy squeezed her and whispered in her ear. Whatever he said made her giggle into her hand, then look at him over the top of her fingers, conspiratorially.

We were like that when we were young, thought Lorna. Me and Jess. Always whispering, always close. Sisters. Her heart contracted; Joyce was right, she should call her. You really never knew.

She counted out the change into the girl's hand, coin by coin, and the children joined in until all three of them were chanting out the words.

'. . . five pence, fifty pence, one pound, two pounds, three makes five!'

'Lorna, is that your sister?' said Mary suddenly.

Lorna's head bounced up. Jess was standing at the door, with an overnight bag in each hand. Her face was flushed and shell-shocked – and looked *wrong* to Lorna.

It took her a moment to realise that Jess had cried off all her eye make-up. That, or she was so distressed she'd forgotten to put on any in the first place.

Lorna hurried the wreckage of her sister into the back office, where she pushed her on to the office chair, put the kettle on, and kicked the door shut for privacy. She held her breath the entire time, waiting for the dam to break, but Jess still hadn't spoken when Lorna shoved a mug into her hands and started adding medicinal amounts of sugar into it.

'Hot sweet tea. Four sugars enough?' Lorna paused, spoon poised. 'If I had brandy to give you, I would, but I haven't forgotten Ryan's eighteenth. Can you even smell it without retching these days?'

'No.' No smile either. Jess cupped her hands round the mug and took a sip.

Lorna had never felt so relieved to hear her sister speak. 'Biscuit?' She offered her Mary's tin of chocolate Hobnobs. 'No calories when you're stressed.'

Jess shook her head.

Lorna sat back on her office chair. The month's unfinished accounts were still on the desk and she shoved them in a drawer. She didn't know what to say. Offering advice to her older sister wasn't something she was familiar with – normally it was Jess appraising and sorting out *her* life.

They sat without speaking for five, ten minutes. Lorna heard the gallery bell jingle. And again. Mary's twittering. Rudy barking upstairs.

How bad *was* this? Her head fluttered with possibilities. When Mum died, Jess had been a torrent of words, a whirlwind of activity and resentment and energy while Lorna had felt numb and wordless. Jess always had plans and action and reactions. Now, she seemed muted, as if all the plans and words had drained out of her.

Lorna desperately wanted to say something, but her mind was blank at the sight of her big sister so defeated. It unravelled her inside.

Finally, Jess put the mug down on the desk. It was empty. 'I need to walk,' she said, and got up.

Jess walked fast at the best of times, but whatever was on her mind sent her powering down the street as if she was heading to a closing departure gate. Lorna found it hard to keep up with her long strides as she followed behind.

At the corner of the high street, where Ryan had failed his driving test twice at the lights, Jess turned down towards the smart villas, the 'Poets Streets' in local estate agent world, and Lorna knew exactly where they were going. She struggled against the memories as they passed the brown towpath sign directing walkers down to the historic joys of the Longhampton–Bristol canal. The canal. She was walking to the canal, where nearly every piece of gossip had been digested throughout their adolescence.

Longhampton's canal ran behind the main streets, hiding a corner of the town that was forever modestly Georgian. Swans glided past the pockmarked brickwork of the banked sides, and the occasional fisherman sat wrapped in green waterproofs, waiting and watching, and ignoring the sniffs of passing dogs. Lorna had spent many mostly unhappy hours slumped on the benches that lined the towpath, reading the rusty plaques dedicated to 'Barry & Cyril who loved this place' or the smug deeds of forgotten councillors. Recent conservation grants had de-shopping-trolleyed the water and weeded the banks, but from the graffiti, Lorna guessed the benches were still a hangout for teens requiring more privacy than the bandstand could offer.

Jess strode past a jogger doing ostentatious calf stretches against a lamp post, and finally slumped down on their favourite bench: 'You and me, and a hot cup of tea. J&L 1985'.

Lorna sat down next to her, and waited anxiously, in case Jess was going to hurl something in the water, or jump in herself.

'Ryan,' she said eventually. 'He's come clean, the lying bastard.'

'About what?' Lorna's heart was in her mouth. She watched her sister's profile as if it might reveal something; Jess was focusing hard on the ducks sailing carelessly down the canal, three yellow ducklings in their wake.

'That girl he was meeting.' Jess gripped her handbag.

'It's not an affair. Jesus. I was about to say *at least* it's not an affair. Ha!'

'So what is it? Is he in debt? Is she . . . ?' Lorna flailed – she couldn't think what else it could be.

Jess turned to face her sister. The purple circles under her eyes stood out against her pale skin. Not enough sleep. 'She's his daughter.'

'*What?*'

'His daughter. She's called Pearl. Pearl Lawson. She's seventeen. More or less.'

'But . . . how? That's impossible.'

Jess didn't reply; she merely raised a weary eyebrow. 'Apparently not.'

'But when did Ryan have *time* to have a daughter?' Lorna struggled to understand. 'She's lying, surely? She *must* be. Is it a scam? He's barely left your side since you were at school!'

Jess sank forward, her head in her hands. 'Not quite. Remember when his family sent him off to work with his brothers in Birmingham? Just after I found out I was pregnant with Hattie?'

'What? Oh . . . no.' None of it made sense. Lorna dug her nails into her palm, just to check this wasn't a weird dream. 'You're joking.'

'Nope. He had a three-night stand, as he put it, in Birmingham with some friend of Craig's. Not that it's his fault, of course. Oh no. Craig and Kyle dragged him out the entire time he was there, trying to take his mind off his little problem back home.' She laughed, but there wasn't any humour in her voice. 'They *made* him go out clubbing with them, tried to encourage him to sow his wild oats. And he did. Very efficiently, as it turns out. Ha! Who knew *Ryan* was such a baby-making machine!'

'But you were pregnant with Hattie! And they knew Ryan loved you!' Lorna couldn't believe it. 'What were they thinking?'

'You know what the Protheros are like,' said Jess, bitterly. 'Kirsten didn't want her precious son tying himself down at eighteen with the girl from down the road, did she? They had hopes for Ryan. God knows even now I swear they think he could have done better for himself. Kirsten has no idea I earn more than he does.'

'But why didn't this woman tell Ryan she was pregnant at the time? Why's this only come to light now?'

'Because Erin – that's her name, by the way – *Erin* had a steady boyfriend in the army. I know! Ironic! She managed to keep it quiet for all these years, but recently there was some kind of illness in the family, and the question of blood groups came up, and Pearl's didn't match . . .' Jess waved a hand. 'I wasn't too fussed about the details, as you can imagine. The upshot was that Erin decided she'd have to tell Pearl that her dad wasn't her real dad, but she overheard something and took matters into her own hands. She tracked Ryan down on Facebook. It wasn't hard – Ryan's useless when it come to internet privacy settings. She got in touch, demanded a meeting. And that's what Hattie saw. Meeting number two.'

'Meeting number two?'

'Yup. The first one was mainly crying, apparently. On both sides.' Jess sounded uncharacteristically bitter.

'I just can't believe this, Jess. Where do they live?'

'Gloucester.'

Not that far away. Lorna felt hollow inside. It was hard

enough to imagine Ryan cheating, even a teenage Ryan. He'd never been the sharpest knife in the box – handsome, yes, but loyal and reassuringly unimaginative. Not a liar. Not a player. 'So . . . what happens now?'

'I don't know. I don't even know what I don't know.' Jess's knuckles were white. 'I feel as if I've been living a completely different life. My children have got a sibling. My husband has another family.'

'But he doesn't *really*,' said Lorna, desperate to mini-mise the pain in her sister's voice.

'He *does*.' Jess turned to her, and her eyes were shining with hurt. She looked unlike herself, damaged by the betrayal. 'He does, Lorna. And she is absolute proof that Ryan isn't the man I've believed he is for most of my life. Which means I'm not who I thought I was either. Have you any idea what that feels like?'

Tears were rolling down Jess's face. Lorna was desperate to stop the pain but she had no words. She could only put her arms round her sister, and hold her.

'I'm sorry,' she whispered. 'I'm so sorry, Jess.'

'I honestly believed Ryan was like Dad,' she sobbed. 'I thought I'd found someone I could trust absolutely, some-one who'd grow up with me and . . . and . . . be the one person I *knew* inside out! How could he do that? How could he shag some random stranger when I was at home, fighting with school and my parents about *us*?'

Because he was eighteen and pissed and panicking, thought Lorna. And listening to his idiot brothers tell him the next seventy years were locked down in front of him. Even predictable men like Ryan managed one freak-out. It was how they dealt with the post-freak-out fall-out that mattered.

'So is he still at home?' She stroked her sister's back. It was like talking about someone else, not Ryan. 'Is it *over*?'

There was a long pause. 'No. But I've told him to pack his stuff and go somewhere for a few nights, so I can try to get my head around it. He's told the kids he's at a conference. They think I'm at a spa today. Ha! Early Mother's Day present.'

'And Hattie?'

'Oh, Hattie's devastated. Blames herself for stirring it all up. I've asked her *not* to get in touch with Pearl on social media but what can you do? It's how they live their lives, on bloody social media.' She covered her face with her hands. 'I've not dealt with this well, Lorn.'

'What? What did you say?'

'Oh, I did what Mum and Dad did, whenever something happened. Closed ranks. *Let us deal with this.* Like I knew better than she did. When I don't. I don't have the first idea what the hell to do.'

That was the final straw. Jess's shoulders slumped, and she began to sob properly.

Lorna tried to take her sister's hand. Jess resisted for a moment, but then she relaxed and let her. Their fingers wrapped round each other's, squeezing tight until it felt as if they were joined by the knuckles. They sat watching the slow water in the canal, barely moving, not speaking, because Lorna couldn't think of anything helpful to say, and Jess seemed exhausted.

My heart's safer on its own, thought Lorna. Why expose yourself to this? Ripping your life apart, because another human being dared to do something out of character, nearly twenty years ago? You couldn't balance your entire sanity on someone else. You couldn't.

'Remember what we used to say?' she murmured into Jess's hair. 'I've always got you. You've always got me.'

'I know,' said Jess. Her voice was almost inaudible. 'I know.'

They walked back slowly, in silence, and when they turned on to the high street, Sam was parked opposite the gallery in his Land Rover, waiting for her.

Their eyes met across the road, and Lorna knew at once that he knew. Ryan must have called him in panic, looking for his wife. It was written on his face: apprehension and sheer awkwardness when he realised Jess was with her.

She shook her head as he went to open his door to get out, and he stopped, his gaze still locked with hers. Jess hadn't seen him; she was lost in her own thoughts. Sam raised his hands in the car and Lorna struggled with a powerful impulse to talk to him – who else would understand?

But I can't trust him, she thought. He knows because Ryan's called him to warn him, he's probably got a whole other side of the story ready. And what if Jess decides she needs to talk to him? To grill him about what happened between the Big Talk and Ryan coming home for the last few months of her pregnancy? Suddenly she was back there again, the little sister left out of their trio, tagging along behind, never getting the whole story.

Sam mouthed something, but she shook her head again.

We need to stick together, me and Jess, she thought, and put her arm around her sister. She turned her back on Sam, and ushered Jess into the gallery.

Then she turned the shop sign to Closed and heard the sound of a car engine starting outside, and pulling away.

271

Chapter Nineteen

Jess went home later that night, once she'd sat in Lorna's bath for an hour, and smoothed herself back into her recognisable shape.

'Don't tell Sam,' she said as Lorna leaned into the car for a final goodbye. 'Let me . . . let me deal with it.'

That meant Jess wanted to pretend none of it was happening, thought Lorna as the Golf disappeared around the corner. She was incredibly good at willing things out of existence if she didn't like the sound of them. Watching from the sidelines during that surreal summer, the teenage Lorna had seen the light go on and off in their mother's studio, where she'd set up a bed so she could work all hours, and wondered if she was doing much the same thing: painting herself into a universe where none of this was happening.

Lorna wasn't sure if she wanted to talk to Sam about it, anyway. She was never sure which Sam would turn up these days.

Jess sent a brief text to the effect that Ryan was 'back' and they were 'talking things through' but about an hour after, Hattie asked if she could come and help out at the gallery at the weekends, so clearly things weren't completely back to normal.

Hattie herself said as much when Lorna collected her

from the station on Friday night. 'Mum's stopped pretending everything's fine. She didn't even take Tyra to
ballet this week, that's how much she's lost it with Dad.'

'How do you mean, lost it?'

'They're not talking. They're pretending to – like,
"When will you be in tonight?" but they're not *talking*.'
Hattie looked wretched. 'They never make a coffee for the
other if the kettle's on.'

It had started to rain again – light spots, but soaking –
and for once, there was a space right in front of the gallery.
Lorna reverse parked in one go, and then turned off the
engine. The sun had just set, and the street lights were
starting to shine out of the dusk. Longhampton high
street was always prettiest when it was deserted, when the
evening light blurred the rust and the dirt and all you
could see were the hanging baskets and the carved stone
apples on the lintels.

The engine ticked, then fell silent.

'Are you mad with me?' asked Hattie in a small voice.

'With you? Of course not!'

Hattie hugged her bag tighter. 'I'd understand if you
blame me if Mum and Dad get divorced. I mean, if Milo
and Tyra end up—' She bit the words back, pressing her
rosebud lips in on themselves.

'No one thinks it's your fault!' Lorna squeezed Hattie's
knee. 'You were *right* to tell me, and *I* decided to tell Jess.
We had an agreement, years ago, your mum and me. We
tell each other everything.'

'Everything?'

'Everything.' Apart from that one major secret Jess
hadn't told her, thought Lorna. Because everyone thought
she was too young to understand.

273

'Pearl's my sister,' said Hattie, staring out at the empty street. 'I've got a right to meet her.'

'I'm not sure you could call it a *right* . . .' Lorna started, but Hattie twisted in her seat to face her.

'Don't you think I'm entitled to know my own sister? She's half me. She's like . . . practically my twin! We're nearly the same age!'

Lorna winced. The timing of it was so cruel. There could only be months between the two girls. *Ryan*, she thought. Seriously, what were the chances?

'Hattie, try to see it from your mum's point of view,' she said. 'You were a wanted baby, but you were a . . . surprise. You changed everyone's lives: your parents', mine, your grandparents'.' She wasn't sure how to put this delicately: Pearl was proof Ryan had thrown Jess's trust, the sacrifice of her big academic dreams and the plans she'd made to travel the world, right back in her face. How did you forgive that, when time had added even more responsibilities?

Hattie rolled her eyes. 'I get that, but it's different for me. Me and Pearl, we could build bridges between our families.' A dramatic glow lit up her face and Lorna knew what Hattie was seeing in her mind's eye: selfless teen diplomat, bringing together the sulking, wounded adults with her pureness of spirit and social media skills.

This is what happens when you don't talk, she thought, and the irony of Jess priding herself on her terrific communication with her kids, only weeks ago, wasn't lost on her. No wonder she felt as if she'd woken up in someone else's life.

'You'll talk to Mum, won't you?' Hattie grabbed her hand. 'About me meeting Pearl?'

At least she was asking. It would only take ten seconds

on Facebook to bypass any kind of parental permission. How long before Hattie got sick of waiting?

'Hattie,' she started, 'I don't think it's a good idea for anyone to—'

'Yeah, yeah, hang on, Auntie Lorna: look at Rudy! He's so pleased to see me!' Hattie pointed upwards. One storey up, in the kitchen window, Rudy was barking furiously but silently, his barks swallowed up by the double glazing as he wagged his tail. Was that delight, or anxiety?

Oh, Rudy, thought Lorna, I know how you feel.

It was when Lorna took delivery of a pile of fliers for Art Week, featuring her bandstand idea on the front page, that she really started to get nervous about her event.

It was hard to practise something so random, but she did her best. The night before the big event, Hattie, Lorna and Tiffany stood in the kitchen, listening to Vivaldi's *Four Seasons*, trying to decide on the colour of a cello.

'You're sure this is what a violin sounds like?' Tiffany stared at the paper covering the table, now covered in wild splashes of green and yellow paint.

'If that's what it sounds like to you, then yes.' Lorna checked off the delivery slip from the suppliers one final time. Canvas boards, fifteen, downstairs. Brushes, fifty, various sizes. Paints, in different textures, in every colour of the rainbow. Sponges, palettes, pens. The cost had mounted dramatically but somehow that paled into insignificance compared with the small matter of making it all work.

'I think I'm hearing a different violin.' Hattie swirled a long motif down the side of the paper. She had taken to the task unquestioningly, with an elegant style that Lorna envied. 'Mine's blue.'

'To be honest, I don't care what colour your violin is,' said Lorna, 'as long as none of it ends up on the floor. Or the dog.'

Tiffany marched a series of leaves down the page, stamping with the print she'd made from a potato.

'Ooh, that's good. Did you do art at school?'

'Nope,' she said. 'Let's just say I've spent a *lot* of time cutting shapes out of potatoes in the last few years.'

Hattie squinted critically at the mess. 'You know what it needs? Some gold.'

'Yes, gold would be great!' Tiffany agreed. 'Have we got any?'

Lorna looked up from the invoice and made a panicked noise. 'No! This is already *way* over budget.' She knew she shouldn't have got the special easel to display Joyce's painting but she wanted to honour her properly – to make it clear where the inspiration had come from.

'Won't there be trumpets?' asked Hattie. 'They're gold.'

'It's a school band,' Tiff reminded her. 'And that's a whooooole load of recorders. And recorders are definitely not gold. They're more . . . acid yellow?'

Lorna gazed at the mess in front of her. This wasn't what she'd pictured. Her heartbeat skittered, as if she'd drunk too much coffee. 'You think we need gold paint? Bollocks. What time does Hobbycraft shut?'

An awkward silence fell over them as the massed violins of 'Autumn' sawed away in the background and the madness of what they were attempting sank in.

'Don't worry, Lorna, it'll be fine,' said Tiffany reassuringly.

It really was a mess. It was nothing like the fliers. 'It's too important to be "fine", Tiff.'

'Why? Because of Joyce?'

'Partly. It's the first piece of public art she's created in years. I hoped it might inspire her to start painting again. If it's a disaster, she'll think I don't understand what she's trying to do. And if it looks crap, no one will join it, and it's so *public*.'

'Don't worry about people not joining in. We'll drag them in if necessary,' said Hattie. 'And Mum's coming, and Milo and Tyra . . .' Her expression tightened. 'And Dad.'

Lorna pretended to look pleased. It was great that Jess wanted to support her, but she could have done without the added stress of the Big Family Outing. Keeping an eye on Ryan and Jess, as well as everything else, was something she could have done without.

'And I'm worried it'll rain,' she blurted out. 'There's a fifteen per cent chance, and all Calum's given us is one tiny tent.'

'*Prrthph*. One in six,' said Tiffany dismissively. 'It won't rain – weather forecasts are just guesswork. It's going to be fine.'

Lorna couldn't bear to look at the catastrophe on the table. She turned, and her eye fell on Betty's framed medal, hanging between the two big windows. For the first time in too long, she thought of Rudy's glamorous mistress, reckless Betty standing on the rooftops in her man's peacoat, sticking up two fingers at the Blitz, and she felt stupid, and a bit ashamed.

Betty would laugh at this. A bit of rain? It was nothing in comparison. Absolutely nothing to worry about. And yet . . .

'Wait! I've got an idea!' Hattie ran out and returned with a can of gold body glitter, which she started spraying on to the canvas. It brought the whole thing into a new focus, scattering a fine mist of autumnal shimmer over the textured leaves. 'There!' she said, and beamed.

Mum's creativity, thought Lorna, with a pang, it's skipped a generation.

The first drop of rain fell when Lorna had just finished setting up Joyce's painting on its easel.

It landed on the burst of iridescent paint, bulging a rosebush into life. She stared at it in horror.

'All set?' Calum jumped down from his photo position on the bandstand, taking care not to spill his breakfast espresso. He was wearing a hoodie and a new pair of thick-rimmed glasses that made him look more like an art dealer than Lorna. 'Love the easel!'

'Calum, it's raining,' she said.

He held out a hand, waited, then shook his head. 'No, you're imagining it.'

She pointed at the looming clouds. 'It's definitely raining.'

'Nah, that's just . . . dew?' He looked hopefully at the sky. Lorna had never seen a townier person, even in EC1. 'Pop your stuff in the bandstand if there's a bit of drizzle – the kids won't be here till half nine at the earliest. Can I leave you to it? There's a pottery throwdown in the town hall I need to check in on.'

'But what about . . . ?'

Luckily for Calum, someone called his name before Lorna could finish, and he was jogging across the park towards a woman carrying three carrier bags of pineapples and a sign saying 'Fruit Installation'.

'I'll put it in the tent.' Tiffany threw a plastic sheet over the canvas, and began bundling it towards the mini-tent they'd set up without instructions while Calum was taking 'Before' shots of the park. It was lopsided and didn't seem to have enough parts.

'Careful!' Lorna reached out to protect an exposed corner bumping on a crate. She hadn't told Tiff how valuable the bandstand painting was – she thought it would freak her out, and also provoke a lecture about including it on the house insurance, which Lorna couldn't afford to do.

'Chill out, Lola.' Tiff frowned at her. 'Did you get back to Sam yet?'

Lorna's phone had buzzed a couple of times on the way over but she'd ignored the calls. 'No.'

'Why not?'

'Because it'll be about Ryan, and I can't deal with that today.'

Tiffany sighed. 'How do you know?'

'What else will it be about?' Lorna felt another two raindrops on her face. Why hadn't she brought a coat with a hood? 'He knows they're coming – he's probably had a whole different story from Ryan and wants to tell me so I can tell Jess. It's like being back at school.'

'Whatever it is, he's been trying to see you all week.' Tiffany propped the painting against a plastic crate and pulled up the hood on her raincoat. It was yellow, with massive white daisies on it. 'I told you he came round while you were out with the dogs. Just talk to him, will you? It's obviously something important.'

Lorna hunted in the big bag of food they'd brought, so Tiff couldn't see her face. The bandstand idea was too close to the sort of art Sam thought was pretentious bollocks. She didn't want another lecture about persuading

Joyce to look into retirement homes. She didn't want to hear some cock-and-bull story about poor Ryan. There was no version of Sam that would be helpful right now.

A phone was ringing, and Lorna felt a mobile being shoved under her nose.

'From the gallery,' said Tiffany shortly. 'Mary.'

'Mary?' Lorna took it. 'What's wrong? Is Hattie up yet? Can you tell her to get herself out of bed and down to the park, please?'

'Hello, Lorna.' Mary sounded flustered. 'I didn't know Hattie was still here. I'll give her a shout . . . I've got some-one who wants a word.'

Before Lorna could ask who, the phone was passed over. 'Sam here,' said Sam. 'I've been phoning your mobile since eight this morning!'

Lorna's pulse quickened in her chest at the sound of his voice. 'I'm busy. It's my event today, the one in the park.'

'I know that,' he said. 'It's why I'm ringing. It's raining – do you have enough wet-weather provision?'

'Um . . . no. We don't.' How did he know? And how had he remembered about her event? She'd only men-tioned it in passing over the dinner table that night, before they got on to his plans for Joyce's house.

'Thought so. I took Mum to something similar last year and it was just the same – everyone soaked. No one ever thinks to hire tents. Wine, but no tents. Typical arty types. I'm assuming you can't exactly relocate if it pours down?'

'Is it going to pour down? Do you have some kind of special farmer antennae? Is your bladderwrack quivering, or whatever?'

'I'm not that kind of farmer. Look, do you need a small

marquee, or not? It's just that I thought of you this morning when I was in the barns – there's an events company renting space at the moment and I'm sure they'd be fine about us borrowing one for the afternoon. For the advertising.'

The rain was getting heavier. Lorna could hear fat drops starting to flick the fabric over her head. Joyce would need somewhere too, if she was going to join them. Hadn't she said; *And if it rains, I'm not coming*? Another lead weight in her stomach.

Still, something made Lorna hesitate. Was this going to end up in a favour being demanded in return? Was Joyce going to suffer, indirectly, if Sam now felt she owed him one?

Tiffany nudged her, and frowned – hard. 'He's got a marquee? Get the marquee!' she hissed.

Lorna swallowed. Of course. It was kind.

'Yes, please,' she said. 'And . . .'

'What?'

'Thanks for thinking of me,' she said.

'No worries,' said Sam. 'I'll see you in half an hour. Can't help you with earplugs for the band, mind. Gabe says the kids are playing their recorders.'

True to his word, Sam arrived at the same time as Tiffany was returning from the coffee cart with fresh supplies. Coffee, and 'something to cheer you up'. No croissant in the world was that big, Lorna thought, biting off the end.

'Clearing up, I see?' Sam called ironically as he and Simon the grumpy gamekeeper jumped out of the Land Rover and began unloading canvas and poles. 'Where d'you want this?'

The early drops had turned into a shower, knocking the petals off some of the flowers in the beds. The parents starting to gather with cello cases and music bags by the bandstand wore waterproofs and resigned expressions as water dripped off the plastic bunting.

'Over here would be good.' Lorna put her coffee down and went to show him. 'We need to be able to see and hear the band . . .'

'Right. Got you. Simon, pass us that pole?'

Sam worked quickly with Simon, and when the marquee was up, he helped her and Tiffany move their boxes from the tiny tent. It smelled of damp grass and tea, but it was dry.

Would Joyce come if it carried on raining? she wondered, seeing yet another tiny detail she'd missed in the painting: a fat silver pigeon's coo. It was so full of surprise and wit. Nothing like their attempts.

She was conscious of Sam near her, a few feet away, waiting to speak.

Tiffany, propping up the first canvases, realised that he wanted to talk to Lorna alone and coughed. 'Simon, can I get you a coffee?' she said easily, steering him out of the tent. 'You must be hungry . . .' Their voices trailed away, and there was Sam, in front of her.

'I know you're avoiding me but we need to talk.' He gazed at her, his eyes steady on her face, seeking her confidence. 'Ryan phoned me, told me what's happened. I'm sorry. It's . . . surreal.'

Lorna raised an eyebrow; she couldn't help it. 'You knew nothing?'

'Nothing!' Sam looked surprised she was even asking. 'I barely saw him when he was in Birmingham that summer – his brothers bundled him off. And I was at university after, so we didn't see much of each other . . .'

'Pardon me? Lorna?' One of the orchestra organisers popped his head in, waving a plastic wallet. 'Can I give you a copy of the final set list?'

'Yes, great!' She reached out and took the folder. The sight of the eight pieces and a start time in under an hour set the butterflies wheeling in her stomach.

Lorna turned back to Sam, and tried not to notice the hollow of his throat under his unbuttoned collar, the smell of him close to her in the warm marquee.

He ran a hand through his damp hair. 'I don't see any point in taking sides, not now. Ryan's broken. Jess sounds like she's in major denial. God knows what the kids are making of it.'

'I can tell you what Hattie's making of it. She's spending as much time here as she can. And Jess isn't in denial, she's in shock. She trusted Ryan – she gave up everything to be with him. Things were never the same with our mum and dad afterwards, you know. They always saw us as really happy children, then suddenly Jess is pregnant and leaving, and they don't know how it happened.' Lorna swallowed. 'Dad never got over it, and Mum . . . Things changed. You could see it in the work she was doing. No more fairies after Jess left. We weren't in her work anymore. And, yes, we noticed.'

She hadn't meant to let that slip; it had come out on the rush to defend Jess. Lorna flushed, embarrassed. She'd never told anyone, not even Tiffany.

They stared at each other. Sam seemed conscious that she'd shared something she hadn't meant to. 'I'm sorry,' he said.

'Don't be.' She sounded harder than she felt. 'If they hadn't been so wrapped up in each other Jess might not have been so keen to find her own family.'

He reached out a hand, his eyes soft and sympathetic. 'And what about you, Lorna? I should have—'

Lorna swallowed and watched Sam's hand touch her arm. No one ever really asked how she'd felt, when her best friend became someone else's mum, and her parents folded in on themselves. Only Sam, only now.

'There you are!'

They both spun round. Jess and Ryan were standing at the door of the marquee, peering in as if they were visiting Santa's Grotto. But with no chance of a nice surprise at the end.

Chapter Twenty

For a couple whose seventeen-year marriage had just been revealed as merely half a story, the Protheros seemed surprisingly together. Eerily so, in fact, thought Lorna as she inspected Ryan and Jess's faces for clues of recent harsh words or tears.

Jess ushered Tyra and Milo into Lorna's marquee, out of the drizzle. 'I know we're early but we wanted to get the best seats,' she chirped in a voice that sounded a bit too cheery. 'You didn't tell me we should have brought an ark!'

'Ha ha!' said Lorna, at the same time as Sam managed an almost convincing guffaw. They side-eyed each other simultaneously, in a cartoonish way that would normally have made Lorna's stomach flip at how in tune they were, but Sam's eyes didn't crinkle as they usually did when something like this happened. He looked tense.

Jess was meticulously turned out, which was always a sign that things were wrong. Her dark hair was blow-dried straight, and she was wearing an entire page from the Boden catalogue in one go: cropped red jeans and white plimsolls, a crisp blouse with a blue cardigan, topped off with a jaunty rain mac.

Ryan, in contrast, was a wreck. His hair was grown out, there were bags under his eyes and he seemed creased from head to toe. He couldn't look further from the teenage Lothario. He looked like a teenage Lothario's weary dad.

'Put that down, Milo,' said Jess, and grabbed a jam jar of water from his curious hands. 'We look with our eyes, not our hands.'

Tyra and Milo were just as ever. Bright, confident, fiddling curiously with the art materials on the trestle tables. Thank God for that, thought Lorna, and ignored Tyra's forceful squashing of some paint tubes.

'Hey, Tyra, nice wellies,' Lorna observed. 'They new?'

'Yes. Mine are frogs.' Tyra pointed to her brother. 'Milo got ladybirds. Dad bought the wrong ones.'

'Dad always buys the wrong ones,' muttered Ryan.

'No reason why girls can't have frogs,' said Lorna brightly. 'Or ladybirds.'

'How are you, Sam?' asked Jess, swinging round to him, deliberately blocking Ryan so there could be no secret communication. 'Haven't heard from you in a while.'

Sam rocked back and forth on his wellies. 'I've been up to my knees in bird seed and DIY, trying to get the farm into the black.'

'Sam lent us this marquee,' Lorna piped up. 'Saved the day! Isn't that great!'

The tension was building to a nearly unbearable level when the flap rustled and a tray of coffees appeared. 'Lorna, I got you a . . .' The coffees were followed by Hattie. She saw her parents and froze, unable to back out.

'Ah, there you are! Just in time to tell your mum and dad about our event!' Lorna removed the tray from her grasp and gestured at the tables. 'Go on, show them how it works . . .'

Hattie's body language was more eloquent than her explanation as she ran through the spiel they'd rehearsed for visitors. Her shoulders hunched, and the pantomime eagerness with which Ryan was listening made Lorna tense up on her behalf. Each step her dad took towards her forced Hattie back another step. Jess was pretending to listen, but Lorna could see her attention drifting towards Ryan over and over when he wasn't looking – her eyes were hurt, and kept flicking away, as if she had to keep reminding herself he was the man she'd married.

Lorna checked her watch; after a morning of time passing glacially the second hand had suddenly jerked forward, and the concert was due to start in exactly five minutes. Her chest tightened with nerves.

Right on cue, Calum Hardy pretended to knock on the marquee door. 'Hello, hello! Lorna, we're on stage in two.'

On stage? Also, *we*?

'I need to introduce you and your event at the same time as the band . . . Oh, hello! Already found some willing volunteers? Cool!' He smiled at Sam and the Protheros, and then held out his hand. 'Come on!'

Sam gave Calum a funny look as he grabbed Lorna's hand, and Lorna wanted to explain, but she had no choice but to follow him out into the cooler air. The rain had stopped, but the sky remained uncooperatively leaden.

He kept hold of her hand until they reached the bandstand, and Lorna was slightly sorry when he dropped it.

'I was hoping Joyce would be here,' she said. The park had filled up, and a reasonable crowd was now gathered by the chairs, most of them still huddled under umbrellas. 'You'll mention it's her idea . . .'

Calum was grabbing a microphone from a volunteer.

'Thanks, Ben.' He turned and grinned at her. 'All set? Let's go!'

'What? No . . .' Lorna watched with dread as Calum jumped up on to the stage and beckoned her to follow him.

She shook her head – no way did she want to get up on stage. There were a *lot* of people now. Lorna counted her breaths – in, slowly, out, slowly – as she scanned the crowd for Joyce, but she wasn't there.

Her heart sank. Had it been too much to ask? Was she angry with her for taking her idea? Had the association with Ronan been too painful to deal with in public?

Calum held out a hand, and smiled at her so encouragingly – and so unexpectedly – that Lorna took it again. Then suddenly, whether she liked it or not, she was on stage, and it was starting.

'Ladies and gentlemen, it gives me tremendous pleasure to introduce the highlight of our Art Week events!' He swung his arm towards her. 'Lorna Larkham of the Maiden Gallery, and the band of Longhampton High School! Now, as well as enjoying the talents of our young musicians, we are privileged to be part of a truly experimental art event here this afternoon . . .'

Calum was good in front of a crowd. He made her event sound fun and trailblazing – proper art, in other words. Lorna worried he was talking it up too much, though. Everyone was looking at her: the orchestra behind, the crowd in front. By the marquee, Jess and Ryan and Sam were staring too. Lorna had never ever done anything that involved people looking at her; she hadn't even been in school plays. Her mouth was so dry her tongue was sticking to the roof of her mouth.

'. . . and if you head over to the Maiden Gallery's marquee in . . .' Calum made a big show of looking at his watch. '. . . two minutes, Lorna will equip you with all you need to be part of Longhampton art history!'

He turned and smiled at her. Lightheaded with adrenalin, Lorna smiled back. Calum's eyes were twinkling behind his glasses, as if they were sharing a joke, and she felt . . . an uncomplicated happiness. As if Lorna Larkham were in the crowd, watching the art-event organiser, and she were an entirely new adult person, who'd stepped fully formed into this situation with none of her laughable career record trailing after her like toilet roll stuck to her heel.

As if she was in control, for once.

The feeling didn't last long. At the marquee a queue of curious onlookers had formed, headed up by a photographer from the local paper. Hattie and Tiffany were policing the line while Ryan and Jess talked to one child each, to avoid speaking to one another.

Ten white easels stood like an army inside the marquee. Blank and arrogant and perfect. Lorna took a deep breath and stepped inside. As she did, the photographer grabbed her.

'Right, I need a nice one of you putting the first touch on the canvas,' he said, moving people around to get a clear shot. 'Quick, they're going to start. Here, grab this.'

'No, no, I'm not the artist.' Lorna raised her hands against the proffered brush. 'I can't go first.'

The canvas loomed, exactly like the one in her spare room that she'd never found the courage to spoil with paint. Behind her, the rustle and whisper of the band faded away as the conductor shushed the children's orchestra and raised his baton. Tiny ants swarmed around Lorna's chest, up into her throat, and every nerve in her arm flickered. Everyone was looking at her. Calum Hardy, Tiffany, Jess. Sam. Sam was still here, standing towards the back of the crowd, looking at her.

What was she supposed to do?

Lorna buckled. She grabbed a couple of brushes and bent down to Milo and Tyra's level. Kids always made a better photo, she told herself. And whatever they painted would be more interesting than her anxious overthinking.

'When the music starts,' she whispered, 'paint what you think it sounds like, on this canvas.'

Tyra's eyes widened. 'Me?' She pointed to herself dramatically.

Lorna nodded. 'Just choose the colour you can hear in your head and put it on there.'

Neither Milo nor Tyra questioned what she meant. Instead they swivelled happily to the rainbow of paints on the side.

Lorna picked up a brush herself, more to give herself something to do with her hands, and held her breath.

And then the music started – the first simple, rocking-chair chords of 'Imagine' – and something happened. Lorna's brush reached instinctively for the purple paint, and there it was.

As the school band honked and parped their way into the first verse, she looked at the mark on the white canvas. That's what it sounded like: a calm purple wave and she'd made it.

Lorna suddenly felt like a transparent balloon against a cloudless blue sky, the music and the colours passing through her into her hands. She reached for the paint and squelched her brush in it before the sparkle left her – something about the regular heartbeat of the melody really did feel purple and she drew a pulsing line along the base of the canvas, relishing the slippery ease of the paint as she went, the breathy feathering as the paint ran out.

Next to her, Milo and Tyra splodged away with enthusiasm, a brush in each hand with different colours. They didn't care about being wrong or right. Milo was bouncing as he painted, and Tiffany had flipped into nanny mode, moving paints out of reach before red brushes could be plunged into yellow paint ramekins. Within moments, the canvas glistened as the colours erupted across it like fireworks, colour and sound in one.

Lorna stepped back to look at what she'd done, and a child pushed into her space to add an arching red shooting star as the violins soared behind them. His paint dripped down into the pretty feathering of her purple wave, but she didn't mind.

A magical thing was taking shape right in front of her, a machine powered by imaginations working together and separately, and Lorna wanted to float away with excitement. Even if it was a huge mess, she'd achieved something she never thought she would. She'd beaten a white canvas in a staring competition. Finally!

So this is what it feels like to be an artist, she thought, and the words sent a flutter of silvery elation across her skin as she reached for another clean brush.

The sun came out during the next piece, and the marquee began to fill up with people eager to have a go at expressing 'Eye of the Tiger' in poster paints. Tiffany had to organise a one in/one out system at the easels, as Hattie washed brushes as fast as she could. The photographer moved around taking pictures, people gathered to watch the artists working, and the buzz of interest rose, along with the smell of trampled grass in the marquee.

'Let me guess – was that the John Lennon?' said a voice next to her elbow. 'I would say so, from the waves?'

Lorna turned round. Joyce was standing next to her, with Keir following close behind. She was resplendent in a man's black jacket over her trousers, with a trilby tipped at a rakish angle. A hammered silver brooch finished off the look. Lorna had never seen Joyce so dressed up; clearly, she'd gone to some effort, and Lorna felt honoured, if a little disappointed that Joyce had missed the chance to make the first mark.

'Hello!' she said. 'Were you waiting to see if the rain stopped?'

'I was waiting for you to start, Lorna,' said Joyce. She squinted at the three finished canvases. 'What joyful colours. This has all worked out even better than I'd imagined.'

'Would you care to join us for the *1812 Overture*? We've been saving a canvas for you.' Lorna tried to sound light, but held her breath. Had Joyce changed her mind about joining in? Was that why she was late?

Their eyes met. Joyce paused, then to Lorna's relief, she nodded, with a twinkle.

The queue stepped back as one when Joyce approached the painting area – she had an aura, Lorna thought, fascinated. A calm intensity, like the gathering weight in the sky before snow, her creativity suspended somewhere between her imagination and the canvas.

Joyce picked up a brush and moved it gently in the air, her gaze fixed on the easel as if the colours were already appearing to her.

'There you are!' Calum Hardy popped up out of nowhere, and within moments he'd organised a photo call with Joyce and Lorna, volunteers in Art Week T-shirts and, of course, himself in the middle. Joyce made the elegant first touches to the *1812 Overture* canvas (bright yellow peaks, three inscrutable red circles), and gave the local paper a few quotes about how inspirational the area had been for her, but she declined to be photographed next to her own painting, Ronan's bandstand.

'Lorna is a generous curator.' Joyce touched her arm, nudging her forward to give her the moment. 'I'm honoured to be involved.'

Calum went off to talk to some more journalists, and Joyce and Lorna were left alone for a moment, observing the activity from a distance.

'So what did it feel like, that first stroke?' Joyce regarded her from under her trilby. 'With everyone watching you?'

'Scary,' Lorna admitted. 'I have no idea where it came from, the colour or the shape.'

'Who does? It was very brave.'

She suspected Joyce was being kind. 'Hardly *brave*. I didn't have time to think. The music started, so I had to.'

'All first leaps require courage. And it's hard to be watched while you're working, I know.' Joyce's gaze didn't flinch. 'It was a sterling effort.'

'Thank you,' said Lorna. 'And thanks for making me do it. You're right, it had to be my responsibility. Even if you'd have done it better.'

'I don't know about that. You have your own vision,' said Joyce. 'You're a very creative person, Lorna. You just have a rather narrow idea of what form creativity can take.'

Neither of them spoke. Suddenly it felt as if the world had shrunk into the damp space of the marquee, and they were back in Rooks Hall, talking in front of the fire with the ticking clock, the smell of firewood and dog hair. She bloomed with pride. If I had to paint this emotion, she thought, it would be a deep, warm red.

'None of this could have happened without you,' said Lorna. 'You, and your beautiful bandstand painting.'

Joyce turned to the painting, displayed proudly in the corner of the marquee. Two children were gazing in wonder at it, pointing out details to their dad with stubby fingers. Lorna suddenly felt the depth of Joyce's sacrifice: to give Lorna a project, this private woman had opened herself up to a public examination of her most precious memories.

'I think . . . I think Ronan would have enjoyed this, Joyce,' she said. 'If you don't mind me saying so.'

Lorna's words hung in the warm, grassy air: intimate, brave. Much braver than just starting a painting.

Joyce turned. 'And, if you don't mind *my* saying,' she replied, 'your mother would be proud of your vision.'

Lorna caught her breath: what *would* Mum have made of today? In her mind, her favourite memory rolled like Super-8 film, her mother turning from her tilted drawing desk, detaching from her work for a moment to smile down at Lorna, praising her choice of crayon, the neatness of her colouring. She'd looked like a bright goddess, her dark hair messy and her face alive with energy. How much Lorna had longed to be like that. Alive with energy, inspired with other-worldly power.

'Thank you,' she said. 'I think that's one of the nicest things anyone's ever said to me.'

The park started to empty at teatime. Tiffany and Hattie helped Lorna stack the materials into plastic crates to be taken back to the gallery. There was just the marquee to be taken down; Sam texted to say he'd be there as soon as he'd finished at the farm. She wasn't to start without him, apparently.

'You two go home,' Lorna said as they loaded the final piece into the back of her car – Joyce's painting. 'I'll wait for Sam; he won't be long.'

'Mum and Dad are coming back at six,' said Hattie. 'Please don't be late.'

'I won't.' Lorna patted her arm; she looked apprehensive, and Lorna couldn't blame her. 'I won't.'

'There he is now.' Tiff nodded at the Land Rover pulling up by the gates. Sam was on his own in the front. 'I'll see you back at the gallery.'

Lorna waved them off, and squinted into the late afternoon sun as Sam jumped out of the Land Rover and strode across the grass towards her. He looked as if he'd driven over in a rush; he was wearing rough jeans and his dark hair was a mess.

'Right.' He pointed at the marquee. 'Let's get this thing down. Start with this bit here . . .'

They worked together well, and it didn't take long before the marquee lay in pieces around them. Lorna enjoyed the methodical way they peeled it apart, stacking the components in neat lines, talking without having to look at each other.

'This saved the day, you know,' she said. 'Apart from

keeping everything dry, everyone loves a marquee. It's intriguing.'

'Glad to help.' Sam heaved the rolled-up tarpaulin into the back of the Land Rover with a grunt. 'Not pretending I understand what on earth painting sound is, but it looked fun. I hear you had queues around the block.'

'Well, people wanted to keep dry.' She was disappointed Sam hadn't seen it for himself. But maybe the farm had been busy, Lorna told herself. It didn't mean he thought it was pretentious bollocks, not necessarily.

He turned, and gave her an appraising look. 'I think it was more than that.'

Lorna clanged the final tent peg into the bag. She didn't want to go back to the flat, to deal with Jess and Ryan's simmering drama. Not just yet. 'We've got some cake left over and I could do with a sit down.' She nodded at the bandstand. 'Can I tempt you?'

'With cake?' Sam patted his stomach. 'Sadly, yes.'

By now the park had returned to normal, the dog walkers appearing on the paths and a few joggers weaving around them. Lorna had half a flask of coffee left, and they shared it on the bandstand steps with some squashed Victoria sponge.

'Your mum would have loved your event, you know,' said Sam out of nowhere.

'Do you think so?' Sam had only met her mother once or twice; Mum had been shy, and their house hadn't been one of the teen hang-outs. Maybe it was the Teacher Dad vibes.

'Of course. What artist wouldn't love something like that? And the way you got everyone involved, even people who wouldn't normally do something so wacky. Can I call it wacky?' He lifted his eyebrows, then turned more serious. 'That's much harder. Creative and practical – that's you.'

Lorna almost said, it was Joyce, really, but stopped herself. Pride fluttered in her chest. 'Thanks. But Mum was a proper artist . . .'

'What's proper?' He made a dismissive noise. 'So were those pretentious tossers in London who scammed you of your inheritance.'

Lorna flinched, and Sam looked repentant. 'Sorry,' he said. 'I just get angry sometimes, thinking about it. Sorry.' He stretched out his legs on the bandstand steps. 'Let's not go there again.'

He got *angry*? Lorna stared at him, surprised. He'd never told her that. But then they'd never talked about it; she'd never wanted to see Sam again when his advice had turned out to be spot on. Not to mention the rest . . . 'I thought you just thought I'd been stupid.'

'That too. But that wasn't art, Lorna. I know nothing about it, but what you did today – that's worth a million times more.'

'Really?'

'Yup.'

'So when did you see the finished paintings? I thought you were tied up on the farm all day.'

Sam brushed cake crumbs off his jeans. Lorna didn't know why: they were already paint-spattered. 'I, um, I popped back. Just briefly.'

'You should have said!' She nudged him. 'Were you afraid we'd make you paint?'

Their eyes locked, and then very slowly, as if two magnets were drawing them together, Lorna felt herself leaning closer. She wasn't conscious of making any decision at all; it was just happening. Nothing else was touching, no hands, no knees, no other connection, apart from the electricity sparking in the space between their faces which was closing, closing, until Sam's lips, soft and firm at the same time, were on hers and he was kissing her.

She was kissing him. And it was exactly like she'd imagined, a normal kiss multiplied by a sense of time absolutely stopping. He tasted of coffee and a strange familiarity; he smelled of warm skin and damp jackets. Lorna's heart expanded inside her, a perfect rose gold behind her eyelids, and she wanted to stay in this bubble for ever.

And then she became aware of a ringing noise, by her feet. Her phone, in her bag. Lorna pulled away, automatically, and immediately wished she hadn't.

'Your phone.' Sam pointed at her bag.

'I don't have to answer it,' she said. But the moment had broken. Now they'd have to discuss it, with awkward words.

'What if it's Jess? Are you meant to be somewhere?'

'Dinner, with the family. You want to come?' Lorna dug half-heartedly in her bag. Her heart was still hammering. Way to destroy the moment. She didn't really want to talk to Jess right now.

'I would.' Sam's voice sounded different. 'But I've got a call at home later. About work.'

'Pigeon fancier? Or holidaymaker?'

Sam didn't answer at once. Lorna turned to see him fidgeting with his own phone.

'Sam?'

'With a mate who's a headhunter, if you must know. I've got a few options lined up.'

A headhunter? That wasn't what she'd expected. 'What sort of options?'

'In London.' He tried to shrug it off. 'I've got the diversification plans set up now; Gabe knows what he's doing. Well, more or less. I was only ever going to come back in the short term, just to get things turned around,' Sam added defensively.

She stared at him. 'Do your parents know that?' It wasn't the impression she'd got over the dinner table. They seemed pretty happy, the farm safe for another generation.

'Yes.' Sam stared back, but his gaze faltered. 'Oh, Lorna, come on. Neither of us suits this sort of small town life. I bet you if you got offered a job running a gallery in Manchester or somewhere, you'd be off like a shot.'

'Would I?' I don't know this man at all, she thought. He's just kissed me, knowing how much I've wanted it for so long, but he's already planning on leaving. Leaving me here. She pushed herself off the bench and grabbed her bag. Her skin was rippling with panic, just like Rudy's. 'I need to get back to the flat. Thanks for the marquee, Sam.'

'Lorna!'

She heard him calling her, but she didn't want to turn back and see him. She just kept marching and marching until she was out of the park, and back on the high street.

Chapter Twenty-One

'So . . .' Calum Hardy leaned forward on his elbows and fixed Lorna with his most art-dealery look. 'Here's where we are. Devolved creative autonomy – it's in our hands. Or rather . . . your hands.'

As he said that he turned his own hands round, raised his forefingers and pointed at her.

On the other side of the restaurant table, Lorna bit back a smile and tried to arrange the words in an order that made sense. Calum Hardy began every sentence with the word 'So . . .' It was like a red flag to announce the importance of what was to follow, but it had stopped being irritating once she'd decided to imagine him as he probably imagined himself: as a man constantly being interviewed by the BBC's Culture Editor. A man single-handedly bringing art to the outposts of civilisation, one community event at a time.

They were having lunch again, at Calum's invitation, this time at Longhampton's second most popular establishment, the gourmet burger bar known as Crazy Patty's. Lorna and Tiffany had found it impossible to get in on the three occasions they'd tried. It was always rammed with luminous teenagers wrestling juicy handfuls of beef and brioche, then taking selfies of themselves next to the neon Crazy signs.

Lorna moved her plate away. Her burger had been perfect, although it had made her think of the cows outside the farmhouse. Thanks, Gabe.

'Everyone in the office is still buzzing about the bandstand,' Calum went on. 'It worked on so many levels – bringing people together, sharing a communal experience, and making art in the process. All the feels.'

Lorna nodded. *All the feels.* Meaning? She'd have to check with Hattie that that was a good thing. 'I had no idea it would go that well, to be honest.'

'But it did!' Calum beamed at her, and the realness of his smile warmed her. His positivity was nice to be around and he seemed genuinely interested in her ideas. 'You went for it, everyone raised their game . . . you made the sun come out!'

'It helped that we had a marquee.'

'Marquee was great. Love that you can just rustle up a marquee. So. Where do we go next?'

'*We?*' said Lorna. 'I thought that was it for Art Week.'

He twinkled at her. 'I've been tasked with co-ordinating the regional entry for a national community art prize.' His voice dropped to indicate how serious he was being. 'The submission has to reflect the place we live in, it has to bring people together, and if we hadn't already done your Paint the Music project, that would have been exactly what they were looking for.'

'Can't we do it again?' she asked. 'With, er, dogs or something? We could make the dogs run around to music on canvases!'

'No, it's got to be fresh.' He signalled to the waitress for another milkshake, then pointed at her empty coffee cup. Lorna nodded. Why not? There wasn't enough

301

caffeine in the world to keep up with Calum's mile-a-minute conversation.

'I can tell you what hasn't worked,' he went on. 'Film projects, nope – people get shy or weird. Or, in one case, obscene – but, you know, in an interesting way . . . Murals, nope – you can't stick a wall on a truck and take it to an awards dinner. Community poetry, nope – God, don't even start me. Don't even. The *things* people think! And the rhymes!'

What was she supposed to say? Lorna could already imagine how Joyce would be rolling her eyes at this.

Calum pointed at her again. 'I know what you're thinking – you're thinking, this is going to take up a lot of my time.' He tilted his head. 'I hear that. But, apart from the satisfaction of making a difference to a town that, let's face it, needs a bit of help to locate its creative side, there is a prize, to be spent on art facilities, obviously, plus some fantastic publicity for your gallery. The council will pay any out-of-pocket expenses – within reason, of course.'

The coffee and the milkshake arrived. Calum thanked the waitress, then, as an afterthought, ordered some chocolate truffles too. Truffles, obviously, were a reasonable expense.

Lorna was conscious that she wasn't saying very much. 'But isn't this something you've done before?'

'It is, but I want to tap into *your* experience here. This is right up your street.' Finally, Calum sounded natural. 'I understand you used to work with art in hospitals? I've read the brief and I reckon the key to it is seeing art as something that makes the world happier.'

He'd researched her: how flattering. 'It's a strong idea. Art can be healing in ways we don't fully understand, but

my experience is really in distributing it, rather than actually making it.'

'Get out of here.' Calum boggled, as if she were being
modest. 'You made the bandstand art. And it won't just be
you, it'll be the whole town.'

'So I can blame them if it goes wrong?'

'Ha ha!' Calum pointed at her again, with a cheeky
wink. 'So, the deadline for the project is the end of the
year. We'd need to announce whatever it is you're planning to do in a couple of months – that will give us six
months to complete it.' He raised his hands. 'Over to you,
Lorna.'

The truffles arrived. She put two of them in her mouth
at once without even thinking about it, before he could
change his mind.

'I haven't got a clue what he's talking about,' said Lorna.
'Even if I wasn't completely out of ideas.'

'I doubt Mr Hardy has the first idea either,' said Joyce.
'And that's exactly why he's passed the buck to you. Forgive the jargon. So much jargon these days. Ugh.'

'He wants me to give him some ideas to "bounce around"
by the end of next week.' Lorna leaned back in her chair
and Rudy jerked awake from where he'd been lying at
her feet, but she barely noticed. She couldn't work out if
the sinking sensation in her stomach was dread or excitement. Calum had looked at her as if she was someone
who could organise mass art events. He had no idea that
she couldn't.

'I'm sure something will come to you,' Joyce went on,
her needles slipping and clicking as she knitted. These
days she never seemed to stop knitting. Every time Lorna

called in, she'd started a new item. 'Something always pops up.'

'Does it?'

'Oh, yes. Inspiration is a funny thing. Sometimes it refuses to come for months; sometimes it hears an alarm clock you can't.'

'I thought you said it had to come from here.' Lorna patted her chest, above her heart.

Joyce gave her an inscrutable glance, then returned to her needles. 'I didn't say that it's the *only* place it can come from. This Calum Hardy . . . you're quite keen to impress him, aren't you?'

Lorna concentrated on her own knitting: a dog jumper for Rudy, which was not progressing as fast as Joyce's. 'Well, yes. He's got a lot of useful connections – Calum knows some of the big artists working in Birmingham and London. I could do with a few of their paintings in the gallery. I know it's nice to keep things local, but I'm not exactly going to be retiring on what we're making on felt brooches.'

That was putting it mildly. Monday's takings hadn't even covered Mary's bulk-buying of biscuits for the month, and the bandstand materials had gone on Lorna's own credit card. It was nearly April, almost a third of the way through her year.

Joyce turned her row over. 'He has a high opinion of you, evidently. You could be the golden art couple of the West Midlands.'

'I'm not trying to impress him like *that*,' Lorna insisted. She put her knitting down. 'I don't have time to get distracted with men. I'd rather get the gallery established.'

Although . . . Her mind slid sideways to Calum's smile across the table, the genuine enthusiasm once you got past

304

the hipster exterior. The thing about Calum was that he didn't actually know her – he just knew the Lorna she was now, the gallery owner, straightforward and competent. He didn't know she'd failed as an artist, that her degree was really in Sociology.

Which made her think of Sam. He hadn't called since the weekend, and she hadn't called him. Not even to report on the strained family supper she'd had with Jess and Ryan.

Bernard raced to the window and barked so hard his fur vibrated; the postman was making his way up the path, shooting narrow glances towards the house as he went.

'Have *you* got any ideas?' Lorna asked Joyce. She tried to make it sound casual.

'My mind's a perfect blank. I'm afraid I always shied away from those *collectives* people used to go in for. I prefer to work alone.'

Lorna wasn't sure what to make of Joyce's neutral tone. Didn't she want to help? Was she asking too much now?

She looked around the room, and her eye fell on the canvas leaning against the low coffee table. She'd noticed it when she'd arrived but had been so caught up in telling Joyce about her meeting with Calum that she hadn't asked why it was there.

'Is that your garden?' Lorna gestured towards the canvas; it had to be the painting Joyce and Bernie had designed together to map out their year-round cottage flower festival.

Joyce nodded. 'I painted, my husband planted. Of course, there's a little artistic licence . . .'

The letterbox rattled and Bernard and Rudy scooted out into the hall, their barks overlapping, deep and sharp.

Lorna found it impossible to tear her gaze from the painted garden; something about it snagged a half-buried memory, hooking it out from her subconscious the same way the clifftop cottage had. Joyce's sweeping brush-strokes outlined the landscape around Rooks Hall – the trees, the fields, the sky looming outside – but within the brick walls, the world tilted and sharpened, the same tender focus on every leaf and flower as in the bandstand painting Joyce had created for Ronan. It was a big canvas, and every centimetre was layered with thought.

Lorna glanced towards the fireplace to check the clifftop cottage she thought of as 'hers' was still there and saw it was. But the three lino prints that hung in an ochre column had gone, their absence marked by ghostly rectangles on the wall. That was why she felt the room was different. The sharp shards of colour were missing.

'Are you reviewing your collection?' she asked. 'Let me know if you'd like me to give you a hand moving paintings around.'

Joyce put her knitting down on her lap. She pressed her lips together, as if gathering the words for a complicated speech.

'Joyce? Is everything . . . all right?' Lorna faltered as the dogs went quiet outside.

'If you don't mind, Lorna, there's something we need to talk about.'

The blood rushed from her stomach. 'Of course . . . Should I make some tea?'

'No, no tea.' Joyce straightened up in the armchair. 'And I want you to hear me out before you say anything one way or another.'

Bernard and Rudy slunk back into the room, as if they

sensed something was coming, something they needed to chase away.

Joyce spoke calmly. 'I have to leave this house.'

What? Lorna's mind raced. The letter she'd seen on the side. It must have been about the tenancy. The Osbornes hadn't bothered to wait for her 'conversation' with Joyce after all.

'Oh no. Really? Why?'

Joyce shrugged. When her shoulders dropped, the brooch on her cardigan drooped a bit more than usual; there seemed to be less of her filling the fabric than before.

'It doesn't matter. I have to move out. And I would rather seize the decision to leave here myself, rather than be dragged, kicking and screaming. Dignity, you know. No, don't, let me finish . . .' Joyce held up a hand to stop Lorna's protests. 'It's left me with a dilemma. I'm limited in where I can go with Bernard.' She gestured towards the loyal dog standing guard at her feet. 'There's sheltered accommodation, but with a waiting list, naturally. Keir is keen to shuttle me off to that old folks' mausoleum, but I can't take the hound, so that's out. He's been with me his whole life, asked for nothing but my company. I'm not putting him up for rehoming at his age.'

'No, of course not. Poor Bernard. He would miss you. Rudy still misses Betty, don't you, Rudy?'

Lorna bent down to stroke Rudy's scruffy beard; the idea of Bernard in a concrete kennel was awful. Not quite as awful as Joyce packing up the house she loved, though. A furious chill shivered down her spine. How could Sam let this happen? How could he go through the charade of putting in those handrails if all the time he meant to get Joyce out, like a . . . squatter. Surely she had rights?

She sat up, and tried to look positive. 'Well, you never need worry about Bernard. There'll always be a spot for him with me and Rudy, whatever happens.'

'I was rather hoping we could both come.'

'To my flat? Above the gallery?'

'Until I find somewhere else.' Joyce folded her hands in her lap. A neat, submissive gesture, one that Lorna didn't associate with Joyce at all.

'Oh.' Something about the way she'd come out with that made Lorna wonder if this had been rehearsed. 'I mean, you're very welcome, of course but . . . are you sure you wouldn't be happier somewhere more peaceful?'

Joyce glanced over at the garden canvas. Her chest rose and fell with two, three deep breaths, as if she was communing with it, then she said, 'If I'm honest with you, Lorna, that week I spent with you and your friends – it seems to have shaken something inside me. I've woken in the night with ideas, for the first time in years. I feel as if there's something stirring, something I want to get out while I still can. Before . . .'

She made a stiff gesture towards her face. Lorna guessed she meant her eyesight.

'Are you being polite?' she said. 'I thought we'd driven you half mad.'

Joyce laughed drily, and turned her head towards the window. 'There's an apple tree in the corner,' she said. 'I don't know if you've noticed it – well, you won't have done. Bernard planted it for me the year Ronan was born. I thought it was dead. There's been no fruit on it for years. I could never bring myself to dig it out, though. This spring, for some reason I don't understand, there was a little blossom. I thought it had blown off something else, but no. It was the apple tree. A little pink blossom.'

Lorna leaned forward.

'I would like to create one last beautiful thing,' said Joyce. 'There's one last beautiful thing inside me, and I need to be somewhere with conversation and colour and people.'

'All right . . .'

'And I will strike a deal with you. A painting for each month I stay. How about that? I thought . . . perhaps the first one could be the garden. What do you think? Do you like it?'

'Of course I like it – it's stunning, but Joyce, I can't take that. It's *far* too personal.'

'Why not? You're the only person I know who knows the story of it. To anyone else, it's just a garden. In fact, to anyone else, it's a rather odd deviation from my usual style. Probably not worth as much.'

Lorna gazed at the defiant old lady in the chair. She didn't know what to say: the emotions swirling in her were too messy and important for words.

'Oh dear,' said Joyce. 'You're embarrassed.'

'I'm not embarrassed, I'm just . . . surprised.' Lorna struggled. 'Of course you can come to stay. Of course. It's just . . .' She looked around the room. It was full of a life; how hard would it be for Joyce to dismantle this? 'When do you have to move?'

'Fairly soon.'

Lorna bit back her outrage. How could the Osbornes treat Joyce like this? A marriage lived out here, a son grieved for, a husband lost, a lifetime's work dreamed and created and waved off. And in the end, a matter of days to pack it up.

'No,' she said. 'We can't let this happen. Joyce, whatever anyone's said to you, you don't have to leave this house. It's *wrong* to make you leave. Keir must be able to help; surely there are protections . . .'

Bernard jumped up at the angst in Lorna's voice, and began barking and bouncing.

Joyce raised a hand. Pride made her sharp. 'Please, Lorna. You're the only person in my limited circle who doesn't treat me like a senile old fool, so don't start now. If I take *you* seriously, then kindly take me seriously too. One of the first privileges you lose as you get older is the chance to make your own decisions. I'm not at that stage yet.'

Lorna flinched.

'Would you mind taking Bernard for a walk?' Joyce asked. 'Have a think and let me know what you've decided when you come back.'

Lorna harnessed up both dogs and headed down the path, along the road and up the footpath that ran alongside fields that were now springing with green grass.

Thoughts pushed into her head, one replaced by another before she had the chance to examine them properly. The paintings. Joyce's steely eyes. The spaces on the walls. Her space, invaded. Joyce's space, lost. An elusive feeling that this wasn't the whole story was driven out by her indignation on Joyce's behalf – how could Sam let this happen?

As Lorna rounded the corner she saw a quad bike bouncing down the field. She waved it down before she could even think. If that was Sam, perfect – she could tell him exactly what she thought about this, without marching round to the farmhouse and making a scene in front of his family. Although right now, she was quite prepared to do that.

Bernard and Rudy both barked and strained on their leads as the bike approached, and Lorna saw that the figure on it was bigger than Sam. It was Gabe, a baseball hat rammed on his head. Irrationally, the baseball hat made Lorna dislike him even more than she already did.

He spoke before she could. 'What are you doing on here?' he yelled. 'Livestock in the field.'

'I'm walking the dogs, and they're on leads, and this is a public footpath,' she yelled back.

He pulled up a few metres from her and nodded at Bernard. 'You want to watch that one. Old Ma Rothery's, isn't it? Little bastard. He's lucky not to have been picked off by Simon; out of control round animals.'

Simon, sneaky Simon, must have told them she'd lost Bernard. Gabriel smirked, as though he was remembering a good joke, and Lorna hated him even more. If Sam was going back to London, Gabriel would be in charge of everything. It was a horrible thought.

'That's not going to be a problem for much longer, though, is it?' she snapped.

'And what do you mean by that?'

'That you'll soon have Rooks Hall to do up for tourists. I hear Joyce is moving out.'

'Apparently so.'

'Well, I think it's a disgrace.' She lifted her chin. 'It's not easy for an old person to find somewhere new to live, especially with a dog.'

Gabriel dropped the smirk. 'Yeah, you think we're just

looking after ourselves, do you? Evil farmers, only caring about the bottom line.'

'Isn't it?'

He made a dismissive noise. 'You want to take it up with Sam, not me. Sam's the one who's making the decisions around here these days. We just jump to his tune, don't we? If Sam says we need them cottages making more money, then that's what happens. No point getting uppity with me.'

Lorna's words evaporated on the white heat of her anger, and she felt a surge of energy run through her body, bigger and stronger than anything she'd felt before. It was all she could do to stop herself slapping the smug grin off Gabriel's face. She clenched her fists by her sides, and the dogs yapped at her ankles, sensing her tension through the leads.

'What?' He looked at her from his quad bike. 'Going to hit me?'

Lorna shook her head and forced the words out. 'I think it's disgusting. And you can tell Sam that. Since he's your boss.'

And as she turned, Lorna was already deciding how best to rearrange her flat to move Joyce into it. As soon as she wanted.

Chapter Twenty-Two

Lorna's idea came to her unexpectedly, when she was thinking more about the woeful state of her toenails than how she might wow Calum Hardy and the art judges.

It was Tuesday evening. Tiff had gone out to do some cash-in-hand babysitting for Keir's boss, and Lorna was taking advantage of the empty flat to do some yoga. Her creative thinking room was now a bit of a mess, with easels folded up against the walls and spare bed linen stacked by the door, but she managed to unroll her mat and was stretching out her hamstrings, letting the sounds of Longhampton's evening drift through the room.

The weather had been unusually hot for April and Lorna could smell grilled meat, and the wet greenness of the town's hanging baskets as they were watered by a man from the council on a cherry picker outside her window. Somewhere a dog was barking – a dog was always barking somewhere – and her mind wandered to Joyce's painted garden, propped up against the fireplace behind her.

Joyce had wrapped it up while she was walking the dogs and when Lorna stormed back full of Gabriel-inspired rage and said yes, Joyce could come and stay in the flat, Joyce had nodded, and then insisted on Lorna loading the painting into the back of the car.

The deal was done.

Lorna hauled herself into a shoulder stand, locking her gaze on to the fireplace to stop herself wobbling. Viewed from this angle, the painting had quite a spooky feel: the broad battleship-grey strokes of the sky took on a blunt menace against the tender detail of the garden – there was so *much* detail it seemed to be alive. The delicately petalled roses; the glint of the cat's eye as it hid in the bushes, spying on the nest of pink-beaked chicks squawking in the apple tree. Everything in the garden was bright and pulsing; everything outside was looming and dark, held at bay by the meticulous care of the gardeners.

But it wasn't just the dark skies that were spooky, Lorna thought. The *garden* was spooky too. When you looked closer, you saw red tulips blooming next to pearly mistletoe next to blowsy peonies next to lion's mane chrysanthemums next to wintry snowdrops, tortoiseshell butterflies enamel-bright against the frost – all the seasons at once, clamouring for the light. Time and nature rearranged by the painter until it fitted her requirements, guided by an invisible gardener advising on beds and soil and sunlight.

Lorna flopped down and sat cross-legged, staring into the garden. It was bright and clever but there was a discord she couldn't put her finger on. What was the key, the clue that would unlock this garden's secret? And then, in the corner, she saw it: a tiny tree that had glossy fruit and blossom and shady leaves. It was the apple tree Joyce had talked about, the one that had bloomed unexpectedly this year.

Her heart skipped as she realised what it represented. There it was: the secret grief in the garden's exploding cornucopia of lushness; a desperate need to make time stand still with constant motion.

As if two people were determined never to let winter's

darkness come to their doorstep again. As if two grieving parents were determined to defy time and sadness and darkness with colour and scent and fruit and berries, always popping, blooming, reaching for the sun.

That motion. It ticked in Lorna's head like the mantel clock in Rooks Hall. Flowers constantly budding. Berries always bursting. Needles clicking. Wool winding and knotting. Emotions, clouds, rain, sounds, love – Joyce plucked those fleeting sensations out of the air, pinned them down, owned them. She could stop time with her eye and her brush, flip memories, make roses bloom in snow, turn single strings of yarn into wings and ears.

And then it appeared in Lorna's head as clearly as if someone had just pushed it in front of her. How she could make the community art project something truly incredible.

The idea spread out across her imagination, unrolling the details and images by itself, each one answering a question before she could even ask it, and her heart sped up. She felt a powerful urge, a *need*, to see it right now, finished. Before anything could spoil the perfection of its potential.

Lorna lay flat for a moment, savouring this unexpected euphoria, feeling the pressure of the floorboards against her spine, savouring the scent of the evening air, hearing the slam of car doors and chatter out in the street: herself, in this moment, at the top of a wave.

Then she rolled herself back to sitting, and scrambled to her feet, reaching for her laptop to start making it happen.

'Obviously, it won't look like that when it's done properly.' Lorna adjusted the flower on the desk. The petals were different sizes and you could see the paintbrush inside the green stem, but the general idea was there. 'It'll be neater too,' she added. 'Although part of the charm will be that they're all different.'

'And how many of them will you need?' asked Tiffany.

'As many as it takes.' Lorna turned to Caitlin, the yarn-bomber who'd made a special trip over to Longhampton after a series of excitable emails exchanged over the past few days. Caitlin's enthusiasm had gone a long way to convincing Lorna that her concept might work. She also kept helpfully late hours. 'How many do you reckon, Cait? For a really dramatic display?'

'I don't know.' Caitlin shoved a hand into her curly lion's mane of hair and scratched her head. 'A thousand? Five thousand? I've never actually done anything like this before. I've just read about it.'

'Oh, I think *more*,' said Joyce. 'Why not? Ten thousand!'

Tiffany made a gurgling noise.

Joyce gave her a nod of encouragement. Lorna had asked if she could run the idea past her first, but Joyce had insisted she present it to all of them at the same time. 'You must own the idea,' she'd told her, more or less holding her hands over her ears to stop Lorna telling her. 'You must *believe* in it. Art by committee is egregious.'

'They won't all be like this,' Lorna continued. 'We'd knit lots of different types – flowers from every season. Roses, daisies, poppies, sunflowers. And apples! We could make stuffed apples and pears and hang them from trees.'

'And pineapples,' said Joyce. 'And bananas.'

'Bananas? In Longhampton?' Tiffany frowned. 'And it'll be winter. Won't it? Shouldn't you do something Christmassy? Like . . . a partridge in a pear tree?'

'No, that's the point. No seasons, no limits. We'll be turning the whole of Longhampton into a secret garden for one day, in the depths of winter. Like magic! Can you imagine the high street going to bed all grey and dull and wintry, then the next morning everyone wakes up and wow! It's the Chelsea Flower Show!'

'But ten thousand flowers . . .'

'It's for the whole town. Everyone will be able to join in – we'll run workshops here, and hand out knitting patterns, and wool, and go into schools and maybe get them to knit a special easy flower, or make metres of stems with those knitting dollies? And we can tap into the knitting talent in the local residential homes . . . It's something everyone can do, and it's quick and it's easy and it's . . . it's . . .' Lorna ran out of breath, and out of words to convey how excited she was.

No one spoke. Behind them a customer came into the gallery and headed for the display of silver jewellery. Everyone liked the silver jewellery.

Joyce finished the sentence Lorna had left hanging in the air. 'It's *art*,' she said, and put down her knitting to clap. She held her hands elegantly, high and vertical, as if she were applauding a virtuoso musician.

Lorna smiled so hard her cheeks ached. *Art*. She felt light, light and floating on the possibilities spreading out before her.

'Well, I love it,' said Caitlin. 'I absolutely, totally love it. You're a genius. When can we get going?'

Lorna reached for her notepad. 'I've drawn up a proposal – look, these are the sites that I think we could use. The trees down the high street, they'll be bare in winter so the flowers will stand out in the branches, and we can make flower

317

beds from the railings around the town.' She pointed to the map she'd downloaded and marked up. 'We can hang some tall sunflowers around the library and some kind of climbing rose bush around the town hall façade. We can do it on a big net.'

'It's all very well for you expert knitters, but have you got patterns?' asked Tiffany. She pointed at the poppy, with its curling red petals. 'I'm looking at that, and I'm thinking that's intermediate level. Minimum. I'd need to have that *explained*.'

'We can make patterns, can't we?' Lorna turned to Caitlin. 'Is there an online community that might be able to make some for us?'

'I think so. I think there are . . . apps? We'd need drawings.'

'I will draw the flowers,' said Joyce. She reached out and straightened the poppy, curling the leaf over. 'That will be my contribution to this project.'

Lorna caught her eye, and saw the smile at the edge of her lips. This was Joyce's beautiful thing. The burst of creativity that was boiling away inside her, urged on by that little apple tree surprising her with its blossom confetti. She wanted to share it with Lorna – what an honour.

'I'll take the inspiration from my own garden,' Joyce went on. 'They won't be detailed drawings, obviously, as my eyesight isn't up to detailed work any more, but perhaps that's for the best.'

'Exactly,' said Lorna. 'The simpler the better.'

'Very, very simple,' said Tiffany. 'Please.'

Lorna would have driven Joyce back to Rooks Hall, but Keir had arranged to have Shirley the volunteer driver do the honours, via an appointment at the hospital which Joyce did not wish to discuss but which was, Keir muttered while Joyce was browsing some new arrivals in the watercolour section, just a routine check-up following her fall.

'They wanted to run some tests,' he whispered, keeping one eye on Joyce's back. 'Just to make sure she's eating properly. Or maybe to find out what she *is* eating to keep her so . . . determined. Then we can put the rest of the old dears on the Joyce Rothery diet.'

Lorna felt sorry for the nurses up at the hospital. The Zimmer frame stood in the back yard, still in its plastic wrapping, furiously exiled. 'Listen, Keir, I need to discuss something with you, something about Joyce,' she said, under her breath. 'It's about her tenancy – apparently she's been kicked out!'

'Shirley's here!' Tiffany announced as a car hooted outside. 'And she's on a double yellow again!'

Keir gave Lorna a harassed glance. 'I'll try and call later,' he said. 'I'm in and out of meetings all day – it's like people have saved up their crises for the nice weather.'

'Goodbye, goodbye!' Joyce waved to everyone as she swept out, and suddenly the gallery seemed like a much quieter place.

'Wow,' said Caitlin, clutching the dog coat Joyce had finished while they were talking. It had a unicorn horn *and* wings. Joyce's imagination was running wild. 'Mrs Rothery is . . . wow.'

'She certainly is,' said Lorna.

The rest of the afternoon passed without much to distract Lorna from her internet research. She sold three birthday cards and a shell necklace, but mainly she found ways to turn pictures into knitting patterns. At four, the bell jangled and Lorna looked up to see a tall figure coming in, and as always her heart skipped ahead of her, before her brain even had time to react.

It was Sam.

She closed her laptop and tried to arrange her thoughts. She hadn't seen Sam since the art event and pride had stopped her getting in touch. The kiss – the perfect, spoiled kiss – had played on her mind for days after, but she'd made a decision to lock it away. And clearly he had too, because he hadn't tried to get in touch either.

Maybe this was the moment, she thought. He'd come in to have yet another mortifying conversation with her.

She slipped off the tall stool, pulling herself up to her full height. 'Hello,' she said, and her voice sounded awkward.

Sam gestured to the wall of paintings behind them. 'I'm in the market for some of your finest artwork. About twenty-five of them. Various sizes and colours, please.'

Oh. Lorna hadn't been expecting *that*.

'Yes, but what subject matter? What style? What artist?' She indicated some pastels she'd just hung, a young artist from the college who specialised in oily abstracts. 'What medium?'

'Medium is fine,' said Sam gravely. 'But I'd also like a couple of larges, some smalls, and one extra large.'

'Ho ho.' Lorna needed something to occupy her hands. 'Tea? I was just about to make some.'

'That'd be nice, thanks. Is this all your stock?'

'I've got more in the back.' Lorna moved towards the office to flip the kettle on. She was biting her tongue to stop herself asking how the headhunter conversation had gone. When he would be leaving. 'Does it have to be countryside animals? I'm nearly out of cows, but I might have some sheep coming in.'

Sam followed her through the gallery. 'No animals. Maybe . . . peaceful local scenes?' He was more serious now. 'Everything's white, basically. Mum picked up some of those fancy paint cards which are fifty shades of cream. I know how a polar bear feels now – snow as far as the eye can see. I don't suppose you do house calls, do you?'

Lorna swilled out the teapot and dropped two tea-bags in. Mary had zero rules for her gallery but strict rules about brewing tea: no bags in cups, always warm the pot. 'So is this for you? You're doing up the farmhouse?'

As soon as she said it, she knew he wasn't. She wanted him to say it – or maybe she wanted him to tell her Gabe had it wrong.

'No, the holiday lets.'

She fiddled with the tea caddy. *I'll have to say something. I'll have to say something.* Lorna hated scenes; she hated unpleasantness. But her friendship with Sam had been so pure, the one solid trust in her life, like Ryan and Jess. She couldn't believe he could abandon his kindness so easily. It made her question everything she'd thought of him, every standard she'd held other men to since.

The words burst out. 'I hear you've got another cottage to make over soon.'

The kettle boiled and clicked off, and silence filled the small room. The only noise was Rudy, breathing heavily in the basket under the desk. He didn't get up and bark at Sam, but then he never had.

Sam sighed. 'I hear you bumped into Gabriel.'

'I did,' Lorna said. Her voice sounded clipped, not her own, and she didn't like it. 'He didn't seem particularly bothered about making an old lady homeless. But still, it's going to be a lovely cottage for someone. Lovely garden, if he doesn't Tarmac it over for cars.'

She swept towards the fridge to get the milk, her stomach churning. In her head she saw the big pan of fudge Mum used to make on birthdays and on holidays, the molten sugar bubbling like lava, sweet but so dangerously hot a premature taste could blister your tongue for days. Lorna's indignation boiled and plopped, great bubbles of it rising and bursting. Waiting to burn her.

'Wait, what? Making an old lady homeless?' He caught her arm as she swept past.

Lorna turned. She didn't want to shake off the hand; she didn't want a row. But she had gone too far to stop. 'Joyce has to leave her house. She's in reasonable health, apart from her eyesight, so there can only be one reason – her lease has been ended by landlords who've made no secret of the fact that they want her home back to put on the market. I think that's a lame way to treat a tenant of her age. I told Gabe that. And he *laughed*.'

'I'd agree with you, if it were true,' he said.

'What's not true? That Joyce is leaving? I can assure you she is.'

'No, that we made her leave.'

'Is that just semantics? "We didn't make her leave, we just made it really clear that we'd prefer to let her house out for more money"?'

'No, Lorna.' Sam seemed impatient now. 'Joyce ended her tenancy. She wrote to us, informing us that she wanted to break her rental agreement. She gave us a month's notice.'

She had started to pour the tea, to give herself something to do, but her hands were shaking and she put the pot down. 'Joyce ended the tenancy?'

'Yes. Last week. She didn't tell you?'

Lorna faltered. 'She didn't go into detail. She's a private lady.'

'Right.' Sam regarded her critically. 'So you let rip at Gabriel because you assumed we were bastards and Joyce was some helpless old dear who needs protecting from everyone else? I'm not saying he isn't an arse, but did you really think we'd do that?'

By *we*, he meant *I*. His eyes said it very clearly.

'It's not unreasonable. You more or less told me you were trying to get her out! Round at your house!'

'*Mum* said that. I didn't. Why did you think I'd bother fitting that bloody safety equipment if I was planning to kick her out? Wouldn't I just have given her notice then? When I could have got the social worker – what's his name? – to say the place wasn't safe?'

They were glaring at each other. Lorna felt the surging, sweeping sensation in the pit of her stomach, the danger of the wrong words coming, and ruining everything, and she felt herself scrabbling to keep it at bay. She had no tactics for rows. They'd never heard a cross word at home; Cathy and Peter had never so much as raised their voices with each other.

Sam broke first. 'You seem to think that *I'm* . . .' He ran a hand through his hair, struggling with his patience. 'Lorna, I wish you didn't do this.'

'Do what?'

'*Assume* stuff. I'm doing my best here. I've got to support five people and ten workers on a farm that basically *can't* make money the way it used to, I've got a family who think I'm a townie snob because I don't have any tattoos and won't go lamping, and I've got no one to ask for help because my best mate moved miles away and has turned out to be a complete—'

He stopped, his expression so forlorn that her anger faded.

'Did you speak to Ryan?' Lorna asked. 'When he was here at the art event?'

Sam shrugged. 'Sort of. Wasn't really the right time, was it? How's Jess?'

One brief FaceTime conversation about Hattie's exams and Milo's trumpet lessons, with words that said one thing and eyes that said something very different. It hurt Lorna that Jess wasn't sharing. 'She keeps saying she's fine. She's not fine.'

I'm not fine, she wanted to add. *Everything has changed, including you.*

Sam picked up his mug and stared into it, as if there might be some leaves in there with a clue. 'Sometimes,' he said, 'I think we should give up on this idea that you can ever know someone. Truly know them, I mean. Because when you think about it, don't we all have things about ourselves that we wouldn't want anyone to know? Even our best friends?'

'Maybe.' It was such a sad thing to say. Even though Lorna thought it was true, she couldn't bear to hear Sam say it. It suggested he thought he didn't know her, and that she didn't know him, not properly. 'Real friends probably understand us better than we understand ourselves, I reckon.'

Sam knew her, and her secrets. He sensed the empty space behind her that she was too scared to turn back and look at, forcing her forward because there was no past to prop her up any more, no family to tell her who she was. Sam knew about Jess, and the shattering repercussions of that time, and Lorna had thought she knew him, and his secret that made him different from the other Osborne farmers.

But now? Did she? It caught her under the ribs. She didn't. That was what Sam was trying to tell her. That she didn't know *him*, just like they didn't know Ryan. He was reminding her they'd lived different lives since those adolescent moments on the hay bales, that they'd grown into different people.

Sam looked at her squarely. 'I think people just see the person they always have done. The person they want you to be. And then they're disappointed.'

Lorna met his gaze, crushed. In her head, she saw Joyce's bright yellow mountains from the art event, spiking into the whiteness, separating and linking, separating and linking.

'Are you talking about me?' The voice was brave, not hers. She didn't know where it had come from. Her hands hung like dead weights by her side. Please take them, she thought, but he didn't.

For a second, Sam seemed on the verge of opening his heart. His eyes were miles away. Then he managed a broken smile. 'No, Lorna,' he said. 'It's not always about you. Now can we talk about paintings? I've got eight rooms to fill with the best local art you can supply.'

Chapter Twenty-Three

'This is all you're taking? Are you sure?'

Lorna looked uncertainly at the collection of bags and boxes in front of Joyce. One carpet bag like Mary Poppins's, plump under its zip but not bursting. One plastic crate of books and photograph albums. Her knitting bag, with balls of wool neatly lined up along the top like rainbow peas in a pod. Another crate, of paintings wrapped in throws. And Bernard.

Bernard wagged his tail. He made up approximately one-fifth of Joyce's worldly goods.

Was that enough? It seemed so little, she thought, for a life as long and creative as Joyce's.

'I should think so. You're only giving me one room, aren't you? Not the whole flat.' Joyce peered over her glasses. 'Unless you're angling for some furniture?'

'No!' Lorna burst out, then realised Joyce was trying to make light of this strange day. 'No,' she said again, with the best smile she could muster up under Joyce's scrutiny. 'I just want you to be comfortable.'

A couple of volunteers from the day centre had packed up Joyce's house, and Lorna had come from the gallery to help. Most of the hard work was already done, but even so the half-filleted house had stirred strange feelings inside her, lifting up memories like the dust floating around from unhooked paintings and emptied shelves. It had reminded her – or not reminded her, since she hadn't been there – of the grim task Jess had tackled on her own after their father died. Jess had packed up Peter's possessions from the house that had been his final home. By the time Lorna had arrived, her parents' life had been tidied away, stacked in brown boxes at the back of the storage unit the Protheros kept for Ryan's barbecue equipment and the junk they couldn't fit in the garage.

They were supposed to have gone through the boxes by now, but neither Lorna nor Jess could face it. At this rate, it would be a job for Hattie, Milo and Tyra.

Lorna stared at Joyce's half-empty bookshelf by the fireplace, the irregular gaps like missing teeth, and felt a similar hollow. Gaps, where a memory should be. At the time, she'd been relieved Jess had spared her the experience of handling their parents' personal belongings, but soon after Jess had revealed that there wasn't much to do; Peter had taken it upon himself to shred and burn most of their private papers himself, to 'save them the bother'. Their parents' love letters and secrets had been reduced to ashes. It had felt like a third bereavement, one neither of them had expected.

'Are you all right?' Joyce enquired. 'If you're being glum on my account, don't be. I've always enjoyed a good sort-out. This is therapeutic.' She waved a dismissive hand. 'It's only *things*, when all's said and done. When Bernie died, I gave away so much stuff to the charity shop they practically had to open a second branch. And it was exactly what he'd have done for me.'

'My parents were the same,' said Lorna. 'I wish they'd left something for us to keep.'

'It wouldn't be what you'd want,' said Joyce.

The sight of the empty armchair opposite Joyce's was too much for Lorna. She put her hand on the back of it, where the leather was worn from decades of Bernard's head rubbing the back as he nodded off in front of the fire.

'But what about your chairs?' she asked. 'Don't you want to bring these? We can make room.'

Keir had just walked back into the sitting room, fresh from jamming a large oil painting into the back of Lorna's car. 'We can take Joyce's chairs, can't we?'

'What? Into your flat? No way. I can't carry them up two flights of stairs.' He eyed the smooth arms and high backs, and rubbed his neck. His face was sheeny with sweat above his dark T-shirt. 'I've got a sports injury.'

Joyce regarded him incredulously. 'What sport do you do?'

He affected not to hear her. 'And they won't go in your car.'

'I'm sure you can think of something. I'll make a cup of tea,' said Joyce, 'while the kettle's still here.'

'Wow.' Keir boggled as she headed to the kitchen. 'She's never offered to make tea before.'

Lorna watched Joyce's progress down her dark hall, proud but noticeably shufflier than the first time she'd visited.

'I just wish she wasn't leaving so much.' She gestured at the low sideboard, with the old phone and the vase of paintbrushes. Each piece was dotted with yellow Post-it notes: *storage, charity shop.* 'I think we should make sure she has her chairs at least.'

'Both of them?'

Lorna fixed him with a look. 'Yes. Both of them.'

Keir raised his eyebrows.

'She's already leaving her house,' she hissed back. 'Don't make her leave her memories too.'

'But isn't that her plan? She *wants* to leave. Perhaps her memories aren't tied up in furniture.' He glanced over his shoulder to check Joyce was still in the kitchen. 'We see this a lot when older people move into care. Joyce has made a decision, Lorna. We have to respect that. Just because you'd take everything doesn't mean she wants to.

'Residents get a fair bit of space in Butterfields,' he went on, in a low voice. 'It's not like some of these homes. The rooms are quite large. Space for . . .' He looked around the sitting room, scanning what was left. 'Well, a sofa, definitely.'

That didn't sound very big to Lorna. But she'd seen the website, and had to concede that as old folks' homes went, few were as leafy, wood-panelled or dog-friendly as the one-time country estate of some Birmingham mill owner, ten miles out of town. It was just so unfair that Joyce and Bernard couldn't see out their time together *here* . . .

She caught herself. 'So how long will this have to be in storage? When's the next space likely to come up?'

Keir lifted and dropped his shoulders. 'Between you and me, no idea. I've done everything I can to get Joyce bumped up the waiting list, piled it on about how she can't be separated from her dog, et cetera, but without wanting to be brutal, it's about waiting for a current resident to, um . . .' He still didn't seem comfortable talking about death, despite it being a near weekly occurrence in his placement.

'Die,' said Lorna baldly.

'Yes.'

The idea hung between them. Lorna thought about Betty, and the other residents she'd visited in the hospice who had been so vivid to begin with, then suddenly faded, faded, and then one day, a new face, a new set of post-war wedding photos, a new smell of medicines and a much larger house condensed into a handful of ornaments. But Joyce wasn't fading just yet. Not while she was fanning that unexpected spark of creativity into their joint masterpiece.

'The thing about Butterfields,' Keir burst out, 'is that it's so bloody nice people go there and never leave, because why would you? It gives them a new lease of life! They end up staying for ever!'

Lorna forced herself to smile; no, her flat would keep Joyce bright and sharp, upright in her chair, needles clicking, sharp eyes nibbling up details.

'Don't worry, I'm sure something will come up before too long,' he went on, misreading her tense expression. 'I've got Tiffany on the dog-walking rota up there, so she can tip us the wink if anyone has to be moved out for . . . closer care. And in the meantime Joyce will still get regular care visits from us, so if you need any additional support then just ask – anything you need.'

'Thanks,' said Lorna. 'I think we'll be fine. Joyce is pretty independent and, as you say, she might not be with me that long. If a room comes up.'

Keir glanced over his shoulder again, his expression shifting to an 'off the record' one. 'Can I ask . . .' He hesitated. 'Do you know *why* she's made this decision? Why she's decided to leave now? And come to you? We don't know, in case you were wondering.'

Lorna had been hoping he might tell her. 'No, I don't. Maybe it's like you say – wanting to retain control, leaving while it's still her choice. The landlords definitely want the house back but Sam's adamant this was her decision.'

Keir nodded. 'I guess there's always the company. And being in the gallery, near the art?'

'That too.' Lorna had wondered, privately, if Joyce had somehow intuited that she was having trouble making the sums add up at the gallery – if she'd guessed some rent money would come in handy.

But she wasn't paying rent. She was paying in pictures, pictures worth far more than any rent Lorna could charge.

'Are you discussing me?' Joyce appeared in the doorway holding a tray of tea things. The cups rattled ominously and Keir sprang forward to take them off her before they crashed to the floor.

'Not at all,' said Lorna.

'Oh. Why not? You should be,' said Joyce and pretended to look offended.

It took two journeys to move Joyce's belongings into Lorna's flat. The second journey was for Bernard, who couldn't be fitted in with everything else, and Joyce herself.

When Lorna pulled up outside Rooks Hall, the sun had started to set, and shadows were falling over the front of the house, dulling the windows like weary eyes. Something moved – a slow flash of red appearing behind the green of the bushes – and Lorna realised dog and mistress were in the garden. Joyce was moving slowly around the flower beds, touching the rose petals and pulling the tendrils of honeysuckle to her face to smell them one last time, while Bernard snuffled around the undergrowth in a more subdued manner than his usual frenzied dashing. Joyce was picking a few flowers as she went, shaping them into a fluttering posy.

They were saying goodbye, thought Lorna, and a hand slowly squeezed her heart. She let them wander for a moment in the last sunrays of the day, willing the dark shape of a gardener to appear from the walls to join them. She'd always wanted to see a ghost, one summoned by love and memory. But nothing came. Two swallows dipped and dived around the eaves, and Joyce moved slowly through the garden in her tweed skirt.

Lorna breathed in, and her nose filled with the evening grass-and-cows smell that she and Jess had decided smelled like holidays when they'd first moved here. It still smelled like holidays, and when she closed her eyes it was easy to go back. Far enough to remember uncomplicated pleasure in the warmth of the sun on bare skin, and the salmon-pink sky and no school in the morning. Mum and Dad singing, before Mum stopped singing and Dad looked at them with that sadness etched in his face.

Goodbye, she thought, and didn't know whom she was saying goodbye to.

The next day, Joyce was already up, dressed in a pale blouse and skirt, sitting at the kitchen table with a big sketch pad when Lorna went down to make breakfast.

The felt-tip pens were arranged in a fan in front of her, and in the centre of the pad Joyce had drawn a daisy. Simple and bright, with a yellow centre like a sun.

'Oh, that looks very knittable.' Lorna paused at the door. Joyce was staring at the paper, frowning with concentration, a pink pen in one hand. 'Everything all right?'

'Yes, yes. I'm just trying to work out . . . how you get this into the computer?' She touched the thick paper.

'We scan it, I think. But don't worry about that.' Lorna

gazed at the flower over Joyce's shoulder as she clicked the kettle on. The daisy was beautiful, not neat but confident. Yellow, a hopeful colour. 'Caitlin's found someone who can convert it into a pattern, then we can print it, and hand the pattern out to volunteers to knit. If we knit the first ones – you, me, Caitlin and Tiff – then we can hold a launch party to get some interest going in the town. Calum can get the press along, invite all his cronies.'

'Sounds awful,' said Joyce cheerfully. She pointed at her drawing. 'Is this right?'

'It's lovely.'

'Good. I'm rather rusty.' Joyce allowed herself a smile. 'I thought a daisy chain would be symbolic – of the community element. And we could drape them over railings, they'd be easier to move around.' She had clearly been thinking about the practicalities of the project. 'I'd like to knit wild flowers, as much as planted flower beds. They're so important, much more so than cultivated varieties, for the bees and butterflies. And appropriate, when you think about it – for what we're doing.' She looked up with a smile, as if the neatness pleased her. 'Wild seeds, planting beauty in pavements and so on.'

'Was that something your husband was interested in? Wild flowers?' Lorna asked casually, making the tea without turning around. Outside, the town was starting to come to life, the post van making its way down the street as the bus emptied a load of early office workers outside Greggs.

Joyce started to add delicate pink tips to the daisy petals. 'Yes. He was furious about the plight of the bumblebees. Do you think we could add some bees to the project?'

'Of course.'

'I like the idea of art pollinating beauty through the town. Yes. How apt. Bernard would laugh at that – me knitting bees and calling it art.'

Lorna put a slice of toast down in front of Joyce, and wondered if, for once, Joyce was tacitly encouraging a conversation about her past.

She had carried in Joyce's personal crate of possessions and couldn't help noticing the square photograph on top: a wide-eyed young Joyce with centre-parted hair, holding a tiny baby while a bearded man encircled them both with his arms, wrapping a thick band of Aran knitted jumper around them. They seemed to be by the seaside. The baby had his mother's distinctive eyes, and his father's gappy grin. Ronan. And Bernard. It was as if Joyce's life suddenly had a trail now, a faint vapour trail of a past.

Joyce seemed relaxed, and Lorna opened her mouth to ask other questions – where did Bernard learn to garden? What was his favourite flower? – but the phone rang, and she excused herself to answer it.

'It's me, I'm glad I caught you,' said Sam.

'Oh, hello.' She turned and saw Joyce starting a new sheet of paper. Two drawings, before lunch. Wow.

'Is it too early?' he went on. There was mooing in the background; Lorna guessed he was in the cattle sheds. Well, she hoped he was.

'No, I'm just having breakfast. What's up?' She tensed, not wanting to talk about Rooks Hall with Joyce there.

'I had a call last night from Ryan. He's . . . Well, I think we need to talk.'

Lorna had been dreading this. It had all been too weird at the bandstand event, everyone pretending nothing had happened. It couldn't last. Not even Jess could keep the pieces of her family from flying apart under this sort of strain.

'What's happened?'

Her mind raced through possibilities. I bet Hattie's got in touch with Pearl, she thought. Or Ryan's trying to force a meeting with Jess and . . . what was her name, Pearl's mum?

A guilty panic gripped her. *I should have done this. I should have been more help to Jess.* Even now Ryan and Jess and Sam were sorting it out between them.

There was a deep rumbling moo, some metallic clattering, and a man shouted cheerily at the cows. It sounded like Sam's dad. 'Look, I don't want to get into it now,' said Sam. 'Can I meet you for a drink later? The Jolly Fox? About six?'

'Sure.' Lorna turned; Tiffany had wandered in, and was opening the fridge in search of her probiotic yogurts. She and Joyce exchanged morning pleasantries as if she'd always been there, as Rudy and Bernard circled the table in the hope of toast.

'Thanks. See you then.' He hung up, just as the mooing increased.

'That Sam?' asked Tiff, whirling round to put marmalade on the table.

'Yes.' Lorna stood gripping the phone. 'Wants to talk to me about Ryan.'

'Oh dear.' Tiffany made a wincing face. 'I meant to say, you know Sam's granny's in Butterfields? I'm walking her collie, Wispa, once a week. Nice old thing. Gets all the gossip.'

'Well, don't believe everything you hear.' It whipped

335

out of Lorna before she had time to think. Gossip. It was a trigger word, always had been.

Tiff looked surprised. 'Hey, I just meant . . . I thought she might have some inside track on Sam.'

'Like what?' Lorna knew like what. Whether he'd had a girlfriend back in London. Why he'd left his job so easily to come back to the farm. What he really thought about her. All the questions she wanted to ask, but which actually didn't even matter now. He wasn't staying. That kiss had meant nothing, probably a water-testing move to see if she was up for something casual before he went back to his London life.

The thought stung her, and it showed in her face.

Tiffany held up her hands. 'I seem to have started this morning badly. Would you like me to come downstairs and try again?'

Lorna shook herself. 'No,' she said, with an apologetic smile. 'I want you to show me how to use the scanner, please.'

Sam was sitting by the table they'd met at before when Lorna walked into the pub at six. He'd come straight from the farm, judging by his jeans and shirt, but his hair was damp from a recent shower.

He waved and pointed at the cider he'd ordered already for her, and even though she reminded herself that she didn't care, Lorna felt a little self-conscious as she made her way through the tables to join him, aware of his eyes on her.

She sat down quickly, before he could get up and kiss her cheek – or not. 'So what's happened?'

Sam pushed back on his chair and raked his hands

through his hair. 'Ryan called yesterday wanting to know if he could crash in my flat in London for a few weeks.'

Lorna took a long sip of cider; it was cold and good. So Sam had kept his flat there. He'd never intended to stay; Ryan must have known that from the start. Everyone knew things but her. Nothing changed.

She raised an eyebrow. 'Don't *you* need your flat – for your new job?'

He didn't rise to it. 'Maybe. A friend's staying there at the moment. The main thing is, it sounds as if Jess has kicked Ryan out. She hasn't said anything to you?'

Lorna shook her head. 'Jess's whole life is her family. She'd do anything to keep it together. If he's moved out then I'd say it's his choice.'

'There's something else, though. It's not breaking a confidence; Ryan would want you to know, since Hattie's been spending so much time with you lately . . .' He gazed at Lorna, and the concern in his eyes melted her attempts at coolness. 'Ryan told me he thinks Hattie and Pearl have been meeting up in secret.'

She groaned. 'How's *that* going to help?'

'It's not. Ryan doesn't know for sure, he only suspects, but Jess doesn't know, and when she finds out . . .' He shook his head. They both knew what would happen when Jess found out. 'Don't be mad at Hattie. She's just a kid, she's got no idea what she's doing.'

'I'm not. But you want me to tell Jess? You want me to let her know that her husband's been confiding in his mate, who's been confiding in me, who's decided she ought to know what her daughter's been up to behind her back?' Lorna looked disbelieving. 'No way, Sam. Tell

Ryan he has to talk to his daughter. Then talk to his wife. We can't get involved like that.'

Sam slumped back in his chair. 'Maybe you're right. All this "he said, she said" stuff . . . But I don't know how else it's going to get discussed. Ryan says Jess is stonewalling him, trying to pretend it's not happening. I think we need to sit them down and make them talk properly, you and me.'

'What?' Lorna hadn't expected that. *You and me.*

'We're the only people who really know them. I don't want to get stuck in the middle, taking sides with my two oldest mates.' Sam seemed different tonight, Lorna thought, as if this upheaval of his own past was upsetting for him, discovering nothing had been as it seemed. He wasn't as self-assured as he'd seemed lately. That, or maybe his job search hadn't turned out as he'd planned . . .

'I need to think about this.' Lorna reached for her bag. She'd downed the cider quicker than she meant to. 'You want another?'

'Thanks. Pint of Butty.'

When she came back with the drinks, Sam was checking something on his phone; a frown was creasing his forehead. He stopped when she put his pint down, and said, 'So, what's happening with you? Any new art events on the horizon?'

'Joyce has moved in with me.'

'So I heard!' He winced. 'Sorry, my attempt to change the subject to something less controversial clearly failed there. Please can we not argue about that again? What's happening in the gallery? Any new submissions I should know about, as an official collector?'

Lorna had to forgive him; his expression was so apologetic, and she didn't have the energy to argue either.

Instead she got out her own phone. 'So . . .' she said, aware that she sounded exactly like Calum Hardy, 'this is my Knitting Collective Competition project! This is what Joyce sketched for us today, and this is what it looks like as a knitting pattern . . .'

Sam leaned over to get a better look, and Lorna breathed in shampoo, and warm skin, the old smell of him. She fought back the temptation to lean in and draw a deep breath.

'Wow,' he said. 'You've knitted a whole car-sized tea cosy?'

'No, that's a photo from the internet.' She swiped through some images Caitlin had sent her 'for knitspiration', explaining the project as she went, until she finally reached her own proto-poppy. 'This is what I did.'

'Oh. Er, OK.'

As he was trying to find something positive to say about her knobbly knitting, a text message from Calum appeared at the top of the screen, barging its way over the photo.

Can we talk? I've got some exciting news . . . !!!

Lorna was surprised to see that: Calum didn't normally text her out of office hours.

'Calum?' Sam looked quizzical. He leaned back. 'Boyfriend?'

'No. He's on the council's cultural services team, I'm working with him on the yarnbomb project. Calum's actually an interesting guy, studied printmaking at art school.' Too much information. Shut up, Lorna. 'Probably working late . . .'

'Must be very keen on your project. Or maybe you?'

'It's the project – there's money in it.' Lorna knew she was blushing.

The phone pinged, Calum again. *But need to talk re locations. Call me?*

'I think he needs to speak to you,' said Sam, deadpan.

'Well, I don't want to speak to him right now,' said Lorna, and even as she said it, she knew it wasn't coming out right.

They regarded each other over the table, then both looked down.

'Anyway . . .' Sam pushed his chair back, his pint only half-drunk, and tapped his phone. 'I've got to get back. Dad's entering his cows in a competition this weekend. I said I'd . . . do whatever you need to do with stage cows. Blow dry them, or paint their hooves or whatever.'

'Good luck with that.'

'So what do you want me to do about Ryan? Nothing? Really?'

'Let's see what happens,' said Lorna. 'I'll ask Hattie to help me out in the gallery with this knitting project. She might tell me herself.' She pulled a face. 'It's not ideal but Jess is stubborn. She won't ask for help till she's ready.'

Sam shrugged. 'Fine. But keep me in the loop.'

'Course.' She smiled, but as he was getting ready to go her stomach flipped over, and she held her breath – would he give her a kiss goodbye?

'Night, Lorna. I'm glad we could talk about this. I feel better about the whole thing.' He leaned over, and there it was: a simple, brotherly brush of her cheek, and for some irrational reason, it felt like more of a rejection than no kiss at all.

Chapter Twenty-Four

Up until Lorna was thirteen, birthdays were the one day in the family calendar when she and Jess could absolutely guarantee their parents' full attention, and for that reason, she'd always loved them.

Since Lorna's birthday was at the end of July, in the school holidays, Dad was around and made a point of taking her somewhere special, just him and her. They both liked train journeys so the trip often started at the station, and ended with an ice cream. At home, Mum baked a cake – often with Jess supervising since Cathy could be a bit vague about timings – and they ate whatever Lorna chose for supper, however outlandish.

Best of all, every year Mum drew Lorna a birthday card with her on the front. Lorna kept them all together in her memory box: they started with a cheerful baby, growing into chubby-kneed toddlerdom, then stretching out into hair-chewing, blushing childhood, until the age of thirteen, Lorna's final card. On it, she was laughing in her wrinkled over-the-knee socks and plaid shirt, a teenager at last.

Everything had changed after that summer, when Jess announced her pregnancy and Cathy and Peter went into a kind of shock. There were no more hand-drawn cards after that.

Jess did her best to keep it going into adulthood, even when their parents withdrew into their own world; she had carefully maintained birthday rituals for her own family. Ryan's pizza night was just one. Hattie had a charm bracelet that she'd been adding charms to since she was three; Jess treated herself to a new Emma Bridgewater mug on hers. She tried to impose the same on Lorna, stitching her determinedly into her family tapestry of traditions.

'You have to do something,' she urged Lorna, a week or so before her birthday. 'Even if it's just afternoon tea!'

She'd chosen a bad time to ring. It was VAT night in the back office. Lorna had spent ages trying to make the books balance, until in desperation she'd checked her online banking, just in case someone had accidentally put ten thousand pounds into her account. No one had. Instead, she'd had to transfer another thousand from her savings to pay for the red bills. Her savings were a safety net, outside the money she'd earmarked for the gallery, but there wasn't much and she hated seeing them dwindle. 'Jess, it would be nice but I can't afford it.'

'I'll come to you then, with a cake. Come on,' she urged her. 'Ryan's taking the kids to his mum's next weekend.'

Oh, right, thought Lorna. That's the reason. Jess hated being apart from her children; she'd be looking for something to take her mind off what they might be up to. 'All three?'

'No.' A pause. 'Hattie refused to go. She'll be coming with me. She'd love to see you!'

Hattie had spent quite a few weekends helping out in the gallery, now that the knitting was underway. She seemed keen to help, and Lorna had wondered if maybe the hours on the train were a useful chunk of privacy for the teenager.

She swung on the chair, taking care not to kick Rudy, who was by her feet. 'It'd be nice, but I need to keep this place open as much as possible. We're really not taking enough to justify a day off.'

'Didn't you budget for bad weeks?'

'Of course I did. Maybe I didn't realise how quiet Longhampton could be. I've got enough to cover basic expenses to the end of the year but . . .' Saying it made it real. 'I can't look beyond that,' she finished unhappily.

Lorna was over halfway through her year, and even with her front page bandstand appearance in the local paper, a new website and artists swapping galleries so she could sell their work, she was still barely covering her costs. Sam's big order had helped, but that was last month now, and she'd sold little else since. Two more invoices from artists had arrived on her desk that morning. Money came in, then it went straight out, far faster than Mary's accounts had suggested. The thought of having to give up filled Lorna with real sadness, and now a fear that she would be letting Joyce down, just when she'd come back round to the idea of creating art again.

'I can lend you—' Jess started but Lorna wouldn't let her say what she knew was coming next.

'No,' she said. 'I worked it out. I said I'd give it a year. And after that . . . I'll just have to go back to Anthony and see if he can give me some freelance hours for the charity. I can maybe do both.'

The words felt like raindrops on her hopes, cold and heavy spots of reality spoiling them.

343

'All the more reason to let me bring your birthday to you,' said Jess. 'You need treating.'

Lorna gave in. What else did she have planned for her birthday weekend? She couldn't go away – she couldn't afford to. Jess clearly needed a distraction. Sam had already dropped a hint that he was away that weekend, as if she should care. 'If you're sure . . .'

'I'm sure.' Jess sounded buoyant. 'And is there anything you'd like?'

Three more hours in the day?

Customers who bought more than just one card?

A massive win on the Premium Bonds?

'Surprise me,' said Lorna.

When the big day rolled around, Lorna's birthday got off to a better start than nearly every previous one with the arrival of breakfast in bed, made by Tiffany, and special birthday greetings from Rudy and Bernard – who might just have been following the smell of the toast.

'Sorry it's so little,' she apologised as Lorna unwrapped her present. 'Soon as I get a proper job I'll upgrade it.'

'Why?' Lorna held the multi-coloured wooden needles up to the light – they were fabulously flamboyant. Unicorn needles. 'These are amazing! Where did you find them?'

'Butterfields. You get a different class of knitting fanatic up there.' Tiff tapped her nose and handed her the post, discarding a couple of obvious bills. 'Drink your tea, your sister's on her way.'

Lorna scrabbled through the letters – two fliers for other galleries' summer events, an enquiry from an artist about hanging space, and three cards, there was one from Hattie, one from Tyra and Milo. Jess always sent the maximum number of cards to compensate for the minimal family available to send birthday greetings.

The third card was, to her surprise, from Calum. It had a perfect knitted fuschia on it, created by a modern artist she hadn't heard of, but now felt very intimidated by.

Nothing from Sam.

Well, were you expecting it? Lorna asked herself, and tried to hear a no in her head. Why would he post it, anyway? Much more likely to drop by with it.

Joyce, moving slowly but with determination, was getting the dogs' breakfast ready when Lorna walked in. 'Happy birthday!' she said, and pointed to the card and package on the table. 'No need for excitement, it's just a token.'

'Why are you both apologising? This is way more than I usually get,' said Lorna. Joyce's card was a folded page from her sketchbook, featuring an unmistakeable Rudy, sitting on the sofa with his long nose draped over the arm, gazing out of the frame.

'Waiting for you,' Joyce explained.

Lorna smiled, touched by the observation. 'You really shouldn't have,' she said, unwrapping the small parcel, and then drew in a breath at what was inside.

Joyce had given her a small, unframed watercolour of a white cottage which glowed like an opal under a peaceful turquoise sky. Lorna recognised it from the crate of unframed personal pieces she'd brought from Rooks Hall, the paintings she couldn't live without.

Lorna loved it. Its stillness made her feel she could slip inside the front door and be perfectly safe.

She looked up. 'Oh, Joyce, you shouldn't have. Is this . . . ?'

'Our seaside house on the cliff. It wasn't always stormy.'

'It's beautiful. Are you sure?'

'Well, I know the larger painting struck a chord with you.' Joyce poured herself a cup of tea into the china breakfast cup. 'I'd like you to have it – outside our monthly rent agreement, naturally. This is for you. For your birthday.'

Lorna wanted to go over to hug her, to thank her for the kind thought as well as the generous gift, but something stopped her. Joyce still had a force field of reserve around her bony shoulders. It was part of their understanding that Lorna didn't try to break it.

'Thank you.' She hoped her eyes spoke for her heart. 'I will treasure this for ever.'

'Good,' said Joyce, and then peered out of the window to the street below. 'I think that's your sister arriving, by the way.'

Jess and Hattie clumped up the stairs laden with bags. As usual with Jess, it looked as if she were staying for three weeks, not overnight.

'This is for you,' Jess said, handing her a heavy and smelly bag from Lush. 'Picked by your niece and nephew, paid for with their own pocket money.'

'And this is from us.' Hattie gave her a long bottle bag. 'Put it in the fridge for later.'

Jess seemed eager to investigate the town she'd left behind in such a hurry nearly seventeen years ago. They spent the morning wandering around the shops, investigating the new ones and boring Hattie senseless with stories of what had been there before. Then after an early tea, Jess announced that as a special treat she would be taking her little sister out on the town, starting with a cider and black at the Jolly Fox and finishing 'who knows where!'

'Don't wait up!' she informed Hattie, who was being left with Tiffany and a takeaway menu for the evening.

'Don't show yourselves up,' muttered Hattie, from behind her laptop.

Jess seemed quite impressed with the improvements at their erstwhile teenage hang-out, and after the promised cider and black, she ordered a bottle of Prosecco since it was on offer. They left shortly after in high dudgeon when some hopeful Young Farmers sent drinks over 'to the MILFs in the corner', though not before Jess had downed them in one.

She was drinking more than usual, Lorna noticed. Jess had never been one for getting drunk; she liked being in control too much. The strain of the past few months must be getting to her.

'Where next?' Jess asked, outside the pub. Her face glinted in the street light with the shimmery shadow the baby-faced assistant had applied for her, as part of their joint makeovers on the beauty counter. Flakes caught on the faint new lines around her eyes. 'Is that club on Wye Street still open?'

'It's luxury flats.'

'Then it'll have to be the bandstand,' said Jess, solemnly. 'Via Tesco. Got your dodgy ID?'

'Yeah,' said Lorna, and Jess tucked her arm into hers and started marching them down the high street.

It was a warm evening, and the town's Saturday night

chatter and laughter drifted through open windows and doors, underpinned with faint music from cars and a siren in the distance.

Lorna picked out the bandstand as soon as they wandered into the park: its peaked roof silhouetted against the strings of silvery lights that looped between the old lamps like necklaces. Beds of wallflowers wafted their gentle clouds of fragrance, and as they crunched along the gravel, the smell faded into a swirl of colour, like a breeze breathing across the edges of her thoughts.

'I wonder what colour you would paint that smell,' she said.

Jess looked at her out of the corner of her eye. 'It's purple,' she said. 'Dur.'

'Really? Not a suede brown?' She inhaled spicy wallflowers, cut grass, warm earth. 'Or a dusty ochre?'

'Purple.' Jess clattered up the steps to the bandstand and sank on to a bench inside, putting her feet up against the next one. Her heels hooked against the wood, and she groaned as the weight came off her toes. 'Oof, when did wine stop making heels bearable?'

Lorna sat down next to her and popped the mini bottles of champagne they'd bought. Extravagant, but Jess had insisted. She was glad; it felt like a celebration of them, as much as her birthday. Her and her big sister, together on the bandstand.

'Happy birthday, baby sis.' Jess clinked her bottle.

'Happy birthday,' Lorna echoed. They looked like a Beryl Cook picture – the two of them in a moonlit bandstand, sipping champagne in their glitter.

Jess leaned back against the bench. 'Aaah. This is nice. Are you having a nice birthday?'

'Yes,' said Lorna. 'I am.'

'I used to envy your birthdays with Dad. You got to spend the whole day with him. Mine were always during term time – the best I got was a late night and a choice of takeaway.' She looked nostalgic. 'Plus Mum always made you a cake. She never bothered for me.'

'She never baked for you because you *demanded* one of those giant French fancies every year. Anyway, if we're talking about envy, I always used to envy you for those baby photos of you and them – everyone looks way happier than they do in mine.'

Jess turned to her, the bleak face of experience. 'I was four by then. I was bringing my own brand of hell with me on top of sleepless nights with you. No wonder everyone looks pissed off. I look murderous in Tyra's baby photos. And I adored her.'

Lorna shrugged. 'They did their best. I just wonder, watching you with your kids, whether . . .' It felt traitorous to even say it; Lorna had thought it for years, though, 'whether they really enjoyed being parents. Whether they preferred being together, on their own.'

Jess didn't reply at once.

And that, thought Lorna, silently proved her point: better not to get into it at all.

'It's a big trial of who are you, parenting,' she said. 'I can't imagine not being a mum now, though. I miss mine so much when they're not with me.' Jess was tipsy enough to be getting maudlin; there was a thickness in her speech. 'I know you think I'm being weak, but it would kill me, having to hand my babies over every weekend. If Ryan and I . . .' She couldn't bring herself to say it.

'Have you talked about that?'

'About what?'

'Splitting up.'

'No. I don't dare start the conversation.' Jess traced the ghosts of old initials carved under the gloss paint. You couldn't obliterate the past completely round here. 'But I can't trust a single word he says any more. He says he's going to the shops; I think, *Are you?* Are you going via Erin's house? He says he's in Manchester for work; I check the phone bill for area codes. That's not me. That's not *him*. He's turned me into someone I don't know.'

Years of car cleaning, boring-jumper wearing, regular-as-clockwork bin-putting-out, thought Lorna, did it count for nothing?

'Ryan's been a great husband for seventeen years, Jess. This is something he did once – *years* ago.'

'But it's the secrecy!' She shook her head; it wasn't in the deal that Ryan could behave in an unpredictable way. 'He met up with this girl, and he didn't tell me. For weeks! He let Hattie keep his dirty secret! It only makes me question what else I don't know about him. My Ryan is someone else's dad. Someone else has been in our life this whole time and I didn't know. I feel as if we've been burgled.'

Lorna watched her expression. Jess seemed aggrieved, as if she'd been tricked, rather than betrayed. Security, that's what she'd wanted more than anything from her life. The security of knowing her own little family loved her and she loved them.

'I don't know, Jess. Something about this is so Ryan.' Lorna felt her way slowly around the thoughts in her mind. 'He always tries to do the right thing, doesn't he? When you found out you were pregnant with Hattie, he never hesitated about standing by you. No teenage boy means to settle down at eighteen. I mean, you didn't either, did you? You had to give up everything.'

Lorna could remember being glued to the sofa in disbelief as Dad uncharacteristically listed exactly what Jess would be 'throwing away' – her magnificent grades, the chance of a law career, the respect of her peers, the 'best part of her life' . . . He rarely sounded like a teacher at home, but then he'd been totally headmasterly. The implication that having kids would ruin Jess's life wasn't lost on Lorna, his other daughter. 'And us, Jess,' he'd pleaded at the end. 'What about *us*?'

He hadn't specified how, exactly, an unexpected grandchild would impact on him and Mum, but the tone indicated it wouldn't be in a way they'd particularly welcome. It had shocked her. Mum's reaction had shocked her too. She'd sat there, as if she were sitting behind a thick glass screen.

Lorna had wanted to yank on her mother's sleeves, the way she had as a kid, and make her say something nice to Jess, because the sterner Dad was being, the more stubborn Jess's face had set.

'That was the end, wasn't it?' she said sadly. 'Of that chapter of our lives. You went away to teacher training college with Hattie, Dad moved schools, and then I went to uni and never came back.' Neither of them had wanted to come home, not after that. Not when they both realised their parents probably secretly preferred them not to. 'All because of an accident. And that's what it was for this other woman. An accident. It's probably reshaped her life too.'

A shadow crossed Jess's face.

'What?' said Lorna, and she sensed Jess was holding something back from her.

'It's *not* the same. I wanted Hattie,' she burst out. 'I . . . *wanted* her. This woman, she was just some one-night stand.'

'It comes down to the same thing – no one *planned* it.' As far as Lorna knew – which wasn't very far – Jess had taken matters into her own hands and acquired a covert supply of the Pill from the Family Planning Clinic. Not their GP's surgery.

But what if . . . A strange thought occurred to her, and Lorna turned to her sister. Their shared bathroom, the cabinet above the sink that smelled of mouthwash. The gold strips of tiny pills that counted off their school week, apart from the occasional one left, like a whitehead in the plastic. 'Jess, did you . . . did you deliberately get pregnant with Hattie?'

It was so far out of everything she knew about her big sister, the academic achiever, the smart, ambitious one whom everyone consulted when it came to directions and school rules. Or was it? Had that been Jess's way of making herself the centre of her own family?

Jess wasn't saying anything. She was gazing out into the park, where the moon was starting to glow in the navy sky, and her face was lost in thought, as if retracing her own steps through the past.

'*Jess?*' This put a very different slant on things.

'What? Of course I didn't,' said Jess. 'I think it's time we got back, I need to text the kids before bed.' And she pushed herself off the bench and wobbled down the bandstand steps.

*

Back at the flat, Hattie and Joyce were sitting at opposite ends of the kitchen sofa, knitting, when Jess and Lorna walked back in. The dogs had curled up between them, and there was a pot of tea on the table, the remains of the cake Jess had brought and a gift bag.

The pair of them were engrossed in their work and, for a second, Lorna had a glimpse of what her mum and Hattie might have looked like, sharing their skills. But Mum would never have helped Hattie the way Joyce did, Lorna realised; her art had been very personal.

Somewhere in the flat, an animated conversation was taking place between Tiffany and a familiar woman's voice.

Hattie put a finger up to her lips. 'Shh.'

'We have a bet,' Joyce said drily. 'Tiffany asked us to count how many times her mum said . . . what was it, Hattie?'

'Tiffany, you've lost your mind,' repeated Hattie in a perfect TOWIE accent.

'We're up to . . . seven. And she's only just told her that she's not going back to the agency.'

So the moment of truth had arrived. Lorna helped herself to cake, cut another slice for Tiffany, and followed the sound of the argument into the sitting room.

Mrs Harris was ranting on Tiffany's iPad, which was propped up against the window. She was tanned from her cruise, but any Zen calm had gone, washed away by a tidal wave of incredulity at her daughter's crazy behaviour.

'Mum,' Tiffany was pleading, 'would you listen? I'm working on an important charity project, while I build my CV . . .'

'You have thrown away the chance of a lifetime! You had a career! You had openings!'

'I had dangerously high blood pressure, Mum. I've made my mind up. This is my new career. I will pay you back for the course and—'

'You've broken our hearts, Tiff. I could have got you so many jobs on this cruise, with some smashing families.'

'I don't want to work for people who basically avoid their kids, Mum, I want to help people who actually want my help.'

'You. Have. Lost. Your. *Mind!*'

Mrs Harris looked as if she was going to explode and Tiffany made the imperceptible gesture that was their agreed sign to facilitate 'an unexpected Wi-Fi problem'.

Behind the iPad, Lorna pulled the lead out of the router and Tiff's mother's face froze, mouth wide like a letterbox.

'Well, that's done.' Tiffany's bright smile didn't completely cover her strained expression. 'Can't say it was a popular decision but . . . I've told her.'

'Good on you,' said Lorna, offering her the plate of cake. 'How long till she gets here with the sack to put over your head to bring you home?'

'Long enough for a drink. Did you get the parcel from Sam?'

'Oh? The gift bag's from Sam?' Casual. Be casual.

'He dropped it off on his way past – said he was sorry to miss you. He's off to London tonight, got an interview on Monday.' Tiff wandered back into the kitchen, flicking the kettle on as she went. 'Didn't say where. Or what. More tea, everyone?'

'Yes, please,' said Joyce and Hattie from the sofa.

Lorna tried not to think about the interview as she opened the bag and took out the parcel, wrapped in the expensive handmade paper they sold downstairs. It felt like a small painting, and part of her dreaded what Sam might have decided an appropriate painting was. Would it be another pointed verdict on What Was Art? At least he'd spent a good tenner in the gallery, just on the card and wrapping, she thought, undoing the Sellotape carefully.

'What's he given you?' Jess asked.

Lorna stared at the present in her hands. Sam had given her a home-burned CD, framed in one of Archibald's archive frames. His neat adolescent writing was all over it in Sharpie, a list of the tracks he'd downloaded and burned on to what she realised was a mix CD, exactly like the ones they'd played in Ryan's Renault while they'd driven all over Longhampton – she, Sam, Ryan and Jess, back in 2001 before . . . Before.

I burned this for your birthday years ago, he'd written in the card, and now the writing was older, less careful. *I never gave you it, so here it is now – I thought you'd appreciate it more if I put it in a frame and made it Art. Love, Sam x.*

Had he found this at home, in his old room? The thought of him taking time to choose the songs from their own favourites, make the CD, write every track so meticulously on it – it touched Lorna, and made her teenage self wriggle inside.

Each one brought a taste of that summer back: 'Teenage Dirtbag', 'Bohemian Rhapsody', 'I'm Free', 'Pure Shores'.

She turned the card over. It had a cow on it, with a party hat. Not one of the better ones in the shop, but still.

Lorna looked up; Tiffany was grinning at her. She waved the card in a 'you did this?' way, and Tiff gave her a thumbs-up.

'Thanks,' she said.

'Happy birthday,' said Tiffany.

Chapter Twenty-Five

Lorna didn't have time to dwell too much on either her birthday, or Jess's evasiveness, or who Sam's interview in London might be with, because first thing on Monday morning, a graduate from the art college arrived with his work for a mini-exhibition she'd arranged, in time for any summer tourists: pastiche paint charts, but for selecting emotions. A hundred shades of green ran the spectrum from Disinterest to Envy, while Lorna's own favourite piece calibrated Delight in shades of metallic gold.

And, as Tiffany reminded her when Lorna came into the back office for a tea break after hanging the framed cards, the deadline for their yarnbomb trial was practically there.

'Four more daisies by lunchtime,' she said, shoving her unicorn needles into her hands. 'Go go go.'

There was only one day left before the meeting with Calum, where they'd present the yarnbomb trial, and – if he liked it – he would transfer the funding for the mountain of wool required to create a townful of flowers. According to Lorna's spreadsheet, they were still thirty daisies and two and a half sunflowers short, and all their finished petals needed to be sewn on to the big crocheted net, so they could cover a whole brick wall with a trellis of tumbling sweet peas.

All hands were now on deck. Caitlin had come round to help with the final push, and the sight of her, Tiffany, Joyce, Mary and Lorna sitting in a circle, chatting and knitting as fast as their needles could move, was drawing people into the gallery to watch. Lorna felt proud of the camaraderie buzzing throughout the gallery. All day she made tea, passed around Mary's biscuit tin, and took Spotify requests to keep everyone's spirits up – who knew, she reflected, that Joyce would be such a fan of the Supremes? The conversation ebbed and flowed, according to how complicated a stage people were at in their patterns, but the atmosphere was friendly and – the part that made Lorna's heart hum with happiness – it felt creative.

This is exactly what I wanted my gallery to be, she thought as Caitlin triumphantly waved the newest pattern, Joyce's bold trumpet lily. It had taken nearly seven months to get going, but something was happening at last. Whether it would be enough for her to stay for another year . . .

Lorna didn't want to think about that just yet.

Next morning, Lorna and Tiffany packed the flowers and their assembly kit into boxes and loaded them into the car, along with the instructions Caitlin had found on the internet about installing them securely. Calum was meeting them at eleven, and the idea was that they should transform the space they'd chosen to yarnbomb as stealthily and quickly as possible, for maximum impact. Mary was left in the gallery, with strict instructions not to accept any offers of pottery or felted clothes.

Joyce hadn't appeared for breakfast, but she surprised Lorna by appearing at the door with her handbag on her arm, and Bernard on his short lead. 'May I come too?

I want to see how my flower designs work outside,' she said. 'Plus, Bernard needs to get out.'

Bernard wagged his tail. Unlike dachshunds, Border terriers always seemed keen, regardless of the plans.

It was more noticeable downstairs in the grey-walled gallery, but Lorna thought Joyce was looking paler than she had for a while. The colour had come back into her cheeks when she'd started working on the flowers, but now her brow was creased, as if she was worried what she'd designed wouldn't be right. It was a warm day, forecast to get hotter. 'Are you sure?' she asked. 'We can take pictures if you want?'

'It's not the same as seeing it in real life!' said Joyce. 'I need to be able to make changes before we finalise anything . . .' She paused. 'I don't want it to fail because my initial designs aren't quite right.'

Lorna admired Joyce's stubborn perfectionism but she also noticed the way she was sharing her concerns with her. They were collaborators. 'Then please do come.'

'Just don't make me go up that stepladder.' Joyce swept out of the gallery. 'Come on, Bernard.'

'They're watching us,' panted Tiffany as she balanced on Lorna's shoulder to fix the net of flowers to the top of the wall outside the council-office car park. 'Up there, they're trying to work out what we're doing.'

From the back of the air-conditioned car, Joyce indicated that the netting wasn't straight.

'Don't look at them, just get the bloody clips in.' Lorna gave Joyce a fixed grin and nodded. 'You'd better speed up. The guide book says yarnbombers have to work fast and in black clothes. For the surprise factor.'

Tiff yelped in derision. 'Seeing all the lamp posts from here to the town hall dressed as sunflowers is going to be a surprise enough. They're going to think they've put something in the water. Done! You can let me down.'

They staggered backwards to admire their handiwork. The concrete courtyard was now a knobbly florist's shop: double-size sunflowers stretching up between the lower windows, blood-red poppies climbing the corrugated sixties façade, and a trellis of tendrils and pink petals. It was a joyful riot of colour and Lorna's heart swelled with pride that they'd knitted every stitch. They'd turned plain wool into . . . magic. And every flower had a distinctive Joyce Rotheryish boldness in its shape. It was special. Proper art.

Joyce buzzed down her window. 'It looks marvellous,' she said. 'But I think I know what's missing. Butterflies!'

'Here's your man.' Tiffany nodded to the doors.

'Can I look?' Calum came bouncing out of the main doors and took a step back when he saw what they'd done. His expression registered pure amazement. 'Lorna *Larkham*!'

'You like it?' Lorna smiled till her cheeks ached.

'Like it? I love it! I really, really love it! Come here! I'm sorry, but come here.' And without warning, Calum threw his arms round her and pulled her to his chest.

He was slight but strong, and he gave her a proper hug, not the social clasp she'd been anticipating. She wasn't expecting the affection in it.

'And me?' Tiffany put herself forward, and Calum hugged her too, but not, Lorna noticed, quite as tightly.

'Amazing. I am just . . . blown away. And Joyce too?

Hello, there . . .' He stepped towards the car and Bernard warned him off with a sharp yap.

'Do not embrace me,' said Joyce. 'Or my dog.'

Calum raised his hands and backed off. 'Congratulations, Joyce, it's a triumph. I hear you'll be exhibiting the original designs?'

'If I may.'

'Oh, I'm seeing a separate installation in the town hall,' he reassured her.

'So we can go ahead?' Lorna needed to hear him say it.

'Full speed ahead. I'll get the grant paid to you today. Just tell me how you'd like us to organise the schools' involvement we discussed, and how we can co-ordinate the other volunteer groups and . . . Do you mind if I . . . ?' Calum touched a petal wonderingly. 'You knitted this?'

Lorna turned to Joyce and smiled. 'Yup. We knitted every last petal.'

Her art collective, in her gallery. She wanted to press this moment into a painted image, to hold it for ever.

If Mum could see this, she started to think, and for the first time, in a council car park, so many years after her mother had died, Lorna felt a stab of realisation: she never would. Mum would *never* know she'd done this.

The pain reverberated through her like a gong, and Lorna floated above herself as Calum rattled on about mailing lists and drop-off points. She'd come to terms with her mother's death, of course, and she'd grieved, but she'd never believed there'd be a moment when they *could* have connected like this. Finally, Lorna had made something she considered art, as worthy as the beauty her mother created, and she couldn't share it with her, or talk about how it felt to create something no one else could.

My mum's gone, thought Lorna in shock, and her soul twisted. She's gone and I'm still here, and she'll never know that I finally found something that made me happy.

Lorna stared blindly at the flowers, bright and static on the brick wall, and tears pricked the back of her throat. Not just for her mother, but for the knowledge that this was the first time in so long that she had been happy. Truly, unconditionally happy with herself.

Calum was as good as his word, and by the end of the week, the grant for the knitting project arrived in the gallery's account, along with a link to the colourful web page the council web geek had created for volunteers to sign up, and an invitation to lunch, to liaise with the press team. And Calum, obviously. *We need to get the ball (of wool!!) rolling!* he emailed.

'It's at Ferrari's,' Tiff observed. 'He either wants to impress you, or the press officer.'

Lorna launched into her action plan.

The first stage was to publicise the daily knitting workshops in the back room, to give away free needles and balls of wool to volunteer groups, and to drop into schools, hospitals, coffee shops and craft groups to explain her project and get local people inspired by the possibilities of turning the town into a woolly paradise.

It meant a lot to Lorna to feel *she* was creating art in places where before she'd only distributed other people's. The first time she carried a box of wool, needles and poppy patterns up to the hospital, she remembered every ward she'd walked through with her art catalogue, deciding what paintings would cheer up sterile waiting rooms, matching tranquil pieces to bleaker places. Now, not only was she bringing that art to the patients in the beds, she was helping them create it for themselves.

'It passes the time,' confided one old lady, tethered to a bed with tubes and drips. Like Joyce, she knitted rapidly without looking, and had finished a lily by the time Lorna was ready to leave. It lay on the green blanket, perfect, and the old lady smiled.

Joyce kept drawing flowers for Caitlin to turn into patterns, and sometimes drew the dogs, for her own amusement. Her inspiration sometimes ran ahead of her eyesight, and the detail wasn't always precise, but Joyce could capture mood in a few pencil strokes. Little sketches were left on the kitchen table: Rudy, asleep and dreaming; Bernard staring out of the window, shaggy paws up on the windowsill. Nothing was said, but Lorna knew they were left for her to find.

'Would you like these to go in our summer exhibition?' Lorna asked her very casually one morning.

'No, they're just silly things.' Joyce waved her hand, her stiff 'no, no' gesture, but Lorna detected the glimmer of satisfaction, and secretly sent them to Archibald for framing. When Joyce's pencil dogs came back from the workshop in matt black frames, Lorna caught her admiring them, and she fought back her instinct to tell Joyce how proud it made her to be part of this Indian summer of creativity.

But she didn't. That was their agreement. And on the first of September, Joyce left Lorna another rental payment – the fourth picture. It was a pencil sketch of a chubby toddler in denim dungarees napping in the corner of a sofa: Ronan, drawn by his mother. The detail in his tiny fingers and downy hair was exquisite, a masterpiece of love controlled with precision. The emotion here, in its quiet tenderness, was just as powerful as Joyce's huge oils, and it made Lorna's heart ache.

It was too much.

She knocked on the bedroom door, and when Joyce opened it, she said, 'I can't take this. You can't give it away.'

'I can, and I want you to have it,' she replied firmly, and closed her bedroom door.

Lorna stood there for a moment. It felt almost as if someone had put a real live baby in her hands. Then the door reopened, just a crack.

'Mothers don't always show their love in words.' Joyce's face wasn't visible. 'But it is eternal. And I think you will appreciate that picture more than anyone I know.' And the door closed.

The weather stayed warm, and the humid nights didn't help Lorna's insomnia. Her dreams about boxes started again; always the same one – that she was searching through boxes and boxes, looking for something as a clock ticked in the background, but every time she opened a box, she forgot what she was looking for.

She had a good idea what was causing them: her brain was looping in circles that never resolved, before moving on to the next dilemma. How to help Jess, but what help did Jess need? How to let Sam know how she felt, but how did she feel? And all the time, she felt herself getting nearer to the end of her year, to the time when she'd have to be realistic about carrying on. Time was driving forward, but she was still circling, a little boat caught in a whirling stream heading for the waterfall.

Knitting helped stop the thinking. On nights when she

gave up on sleep, Lorna got up and sat in the kitchen with her needles and a pattern, and created a poppy or a broad leaf. Sometimes Joyce slipped in and joined her. Lorna didn't ask why she couldn't sleep, and Joyce never mentioned her own reasons for wakefulness. Sometimes they talked in snippets about Ronan or Lorna's mum, and a long silence would fall, but it was a companionable silence.

One very late night, or early morning, in the second week of September, Lorna was in the kitchen with Rudy snoring on her lap while she added stitched details to some daisies she'd knitted the previous day. Joyce drifted in, wrapped in her vivid Liberty print dressing gown, and sat down at the table.

After a few minutes, she said in her brisk voice, 'Lorna, could I ask a favour of you?'

'Of course.' Lorna tied off the end of the flower petal. This was her best daisy yet, with delicate pink tips she'd embroidered on with cotton. The daisy chains were going to be woven through the fences around the municipal gardens: sunshine yellow and cloud white against the ironwork.

'Could you run me into the hospital tomorrow, please?'

Lorna glanced up. Joyce's face didn't have its usual small-hours blurriness; she seemed focused. 'Sure, what time? Has Shirley Wheels had her car clamped? One double yellow too many?'

'No, Shirley Wheels is very much still on the road but I'd rather . . . If you don't mind, I'd like you to come into the appointment with me.'

It wasn't their usual way, asking direct questions, but Lorna instinctively broke the rule. 'Is something wrong?'

'Everything is fine, but I'm afraid it's one of those

appointments at which the well-meaning social team encourage you to "have someone with you".' Joyce didn't need to mime the inverted commas; Lorna could hear them. 'There'll be some medical details, for which I apologise, but I'd very much appreciate it if you'd be there. Keir is unable to attend, which I must say is rather a relief. He does fuss.'

Keir was on holiday, a 'wellbeing break' in Italy. Tiffany had had a postcard, outlining all the problems he'd encountered since the plane took off. She'd become something of a shoulder for Keir to moan on.

'I'd be happy to take you.' Lorna tried to gauge how concerned Joyce wanted her to be. 'But if there are things I ought to know in advance please do tell me. So I can be helpful.'

They looked at each other. There was an honesty here that was easier than Lorna had imagined. Joyce wasn't her mother, she wasn't her responsibility. She wasn't Joyce's carer. She was her friend, though. The heart of her artistic inspiration. Lorna felt something sliding in the flat, something sliding away, out of her control.

'The only help I need,' said Joyce, 'is to be treated like a woman who knows her own mind.'

'Well, I can do that,' said Lorna, although her heart sank.

Joyce insisted that Lorna didn't need to do anything other than turn up and listen – 'so they don't make a big fuss about my geriatric brain not getting it' – but from the moment she and Joyce sat down in the airy consulting room she sensed there was something ominous about the meeting.

The room in the new wing of Longhampton Hospital was too nice, with comfy chairs and a view of the car park outside, and a bright pink gerbera in a silver pot on the table. The giveaway, however, was the box of tissues next to it.

Mr Khan the consultant – he didn't say what he was a consultant in, assuming Lorna knew – was friendly, as was Ali, a social worker colleague of Keir's who'd been drafted into the meeting in his place. Like Keir, Ali had bundles of papers and files, and a phone that never stopped buzzing. There was another pleasant middle-aged woman too, who introduced herself as Tina as if Lorna should know her.

Lorna noticed that they all referred to Joyce as Mrs Rothery, right from the off. How long had Joyce been coming here? How much had she kept to herself?

'Well, Mrs Rothery, it's good to see you walking in here so easily!' said Mr Khan, checking and then closing his notes. 'The physio says you're almost back to normal.'

'We'll have you running the marathon in no time!' chirped Tina, but then seemed to think better of it.

'So that's great news. However . . .' Mr Khan's tone changed, a shade of solemnity over the jovial warmth. Elephant grey, thought Lorna. 'I'm afraid we're going to have to talk about these results.' He pulled a file across his desk and opened it. 'You remember at your last appointment, we decided to do a scan and run some blood tests, just to confirm a few niggling concerns we had.'

'*You* decided,' said Joyce. 'I was quite prepared to take my chances in blissful ignorance.'

'Yes, you're quite right: *I* decided.' He smiled briefly. 'Anyway, we . . . you had a CT scan, as well as some other diagnostic tests, and I'm very sorry to say that my suspicions proved correct. The scan has shown up some abnormalities in your pancreas.' He pressed his lips together.

An invisible heavy hand grabbed Lorna by the back of the neck, temporarily shaking her centre of gravity. *Abnormalities*. That could only mean one thing.

She glanced at Ali and Tina. They must hear this all the time, she thought, struggling to keep her own expression straight when every nerve was straining not to grab Joyce's hand in hers. What were the signs? How had she missed them?

'I see,' said Joyce, as if they were discussing the weather. 'And how advanced is it?'

'We would need to do a few more tests to pinpoint that.'

'Has it spread?' She looked impatient. 'Doctor, I have had friends with . . . abnormalities, as you call them. I'm not frightened by the terminology.'

He seemed respectful of her vim. 'There are indications of metastases, in the bone and liver. But, again, I'd prefer to do some further tests so we can be absolutely precise.'

Joyce raised her hand. 'I know you're duty-bound to offer me a series of treatments and solutions but I don't want them. I'm beyond being poked and prodded, just to save a few months.'

The social worker, Ali, leaned forward. 'Joyce . . . Mrs Rothery, you don't have to make any decisions today. Why not just listen to the options? It's not all aggressive surgery, you know. You might not even have to lose your hair!'

Joyce gave her a withering glance. 'My dear, how do you know this isn't a wig already?'

Ali shrank back, with an 'I warned you' glance from Tina, and Joyce returned her gaze to the consultant.

'But there *are* treatment options?' Lorna couldn't hold it in any longer. 'Aren't there? Maybe not chemotherapy but perhaps radiotherapy?' She was racking her brains for any scraps of anything she'd ever known about cancer. There *had* to be options, even at Joyce's age. Doctors worked miracles these days.

'Yes, um . . .' He tried to check the notes for her name, without being obvious.

'Lorna.' Mr Khan was obviously assuming she was Joyce's granddaughter, or great-niece, and she was about to explain before suddenly realising that might limit how much he'd tell her.

Joyce had no one apart from her. No sister, no child, no husband: she was alone at the edge of this cliff, looking down into nothing, not knowing when she might fall. It caught Lorna in the throat.

'Lorna.' He smiled. 'Of course, there are quite a few things we can try.'

Joyce huffed. 'As we've already established, I'm practically eighty so I don't have much time left,' she said. 'Can we please cut to the chase? I want you to be honest with me, Mr Khan. You must know roughly how advanced my . . . condition is.' The faintest trace of fear scudded across her pale blue eyes, to vanish instantly. Joyce raised her chin, facing it. 'How long do I have?'

Finally, the doctor conceded he was in the presence of a stronger will than his own. 'We'd need to do more staging tests. Pancreatic cancers are hard to detect so you may have had this for a while . . . It could be a year. It could be a few months.'

A few months. Lorna stared in shock at Joyce. A few months wouldn't even take them to Christmas!

Christmas. Who cared about Christmas? It wouldn't even let Joyce finish her yarnbombing project.

Joyce turned her head and met Lorna's anguished gaze. And she smiled, more sadly for Lorna's shock than herself, then reached over and squeezed her hand.

They had been sitting in the car for ten minutes without speaking, and Lorna couldn't bring herself to start the engine. Driving home to the gallery, to the piles of knitted petals, to a life that now had a stopwatch on it – it made everything real. She couldn't bear it. That dark shadow at the back of her mind: she hadn't been able to sit with Betty at the end, or her own mother. And now Joyce would be sitting in her room, knitting and patiently waiting for death to come, instead of barring the doors and fighting it away.

Finally, she made herself ask. 'Did you know?'

Joyce was watching the people walking into the hospital. An older couple with a helium balloon of congratulations, rushing up the stairs as fast as they could behind a couple of a similar age; the man's arm around the woman's bowed shoulders told a different story. A toddler and his mum. A pair of teenagers, hugging in tears.

'Yes,' she said. 'I think I did.'

'How? Did Keir take you for tests? Why didn't he say something? I mean, I know there's patient confidentiality but he knew you were moving in with me! He should have let us all know in case . . .' She didn't know in case what.

'Keir doesn't know.' Joyce turned her gold wedding ring round on her finger. 'I've spent my whole life tuning into impulses I don't understand. I let my body respond to instincts I can't rationalise. Hand moves, brain responds.'

She mimed painting, then let her hand fall. 'I knew something wasn't right. I just didn't know what it was.'

'So why didn't you say something sooner?'

'Because these doctors always want to *treat* things,' Joyce replied impatiently. 'You can't treat *life*. They'd try to get me into some fast-track treatment programme, blast it out of me with chemicals and lasers – whatever it is they do. I didn't want that. I didn't want to leave my house in an ambulance, then be blasted and poisoned, and sent back a wreck. Or worse than that, never allowed back at all.'

'But it's not like that.' Lorna couldn't bear the finality of Joyce's attitude; she couldn't bear the thought that in months, weeks, this sharp mind would be gone. 'Won't you even consider the options?'

'No, Lorna.' The tone was more like the old Joyce. Quite snippy. 'Please.'

They lapsed into silence again.

'Is that why you wanted to move in with me? So I could look after you?' Lorna's chest tightened. 'So you could die in my house and not in a hospital?'

'No. That sounds . . . Oh dear. No.' Joyce meshed her fingers in her lap. 'I wanted to move into your flat first because I thought it would be good for us both.' She turned, so Lorna could see the honesty in her eyes. 'I've lived my life on my own terms, since I was a young woman. I paid my own art-school fees because my parents thought it was a waste of time. And I did all manner of jobs before my paintings sold, to put food on the table. I didn't want matters taken out of my hands now I'm on my own. You've seen the social workers fussing around, telling me what's best, as if I don't know my own mind. You needed quality art for your gallery, and I needed a little room with civilised company, and Bernard would get . . .' At the mention of his name, her composure wobbled. 'Bernard would be somewhere he knew and trusted when I was no longer able to take care of him.'

'I can do *that*, Joyce.' Lorna tried not to think about Bernard, and how bewildered he'd be without his mistress. He knew exactly where Joyce was, even when he looked asleep. His nose twitched, following her.

'I appreciate it's a lot to ask.' She tapped her hand on the gear stick, clicking her rings against the plastic. 'But as the care nurse said, I should be fairly fit for a while. I haven't had many symptoms up until now, and when it does . . . start to affect me more, there are nurses who can call in.' She sensed the horror on Lorna's face, and pulled back. 'But we can take it as it comes. My room in Butterfields might come up at any moment.'

Lorna knew it wouldn't. Butterfields required its residents to be 'in independent health'; it would be the hospice, when that time came.

'The main thing is,' Joyce went on, 'I am absolutely determined to finish our project.'

'You came up with the idea, not me. It was your garden painting that inspired it.' Lorna was close to tears. That beautiful garden, where she'd first met Joyce. It seemed so long ago that she'd broken into Rooks Hall with Keir, so long since she'd walked behind Rudy and Bernard, snuffling through the hedges, and found Sam again.

'We both did.' Joyce looked at her and there was a flash of understanding between them that stopped the tears in Lorna's eyes. Joyce was focused, not wallowing in sentiment; she seemed clearer now than she had been on the way in. 'I want to finish *our* project. I want to see Longhampton bedecked with glorious colour on New Year's Day.'

Lorna threw caution to the wind. 'So why won't you even consider treatment that might give us more time?'

'Because we all have to die sometime,' said Joyce. Her tone was matter-of-fact, but not unkind. 'I want to do it on my own terms. As an artist.' She managed a sad, proud smile.

'All right,' said Lorna. She didn't understand, but there didn't seem much point arguing.

More people walked up the hospital steps, and she thought of her parents, dying on their own terms, alone and unnoticed, ready to go. That won't happen to Joyce, she thought, she'll go out loved and celebrating. Her heart lurched with sudden emotion.

I don't want you to go yet, she thought. *We've only just started to get to know one another.*

They sat for another moment, then Lorna started the car. 'Let's get back,' she said. 'We have flowers to knit.'

Chapter Twenty-Six

'So, when you're not knitting, what do you do?' Calum offered Lorna the bowl of sugar crystals. When she shook her head, he tipped two spoons into his espresso, letting it sit on the thick crema before it sank down. The sign of a decent coffee. She knew he'd be thinking that; they'd talked about coffee, as well as New York, and arts funding, and Japanese food, and cartoons. Calum was easy to talk to.

'That's all I do these days,' she said, honestly. 'I knit.'

He grinned. 'Come on, we're off the record now. You don't have to convince me you're working to timetable. I mean, what do you like doing? Are you a sculptor? A sketcher?'

She pushed a stray strand of hair behind her ear. 'Seriously, I haven't done anything apart from knit, dawn till dusk, ever since we started,' she said. 'I love it. We sit and chat, me and my flatmates. It feels very communal, actually.'

'Then you're a textile artist.'

'Maybe I am.' She smiled over her coffee cup, and liked the way Calum's eyes smiled back.

They were in the wine bar on the corner of the high street, on an outside table, and Lorna wasn't sure if she was on a date or not. Tiffany said she was; Calum had asked to meet her for a drink after work this time, and he'd made a casual reference to getting something to eat. That meant nothing in Lorna's opinion. It was probably so he could expense it.

'He's asking you out for dinner, so go.' Tiffany rolled her eyes. 'Why wouldn't you? Calum's cute; he likes the same arty nonsense you do. And he's been trying to ask you out for ages – give the guy a break.'

'But what if it goes wrong and work gets . . . ?'

I'm about to say, *Don't mix business with pleasure*, she thought, and her teeth clenched.

'Lorna.' Tiffany looked incredulous. 'How many dates are you currently getting? Just go, for God's sake.'

And so here she was, in a black dress with her hair wound in a bun, flirting pleasantly with the only other Longhamptonite who had an opinion on pointillism. She'd stuck to espresso so far, just in case, but the next drink, she decided, would be a glass of wine.

'You mentioned something about a gallery in London?' Calum waved his spoon at her. 'Who were you working for there?'

'Me. I started a pop-up.'

'Wow. Who were you representing?'

She started to tell him, and instead of looking appalled at her naivety, he leaned closer, taking in every detail.

'But no one bought anything and then Zak disappeared with what money was left,' she finished, and waited for him to ask the usual questions: *How much did you lose? Was it humiliating?*

Calum didn't ask any of them. He just shrugged. 'It happens. If it had worked out, you'd be a millionaire and everyone would say you were a visionary. At least you tried.

Someone's got to go out and bat for the artists. Do you fancy something to eat?' He checked his watch – they were well into 'out for dinner' time now. 'I've found – don't laugh – a good little tapas place behind the sports centre. What are your feelings about tapas?'

'I'm willing to take a *gambas* on it.'

'Ha!' He pointed at her. 'Funny girl.'

Something was growing in the space between them, Lorna sensed it, like wispy sweet peas sending out tendrils to wrap around common ground. She could feel herself going into date mode, sifting through her personality to present the bits she thought Calum would like.

Without warning, Calum reached across the table and laid his hand over hers. The contact made her tingle with surprise. 'This is great,' he said. 'Best evening out I've had since I got here.'

Lorna didn't know what to say. It . . . was great, actually. She smiled. 'Yes, it is.'

Someone coughed behind her and she swivelled her head round. Sam was standing there, and he looked awkward.

'Sorry to interrupt,' he said, deliberately not looking at Calum. 'I was on my way to the gallery but since you're here – I need some more paintings for the cottages. Can you bring a selection over some time this week?'

'Of course.' Lorna pulled her hand back and twisted further round. 'What kind of subject matter do you want? Landscapes? Sheep?'

Sam shrugged. He wasn't even pretending to care about content this time. 'I'll leave it up to you,' he said. 'Some big, some small. Whatever goes with Calico White. You know the budget – email me the invoice.'

'Charming,' said Calum as Sam strode off towards his parked car.

'Yeah.' There was no need for that. Lorna watched Sam's retreating back with mixed feelings, then reached for her bag. 'So, tapas?'

It pained Lorna to admit it, but Sam had done a decent job on the holiday homes around the farm's estate. Over the summer, tradesmen had stripped and rebuilt the stone cottages: the walls had been replastered and painted milky white and sky blue, and the floorboards sanded and oiled to a honey-coloured smoothness. The sash windows were repaired and hung with curtains in oatmeal linen, and if the claw-footed baths and brass-framed beds upstairs looked authentically Victorian, the original farmhands certainly wouldn't have recognised them as anything they'd have used.

The final touch would be, of course, some local art. Since Sam had made it clear he didn't care what she brought, as long as it filled the walls of the three-bed cottage, Lorna cleared the gallery out of all the remaining cow close-ups, large flowers and other 'waiting-room mindwash', as Joyce put it. This would put her in the black for the month and they weren't even halfway through, which would leave her free to focus on organising the knitting workshops and events that were happening around town.

Hattie had started coming every other weekend to work in the gallery, and Lorna was glad of her help; another pair of hands, especially nimble ones like Hattie's, were always welcome. It was nice to have Hattie around, sharing in the business side of things and teaching her snippets of art history here and there. It gave her something to do, and, Lorna hoped, something to think about other than her mysterious half-sister; everything seemed to have gone quiet on that front, and she wasn't about to start asking questions. That afternoon, she'd helped Lorna wrap up Sam's paintings, ticking them off against the invoice, then cross-referencing with Mary's archaic filing system.

Lorna parked outside Nightingale Cottage, as per Sam's instructions, to unload the plastic crates of bubble-wrapped art. The curtains were open, revealing the newly painted sitting room with its leather sofa, and piles of plastic packaging from a luxury bed were heaped on the mown lawn.

She tried not to think what sort of state Rooks Hall was in right now. Whether Sam had rollered bland magnolia over Joyce's colours, each room's different mood razed to a monotone neutral throughout. Whether the garden had been bulldozed for Gabe's double drive; whether the fireplace had been filled with a prosaic wood-burning stove.

No one answered when she knocked on the door, so she turned the handle and pushed it open. 'Hello?' The smell of brand-new tiles and fresh gloss rushed out at her. 'Anyone in?'

A voice came from somewhere at the back of the house. 'Kitchen.' It sounded like Sam. Lorna lugged the first box in, and down the hall.

Sam was by the back door to the pantry, fitting new lights. When he saw her, he climbed down off the chair he was standing on and put the screwdriver in his back pocket.

'Hi,' she said. 'Art delivery, as requested.'

'Great. Thanks.'

It was awkward, and she knew why. Lorna had never

told Sam she was going on a date with Calum; but then he'd gone off to London for an interview, and never even told her what the job was.

'Sorry if I interrupted your date the other night,' he said. 'I take it that was Calum from the council?'

Lorna nodded, and was going to say, It wasn't really a date; then she thought, No. Why should I? It *had* been a date. And more to the point, it had been fun. 'Don't worry. He was impressed to see me getting orders even out of shop hours. Where do you want your paintings?'

'Wherever. Do you need some help hanging them?'

'Not really. Do you want to choose what goes where?'

He shrugged. 'You're the expert.'

So it was going to be like this. A corner of Lorna's heart shrivelled. 'Leave it with me then,' she said, and went to get her hanging kit from the car.

They worked for half an hour or so in different rooms, Lorna in the hall hanging a crop of framed bird studies up the stairs, and Sam in the kitchen, banging nails in and occasionally swearing. Aware of each other, probably listening to one another, but neither speaking.

Lorna had been intending to confide in Sam about Joyce's illness but something was stopping her now. She didn't want to tell him anything. Her mind worried away at those interviews, and what he'd done up in London; it shifted the balance between them, until yet again he was the one who was escaping while she was stuck here, outside everyone's plans.

She'd just hooked the final bird on its string when a car pulled up outside, and a minute or so later, footsteps crunched up the path.

'Hello?' Lorna smelled Gabriel before she saw him. Old sweat and a faint trace of cows. She wrinkled her nose.

'Not sure about that.' He was standing right behind her, too close. 'Shouldn't they be in a line going up the stairs, like?'

'No.' Lorna had hung the birds gallery-style on the wall, in an asymmetrical flock. They were originals and, in her opinion, a bargain. She'd had to talk herself into letting Sam have them for the cottage. 'They work better in a group.'

'I prefer them in a line.' He stared at her, challenging her to disagree.

'You want me to take them down?' She nodded at the wall. 'It'll spoil the plaster. I've knocked nails in.'

Gabriel looked thwarted. 'I could charge you for replastering, I could. Should have waited on instructions from the boss.'

The boss. The idea of Gabriel being the boss when Sam left made Lorna's skin crawl. He'd love that. He probably walked by the byres every morning to remind his dad's cows that he was in charge.

Something made her twist the knife. 'I did get instructions from the boss. Sam told me to hang everything as I thought right.'

'Did I say Sam was the boss?'

'What's going on?' Sam appeared from the kitchen, looking between them. 'Gabriel? Everything all right?'

'You like these paintings like this?' He gestured contemptuously at the chaffinches and swallows. 'Seems messy to me.'

Sam shrugged. 'I'm not the expert, Lorna is. We're aiming for that boutique feel. It's the style.'

Gabriel pulled a face that suggested that such people hadn't a clue, then turned back to her. 'Anyway, now you're here . . . I've been meaning to have a chat with you.'

'Really? About what?' She didn't like the way he was looking at her, that sly 'I know something you don't know' gloat. 'If it's about invoicing for the paintings, let me know if you want the bill made out to a management company, rather than a personal address.'

'It's not that.'

'Oh?' She leaned against the banisters, hammer on her hip.

'Our nan had an interesting conversation with your friend Tiffany the other day,' Gabriel went on. 'When she was visiting her in her residential home.'

'Up at Butterfields? Yes, Tiff mentioned she'd been in to walk some dogs.' Lorna glanced over at Sam. Tiffany was good with the older residents, very chatty and unfazed by physical quirks. 'Wispa, isn't it? Your grandma's collie?'

Sam nodded, but seemed reluctant to join in. Lorna's friendly expression faded into a quizzical one, but he didn't respond.

'Tiffany was telling Nan that that Rudy of yours is quite a wealthy sausage dog,' Gabriel went on. 'Earns more than she does, Tiffany reckons.' He paused and the sly look intensified.

Oh, right. Lorna knew where this was going, but she pretended she didn't. 'That's not hard. Tiffany's not earning anything at the moment.'

'Rudy's got his own bank account, I hear,' Gabe persisted. 'Enough to pay for anything his new owner requires. Very generous for a little dog. I expect he eats quite well, does he? Fillet steaks and such like.'

'Stop right there.' Lorna raised her hand, the one without the hammer in it, trying to keep her indignation under control. She knew he was trying to goad her, and she didn't want to look defensive. 'Someone's got their wires crossed. Rudy's owner, Betty, left money in a trust to cover his insurance and his food. Nothing else. Nothing for me, if that's what you're insinuating.'

Gabriel raised an eyebrow. 'And how did you get to know this Betty?'

'Through a volunteering scheme. In a local hospice, not that it's any of your business.' Lorna resented the implication. She could feel Sam staring at her, and her cheeks started to burn. 'What's your point?'

'No point. Just that it's a bit of a coincidence that you've got another old lady with a dog in your house now. Not saying we know much about Mrs Rothery's finances but I wouldn't be surprised if her dog came with a pension plan too. In the event of him being in need of a new home.'

That was outrageous. *Mrs Rothery.* As though Gabriel was concerned about her!

'Oh, for . . .' Lorna turned to Sam. How could he stand there listening to this with a straight face? 'Sam, explain to your brother that I don't go round targeting old women to steal their money by befriending their dogs.'

'No one's saying that.' His voice was even, but Lorna realised, to her absolute horror, that he didn't sound convinced.

'I told Nan to mind out with Wispa,' Gabriel went on, in his mirthless 'banter' tone. 'She don't want your mate bopping her on the head to get hold of Wispa's stocks and shares. Not that he's got any, like. So you can cross him off your list.'

'Sam?' Lorna ignored Gabe; she couldn't believe Sam wasn't saying something. Had they discussed this already? Normally Sam didn't take any notice of Gabriel, but his jaw was set firm and he was looking at her in a strange way.

He uncrossed his arms, then crossed them again. 'Out of interest, what is the arrangement with you and Joyce? Is she paying you rent?'

'You know what the arrangement is. She's waiting for a place at Butterfields, so she can take Bernard with her. Until then . . .' Why am I even telling him this, she wondered? Because it was better to be open, since she had nothing to hide. 'Until then, she's giving me a couple of paintings, and advising me in the gallery. She's not paying me a penny.'

'Interesting,' said Gabriel, clearly relishing his new role as moral policeman. 'I'm not sure what the taxman would say about paintings, would you, Sam? Especially valuable ones like Mrs Rothery's.'

Sam shrugged. 'It's a grey area. But I'm sure Lorna knows what she's doing.'

Lorna's head swivelled between the two of them, unable to believe what she was hearing. As if Gabe suddenly had financial knowledge of the current art market. As if he cared.

'You're insulting me, and you're insulting Tiffany.' She started packing her kit up, before she hammered nails into Gabriel's fat hands. 'You can tell your nan that any help offered with looking after Wispa is done with nothing but the purest intentions. I'm outraged that you could think I'm trying to exploit Joyce.'

Lorna glared at Sam, barely controlling her furious shame, and he had the grace to look embarrassed.

'I'm also surprised, given that you've both dealt with Joyce, that you even think she's capable of being exploited,' she added spikily.

'We're only looking out for vulnerable old people,' said Gabriel, with a pious shake of the head. 'It's part of our remit as responsible landlords.'

'Ha!' Lorna stopped, midway through shoving the hammer back in her bag, and the laugh burst out of her. 'You wouldn't even be a landlord if you hadn't fallen under your own baler. And if your dad didn't own the farm in the first place.'

'Hey!'

'Good luck with that,' she said to Sam, with a nod towards Gabriel. 'Must be a relief to know that you're bailing out of the family business and leaving your holiday cottages in such experienced, diligent hands. I'll email you the invoice for the artwork.'

'To me, please, Lorna,' said Gabriel, pointing at himself. 'I'm the estate manager now.'

'No problem,' she replied. 'I'll make sure I get it absolutely correct. I'd hate to undercharge you and get you in trouble with the taxman.'

Her phone started ringing when she was nearing the outskirts of Longhampton, and she ignored it at first.

Lorna didn't want to talk to Sam. She was too furious. How could he even think that of her? Even if Gabriel had put two and two together and made fifteen million, Sam should have put him straight.

But the phone kept ringing, and eventually she pulled over outside the church at the top of the hill and answered it.

It was the gallery number, not Sam. 'Hello?'

'Hey, Lola.' It was Tiffany, and she was doing her 'every-thing's fine' voice, which set Lorna on edge at once. 'I don't suppose Hattie's with you, is she?'

'No.' She frowned. 'I've just left the cottages. Why?'

'Oh, right.' There was an unmistakeable 'you're not going to like my next comment' pause.

'What's happened?'

'Well, the thing is . . . you know she went out for lunch just before you left?' said Tiffany. 'Well, now it's half four, and she's not answering her phone.'

'I'm *so* sorry,' said Tiffany, for the hundredth time. 'She told me she was just nipping out to get some lunch, which seemed perfectly normal, and then the gallery was busy, and quite a few people came in for wool and patterns because they'd seen that article about you in this week's paper, and suddenly it was half four and I realised she hadn't come back and . . .'

Lorna held up her hands. 'Stop apologising. She might just be drifting round the shops. You know what teenage girls are like.'

'There aren't four hours' worth of shops in Longhampton.' Tiffany chewed her lip. 'And when I went up to the flat to see if she was there, I noticed her rucksack had gone too.'

'Oh.' That put a rather different complexion on things.

They stared at each other for a moment; then Lorna flipped the shop sign over to Closed and steered Tiffany towards the back stairs. 'Let's make a cup of tea and think about this logically.'

Upstairs, the kitchen table was covered in knitted sweet peas, laid out on the crocheted trellis so they could get an

385

idea of how many would be required for a whole wall. The effort of folding it up was too much for Lorna to bear so she made the tea and then took it through to the sitting room, where Hattie had been sleeping on the sofa bed.

Despite being immaculately turned out, Hattie moved through life leaving a trail of make-up, discarded socks, nail varnishes and mugs with soggy herbal teabags behind her. There was nowhere to put their tea, or even sit down.

'Let me tidy up a bit,' said Tiff, seeing Lorna's tense expression. She swept the magazines off the coffee table so she could put the cups down, and grabbed the duvet, left in a heap. But as she moved it on to the other chair, something fell out – Hattie's iPad, which she'd left bundled up in its folds after watching Netflix late into the night. It fell on the wooden floorboards with an ominous crack.

Tiff tsked. 'We could have sat on this! These screens smash so easily.' She picked it up, checking that it wasn't broken. 'Honestly. She doesn't know how lucky she is, having stuff like this . . .'

'Ryan gave her it,' Lorna said. That's why it was so carelessly treated, unlike the precious make-up Hattie bought with her shop wages. 'You can't say he isn't *trying* to buy her love back.'

'It'd work with me,' said Tiff. 'This is one of the brand-new ones . . . Oh.' The iPad buzzed, and she looked down at the screen, then looked at Lorna. Then she handed it to her, without commenting.

The screen was locked, but a conversation in messages was clearly visible: *Hey P! On my way! Be with u abt 6 xxx*

Someone – *Rosie*, according to the icon – had replied: *Bus stop? xx*

Cool! xx

Hattie. That was Hattie texting, presumably from the phone she had with her. She must have linked up her phone and her iPad messenger – well, Lorna knew she had, she'd seen her FaceTiming Jess from her iPad.

Lorna held it in her hands, staring at the messages, feeling torn. Her over-riding instinct was to turn it off – it was wrong to pry into her niece's private messages, of course it was – but at the same time a black hole in the pit of her stomach was opening up and it made her freeze.

Hattie's icon showed three little 'thinking' dots, then:
Bus is so rank sitting next to a total weirdo haha xx

Dont talk to him! U know what happens when u talk to weird men! Lol xx

Hattie was on a bus next to a weirdo! Lorna felt sick. Why hadn't she said? If she'd wanted to go and meet a friend all she had to do was ask; she wouldn't have forced her to stay, just taken a contact number and asked when she'd be home.

The name of the other person kept flashing up over the dots: *Rosie*. The icon was a blonde girl, Instagram pretty, with a glossy pout and Snapchat cat ears. But Hattie had said, *Hey P!*

'Who's Rosie?' asked Tiff, reading over her shoulder.

'I don't know. She's never mentioned a Rosie. I don't understand why she didn't just tell me she wanted to meet a friend. Do you think it's a boy? Why's she been so secretive?'

'She obviously doesn't want you or Jess to know, so the obvious answer is . . .' Tiff grimaced and pointed to the *Hey P!* message. 'Do you think she's arranged a meeting with her sister? And she's called her Rosie because Pearl's quite a distinctive name Jess might spot?'

Oh God, that was it. And the iPad was buzzing again.

Cool. What's ur postcode case I get lost? I am so bad at directions lol xxx

Rosie's dots flashed. And there it was: the postcode. 'Write it down,' hissed Tiff. 'Quick!'

Did you tell ur mum I'm coming? asked Hattie, and Lorna and Tiff both groaned simultaneously at the answer.

Kind of. Said u were a friend? She'll b cool tho.

Lorna stared at the screen. No, Pearl, she is *not* going to be cool, having her family secret turning up on the doorstep. And, Hattie, *your* mum is definitely not going to be cool.

I think its the best way to be honest. My fam are just ignoring the whole thing. It's so unfair – its like we don't matter? xx

Lorna's own phone rang in her bag, but she ignored it. What did she need? Phone, cash . . . Should she tell Jess? She wavered. No. This was something she could handle better herself.

'I'm going to get her,' she said. 'And if Jess rings, tell her to call me.'

Chapter Twenty-Seven

The drive to Gloucester seemed to take for ever, and Lorna argued aloud with herself for most of the way about whether she should call Hattie to tell her she was coming, or not. She might be able to stop Hattie plunging herself into a mess she couldn't get out of, but it would mean confessing about the iPad.

The situation resolved itself for her when her phone rang on the hands-free and the baby photo of Hattie in her yellow-duck romper suit flashed up. Lorna nearly knocked it out of the cradle in her eagerness to answer.

'Auntie Lorna?' The voice was small.

'Hattie? Are you all right?'

'No. I need you to come and get me. I'm . . .' A ragged breath. 'I've done something a bit stupid. I'm in—'

'I know where you are,' said Lorna. Her heart was pumping protectively. 'I'm on my way. Don't worry, sweetheart. Just go into the nearest coffee shop, or pub, text me the postcode and wait for me.'

Hattie was huddled in the corner of a McDonald's when Lorna found her, an untouched Happy Meal arranged in front of her like a protective wall. The strip lights threw harsh shadows on her face and she seemed younger in her big hoodie, the sleeves wrapped over her fingers.

Lorna slid into the booth and hugged her, but Hattie

389

didn't burrow into her the way she expected. Her body felt rigid, as if she were holding herself very firmly together.

She'd been expecting tears, or hysteria. If anything, Hattie's expression was grim. 'So, then,' said Lorna, picking at the uneaten chips to downplay her own tightly-stretched nerves. 'Hadn't you better tell me what's happened?'

Hattie looked down.

'Come on. No secrets, right? What's been going on?'

She didn't answer, so Lorna said, 'Fine, I'll start. You met up with Pearl, yes? Where?'

'How did you know?'

'Well? Did you?'

Hattie rubbed her eyes and gave up. 'Yeah. We'd been talking on Snapchat for ages. We've got so much in common, it's like I've known her for ever! I told her about how Mum and Dad were pretending like nothing had happened. And we thought since it's really about *us*, we should just start the conversation ourselves. Because it's wrong that we're the only people who don't get a say. And we're, like, family in a way they aren't! Do you know what I mean?'

There was a simplistic logic to it that Lorna couldn't deny. But telling Hattie how selfish it was wouldn't help right now. 'So you decided to meet up?'

'We didn't plan it to hurt anyone's feelings or anything. Pearl said I was a friend coming to hang out, because, like, I was? And we thought we'd just, you know, tell her mum, so she could see it was no big deal for us, so it shouldn't be for them.'

The big dramatic reveal, just like every season finale on reality television. Lorna winced for everyone. 'Could you not have prepared Pearl's mum a bit first?'

'She *was* prepared.' Hattie's eyes widened with indignation. 'She knew Pearl was Dad's daughter. She knew Pearl
had been in touch with him, so it was just a matter of time
before we wanted to meet. She could have dealt with it
herself, instead of leaving it to us.'

'Was her dad there? Pearl's real dad, I mean?' That
wasn't the right phrase but Lorna brushed over it. 'What
did he say?'

'I can't really remember exactly what happened.' Hattie
sawed the straw up and down in her Diet Coke cup. It
made an ugly noise, like a seal barking. 'We were talking,
and Pearl's mum came in and guessed who I was, and
started shouting at Pearl, and then her dad came in to see
what the problem was and he was mad at us for upsetting
her mum. Then Pearl's brothers started crying too. She's
got two brothers, Freddie and Alfie.' Hattie's bemused
expression made it obvious that she hadn't really banked
on anyone being upset.

'And they threw you out?'

'No, I left when everyone started yelling.' She rubbed
her eyes. 'I've never heard Mum and Dad yell like that. It
was . . . so loud. I wanted to run away but I didn't know
where I was, and I didn't know what to do. I didn't mean
to upset anyone. I just wanted a sister, like you and Mum
have got each other. It doesn't matter what happens with
everything else, you've always got each other. Is it so bad I
wanted to know my sister too?'

She hiccupped. Lorna reached out and covered her
hands with hers. It wasn't the time to remind Hattie that
she already *had* a sister, one who might end up being a
wonderful friend one day. That was probably part of the
problem.

'Hattie. I know you were trying to do the right thing but sometimes it's better to . . .'

'To lie?'

'Not lie, but to . . .'

'You're saying it's better to cover things up?' Hattie's expression verged on pitying. '*We've* got nothing to be ashamed of. You can't pretend things don't exist just because they don't fit in the way you want. Maybe in the old days, but life isn't like that any more.'

'No one was pretending anything, Hattie. Everyone's just trying to work out the right thing to do. It's not that simple.'

Hattie looked down at her bitten nails and didn't speak for a moment. 'Pearl's mum said . . .'

A gaggle of teens crashed through the doors, swept up on their own energy, laughing and yelling at each other.

Lorna struggled to make herself heard over their noise. 'Pearl's mum said what?'

Hattie glanced up from under her thick lashes. 'She said that Mum tricked Dad into getting her pregnant because she wanted to leave home because Grandma and Grandpa were weird.' Her face crumpled. 'Is that true? Why would she say that?'

'It's not true,' said Lorna reflexively.

'But weird. What did she mean by weird?' Her expression contorted with lurid fear. 'Grandpa was headmaster of a boarding school, wasn't he? He wasn't one of those . . . ?'

'*No.*' It came out of Lorna with such force the teenage boys at the counter turned to look at her in surprise. 'No,' she said, dropping her voice only slightly. 'Grandpa was nothing like that. Your grandparents loved each other, and they loved me and your mum. If they were weird,

392

then I'd rather have that than . . . than non-weird parents any day.'

'But we never saw them.' Hattie had obviously been rolling it around in her mind. 'Not like we see Granny and Grandpa Jack. I don't know anything about them, really.'

'That was because . . .' Lorna stopped. Why was that? How did you explain that relationship to a teenager? 'Well, they lived a long way away, didn't they?'

Hattie gazed at her, disappointed but also curious. 'Didn't they want to see us? Weren't they interested in us?'

'We need to talk about this at home, Hattie. Not here.' Lorna grabbed her bag and got up. There was one more awkward conversation to have today. 'I think we should try to smooth things over with Pearl and her mum,' she said. 'But you should stay in the car.'

'Not *we* at all then,' said Hattie sulkily. 'You.'

Lorna looked over her shoulder at her niece. Tonight, she looked a lot like Jess. 'Yes,' she said. 'I think you've given it your best shot already.'

Pearl's family lived in a terraced house in a not particularly nice residential area of Gloucester. Number sixteen, with a blue door and dried-up window boxes outside. When Lorna rang the doorbell, she could hear raised voices inside, although it might have been the television. She hoped it was, anyway.

She took a step backwards, glancing up to the bedroom windows. A curtain moved, but whoever had twitched it was keeping well out of sight. Lorna got the feeling she was being watched from the house, as well as from the car — which she'd parked well away from the door, just in case.

The door opened halfway, and a woman's face looked out, staring at her with red-rimmed eyes. Ash-blonde hair, two earrings in each ear, girlish features that had coarsened with age and sleepless nights, a shell-shocked expression. Erin. She wasn't what Lorna had been expecting but then . . . what had she been expecting?

'Don't shut the door on me, I'm Hattie's Aunt Lorna,' she said quickly.

'Oh, for f—' Erin nearly slammed it on her but Lorna had her foot in the way. 'Don't you think your family's caused enough trouble today?'

'I apologise if Hattie's created problems tonight. She means well, but they don't always think things through.'

Erin rolled her eyes. 'No shit. No, she's only set my husband off again, after he'd just about calmed down from the time Pearl told us she'd met up with Ryan. My boys keep asking if they've got any more secret brothers and sisters. And how come Dad's not Pearl's real dad?'

'They didn't know?'

'Why should they?' Erin retorted angrily. 'They're babies, they don't need to know about stuff like this. Me and Andy have been together since Pearl was a toddler. He's her dad. I'd never have got in contact with Ryan at all if it wasn't for the medical thing.' She sniffed. 'Wasn't exactly the romance of the century for me either.'

'Well, I'm sorry you've had to deal with this. But there was no need to tell Hattie those lies about her mum.' Lorna lowered her voice. 'That was just cruel.'

'Was it though?' Erin tilted her head. 'Lies? Not what he said to me. Or his brother.'

'Amazing the things that seem to have stuck in your

mind.' The anger from her earlier confrontation with Gabriel was still coursing through Lorna's blood.

Erin narrowed her eyes. 'Listen, I love the bones of my Pearl, I wouldn't change her for the world, but as far as Ryan goes, it was a mistake. A mistake we can draw a line under. At least I'm not fooling anyone about that. Unlike your sister.'

And she closed the door in Lorna's face.

Lorna stared at the blue gloss paint. She could see the shape of her own face in the reflection, while her ears rang with one word: *mistake*. Mistake. Mistake.

Jess never made mistakes.

'I need to make a call,' said Lorna when they'd driven some way away. She'd parked up in a garage forecourt so she could think, and now she'd made up her mind.

Hattie was sitting subserviently in the passenger seat now. She didn't even have her phone out, and she looked ready to sleep or cry. Or both.

This needed to be sorted out this evening. It couldn't wait until the morning.

Lorna dialled her sister's number, and she answered straight away, as usual.

'Jess, we need to have a talk.' Lorna went straight into her prepared speech. 'Hattie's been doing some . . .' She glanced over at her. '. . . some detective work, and frankly, I think it's about time everyone just sat down and cleared the air about a few things.'

'Lorna, I'm at the cinema,' Jess whispered. 'We're in the family showing of *Despicable Me 3*.'

'I don't care. Where's Ryan? Is he with you?'

A barely audible snort. 'No. At his mother's.'

'Fine, I'll tell Ryan to drive over to my house and I'll expect you by eight.'

'But what about the kids?' Jess was still whispering and Lorna could hear her being shushed by other cinema-goers.

'Bring them. I have a live-in nanny who's happy to entertain them for money. I'll see you soon.'

'This had better be really important.'

Lorna looked at Hattie, half the spitting image of her mother, a quarter the spitting image of her artist grand-mother. Her own blood and spirit, the future of their family. 'It is,' she said.

Milo and Tyra were delighted to be herded upstairs for a surprise bedtime story session with Tiffany. They were still full of Haribos and popcorn from the cinema, and Lorna could tell from the bumps and squeals emanating from overhead that Tiff was using her full range of profes-sional skills to contain their excitement. Joyce had gone for an early night.

Jess looked less delighted to be there, especially when she walked in to see Hattie glaring at her from across the table and Lorna told her why she'd dragged her across the country. She looked even less delighted when Ryan appeared, ten minutes later.

He seemed as anxious as ever, but noticeably less hag-gard than the last time Lorna had seen him. His jumper was stretched over the beginnings of a belly, and his face had filled out.

'I see your mother made you dinner again,' Jess observed tartly.

'I'd almost forgotten what a roast dinner tasted like,' he shot back.

'Stop it!' Lorna held up her hands. 'Stop it. This has gone on long enough. You need to talk. Ryan, sit down.' She pointed at the chair at the table. 'Jess, you sit there, please. Hattie? I think you should go and have a bath.'

'What? Why? You're kicking me out?'

'Yes.' Lorna could understand her indignation but it wouldn't help. Jess and Ryan needed to be honest, more honest than a child should hear, probably. 'Have a bath, and by the time you're done, you can sit in for round two.'

Hattie looked instinctively at her mum, but quickly looked away again, as if she was seeing someone different sitting in her place. The betrayal in her eyes was painful to witness. 'Mum?'

'Lorna's right. Give us ten minutes.'

Ryan snorted, as if ten minutes wasn't going to fix anything.

'Use my good bath soak,' said Lorna. 'Use Tiffany's body butter. Whatever you like.'

'Fine.' With a final huff, she spun on her heel and stalked out.

'And no Snapchat!' Jess called after her. 'What? She's going to be straight on there moaning about what Nazis we are.'

'I don't think so.' Lorna didn't know what she was supposed to do now. She sat down at the table, between them. 'Listen, you two need to sort this out. I have no idea how couples counsellors work, I've never had a relationship last long enough to get to that stage. But I grew up with two parents who kept secrets from me – maybe not intentionally, and maybe they didn't even know they were doing

397

it – and you're doing that to Hattie now. You're pushing her out. And she's going to start looking elsewhere for her family if you keep doing it.'

Silence. Neither wanted to go first. Lorna wondered desperately whether she should get the pens and paper out, make them draw their issues.

Then, to her surprise, Ryan spoke. He'd been staring at his hands on the table, focusing on the thick gold band he'd worn since he was a teen. It had come from the jewellers, five doors down from where they were sitting.

'What did Erin say when Hattie went round there?' It sounded like he already knew the answer.

'She told Hattie you only married Jess because she tricked you into getting her pregnant.'

'What?' Jess's reaction was swift and hot. A fraction too much so, in Lorna's private opinion.

'And that Jess only did it to escape our freaky family,' she went on, and this time Jess's face fell in real shock.

'Ryan? Did you say that?'

He didn't reply at once. Ryan had never been one for repartee or jokes; that had always been Sam. Now Lorna could almost hear him putting the words together in his head, carefully, and she realised it was out of kindness, not slowness. Ryan never wanted to make the wrong impression.

'I was eighteen at the time so probably not the most mature thing to do,' he replied. 'But yes, I think there was a bit of that in there, don't you? If you're completely honest.' He looked up, meeting Jess's eyes straight on, and she reeled from the unexpected challenge in his placid face.

'Our parents weren't *weird*,' she spluttered. 'They were in love, too in love maybe, but Mum was an artist. Just because there weren't any other artists around, she wasn't weird . . .'

'You did want to escape, though. I sensed that from the first time I met you. You wanted your own family and when you told me you were pregnant . . .' He shrugged. 'Well, I can't say I was surprised.'

'You don't think I did it on purpose, do you?' Jess turned to Lorna, appealing to her for moral back-up. 'Lorna? You don't think that too, do you? Oh my God.' She looked furious, defensive. 'It's all coming out tonight, isn't it?'

'What does it matter now?' Ryan shrugged. 'Who cares? We both wanted Hattie. Things worked out. You don't want to think of yourself as the kind of girl who traps a lad with a baby but I didn't mind being trapped, to be honest. I loved you. And I was glad not to have to stay and work for Dad. The only thing that's bothered me is . . .' Finally, he stopped, teetering on the edge of his own honesty.

'What?' Jess pressed him.

Yes, what, thought Lorna, gripped. The hidden depths of Ryan Prothero were a revelation to her too.

'I sometimes wonder if anyone else would have done.' His open face was strained, and Lorna saw Ryan had lived with that corrosive doubt in his heart for seventeen years. 'You wanted out, and you knew I was the kind of guy who wouldn't walk away from a child.'

'No!' Jess's hand shot across the table and grabbed Ryan's. Her voice rang with pain. 'Ryan, *never* think that. That is not true. If I only wanted a way out of Longhampton, why would our marriage have lasted so long? Why would we have had Tyra? And Milo? And our life together? I can't believe you'd think that.'

He gazed at her, sorrowfully, and pulled his hand away. Jess flinched. 'You wanted a reliable man; you knew that's what I was. So why were you surprised when I discovered I had responsibilities to another child? I couldn't walk away from Pearl, even though this really was a mistake. A mistake I made when I was too young to understand what a father should be, and I will always be sorry for it.'

He pushed on. 'You know what hurt me most, though, Jess? Your surprise. Like I could only behave in the boring Ryan routine. You've got no idea how much that hurt, seeing how . . . contemptuous you were of me. It brought it all back. Boring Ryan, the man you could rely on.'

Ryan's words finally ran out, but his pain hung in the air between them.

'I love you now for all the same reasons I loved you then,' he said quietly. 'Nothing has changed for me. It never will. I'm asking you to forgive me, but I'm also asking if . . . if you ever really loved me in the first place.'

'You know I did. I *do*.' Jess's voice was contorted, and she looked ashamed of herself. 'I'm sorry.'

They gazed at each other; then, very slowly, he extended his hand towards hers. She took it, and he gripped it hard.

'Shall I leave you two for a moment?' Lorna pushed her chair away from the table. They needed some space, and frankly, so did she.

Jess came to find her half an hour later. Lorna was sitting in the only quiet place she could find: the back stairs between the flat and the gallery. She'd been staring at the same framed family photo, the one of the four of them on the beach in Wales, trying to find the adult Jess and Lorna in her parents' faces. It was too small to see much.

'Move up.' Jess squashed herself into the narrow stair next to her. 'Thanks for doing that,' she said. 'I wasn't expecting Ryan to say any of it but it's . . . right to talk about it.'

'Like a thunderstorm. Clearing the air.'

'Yeah.' Jess chewed a hangnail. 'He's with Hattie now, talking to her. I wanted to tell you something else though. Something about Mum.'

Lorna turned, as much as she could in the limited space. 'What?'

'I think she was on some kind of medication. Dad managed to destroy most of their paperwork, as you know, but when I was going through the furniture for the charity shop, I found some pills in a drawer. They were hers. I showed them to a friend who's a doctor and he said they were antidepressants. Some kind of anxiety-based medication anyway. He wondered about post-natal depression.'

'Really?' The moods, the need to be alone, the haunted silences. 'Poor Mum. Why didn't Dad say anything to us?'

'He was protecting her, I suppose. Protecting us. Wanting us to think everything was fine, the perfect family – and if it was PND, then it would have felt like our fault.'

Lorna could see that. But she could also see how hiding the problem had only buried it deeper into the heart of the family, so it ate away at them from the inside until there was only a shell left. And Jess had been hiding it again, for years.

'Why didn't you tell me this? Didn't we say no secrets?'

Jess sighed. 'What could you have done? And you were so invested in the idea of them having a perfect marriage, and Mum being the perfect artist. All the things you said about no relationship being worth it if they weren't your soulmate like Mum and Dad . . .'

Lorna raised an eyebrow. 'That's what I thought you were trying to do with Ryan.'

'Ryan? I—' Jess checked herself. 'No. I don't think we're perfect. I don't think anyone is. But we're good enough. You know, it's been strange coming back here. It's made me remember a lot of things. Like how he used to help me climb over gates. How he could drive a tractor.' She smiled to herself.

It took all sorts, thought Lorna.

Jess spread out her hands in front of herself. Her eternity rings glittered in the half-light, their mother's emerald engagement ring a deeper glow on the other hand. She took it off, and put it on to Lorna's right hand, third finger.

'I want you to have that,' she said. 'And I want you to be happy, Lorna. Stop looking for a soulmate. There's a middle ground with a lot of happiness in it.'

'I'm not looking for a soulmate, I'm just . . .'

Jess twisted her mouth. 'I think you know what I'm talking about.'

They held each other's gaze for a long moment. Teenage boys, intense mothers, homework, tractors, haybales, secrets, flew in the air between them.

Then Lorna said, 'I'll make us a cup of tea, shall I?'

Chapter Twenty-Eight

Lorna found out about Sam's new job through Tiffany, of all people. Nan Osborne had been boasting to anyone who'd listen in the day room that her youngest grandson had got himself a top London job and was moving back any day now with a Ferrari.

'His old boss has moved to a different agency and he's asked Sam to join him,' she informed Lorna as they sat with Joyce, sewing broad green leaves on to the sunflower stalks in the gallery. The knitting room had moved into the main area, since it was so popular. 'He can't start until January, for some legal reason Nan Ozzy thought sounded nonsense, but it's been agreed and this time he'll have a much nicer car and more money.'

It was the middle of September; the first cool breezes of autumn were nipping on their morning dog walks. Lorna knew exactly how long it was till January – fifteen weeks – because that was how long they had left to knit several thousand more flowers and several hundred butterflies to dance across the petals. 'So what's he going to do till then?'

'He's started some project there, which is why he's back and forwards.' Tiff raised her head from her leaf. 'She also let slip that it's been rather a relief for all concerned, because Sam didn't leave his last job entirely of his own accord.'

'What?' He hadn't told her that.

'Yup. Made redundant, after something or other that *definitely* wasn't his fault. So, you know, probably his fault.' Tiff winked; she knew Lorna was sore about Sam. She was trying to cheer her up. 'Maybe he *had* to come back to the farm. Maybe he's not the self-sacrificing martyr to the plough he likes to make out.'

Lorna lifted the sunflower: it was one of her favourites. Bright and hopeful and kind of seventies in its yellow and brown flamboyance. 'Good for him. I wish him well.'

'You like him, don't you?' said Joyce. 'Are you going to tell him before he goes?'

Lorna folded the flower up and laid it in the plastic crate marked Bridge Street. They had a big map of the town marked out in assigned beds; she'd cut out the flowers from coloured paper and stuck them on as each section was finished. It was updated daily in the window. Bridge Street was another sunflower extravaganza: bus passengers would wait for the number 32 under a forest of yellow petals.

'No,' she said. She hadn't told Joyce – or anyone – about Sam and Gabe's accusation. 'I think starting a relationship with someone you've known for that long is hard. You're so busy looking for the person they were, you can't always see who they are now.'

She felt a tug in her heart as she said it.

'Ah, well,' said Joyce in a non-committal way. 'Calum the Disco Kid will be pleased to hear that. Shall we start that apple tree now?'

Joyce's health had remained fine as the days passed, and though the community nurse called in to check on her

several times a week, it seemed more routine than anything else.

'It's a wonderful thing you're doing,' Keir said, when he
returned, sunburned. 'It's hard, but being around people
makes a difference when you're dealing with an outlook
like this.'

Lorna had long spells of forgetting what Joyce's outlook
was. 'You think so?'

'Just keep an eye on her. I know she's determined to be
her own woman, but don't let her hide symptoms. Things
can change very quickly, and we want to be ready.'

Lorna had plenty of opportunity to observe Joyce when
she was concentrating on her fluted lilies or red apples.
Her skin had taken on a yellowy tinge, and seemed a little
looser around her knobbly fingers, but her eyes darted
around as rapidly as ever, taking in more than anyone
realised. Lorna knew she would hide any changes, the way
she'd hidden her fading eyesight; the clues, if they were
clues, came more in their conversation.

Neither of them were sleeping well. They often met in
the kitchen, and talked in the small hours about Ronan's
talent for photography, Bernard's rain-stained book of
garden notes, Lorna's mum's illustrations that became
darker as the years passed, sketchy details of Lorna's pater-
nal grandparents and their house, somewhere in Ireland.
Never long conversations, just observation, a question or
two, then the memory would be tucked away again.

One afternoon Joyce and Lorna were sitting in the gallery, starting a big chunk of brown stocking stitch that would
turn the postbox on Forest Street into a furrow-trunked oak
tree. The first spots of rain were flicking against the window,

currently filled with beautiful Japanese noodle bowls made by a talented man in Darton-on-Arrow.

'Lorna, I think I'd like to see the garden at Rooks Hall again, before autumn sets in,' said Joyce casually. 'I'd like to make sure we have all the detail we need for the plan.'

Lorna was concentrating on a knobble in the bark; her knitting had improved but she was easily distracted. 'The plan has everything that was on your original painting. I'm not sure we can change it now. Do you think we're missing something?'

'I'd like to see the garden all the same.' Under Joyce's chair, Bernard stirred; he napped stretched out in a messy line, unlike Rudy's neat circle. 'Just in case. Do you think the Osbornes would mind?'

Something in Joyce's voice made Lorna look up. A draught of unwelcome reality ran across her skin, but she tried not to show it.

'Of course not,' she said. 'I'll ask.'

When she phoned Sam, the background noise sounded like a city. London, probably. She didn't waste time with chit-chat that would embarrass them both.

'Sam, I need to ask a favour of you. It's not for me,' she added. 'It's for Joyce. And before you think it, there's nothing in it for me.'

'Did I say there would be? Fire away.'

'She'd like to see the garden at Rooks Hall – she doesn't mind about the house, just her garden. She says, before the weather turns and everything falls off the trees.'

'Any particular reason? I'm sure you could just drive out and look.'

'I wanted to check with you first.' Lorna knew she

sounded stiff. 'It's for our knitting project. She'd like to walk around it.'

'Well, we've got people staying there this week, but I'm sure we can arrange something. When did you have in mind?'

Lorna had consulted the forecast and rain was due to set in soon, with no let-up into October. She didn't want Joyce's last memory of Rooks Hall – if that's what it was – to be damp and miserable. 'When can we go? I don't want to leave it too long.'

'Weather's not looking great, is it? Leave it with me.'

There was something about Sam's ability to make things happen that lifted her heart. She couldn't help it. She wanted to be offhand with him – and she'd never had any trouble being offhand with other men – but then she heard his voice. 'Thanks. That would be great.'

'No problem.' There was a silence. No easy question about how she was, how the dogs were getting on. None of the questions they'd started asking each other about their new friendship instead of the 'remember when . . . ?' conversations they used to have. All Lorna could hear was Sam's new life in the background.

'Well, I look forward to that.'

'Was there anything else?'

Everything else. There was everything else.

'No,' she said, and they hung up on each other.

Sam texted her an hour later to say that Joyce was welcome to visit Rooks Hall the next day at two o'clock, if it suited, and so the following afternoon, she pulled up outside the house with Joyce and Bernard in the back. Sam's Land Rover was already there.

The house itself was beautifully spruce in the afternoon

sun, thanks to the Osbornes' thorough overhaul. There was a sharp contrast between the black exterior timbers and the white painted walls, and the windows gleamed against freshly glossed frames. Rooks Hall seemed alive in a way it hadn't before. Admiring its refreshed appearance gave Lorna a mild sting of disloyalty; she couldn't imagine how Joyce must feel.

Joyce lingered a moment in the passenger seat when Lorna went round to open her door.

'Do you think I'm being a silly old woman?' She held Bernard on her lap, and raised her face from the silk scarf wrapped round her neck.

'Not at all.' She knew now that Joyce preferred bracing reason at moments like this. 'I'm sure Sam will be pleased to have a few expert gardening tips to keep it looking its best. Farmers know *nothing* about roses, other than you can put horse manure on them.' She nodded to the garden. 'He's here already. Would you like me to go in first?'

'No, I'm quite all right. Would you take Bernard?'

Lorna lifted Bernard down, then offered her arm as Joyce carefully unfolded herself from the front seat.

Seeing them, Sam got out of the Land Rover; when they reached the gate he opened it for them. He was wearing a suit under his jacket, and Lorna wondered if he'd come from the station. There were papers on the dashboard, and his hair was styled in a much more city manner than when he'd been lugging bags of bird feed around. He's gone already, she thought. He's left me behind again.

'Hello, Mrs Rothery,' he said, extending a hand. 'I'm afraid we have people staying in the house at the moment, but I've set up a chair for you in the garden, and it's a nice day, so please . . . take your time.'

Lorna looked up the path and saw a table and chair had been set up in the corner of the garden, nearest the apple tree that had blossomed, to Joyce's surprise. On a white tablecloth was a tea tray with a silver teapot, with cups and a plate of Bakewell tarts. A proper tea.

She looked at Sam, and he nodded, imperceptibly. Lorna wanted to say thanks, for the thoughtfulness, but wasn't sure it would come out right. So she nodded back, and followed Joyce up the garden.

Sam didn't return to the Land Rover. Instead, he stood with his hands behind his back, watching them with an inscrutable expression.

'Oh, this is nice to see,' Joyce said. 'Lorna, this is anthurium – its English name is Painter's Palette. We always had a good display of that, rather an in-joke. And this rose . . . a wedding anniversary present.' She wandered around with Bernard at her heels, sometimes stopping to bury her nose in a flower head or pluck a bloom. Her pace was slow but Lorna left her to it, only popping up by her side if Joyce needed a low-flowering blossom picked, or to hear a story about why she'd chosen the plant or where some guinea pig of Ronan's was buried.

'She's fine to pick the flowers, isn't she?' Lorna muttered to Sam as they watched Joyce stroking the petals of a zinnia, while Bernard stared at something in the hedges.

'Of course. It's her garden.'

That was kind.

'Knitting coming along well?' he asked.

'Yes. Still on target for the end of December.' She turned her head. 'And you? You're on target for then too?'

Sam knew what she was talking about. His eyes

409

lingered on hers, as if he didn't have the right words. 'Yes,' he said eventually. 'An offer I couldn't refuse.'

'You always seem to get those.'

'Not always. Ah, Mrs Rothery, would you like to take a seat?' He stepped forward to help Joyce to the table, steadying her chair as she sat down.

'Tea, Samson?' asked Joyce. 'I'll pour.'

It would have made a surreal tableau for a painting, Lorna thought: the three of them and a Border terrier drinking tea on the lawn. They talked about Longhampton, pedigree cattle herds and Monet, and it was so easy, Lorna let the subtle fragrance and texture of the flowers sink into her mood.

Appropriately it was Joyce who decided the 'at home' had reached its natural end.

She laid her spoon carefully on the saucer. 'Well, that was most pleasant. We should be getting back, before it starts getting chilly. Thank you for the tea, Sam.'

'Yes, thank you,' said Lorna. He knows, she thought. He knows, from somewhere, that she's not well.

If he did, Sam didn't show it in his expression. 'You're very welcome. Thank you, Mrs Rothery, for creating this lovely . . .' He stopped, and leaned forward. 'Mrs Rothery? Is something wrong?'

Joyce had gone to push herself up, but let out a little cry and slumped back down. 'Oh dear.' A fearful expression came over her face and her hands fluttered on the arms of the chair. 'I don't think . . . I don't think I can get up. My wrist feels . . . Oh dear.'

'What? Oh no, Joyce, are you all right?' Lorna panicked. 'Do you want me to call one of the nurses?'

The old lady's skin had lost its colour, and the vein in

her throat was pulsing visibly. She put a hand on her chest, as if trying to hold the strength in her body. 'I'm so sorry, my legs don't seem to have any push in them,' she said crossly.

We've done too much, thought Lorna, horrified. We've over tired her.

Sam flicked the crumbs off his napkin. 'You've been walking round this garden at quite a pace; I'm not surprised you're feeling a bit wobbly. May I give you a hand up?' He stood by her chair, and reached out. 'Here, let me . . .'

Joyce took his hand and got to her feet but she winced as she did so, and swayed dangerously. In one movement, Sam reached forward and caught her, putting his arm around her back. Then, in one easy gesture, he lifted her up as if she were a little girl.

'Forgive the liberty,' he said, beginning to move towards the path, 'but I've helped my grandmother to her room at Butterfields more than once, and in my experience, if we both pretend this isn't happening it'll be over in a matter of seconds.'

Joyce didn't say anything. She closed her eyes, and her face seemed to slacken with exhaustion. It was completely unlike her to submit so easily, and it chilled Lorna.

Sam looked at her over Joyce's head, and gestured towards the car. She nodded, and hurried down the path to put Bernard in the back and open up the passenger door, ready.

Standing by the car, Lorna watched Sam carrying Joyce, talking inaudibly but gently to distract her, and she knew – for all his faults, for all the things he'd said and done lately – she loved him. This was the Sam she'd fixed as her ideal man for so many years: strong and gentle, a man who'd organise afternoon tea for an old lady. But Sam hadn't loved her this way back then; he didn't now. It made her ache.

She moved out of the way as he lowered Joyce into the passenger seat, and did up her belt. Then he stepped back, away from the car and dropped his voice.

'She should be fine, but I'd get her home quickly. Do you want me to call the GP out?'

'Her community nurse is calling in tonight.' Lorna hesitated. If he hadn't guessed how Joyce was, surely he could see now. 'Thank you for this afternoon. You know it's not . . . done for any other reason than to make her happy. She's . . . She's not well.'

'I guessed. And I know you're not after her fortune, Lorna.' He reached for her hand and squeezed it. His fingers were warm, and so were his eyes.

I love you. The words ran across her mind like a ribbon streaming behind a plane in a blue sky, or a ticker tape rattling out. *I love you. I love you.*

Was that what Sam was thinking? His eyes were locked on hers, searching her face, but Lorna couldn't speak. Sam had made a decision to move on; she'd look a fool, yet again.

Bernard barked in the car. It was time to go.

Before September cooled into October, Lorna's flower storm had taken over the kitchen, the bedrooms and most of the gallery storage space. It had also taken over Lorna's brain. Every flower she passed in window boxes, in the park or on a café table, she automatically saw as a knitted bloom, or photographed to show Joyce, who'd sketch it and give it to Caitlin to be turned into a pattern. And then the bobbly two-ply version would appear on the kitchen table. She'd never felt so effortlessly creative: colour and shape seemed to be everywhere.

She'd never felt so much of a team leader either. Longhampton, as one, had fallen in love with the idea of community knitting. Customers called into the gallery with bags of wool and requests to 'donate' a floral area to relatives, or sick friends, so their coverage map of the town spread even further: red and pink and yellow from the railway station to the dog park. Mary and Tiff were the main organisers of the volunteer programme, and Joyce spent her days sitting in the back room, creating petals and tortoiseshell butterfly wings and offering advice on colours. Caitlin was their chief cheerleader; she was staying with her sister-in-law just outside Longhampton, and she came by most days with Eva and the children. They sat on the carved toadstools looping miles of stem on the Knitting Nancies, while Eva – who'd been married to an actor and had connections everywhere – posted photos on Instagram and started some social media buzz for them. Rudy, in his long striped jumper, slowly became the children's new best pal, and a reluctant Instagram star.

'Of course, now you've got your KnitCam going, all you need is some celebs to drop in and start purling,' Eva pointed out as her Instagram photo of the sunflowers started racking up likes.

'Don't remind me about KnitCam,' groaned Lorna. 'It's the reason I can't get anywhere near the bathroom most days, everyone doing their hair before they make their appearance.'

Calum had sent a council IT intern round to set up a webcam in the back room so people could watch the flowers under construction, and dropped in himself for updates – even though he could watch from his own desk.

'He likes you,' Tiff observed after Calum called by with some real flowers for Lorna, ostensibly as a thank you from the council for the traffic KnitCam was drawing to their site. 'When are you going to admit you like him too?'

Lorna said nothing. She had the feeling he did too. Calum was great company, and there had been times when, with one more glass of wine, she might have let a casual kiss go further. He was funny and he knew a lot about modern art. He just wasn't Sam. But maybe that was a good thing. Maybe that was the whole point.

Joyce hadn't changed her opinion of Calum. She still referred to him as 'that strange boy with the waistcoats', but now at least she let him call her Joyce.

The doctor had found no serious cause for her 'funny turn', and Joyce put it down to the emotion of the visit. Lorna could well believe that.

Everything seemed to be going smoothly for a while, when one morning Lorna brought the dogs back in from their early walk to find Joyce already sitting at the kitchen table, with an unreadable expression on her face.

'I've had a letter, Lorna.'

'Oh, really? Do you need another blood test?' Joyce had had her mail redirected to the gallery, and she allowed Lorna to read the various communications from the hospital. The type, she said, with a flick of her hand, was ridiculously small.

'No. It's not from the hospital.' Joyce passed her the envelope; it had a handwritten address on the front, and Lorna wondered for a second if it was some family member – Keir had started to make discreet enquiries about any family Joyce might have left.

Ms Joyce Rothery, c/o The Maiden Gallery, Longhampton. She didn't recognise the writing.

'You can read it,' said Joyce, evenly.

'No, not if it's private, Joyce.'

'I think you should.'

Lorna slid the letter out, but what she read made her heart stop in her chest. It was one folded piece of A4 paper, with just two sentences on it. *Ask Lorna about Betty.* Signed, *A Well-Wisher.*

He'd actually put 'Signed, A Well-Wisher'. Who else but Gabe?

'So,' said Joyce, raising an eyebrow. 'Who's Betty? And why should I know about her?'

The moment stretched out between them, and Lorna's head filled with white noise. What could she say?

Lorna heard Betty Dunlop's impatient tut in her mind. If there was one thing Betty had given her, it was a reminder to be brave, even in the face of losing something precious.

She pushed herself from the table, and went over to the framed medal on the wall, lifted it down and set it down in front of Joyce.

'Betty Dunlop, Rudy's owner. She didn't have any family other than him, and she spent her last weeks in the hospice I used to visit. When she died she left me this in her will. It's her George Medal. We talked a lot about her courage in the war. She saved two people in an air raid.'

'Remarkable,' said Joyce. 'And valuable.'

'Yes.' Was that pointed? 'She also left me Rudy, and some money to look after him. I didn't want the money, I'd happily have taken Rudy on, but she willed the money in a trust, for insurance and food. And that's what I spend it on. Insurance, and food. Nothing else, I swear.'

415

'Who would think otherwise?'

Lorna sighed, and told her who.

'Sam's own brother assumes you're looking after me with a view to inheriting my hidden fortune?' She curled her lip.

'Yes. But I'm *not*.'

Joyce raised her hand. 'Why should I think you would, when it was me who made the deal in the first place? I've no hidden fortune to leave you, in any case. My dear, I would like to write back to this disgusting man and put him straight.' Her eyes were alive with an energy Lorna hadn't seen for several days. 'I'll enjoy that. I may have to get you to type it.'

The medal lay on the table between them, shining on its red satin bed. Lorna tipped it up. 'I don't deserve this.'

'Why do you say that?'

'Because I wasn't brave. I should have been with Betty at the end,' she said. 'My mum died alone, and I've always wished I could have been with her. I saw a counsellor who suggested I volunteer at the hospice and sit with people as they passed away, if they didn't have anyone else.' She bit her lip. 'It's why I had Betty's medal framed and hung where I could see it. To remind me that I had no right to be scared of anything, really.'

Joyce didn't respond at once, and Lorna knew what she was thinking. She was thinking it too.

'I have made a plan for my death, Lorna,' she said. 'No, don't shrink from that word. It's going to happen sooner or later. I don't want to be alone, but I'm determined that it won't be a frightening place for anyone else. I want my departure to be my last creative act.' She managed a smile. 'My *very* last beautiful thing, if you like.'

Tears sprang into Lorna's eyes. She had so much more to talk to Joyce about, so many more conversations to have, more projects to discuss, more advice to file away for later. The way Joyce was talking suggested she knew time was running out.

'I don't want to be rushed off to hospital,' Joyce went on. 'No monitors and tubes and people panicking. Ugh. I'd like to be here with my paintings, and music, and these lovely flowers round me. If you can do that, I'll leave you whatever you like. Sell the lot, and keep your gallery open.'

'Joyce, I don't want anything. It would be an honour.'

'You're worried about the police coming to get you? Or this blackmailer?' She jabbed at Gabriel's letter.

Lorna smiled through her tears. 'No, I'm worried that you'll think it's the only reason I'd do it. I'll do everything I can to make you comfortable, because I care about you. I'm glad we met. I'm sorry we'll have to part so soon.'

She threw caution to the wind and stretched out her hand to cover Joyce's own crooked fingers. After a second, she felt Joyce's fingers curl around hers, and there was an answering squeeze.

'I'll tell you one thing I regret, Lorna,' said Joyce. 'It's not telling Bernard, my husband, that I loved him the very second I realised. I wasted too much time being proud of my independence, when in reality he had me from the start.'

'Are you making a point?'

Joyce shook her head. 'Only if you want to take it as such, my dear.'

At half-term, Jess brought her brood down to visit, and while Tiffany herded the little ones into the frame of the

KnitCam, Ryan took Hattie to the cinema for a dad–daughter afternoon, and Lorna took Jess to Cake Expectations for Black Forest gateau, their childhood treat. Once they were on the vinyl banquette, Jess gave Lorna a potted update of the past few hectic weeks in the Prothero house.

'I phoned her up,' she confessed. 'Erin. I knew Hattie wouldn't leave it alone . . .'

'She *is* your daughter.'

'Yeah, so I said, look, we don't have to be friends, but if the girls want to get to know each other, wouldn't it be heartless to stop them? Erin's got three sisters. I think she saw the sense in it.'

'Well, that's great.'

'At least this way we can keep an eye on things.' Jess squashed cake crumbs under her fork. 'Ryan's set up an account for Pearl for uni fees, if she wants them. Erin won't take any money but you never know, do you?' She shuddered. 'Seventeen years of back maintenance, jeez. I made him sell that fancy bike he bought himself – that's started it off.'

'Good for him. Least he's facing up to it. And you two?'

'We're talking to a counsellor. She told us to go on dates, because we missed out first time. So we are. We got one of those cinema passes but we've had to upgrade because neither of us can deal with the limited leg room.'

'Good!'

'And Ryan was talking about going out for a drink with Sam later – he's trying to get hold of him.' Jess looked enquiring. 'How are . . . things?'

'With Sam? You're way out of the loop. Sam's virtually

living in Highgate now. I've kind of been seeing the guy from the council, Calum.'

'And is that going somewhere?'

'Maybe. He's nice. He's here.' Lorna jabbed her cherry on her fork. She'd been saving it for last, on a blob of cream.

Jess didn't respond. 'You know what the problem about saving the best till last is?' she asked, sneaking her fork towards Lorna's plate. 'Sometimes it looks like you're leaving it, rather than saving it.'

Lorna put the cherry in her mouth in one go, before Jess could snatch it.

'That's better,' said Jess approvingly.

Chapter Twenty-Nine

It was the dogs who knew first, long before Lorna or the nurses, or maybe even Joyce herself.

Bernard lost his bounce shortly after the Protheros went home, to the point where Lorna took him up to George the vet to check he wasn't ill.

'This is a fine specimen of a terrier,' George pronounced as Bernard listlessly allowed him to prod and poke him. 'Great nick for his age.'

'How old is he?' Joyce didn't know; he'd been a rescue from the kennels on the way out of town.

'About eleven, I'd say?' George ruffled his scruff. 'Any upheaval at home? Sometimes they can pick up on it. Sets them back.'

Poor Bernard, she thought, wondering when his muzzle had turned so grey.

She took him home via the delicatessen at the end of the high street, and splashed out on a bag of cheeses, Parma ham, a pillowy focaccia, and a bottle of wine. The knitting team had reached a key stage on Lorna's flower spreadsheet – just three more streets to go and they'd have flowers in every major sector of the town! – but that wasn't the real reason for the deli splurge. Lorna wanted to give Joyce a small treat every single day, something that made her glad to be alive. A new soap in her basin, or fresh flowers by her bed, or clean sheets. Treats for her senses.

Tiffany tucked into the picnic enthusiastically, full of stories from Butterfields about the latest arrival, 'with a *wolfhound*, would you believe', but after watching for a while, Lorna couldn't help herself. She had to say something.

'Joyce? Aren't you hungry?' There was a sliver of cheese and a deep pink flake of ham on Joyce's plate, and she hadn't even touched the bread. 'Don't you like it?'

'It smells delicious.' Joyce seemed confused. 'But I'm afraid I just don't feel hungry.'

'Oh, but this is the best Manchego I've ever had!' said Tiffany. 'I don't care about the calories. Go on, Joyce, try a little.'

'I'm sorry, but no. I just . . . have no appetite.'

Lorna's eyes met Joyce's, and a sombre understanding passed between them. Lorna felt a marble knot in her stomach, cold and tightening with every breath.

In his basket by the window, where he was curled up with his sleek dachshund friend, Bernard groaned, and got up. He shook his shaggy head as if he couldn't remember where he was; then, after a second's pause, he walked over to the table and lay down again on Joyce's slippered feet. As close to her as he could get.

The team of carers and medical experts around Joyce swung into action soon after lunch the following day.

Keir arrived with a friendly but practical nurse called Nina who sat with Joyce for an hour, talking to her in a relaxed tone that Lorna knew covered a multitude of jagged questions. While that conversation was going on, Keir took Lorna into the kitchen and opened a file of paperwork that made it pretty clear how the next few weeks were likely to pan out. DNR forms, pain relief, end-of-life care plans, wills.

We're now one of Keir's thick files, Lorna thought in shock, seeing him go through the stack of documents. How quickly it mounted up. How much paperwork was required for something as simple as breathing; one moment you're your own person, the next you need all this.

'Don't worry,' he said as she put her head in her hands to cover a surge of sorrow that seemed to flood her entire body. 'We'll know more when we get these blood tests back. Nina's the best. She's like the SAS of palliative-care nurses. She'll co-ordinate everything for you – hospital, meds, care team, carer's allowance, the lot – so you can get on with the really important stuff.'

'What, like the knitting?' Lorna put on a brave face, assuming that's what he meant. 'It's taking our minds off this nicely.'

'No, just being there,' said Keir. 'We'll worry about Joyce's body; you take care of her soul.' His eyes filled with sadness, and he put a hand over his mouth. 'God, sorry. I'm so unprofessional. But when I think of her on her own in that dark old house . . .'

'She was never on her own,' said Lorna, through her tears. 'She had more than we knew.'

Over the next few days, KnitCam was never still, as Lorna whipped her volunteers into constant action. It was her deal with the universe: if she could somehow get every flower Joyce had designed to spring into woolly life, the inevitable could be held back.

Community nurses arrived daily now, motherly ladies called Sue and Pat who greeted everyone like old friends with their cheerful smiles, discreetly gauging and probing while they chatted away about garter stitch. But even they couldn't stop the silent weeds creeping through Joyce's tough body. One morning Lorna took her breakfast cup of tea in, to find Joyce crying, silent tears of fury running down her face as she slumped on the floor by the en-suite door; she couldn't walk any further.

'I'm trapped,' she sobbed, shaking her hands in a rare flash of bitterness. 'I can't come downstairs to the gallery! I'm useless!'

'We'll come to you, Joyce,' said Lorna, and moved what she could upstairs – paintings, the webcam, the afternoon meeting about stock. Her bedroom was already a still life composed of Joyce's possessions; it reminded Lorna of an Elizabethan portrait, every detail a clue to the subject's character and past. But two days later, Nina had conjured up a temporary stairlift and sent workmen to install it, and the relief on Joyce's face, that her lifeline to people and art and the outside world was still there, gave Lorna a nudge – she had to keep Joyce's world as broad and outward-facing as she could, for as long as she could.

Sam called round when the stairlift was being fitted to see if she needed any help. He knew the situation, even before he saw the workmen; Tiffany had told his granny up at Butterfields, who'd told him. The Osbornes were all very sorry, he said; his parents remembered Bernard's prize-winning roses in the local show.

'Not Joyce the prize-winning artist?' Lorna raised an eyebrow. 'Or the photographer son?'

'We're farmers,' said Sam. 'It's all about the crops.

Speaking of which, let me take you for a run out. You look like you need to get away.'

She glanced upstairs. 'Joyce is having a nap, so . . .'

'Come on,' he said. 'Fresh air. I want to talk to you.'

He drove her out of town. They didn't say much, and Lorna gazed at the countryside as it passed – cotton-wool sheep, stocking-stitch green fields. It was good to be out, she had to admit. She felt too numb for any tingles of romance; she assumed Sam was taking her to Rooks Hall when he turned left towards the farm. Maybe to show her the re-decoration? Or to take flowers back for Joyce's room?

Instead Sam drove up one of the farm tracks, bumping the Land Rover over the grass towards the field where his dad's Belted Galloways were grazing. He pulled up, and chucked her a fleece and a pair of wellies from the back. 'There you go, Cinderella. You're about Mum's size, as I remember?'

'Do you?'

'Pretty sure we had to lend you a pair once. In the dim and distant.' She couldn't believe his teenage self had even registered her shoe size. 'Follow me.'

It was cold, and she wrapped the fleece round her to keep out the November chill as Sam marched confidently towards the cows. They were compact and shaggy, with big brown eyes and the distinctive stripe round their bellies; the way two or three of them approached Sam suggested that they were familiar with humans. His compromise, with his dad. Some of his principles, in return for some of his dad's joy in life.

'They look like they've been knitted,' Lorna observed.

'Don't they? Hello, my lovely.' He scratched one on its head, behind the ridge on its head where the horns would be. It butted his shoulder with its hairy nose. 'They're gentle creatures, cows. I've always found them calming in times of stress. Since I was little.'

'I know,' said Lorna. 'I remember you telling me.'

Sam turned back to the cow. 'I've struggled with the whole "life cycle of farming" thing. But I remember Dad telling me that we've all got a time, whether you're a human, or a cow, or a head of barley. Our side of the bargain was to give that beast the best possible life in the time it had. To treat it with dignity and respect, let it feel the sun and the rain. We argued about that, obviously. Gabriel would say it makes better meat. But when I see these cows in the field, happy and well treated, enjoying every moment to the full extent of their cow-pabilities . . .'

He was trying to make it light for her, but Lorna's eyes filled with tears.

'I just don't want her to go,' she managed. 'I don't want her to go! Not yet!'

She'd been keeping positive for days on end, but Sam's attempt at tenderness broke the dam inside her, and big gulping sobs tumbled out, swallowing her words.

'I'll miss her!' she sobbed. 'I feel like I've only just started to get to know her, and now she's disappearing in front of me! It's so hard to watch her fading and know there's nothing we can do. It's worse than Mum and Dad, in a way.'

'Oh, Lorna.'

'There has to be something – would she be better in a hospice? We never really got a second opinion . . .' Her mind was running wildly, scrabbling for something to hold on to that might stop the time sliding away, taking Joyce with it.

'You can't control this, Lorna.' Sam held her at arm's length so she could see his serious, sympathetic expression. 'This isn't about your mum and dad. You can't make up for what you didn't do then by overriding what Joyce wants now. Be with her, but let her go.'

Lorna gazed at him, struggling for words, and then he wrapped her up in his arms, gripping her tight against his chest. She let him because she didn't care if this was brotherly or not; it was comforting.

'I'm sorry about Gabriel.' He spoke into her hair. 'I bollocked him when I found out what he'd done. Sending that note to Joyce. What a prick.'

'Why would he do that?' She pulled away to see Sam's face. He was staring grimly over towards the farmhouse.

'Jealous,' he said shortly. 'Of you. Of me. Jealous of anyone who does anything out the goodness of their heart. He doesn't get it. He never will. I'm hiring another manager for the cottages. I don't trust him.'

Her heart was beating high and fast in her chest. 'What do you mean, jealous?'

Sam gazed down at her. 'Jealous of you, for having a talent for art. Jealous of me, getting out of here, having a life that's my own. Jealous of us . . . our friendship.'

It hung there. *Friendship*. Did he mean that? Was that all it was?

'Are you moving back to London, Sam?' Lorna asked. 'Do you . . .' She swallowed; the words were sticking in her throat. 'Do you have to?'

'Yes.' He sighed. 'That's where the job is. I can't stay

here, I don't want to. You've got a reason to stay – your heart's in your gallery, Lorna. I'm proud of you. You're making this place better.'

Lorna thought she'd never be able to tear her eyes from his, the beauty in them was so familiar. Please say something else, she begged in her head. But he pulled her close, with no words spoken, and they hugged, and she wanted to cry but there were no tears left.

'Mum looked up at the sky this morning, and do you know what she said?' Sam said over her head.

'Santa's come early?'

'Snow,' said Sam. 'She reckons it's going to snow.'

Back in the gallery, the afternoon passed, and it didn't snow and Joyce rallied. She sat in her chair downstairs and dozed while Tiffany and Lorna worked around her, sometimes knitting when the gallery was quiet, sometimes talking to customers. The dogs slept by her feet, twitching and leaping awake from time to time, then settling back down again.

Once they went quiet, thinking she was asleep, and Joyce muttered, 'Keep talking, I love to hear you talking.'

'What would you like us to talk about?' Lorna asked.

Joyce's eyes flickered open. There was a flash of the old imperiousness. 'Whatever you like. Tell me about your sister, Lorna. The teacher. Tell me how she's getting on with that husband of hers. And Tiffany, tell me about your mother – has she come to terms with your change of career? Has she got a plan for you to meet someone out here?'

'Oh God, I had the *worst* conversation with Mum – she's found out that some duke has a gun-dog kennel about ten miles away.' Tiffany rolled her eyes. 'I should start dog-sitting for the country set. Apparently she's read that the way to a toff's heart is through his cocker spaniel . . .'

Lorna winked. Clearly Tiff hadn't told her mum that Keir had taken her for a vegan meal the other night, followed by a Jean-Luc Godard showing in the tiny arthouse cinema.

'Tell me,' said Joyce. 'Every detail.'

So they talked, and worked, and the invisible strands of friendship that had brought the three women together looped and knotted around them like stitches, pulling them closer, winding their stories into each other's lives, carrying them on to the next row.

Nina had warned Lorna that when the end came, it would come suddenly.

'You'll know,' she said, and reeled off a list of physical changes that Lorna had to admit she could see in Joyce, but by Friday night something in the room had changed. Joyce was sleeping most of the time now, and the atmosphere around her bed was close, as if it was filling with a different sort of air. Souls, maybe, or dreams. Hopes, or memories.

'Don't be surprised if she starts talking about people coming for her,' Nina warned as the nurses moved softly around Joyce, sliding in the pain-relief needle, hiding it thoughtfully under the blanket. 'Her mum and dad, or her husband.'

Lorna wasn't surprised by the idea. What surprised her was the powerful yearning she had to pull her own mother close through the still evening, to feel Cathy's hand on her back as she sat up late into the small hours, keeping Joyce company until the night nurse arrived, as she breathed and dreamed and jerked her stiff hands on the bedclothes as if she was playing with paint, or picking flowers in a garden on the edge of a cliff.

She'd hung the painting of the cottage on the cliff directly opposite Joyce's bed, so it was the first thing she saw in the morning, and the last thing at night. It gave Lorna comfort to sink into its safe white walls; she hoped it was helping Joyce somewhere.

The town hall clock struck three, and Lorna pulled a curtain back to see what was happening outside. She'd stopped feeling sleepy days ago; she seemed to be running on a weird adrenalin.

'I think it's snowing,' she said. 'I can't remember when it last snowed in November. Can you?'

Joyce didn't respond but Lorna carried on. 'I always thought the garden looked warm when it snowed, because we used to use cotton wool for snow when we made models at home. I thought the garden had a blanket.'

Bernard stirred by the bed. He'd given up his frantic bounciness; his sole job now was watching, and waiting.

'Mum never minded us making a mess with our craft things in the kitchen,' Lorna went on. 'Glueing and sticking, and painting. Everything covered in newspaper and glitter.' She smiled to herself. Christmas collages, their annual treat. A rare instance of a childhood activity the three of them enjoyed.

'When I think about my childhood, it's all bright colours. Poster paints and plastic macs and Smarties. I bet Ronan's was too. What a wonderful book of memories you gave him.'

Joyce's breathing was slowing, with long pauses. Lorna moved round the room, putting the portrait of baby Ronan nearer the bed, just in case Joyce could sense it.

Was he there? Was Bernard waiting?

She looked around, in case there was something else Joyce needed. Nina had said hearing was the last sense to go, so they'd been playing the Motown music Joyce had loved in her art-school youth; they burned lavender and rose candles to remind her of her garden. Lorna had moved most of the knitted flowers up to Joyce's room so she'd get an idea of what her last beautiful thing might look like, but as the moonlight fell on to the bare grey of the street outside, Lorna was gripped with a powerful urge to do something bigger. Something better.

Joyce took a long rattling breath, and then . . . nothing. Lorna swung round in panic. Was that it? Joyce's mouth was open; her chest wasn't moving. Oh God, oh God, not yet, she thought, and rushed over to the bed.

'Joyce?' She bent down, grabbing her mottled hand. 'Joyce? Hang on. We haven't finished yet.'

There was a silence, then another laboured breath. Lorna felt the air return to her own lungs as her heart pounded with oxygen.

They had so little time left. No time to waste.

She went through to Tiff's room, where she was curled up in a ball under the duvet, snoring like a kitten. Lorna shook her awake.

'Tiff? Tiff? I want to do it now,' said Lorna.

Tiffany rubbed her eyes. 'Do what?'

'The yarnstorm. We have to do it now, before Joyce . . . before Joyce goes. Please. The night nurse is coming at half three, we can be out for a few hours.'

Tiff sat up in bed. Years of nanny training snapped her awake at any hour. 'What time is it now?'

'Just gone three o'clock. I want Joyce to look out of her window and see her flowers in the trees outside. Come *on*,' Lorna finished urgently. 'We don't have very long. It's snowing; the roads are going to get closed.'

'But, Lorna . . .'

'Come on. *Please*. We need to do this. I don't want Joyce to go before she sees her final beautiful thing.'

Tiffany looked at her as if she might be dreaming the conversation, then sighed. 'Fine. Make me a coffee.'

The plastic crates of knitting were stacked up in the office, marked with the street and the type of flower inside. Lorna grabbed everything marked for the high street, the parts Joyce would be able to see out of her window. A thick oak tree for the postbox outside, some sweet-pea netting, a flock of chalky cabbage whites, bright brave red Flanders poppies for the War Memorial . . .

'How are we going to do this?' Tiff shivered by the car, snowflakes floating and sticking to her hat.

'Do what?'

She pointed at the tree. 'How are we going to get up there? Fly?'

'I have a plan. Just start on the flowers and I'll get on it.'

As Tiff unpacked the first boxes, Lorna took a deep breath and dialled a number. She spoke before he had time to ask who the hell it was. 'Sam, I need your help.'

His voice was croaky. 'At half three in the bloody morning?'

'I know, I'm sorry, I'm really sorry. I'll never ask you for another favour after this.'

'What is it?' His tone changed. 'Oh. Is this to do with Joyce?'

'Yes. Please.' Lorna was barely keeping the tears at bay. 'I need you to help me put the flowers up. I think she's going and I need her to see what she's created, what she's helped me do, before . . . Before she . . .'

'I'm coming,' he said. 'I'll be right there.'

Chapter Thirty

The yellow street lights threw a supernatural glow over the deserted high street, making it look like a film set. The butcher, the baker, the charity shops . . . the snow fell in thick clumps, barely swirling in the still air, and settling in the scoops of electric light.

Sam's Land Rover rumbled down the white road, with ladders lashed to the top. He was wearing his farm coat and a trapper hat, and he pulled off his gloves in a businesslike way that gave Lorna the same reassurance she felt when Nina the care nurse walked in, with her confident, assessing eye fixing problems Lorna couldn't even see.

'So, you crazy woman, how do we do this?' He rubbed his hands together. 'If we need reinforcements I can ring for some – they'll be getting up with the cows. I reckon the girls can wait an hour or two if it's important.'

She gazed at him, sinking into the relief of having him there. A pulse was starting in her heart, pushing the blood around even faster. Time was ticking past, for dawn, for Joyce, for the snow, but they were racing it, matching it breath for breath.

'I want to put apples in the tree opposite Joyce's bedroom,' she said. 'So when she looks out, she'll see Ronan's tree bearing fruit.'

Sam turned round to see where she was pointing. The

bare branches of the cherry tree were dark against the light, spiking into the night. He didn't flinch. 'Right. We can stand on the roof for the lower branches, then I'll get the ladder down for the rest.'

Tiff and Lorna climbed on to the Land Rover with the box of apples and started bunching them in clumps, stringing them on the branches until the boughs were heavy with fruit. They were streaky Braeburns and red Scrumptious, stuffed with chopped-up tights by the primary-school children. When the lower branches were filled, Sam got his ladder out and Tiffany held it as he slung himself up like the tree-climbing country boy he'd been, stretching out with unexpected grace to hang the apples Lorna passed him.

The tree took half an hour, working fast, and when they'd finished it was the most beautiful thing Lorna had ever seen. A ruby-red crop of apples hanging in the branches of a starkly leafless tree, dusted with the diamond sparkle of frost forming around them. It was magical. She and Joyce had brought summer out of winter, conjured up fruit into a dormant wood.

The truly magical thing was how Joyce had woken the creativity in her too. She'd brought *her* to life, sparking talent in her she'd never found before.

'Come on, no time.' Tiffany clapped her hands together. 'Where can we put the sweet-pea nets?'

They pinned and pulled as efficiently as they could as the first traces of dawn began to bleach the sky. The snow didn't seem to hamper them much; it was falling into thick, crunchy piles, and not melting where it lay. The knitting sat on top of it and the glittery whiteness only intensified the colours of the wool. Soon, lilac and powder pink sweet

peas draped with their twisting tendrils over the bus stop;
a brown tree trunk was tugged over the postbox, and the
spriggy mistletoe woven around it. They tied sunflowers
to the iron fastenings of the shop awnings all down the
street, and wrapped lamp posts with coiling ivy. And here
and there, they fastened Joyce's butterflies trembling with
the joy of summer sun on their fluttering wings.

'I think we're done,' said Lorna finally. 'Now we just
have to show Joyce.'

Upstairs the air in Joyce's bedroom had changed again.
Despite the lavender candles that filled the flat with fragrance, a more medical smell was undercutting it: a
mortal, chemical reality breaking into the carefully constructed tableau Joyce had wanted.

The night nurse, Denise, was taking Joyce's tempera-
ture when they came in. Soft jazz was playing in the
background and her lids were closed; Lorna couldn't tell if
she was sleeping or just resting her eyes in the semi-trance
she slipped into more and more.

She spoke anyway. 'Joyce, we've got a surprise for you. We
couldn't wait until the end of December to see what the yarnstorm would look like, so we went out and put it up now.'

There was no response. Lorna felt disappointed, but
why should there have been? Denise indicated that they
should keep talking.

'That sounds lovely, Lorna,' she said. 'Doesn't it, Joyce?
Aren't they good friends, going out in the snow to do that
just for you! Where have you put it up?'

'Right outside the window. So you can see when you . . .'
Lorna was going to say, when you wake up, then realised
she might not. 'When the sun comes up,' she said instead.

'It's snowing so it looks extra magical,' said Tiffany. 'I think it's going to blow everyone away when they see what we've done.'

There was no response from Joyce.

Please, Lorna begged the invisible forces around her. Please let Joyce open her eyes and see what a wonderful thing she's done, so she knows she's leaving the world with a triumph.

'Do you want to have a look?' Sam asked. 'Would you like me to carry you to the window?'

'Is she safe to carry?' Lorna whispered to Denise.

She nodded. 'I'll help you. Be careful.'

Denise unhooked what tubes she could from around the bed, and supported the drips as Sam lifted Joyce from her sheets. She was so light, so brittle now. He carried her across to the window, and stood with her in his arms next to Lorna as she pulled back the curtain.

There was the tree, framed like a picture by the window-panes, decked out in red apples and snow diamonds, resplendent in the street light. Their version of the little tree planted by two grieving parents, which had blossomed without warning that last summer in Rooks Hall.

'Can you see?' Lorna whispered. She took Joyce's cold hand in hers, warming the bones. 'The tree is the most beautiful thing I've ever seen. And look, there's the postbox . . . only it's an oak! And the sunflowers, can you see . . . ?'

She stroked the papery skin with the back of her finger. It moved with each caress, but Lorna kept her slow rhythm, remembering how her mum had calmed her as a small child, and how she'd calmed a shivering, scared Rudy when he'd first come to live with her. Human contact, soft and loving, soothing away the fear.

'Do you like it?' she whispered. 'Did we do your designs justice? Can you imagine what everyone will be saying when they wake up in a few hours' time?'

The street was a riot of colour, the unexpected textures making it a playground of red, yellow and green, the colours of happiness.

'It's your garden come to life,' Lorna went on, murmuring more to herself now. Joyce was obviously slipping away. *As long as she can hear my voice*, she reminded herself. There was no sign from her closed eyelids that she could, though.

'I think we should . . .' Denise nodded towards the bed.

'OK,' Lorna whispered, disappointed. Maybe Joyce knew, on some level, what they'd done. If she was floating outside herself, seeing everything on every plane.

Sam caught her eye. His face said, *We tried*, and she smiled sadly.

And just as she was about to turn away, Lorna felt a gentle pressure on her hand, the faintest response against her skin. Joyce's hooded eyelids flickered, and slowly her glassy eyes opened, unfocused, and stared out at the street as the snowflakes swirled against the window.

Lorna held her breath.

It was clearly taking a huge effort. She had no idea what Joyce was seeing, if she was seeing anything. But the tendons on her neck strained, and the eyes stayed open, and then suddenly her strength ran out and she relaxed into Sam's arms.

'Well done, Joyce,' said Denise. 'Now, into bed with you.'

Tears streamed down Lorna's face but they were tears of joy, not sadness. *She's seen it. She's seen what she's done.*

Sam carried Joyce as gently as he could towards the bed. Denise had pushed it round so it was angled out to the street, and quickly refreshed the sheets, tugging and pulling with expert swiftness so Joyce had a cool nest to be laid in.

'There we are, nice clean sheets.' Denise rearranged the photos so they were at the end of the bed, not on the table. Easier to see. 'Here's your son, is it? And your husband. What a handsome pair.'

Joyce was definitely sleeping now. Her eyelids flickered from side to side, and her hands jerked as if she was dreaming.

'Don't be surprised if she goes soon,' Denise whispered. 'Sometimes they're just waiting for permission, if you know what I mean.'

'Do you want a cup of tea?' Tiffany touched her hand. 'Let me get you something to drink.'

'Yes,' said Sam. 'That'd be a good idea.' The pair of them slipped out and left Lorna alone with Joyce.

Lorna knelt by the side of Joyce's bed with her hand in hers, watching the rise and fall of her chest. The imperious, defensive old lady she'd met in Rooks Hall had swirled up into the cosmos; what was left here were the last breaths of her body.

She felt something soft against her leg and realised Bernard had come back in. He put his paws briefly up on the bed to check Joyce was still there, then flopped down next to it, and looked up at Lorna.

What harm could it do?

Lorna lifted him up and put him at the very end, by Joyce's feet. 'There. One last time.'

Bernard curled up with his back against Joyce's feet,

facing out into the room as if he could guard her from what was approaching.

Outside, the snow swirled in silence. Inside, Lorna felt the air move and fill with something she didn't understand. She willed Bernard and Ronan to come, and she pictured her own mother coming nearer, the intensely imaginative, soft-skinned mother who'd made toffee and drawn dreams in ink as her little girl coloured in by her feet. Her gentle father, with his broken heart no one could mend. Betty too. A gang of them, ready to take Joyce home.

'Thank you, Joyce,' she whispered, through her tears. 'Thank you for showing me the art in everything. Thank you for giving me your most precious paintings. And your memories.'

There was no response. Lorna rested her forehead on the sheets. She wasn't sure who she was talking to now, Joyce or her mum. She was so tired, she wasn't even sure if she was whispering or just thinking.

'And remember you'll always be a part of me. As long as I think about you, and remember what we said, and the times we laughed . . . you're still with me.'

Bernard started growling at something, but there was nothing in the room. He lifted his head and Lorna saw his hackles were up.

She couldn't explain what happened next: it felt as if the room was suddenly filled with a spiralling love, a clear, warm sense of absolute contentment. The snow against the window seemed too bright, the colours of the knitted flowers too vivid for the subdued nightlights that were on. She couldn't see anything but Lorna felt wrapped in something soft and stronger than her, and she wanted to cry as it swept through her body, and then, suddenly, it vanished and she was alone in the room.

Lorna lifted her head, and looked at Joyce's face. It had slackened and was grey, her nose sharp. She was alone. There was just her and Bernard.

With tears in her eyes, Lorna kissed Joyce's forehead. 'Goodbye, Joyce.'

She stayed by the side of the bed for a long minute, not wanting to move but suddenly awake and scared of what came next. Bernard was whimpering softly and instinctively she reached out to comfort him.

There was a cough by the door. Denise was standing there, with Sam and Tiffany behind her.

'I can take over now if you want?' she asked kindly, and Lorna nodded.

Sam held out his arms and she rushed into them, burying her head in his chest as he held her, kissing the top of her head and stroking her back. She could feel his tears falling on to her hair as he rocked her back and forth.

'My Lorna,' he was saying, over and over. 'My beautiful brave Lorna. My girl.'

They stayed like that for a while, letting the barriers between them fall away, like the broken shell of a chestnut peeling back to reveal the bright conker inside. And then Lorna heard someone calling her name.

'Lorna?' Tiffany was standing with her coat back on. She had her phone in her hand, and a determined look on her face.

'What?'

'Let's do the rest of the town.' She grinned. 'Let's finish this. Let's give Joyce something really amazing to send her off.'

Epilogue

Christmas came suddenly, racing up in the background of Joyce's funeral and Calum's hastily revised plan for the competition entry – Joyce and Lorna's Magic Garden evolved into a proposal for a touring show. The Maiden Gallery was full every day, riding high on the viral hit of thousands of retweeted photos of the town bedecked in snow-dusted wool. Queries arrived daily from the most surprising and far-flung places, and the KnitCam was kept going, for volunteers knitting coats for homeless dogs.

Mary had held the fort with Tiffany while Lorna was distracted with the arrangements for Joyce. Not just the funeral, a simple humanist ceremony near the low white cottage by the cliffs, but organising her ashes to be scattered with her human Bernard (canine Bernard to be scattered in the same place in due course). When Lorna returned to the gallery after a long weekend of walking and thinking in Wales, she found quite a few items of grotesque crockery on sale that hadn't been there when she left, complete with an incomprehensible 'practice statement' from the artist which ran to three cards, tacked on the wall next to the display.

'It's the season of goodwill,' Mary had protested.

'That doesn't mean making this place look like a goodwill shop,' Lorna pointed out, but she let most of it go. After all, who was she to decide what someone else found beautiful?

There was one corner of the gallery set up with work that wasn't for sale: her mother's original hand-drawn Christmas cards, framed by Archibald in festive gold and green. Each card was covered in tiny detail, with her and Jess and Cathy and Peter at the centre, surrounded by a thousand clues to who they were and what they were celebrating that particular year.

Lorna had photocopied some, initially to colour in herself, and then, at Hattie's suggestion, she'd turned them into adult colouring books for Christmas. A very limited print run, and only sold to customers who'd appreciate their witty intricacies. She had plans to stage a proper Cathy Larkham retrospective in the new year, once the yarnstorm was over. Hattie was going to help her, to explore her grandmother's legacy – not just in terms of the art she'd left, but what the family had to be proud of.

'I need to stand back and understand Mum as an artist,' Lorna told Jess. 'I've been trying to live up to her all my life, and I think seeing her on equal terms – her as an artist, me as her curator – is good. Then I can start seeing her as a human being, just like us.'

'I want you to do it so we can clear out the garage,' said Jess, but Lorna knew she was joking.

Only Sam was missing from the picture. His new boss had asked him to start full-time in London early, and he hadn't come back. Lorna missed him every day, but she filled every gap with a task before she had time to think too hard. Her life, from now on, was about creating a future, not dwelling on what wasn't there and would never be.

It was the week before Christmas, the busiest of the year, when Lorna was alone at last in the gallery. They'd stayed open an hour later than normal to deal with the final customers, and Bernard and Rudy were yipping and grumbling for their evening walk. It was hard to remember Rudy had once shrunk in fear from anything he didn't know. Now, with his grizzled mate by his side, the whole world was Rudy's to explore.

'I won't be a minute.' Lorna stepped over them as they chased one another round her legs; she had to move carefully round the gallery, turning off lights and checking cabinets. Finally, she was at the door, turning the Closed sign round when she saw a face behind the sign and jumped.

It was Sam. It took her a moment to recognise him: the beard had gone, and he looked ten years younger. He smiled at her through the glass and held up two takeaway hot chocolates in their red Christmas cups. 'Special delivery.'

'Come in.' She undid the bolts and let him in along with a blast of cold air. 'Thank you so much! What timing. We've run out of biscuits. Mary's nervous eating has gone into overdrive this week. The card machine went down and—'

'I don't need biscuits.' He put the hot chocolates down on the desk and grabbed her hand as she walked past. 'I want to talk to you.'

'About?'

He gazed into her eyes. 'About Christmas.'

Lorna freed her hand to pick up her hot chocolate, mainly so Sam wouldn't feel her trembling with nerves. She didn't want to say something stupid *again*. 'Meaning?'

'Meaning, I know you volunteer at homeless shelters to avoid spending it with the in-laws. And there's only so much of my family I can take, given how things have been this year. So I was wondering if you'd like to do something different?'

'Like what?'

He gently removed the cup from her hand, put it on the desk, and held her hands in his. 'Like go somewhere else. Together.'

'Where?'

'I was thinking London, maybe? It's romantic when there's no one else around. We could go ice skating, we could drink champagne in Trafalgar Square . . . On the lions, if you want.'

London. Her heart sank. He was just bored in town, he wanted company. 'Sam, I don't want to go to all the places you go, and then say goodbye and come back here.'

'Oh, Lorna.' He leaned forward until his forehead was resting against hers. 'Maybe I want to say goodbye to some places . . . before I come back here with you.'

She pulled back and looked up. 'What?'

'I miss you,' he said, simply. 'London is no fun when I know you're here. I keep finding excuses to come back and deal with problems on the farm.' He pulled a face. 'Luckily Gabe's making plenty of those for me but . . .'

'You're coming back to live here?'

'Apart from a few days a month consulting, yes. I want to come back. I want to start again properly, you and me.' Sam's eyes didn't leave hers, searching for her reaction. 'I'm sorry I got things so wrong before. I hated seeing you fall for that Emperor's New Clothes art bollocks. I knew you were smarter than that, but I was too arrogant to know how to tell you without insulting you. I could see you were going to get hurt, and I hated myself for not being able to stop it happening.'

'You have to make your own mistakes.' Lorna trod carefully. 'I wouldn't have done it differently.'

Because if she had, she'd never have met Joyce, never

have known the power of four women and some knitting needles, never have made this world for herself, or known what she could do alone.

'I'm sorry too,' she said. 'I've judged things I knew nothing about. This town is your home, not mine, really, and I feel as if I've . . . complicated it for you. Well, my whole family has, one way or another.'

Sam turned her hand over, inspecting the life lines on her palm. Then slowly he raised her fingers to his lips and kissed her knuckles. 'You're what makes this place home for me, Lorna,' he said, looking up at her.

Lorna looked back at him, this man with the beautiful eyes of her childhood crush, but with an adult heart she was just starting to understand. She thought of him stroking the de-horned cows in the field, the patient compromises around the family table, Rudy's instinctive lack of fear when Sam walked in the room. You surrendered a little fear, you offered a little trust and in return, what did you get? As much as you wanted to give.

'Welcome back,' she said. 'I'll stay, if you will.'

And then Sam leaned forward, put his hands on her face and pulled her towards him, kissing her as if he'd been waiting all his life to kiss her properly, and Lorna's mind filled with a shimmering powdery explosion of colour, a million shades of red from crimson to scarlet to palest ballet pink to scorching magenta. As her arms slipped round Sam's waist, pulling him even closer, the reds softened to one: a perfect warm ruby of apples and London buses and children's wellies and the most bombshell old-fashioned lipstick.

The colour of falling in love. The colour of a heart beating in its perfect rhythm.

Acknowledgements

This has been a hard story to write at times, and I'm extremely grateful to the wonderful crowd of people I have around me, cheering me on and supplying round-the-clock tea, good ideas, dog-walking, and kind but firm nudges in the right direction.

At the front of the crowd is the wonderful Francesca Best, my patient and perceptive editor, and all the team at Transworld; thank you for transforming my pile of words into something so beautiful (and chronologically accurate): particularly Sarah Whittaker, who designed the magical cover, Josh Benn, Judith Welsh, Becky Short, Vicky Palmer, Deirdre O'Connell, Janine Giovanni, Lucy Keech and Elspeth Dougall.

I'm extremely lucky to know, and also be represented by, the presidential force of nature that is Lizzy Kremer, and the other David Higham miracle workers: Harriet Moore, Maddalena Cavaciuti, Emma Jamison, Alice Howe, Giulia Bernabè, Margaux Vialleron, Camilla Dubini and Annabel Church. There aren't enough cupcakes in the whole world to convey how much I appreciate all you do for me. Speaking of which, thank you to the editors who have brought Longhampton to places beyond my wildest dreams – especially you, Teresa Knochenhauer.

447

Acknowledgements

It gives me a thrill every time I get an email from a kind reader so if you're reading this and you've tweeted or Facebooked or messaged me to say hello, I promise you, it made my day. Thank you! (And keep in touch . . .)

Contrary to what you might imagine, writers are a supportive and generous group. Well, the ones I know are. They understand the importance of the right pen and the dangers of unlimited broadband. Thank you to the timeless oracles of the Board, the Kremerinos and the SWANS, who all make me roar daily, one way or another, and particularly to Chris Manby, who is a magnificent woman.

I've had a lot of support this year from my family; my brave dad, who read this book, and my sister Alex, queen of the texts; my wonderful husband Scott, who heroically kept me sane and happy and caffeinated, my stepchildren, Katie, Calum and Fiona, who never complained about the pinboard of quite unsettling notes hanging around the house, and Barney, who got some long walks and some shorter ones. I love you all, very much.

Finally, thank you Julie Williams, both for the guidance you gave me about Joyce's medical treatment (any mistakes are mine), and also for the hard and heartbreaking work you do with families living through their loved one's final days. The compassionate support of Macmillan, Marie Curie and Sue Ryder nurses, and all those professionals and volunteers giving end-of-life care, is somewhere far beyond remarkable. I wish I could thank every single one of you, because you are amazing.

Can I draw your attention to a wonderful charity called **The Cinnamon Trust**? They recognise the special bond between owner and pet, and how precious that companionship can be in later years. Their national team of volunteers supports elderly owners by arranging walks if the owner becomes housebound, temporary fostering during hospital stays, and other practical forms of assistance to help keep old friends together. I think that's kindness in action.

So if you love dogs (or cats or parakeets!) but can't have your own, why not spend a little quality time with someone else's? Volunteers are welcome all over the country – contact www.cinnamon.org.uk

Lucy Dillon grew up in Cumbria and read English at Cambridge, then read a lot of magazines as a press assistant in London, then read other people's manuscripts as a junior fiction editor. She now lives in a village outside Hereford with an old red Land Rover and too many books.

Lucy won the Romantic Novelists' Association Contemporary Romantic Novel prize in 2015 for *A Hundred Pieces of Me*, and the Romantic Novel of the Year Award in 2010 for *Lost Dogs and Lonely Hearts*.